# A PRAYER
# FOR THE DAMNED

Also by Peter Tremayne
Works featuring Fidelma of Cashel

# A PRAYER
# FOR THE DAMNED

*A Mystery of Ancient Ireland*

## PETER TREMAYNE

St. Martin's Minotaur
New York

A PRAYER FOR THE DAMNED. Copyright © 2006 by Peter Tremayne. All rights reserved. Printed in the United States of America. No part of this book may be used or reproduced in any manner whatsoever without written permission except in the case of brief quotations embodied in critical articles or reviews. For information, address St. Martin's Press, 175 Fifth Avenue, New York, N.Y. 10010.

www.minotaurbooks.com

Library of Congress Cataloging-in-Publication Data

Tremayne, Peter.
   A prayer for the damned : a mystery of ancient Ireland / Peter Tremayne.—1st U.S. ed.
       p. cm.
     ISBN-13: 978-0-312-34833-5
     ISBN-10: 0-312-34833-9
     1. Fidelma, Sister (Fictitious character)—Fiction. 2. Nuns—Fiction. 3. Women detectives—Ireland—Fiction. 4. Ireland—History—To 1172—Fiction. I. Title.

PR6070.R366 P73 2007
823'.914—dc22
                                                                      2007024874

First published in Great Britain by Headline Book Publishing,
a division of Hodder Headline

First U.S. Edition: November 2007

10  9  8  7  6  5  4  3  2  1

For Paul and Wendy
and the next generation of the Ellis family
Declan and Caleb
but not forgetting Jamie

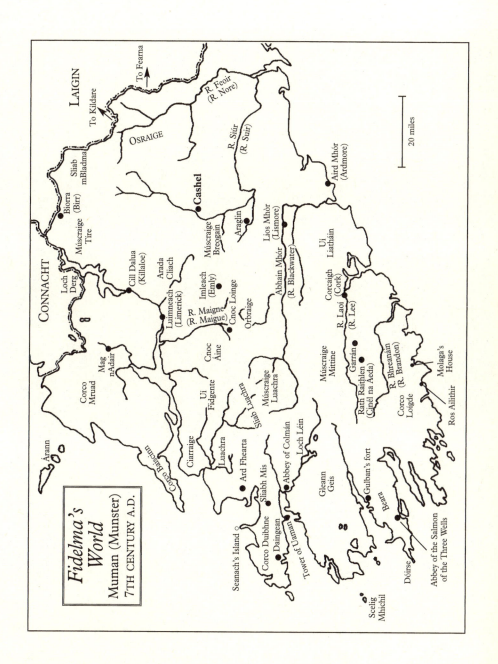

Fidelma's
World
Muman (Munster)
7TH CENTURY A.D.

20 miles

LAIGIN

To Fearna

To Kildare

R. Feoir
(R. Nore)

OSRAIGE

R. Siúr
(R. Suir)

Aird Mhór
(Ardmore)

CONNACHT

Sliab
mBladma

Biorra
(Birr)

Múscraige
Tíre

Loch
Derg

Cashel

Múscraige
Breogain

Araglin

Líos Mhór
(Lismore)

Uí
Liatháin

Cill Dalua
(Killaloe)

Arada
Cliach

Imleach
(Emly)

Abhainn Mhór
(R. Blackwater)

Corcaigh
(Cork)

Luimneach
(Limerick)

Cnoc Loinge

Mag
nAdair

R. Maigne
(R. Maigue)

Cnoc
Áine

Orbraige

R. Laoi
(R. Lee)

Corco
Mruad

Uí
Fidgente

Sliab Luachra

Múscraige
Luachra

Múscraige
Mittine

Garrán

Rath Raithlen
(Cinél na Aeda)

R. Bhreanain
(R. Brandon)

Árann

Ciarraige

Luachra

Ard Fhearta

Abbey of Colmán

Loch Léin

Corco
Loígde

Molaga's
House

Ros Ailithir

Seanach's Island

Coirpre Baiscinn

Sliabh Mis

Gleann
Geis

Gulban's fort

Coirpre Baiscinn

Daingean

Tower of Uaman

Beara

Dóirse

Abbey of the Salmon
of the Three Wells

Coirpre Baiscinn

Scelig
Mhichil

AD 668: *Muircetach Nár rí Connacht .i .mac Guaire moritur*
**Chronicon Scotorum**

AD 668: Muirchertach Nár, King of Connacht, the son of Guaire, died

*Vigilate et orate ut non intretis in dammnare aeternitas . . .*
Gelasius I, **Decretum**, AD 494

Watch and pray that you enter not into eternal damnation

# pRINCIpAL ChARACTERS

**Sister Fidelma** of Cashel, a *dálaigh* or advocate of the law courts of seventh-century Ireland
**Brother Eadulf** of Seaxmund's Ham in the land of the South Folk, her companion

*At the Abbey of Imleach*

**Ségdae,** abbot and bishop of Imleach
**Brother Madagan,** steward of Imleach
**Ultán,** abbot of Cill Ria and bishop of the Uí Thuirtrí
**Brother Drón,** scribe and steward of Cill Ria
**Sister Sétach** of Cill Ria
**Sister Marga** of Cill Ria

*At Ardane in the Valley of Eatharlaí*

**Miach,** chief of the Uí Cuileann
**Brother Berrihert,** a Saxon religieux
**Brother Pecanum,** his brother
**Brother Naovan,** their brother
**Ordwulf,** their elderly father and a pagan Saxon warrior

*At Cashel*

**Colgú,** king of Muman, Fidelma's brother
**Finguine,** his tánaiste or heir apparent, cousin to Colgú and Fidelma
**Brehon Baithen,** brehon of Muman
**Caol,** commander of the king's bodyguard
**Gormán,** a warrior of the guard

**Dego,** a warrior of the guard
**Enda,** a warrior of the guard
**Brother Conchobhar,** an apothecary at Cashel
**Muirgen,** nurse to Alchú, son of Fidelma and Eadulf
**Nessán,** her husband
**Rónán,** a hunter and tracker
**Della,** friend of Fidelma and mother of Gormán

*Guests at Cashel*

**Sechnassach,** High King of Ireland
**Brehon Barrán,** Chief Brehon of the Five Kingdoms
**Muirchertach Nár** of the Uí Fiachracha Aidni, king of Connacht
**Aíbnat,** his wife
**Dúnchad Muirisci** of the Uí Fiachracha Muaide, his tánaiste or heir apparent
**Augaire,** abbot of Conga
**Laisran,** abbot of Durrow
**Ninnid,** brehon of Laigin
**Blathmac mac Mael Coba,** king of Ulaidh
**Fergus Fanat** of Ulaidh, Blathmac's cousin

The main action of this story takes place in the period known as *dubh-luacran*, the darkest period of the year, coming up to the feast of Imbolc (1 February) when the ewes came into lamb. The year is AD 668 and the main events take place immediately after those related in *Master of Souls*.

It would help for a better understanding of the period, and references in this novel, to remind the reader that in seventh-century Ireland a bishop was subordinate in rank to an abbot. Indeed, many abbots held the title of bishop as a secondary rank. It was not until the ninth century in Ireland that bishops slowly started to rise in prominence over abbots.

One other word of clarification: the great river that runs through Tipperary, near Cashel, into Waterford, is called the 'sister river' – the *Siúr*. In the Anglicised form it is spelt as Suir. I have maintained the original Irish spelling. It is not a misprint.

# A PRAYER
# FOR THE DAMNED

# PROLOGUE

The young girl was beautiful. The adjective was not one that Brother Augaire freely bestowed on any object, let alone a person of the opposite sex. However, he could think of no other word to describe the quality that awakened such sensuous delight in his mind. It aroused no carnal desire; Brother Augaire's piety would not acknowledge that. It was a beauty that inspired admiration for beauty's sake and excited only homage.

It had been some time before he had become aware of her presence. He had been sitting in the sunshine on some rocks by the shore of the bay, fully absorbed in his fishing. This was always a good spot to catch bass as it came in to spawn in the estuaries and inshore waters, and he had already brought in a couple of the fish with his rod and line. Then something had made him glance up to his side and he had seen her, appearing as if out of thin air, standing silently on the shell sand of the short beach area and staring out across the calm waters of the bay.

It was the profile that had caught his attention first. While she wore a *bratt*, a flowing cloak of dyed purple wool edged with badger's fur, the hood was thrown back off her shoulders, allowing her golden tresses to shimmer and sparkle in the morning sunlight. He could see the intelligent forehead, the unobtrusive nose, the fullness of her lips, the firm jaw and the slenderness of her neck. Yet no words could express the way those features blended together into a form that surpassed even the great sculptures of Greece and Rome. Brother Augaire was in a position to judge, for he had been on pilgrimage to both those distant lands.

She did not appear to have noticed him and so he took his time with his observation. His eyes fell to her slim figure, a pleasing form even though shrouded somewhat by the cloak. He could make out that she was wearing a tight-fitting purple tunic and a flowing skirt of blue, fashioned from either *sída*, the expensive silk bought from foreign merchants, or *sróll*, a shimmering satin. A patterned *criss* or girdle merely accentuated the girl's slim waist and the shape of her hips. The sun was glancing on a necklace of red jasper that she wore at her neck and, for a moment, she lifted a pale hand to it, showing a bracelet of beaten gold. Brother Augaire even noticed that her shoes were of decorated untanned hide.

Here, indeed, was a girl from a noble family; from a wealthy family.

Brother Augaire glanced round, half expecting to see some companion or a bodyguard nearby. But there was not even a horse waiting patiently along the shore. It was as if she had suddenly materialised there.

He wondered whether to call out a greeting but the girl was looking intently out to sea with an expression of sorrowful yearning that forbade any intrusion into her inner world. Brother Augaire shifted uncomfortably on his rock. He suddenly felt like a trespasser. He knew an impulse to remove himself from a place where he was not wanted.

Then the girl turned and stared momentarily at him; or rather stared through him, because he felt that those deep, dark melancholy eyes did not really see him. But in that moment, Brother Augaire also saw the depth of the suffering on the girl's features. It was an expression that was beyond grief. Its terrible beauty was hardened into a pale mask as if the girl had come to some fearful moment in her life when her very life's blood had frozen and never afterwards resumed its regular flow. Even the tears that had obviously been shed had long dried, but the fearsome abyss in her soul, the dark, cavernous well from which they had sprung, was still there. He could see it in those dark haunted eyes.

Brother Augaire dropped his gaze for a moment. When he looked up again, the girl was walking carefully and deliberately away from the shore and ascending the rocky path to the rising headland beyond. Behind the boulders on which Brother Augaire was sitting, a finger of high rocks stretched out into the sea for over a kilometre. It was called Rinn Carna, the Point of Cairns, because the sharp standing

2

rocks round the small peninsula looked like the mounds which marked the resting places of the departed.

Watching her ascending the path, Brother Augaire felt like an idiot because he had not greeted her. He licked his tongue over his dried lips and called out: 'Take care on the footpath there, my daughter. The path is steep and the rocks are sharp.'

The girl did not bother to answer him or had not heard. She passed on in her self-absorbed melancholia.

Just then, Brother Augaire felt a sharp tug on his line and was soon playing a large bass that claimed his immediate attention. When he had finally brought it to shore, to place in his basket with his other catches, he heard the crunch of footsteps on shingle and glanced up. A younger member of his community was coming down to the seashore.

'*Dominus tecum*, Brother Augaire,' said the newcomer. 'How goes the fishing?'

'Another three fish on my line, *Deo volente*, and we will have supper for all the community,' replied Brother Augaire piously. He paused and glanced round towards Rinn Carna with a frown. 'Tell me, Brother Marcán, did you see any strangers on your walk here?'

'Strangers?' The young man shook his head.

'No sign of a tethered horse, or other conveyance? No one who appeared to be waiting for someone?'

Brother Marcán smiled and shook his head again. 'Why would there be? Apart from our small community, there is no settlement or rath anywhere near here.'

Brother Augaire frowned slightly. 'You did not see a young girl passing by the community? I was sure that she must have come here on horseback and with a bodyguard.'

'A young girl? I have seen no sign of anyone near here this morning. What do you mean?'

'It is just that . . .'

He stopped when he became aware that Brother Marcán was staring over his shoulders, looking upwards, with an expression of utter surprise.

Brother Augaire turned his head.

High up, yet not so far away that he was unable to pick out details, he saw the figure of the girl that he had seen on the shore. She was standing on the edge of the cliff, high above the crashing waves. Her pale arms were held up as if in supplication.

'A strange place to choose for prayer . . .' Brother Marcán began.

But Brother Augaire was already throwing aside his fishing rod and springing to his feet. The shout of 'Stop!' died on his lips as the girl seemed to throw herself outwards, as if taking a dive, her hands still held out before her as if in some entreaty.

'*Deus misereatur* . . .' Brother Marcán began to mumble but his fellow religieux was already scrambling across the boulders along the shore.

'Follow me closely!' he cried over his shoulder. 'There is a small path under the rock face here and we may get to the spot where she fell. The tide is not at its highest as yet.'

Gasping, slipping, stumbling and tearing their robes, the two men darted and scrambled through the rocks and pools that lined the area at the foot of the jagged walls of rock that formed Rinn Carna. They moved quickly, thanks to Brother Augaire's fisherman's knowledge of that stretch of shoreline. Even so, it took a while to come to where the body of the girl lay floating, face down, rocking gently on the whispering wavelets.

The body was bloodied and smashed. There was no need for Brother Augaire to check for a pulse in the slender broken neck, though he did so automatically. She had plunged directly into the rocks, and glancing upwards, with dreadful realisation, he knew that she had not slipped, not fallen by accident, nor even attempted to dive into the water. She had cast herself with deliberation on to the jagged rocks below.

Gently, he raised the fragile body in his arms, and motioned to Brother Marcán to precede him. Slowly and carefully, they made their way back along the bottom of the cliff face towards the shell-sand beach where he laid her down.

'There is nothing to be done, brother,' muttered Brother Marcán as he watched his fellow trying to arrange the girl and her clothing with some dignity. '*Deus vult.*'

'God wills it?' muttered Brother Augaire. 'You are wrong, brother. He cannot have willed this. He was but preoccupied a moment, for

He surely would not have allowed this.'

Brother Marcán stirred uneasily. 'She leapt from the headland, brother. It was no accident. She meant to take her life. That is a sin in the eyes of God. Is it not written that human life is sacrosanct because of its relationship to the divine and to take one's own life must bring on oneself the severest punishment in the next world? The girl must go to an unquiet grave.'

Brother Augaire was gazing at the white face of the girl. The melancholy set of the features appeared to have softened and relaxed in death. Their expression was almost peaceful. He felt a spasm of anguished guilt.

'I saw her look – the despair crying out from her suffering. I should have spoken but I let her pass by in her fearful isolation. God forgive me, but I could have helped her.'

Brother Marcán compressed his lips for a moment and then pointed to where the girl's *cíorbholg*, the 'comb-bag' in which women kept small toilet articles and other personal items, still hung from the girdle at her waist.

'There might be something there that will identify her. She is certainly richly attired.'

Brother Augaire undid the strap of the bag and brought out the contents. Most items were predictable – a mirror, a comb . . . a piece of vellum. This was unusual. He unfolded it with curiosity.

'What is it?' demanded Brother Marcán. 'Some means to identify her?'

Brother Augaire read the words on the vellum and then shook his head. 'They appear to be some lines of poetry . . .' he said.

He handed the scrap to Brother Marcán who held out his hand for it. The young man glanced at it and murmured aloud:

'*A cry of pain*
*And the heart within was rent in two,*
*Without him never beats again.*'

He paused and sniffed. 'It seems some sentimental verse.'

'The girl is dead,' Brother Augaire rebuked him.

'And by her own determination. The rule of our faith aside, suicide

5

is a heinous crime under our native law: the ultimate form of *fingal* – of kin-slaying – which can neither be forgiven nor forgotten in a society such as ours that owes its very existence to the bond of kinship.'

'But surely it must be understood?' cried Brother Augaire.

'What is there to understand?'

'That this young girl, with her life before her, must have been robbed of all hope.' He glanced down again at the pale features of the girl. 'Who could force such a one as you to take your own life? Was it a man who caused you such sorrow?' he asked softly. 'What man could have such power over you?'

Beside him Brother Marcán coughed nervously. 'Whoever such a man might be, the teaching of the Faith is clear. The girl's soul is lost unless there is forgiveness beyond the grave. Come, brother, let us raise our voices in a prayer for the damned. *Canticum graduum de profundis clamavi ad te Domine* . . . Out of the depths have I cried to thee, O Lord . . .'

# CHAPTER ONE

'Have a care, Ségdae of Imleach, lest you be faced with death and eternal damnation!'

As he spoke, Abbot Ultán smote the table in front of him with a balled fist.

There was an audible gasp from those seated on the opposite side of the dark oak boards. Only the man to whom the words were addressed seemed unconcerned. Ségdae, the tall, silver-haired abbot and bishop of Imleach, sat relaxed in his chair with a smile on his face.

There were six men and two women seated at the table in the sanctum of the abbot of Imleach. On one side was Abbot Ségdae with his steward and two of the venerable scholars of the abbey. Facing them was Ultán, abbot of Cill Ria and bishop of the Uí Thuirtrí, who sat with his scribe and two female members of his abbey.

Now, in the flickering candlelight which lit the gloomy chamber, even Abbot Ultán's companions began to look concerned at the intemperance of his language.

There was but a moment's pause after Abbot Ultán's outburst before Abbot Ségdae's steward, the *rechtaire* of the abbey of Imleach, Brother Madagan, leaned forward from his chair at the abbot's side with an angry scowl on his face.

'Do you dare to use threats, Ultán of the Uí Thuirtrí? Do you know to whom you speak? You speak to the Comarb, the successor of the Blessed Ailbe, chief bishop of the Faith in this kingdom of Muman. Imleach has never recognised the claims of Ard Macha. Indeed, is it not accepted that the Blessed Ailbe brought the Word of Christ to

7

this place even before Patrick was engaged on his mission to the northern kingdoms? So have a care with your bombast and threats lest your words rebound on your own head.'

The animosity in Brother Madagan's voice was controlled, the words coldly spoken but none the less threatening for that.

Abbot Ségdae reached forward and laid a restraining hand on his steward's arm. His soft blue eyes remained fixed upon Bishop Ultán's flushed, wrathful features and he let forth a sigh.

'*Aequo animo*, Brother Madagan,' he admonished his steward, urging him to calmness. '*Aequo animo*. I am sure that Abbot Ultán did not mean to imply a physical threat to me. That would be unthinkable in one who has been granted the hospitality of this house.' Was there a slight emphasis, a gentle rebuke in that sentence? 'The abbot was but giving voice to his conviction of the righteousness of his cause. Yet perhaps he was a little over-zealous in his choice of words?'

Abbot Ségdae paused, clearly waiting for the response.

There was a silence broken only by the crackle of the dry logs burning in the hearth at the far end of the chamber and by the winter wind moaning round the grey stones of the abbey walls. Even though it was late afternoon, it could have been midnight for it was *dubh-luacran*, the darkest part of the year. Within a few days it would be the phase of the moon anciently called 'the period of rest', *mi faoide*, which started in contrary fashion with the feast of Imbolc, when the ewes began to come into lamb. It was a long, anxious time in the country.

That very noon Abbot Ultán and his three followers had arrived at the abbey and announced that he was a special emissary from Ségéne, abbot and bishop of Ard Macha, the Cormarb or heir to the Blessed Patrick. Ségéne was regarded by many as the senior churchman in the northern kingdom of Ulaidh. Having been granted hospitality, Abbot Ultán and his companions had presented themselves in Abbot Ségdae's sanctum to deliver their message.

The proposal put forward by Abbot Ultán was simple. Abbot Ségdae, as the most senior churchman in Muman, was to recognise Ségéne of Ard Macha as *archiepiscopus*, chief bishop of all the kingdoms of Éireann. To support the claim, Abbot Ultán pointed out that the Blessed Patrick the Briton had received the *pallium* from the bishop of Rome, who was regarded as the chief bishop of the Faith. Patrick had then proceeded to convert the people of Éireann. He had made Ard Macha his primary seat and it was therefore argued that the bishops of that place should hold religious governance over all the five kingdoms and their sub-kingdoms.

Abbot Ségdae had listened in polite silence while the northern cleric had put forward his argument, which was delivered in such blunt terms as almost to constitute a demand. When the envoy had sat back, Abbot Ségdae had pointed out, politely but with firmness, that churchmen and scholars from the other kingdoms of Éireann would argue that Patrick the Briton, blessed as he was, was not the first who had preached the New Faith in the land. Many others had come before him and one of these had converted Ailbe, son of Olcnais of Araid Cliach in the north-west of Muman, who had established his seat at Imleach. It was the great abbey in which they were presently gathered that was regarded by all the people of Muman as the chief centre of their faith, and when, in recent times, the abbots and bishops of Ard Macha had begun to assert their claims, they were immediately challenged by Imleach and most of the other churches in each of the five kingdoms of Éireann.

It had been at that point that Abbot Ultán, a vain man of middle age, quite handsome in a dark, saturnine way, had pounded the table with his fist, clearly unused to anyone challenging his authority.

Following Abbot Ségdae's gentle rebuke, there was silence round the table. All eyes were upon the arrogant envoy of Ard Macha.

Abbot Ultán flushed as he regarded the open hostility on the face of Brother Madagan and the others who sat across the table on either side of his host. Beside him, his scribe, Brother Drón, a thin, elderly man, with sharp features and birdlike movements, bent quickly forward and whispered in his ear, '*Aurea mediocritas.*' He was urging the abbot to employ moderation: the 'golden mean'. Attack was no way to win an argument when faced with such opposition.

Abbot Ultán finally shrugged and tried to force a smile.

'The words were spoken in the zealousness of my cause and intended no threat, physical or otherwise, to you, my dear brother in Christ, or to anyone here,' he said unctuously. But there was no disguising the falseness of his tone. 'I would simply ask for a moment more in order to clarify my argument, for I fear that I must have presented it badly.'

'We have heard Ard Macha's argument and do not agree with it,' snapped Brother Madagan.

Again Abbot Ségdae laid a hand on his arm and said, without glancing at him: 'My steward, too, is zealous for the rights of this abbey. *Audi alteram partem* – we will hear the other side, for there are two sides to every question. You seem to think, my dear brother in Christ' – Ultán glanced up sharply: was he being mocked? – 'you seem to imply that there is more to set before us for our consideration. Is that so?'

Abbot Ultán nodded quickly. 'My scribe, Brother Drón, will continue for me.'

The sharp-faced scribe, seated at Abbot Ultán's side, cleared his throat. 'I beg leave to read from a sacred book of Ard Macha.' He turned quickly to the fair-faced sister of the Faith at his side. 'Sister Marga, the book, please.'

Thus addressed, his neighbour reached into a satchel that she was carrying and drew forth a small calf-bound book, which she handed to Brother Drón. The scribe took it and turned to a pre-marked page and began to intone: 'A celestial messenger appeared before the Blessed Patrick and spoke to him, saying, "The Lord God has given all the territories of the Irish in *modum paruchiae* to you and to your city, which the Irish call in their language Ard Macha—"'

Abbot Ségdae interrupted. 'Brother Drón, I presume that you are reading from the book that you call *Liber Angeli*? It is already known to us; indeed, we have asked Ard Macha for permission to send a scribe to make a copy for our own *scriptorium*.'

Brother Drón looked up with a frown. 'I am, indeed, reading from the *Book of the Angel*. In virtue of this miraculous appearance to the Blessed Patrick, Ard Macha claims to hold supreme authority over the churches and monasteries of the five kingdoms of Éireann. All the houses of the Faith must defer to the authority of Ard Macha and pay tribute to it both spiritual and material.' Brother Drón tapped the vellum page with his forefinger. 'That is what is written here, Abbot Ségdae. This is why we have come to ask your obedience to this sacred instruction.'

Abbot Ségdae's smile seemed to broaden as he shook his head.

'When I was a young man, I visited your great abbey at Ard Macha.' He spoke slowly, almost dreamily. 'I met with its scribes and scholars.' He paused and for a few moments they waited in silence, but he did not continue. He seemed to have drifted off into his memories.

Brother Drón glanced nervously at Abbot Ultán.

'What relevance has this?' he finally demanded.

'Relevance?' Abbot Ségdae looked up and frowned as if surprised by the question. Then he smiled again. 'I was just thinking back to the time before this celestial message was ever known at Ard Macha. This book and its claims appear to have only recently come to light.'

At that moment, Sister Marga, who had been taking notes, snapped her quill. Brother Drón turned to her with a frown, she muttered a hurried apology.

Brother Madagan ignored the interruption and added cuttingly: 'Not even Muirchú maccu Machtheri, the first great biographer of Patrick, argued that Ard Macha was the place wherein Patrick's earthly remains repose. It is well known that he was buried at Dún Pádraig, and he favoured that place above all others as the centre of his church. If you would venerate the Blessed Patrick, then it is to Dún Pádraig you must go.'

There was no mistaking the anger on Abbot Ultán's face. For a while, he seemed to be physically fighting with himself to prevent a further outburst.

'Am I to take these words back to the *archiepiscopus* Ségéne, Comarb of the Blessed Patrick?' he finally demanded, again making it sound as if the words contained some threat.

Abbot Ségdae inclined his head slightly.

'You may take these words back to the abbot and bishop of Ard Macha,' he said shortly. 'Imleach recognises neither his claims to be *archiepiscopus* nor the seniority of Ard Macha among the churches of the five kingdoms.'

'You should think carefully before you send a final refusal,' snapped Abbot Ultán.

Abbot Ségdae sighed. 'We keep coming to the same end, my dear brother in Christ. How else can we reply when we of Imleach do not recognise the claims of Ard Macha? It is as simple as that. There are many religious houses even in your own northern kingdoms which refuse to accept that Ard Macha is the centre of the *paruchia Patricii*. Why, then, should we recognise Ard Macha if the houses of Ulaidh do not?' He held up his hand as if to stop Abbot Ultán from inter-rupting. 'I know this for a fact, my dear brother in Christ.'

'Name them,' challenged Brother Drón irritably. 'Name those religious houses of the north who would deny the right of Ard Macha to hold primacy in the five kingdoms.'

Abbot Ultán's lips compressed into a thin line and he cast an annoyed glance at his scribe. It seemed that he had already realised that Abbot Ségdae was not one to state something without knowing the facts. Brother Drón might have thought he could call the abbot's bluff, but Ultán suspected that his antagonist did not indulge in bluff.

Again Abbot Ségdae responded with a soft smile.

'The Abbey of Ard Sratha, in the territory of the Uí Fiachracha, denies your claims. Did not the Blessed Eógan build that stone church with his own hands over a hundred years and more ago creating one of the most important centres of learning in the north?'

Brother Madagan, his steward, was nodding in approval.

'The Blessed Patrick himself founded the house at Dumnach hUa nAilello and left three of his disciples there to run its affairs – Macet, Cétgen and Rodan,' he added. 'Their works resound throughout the five kingdoms and the bishops there deny that Ard Macha is more important than they are. In the kingdom of Laigin, the house of Brigid at Cill Dara, in the land of the Uí Faéláin, claims that it should be the chief house of the Faith in the five kingdoms. It is Cill Dara that Cogitosus calls the *principalem ecclesiam*. Why should we not recognise Cill Dara rather than Ard Macha?'

Abbot Ségdae held up his hand for silence when it seemed that Brother Madagan would continue. He looked directly at Abbot Ultán with a challenging smile.

'I am sure that you do not wish us to continue the listing of all the foundations that do not recognise the claims of Abbot Ségéne to this title *archiepiscopus*?'

Abbot Ultán's face was crimson. He did not reply immediately.

'Although we may dwell here, in the south,' went on Abbot Ségdae, and his tone was not devoid of a certain satisfactory relish, 'we are not without eyes to see and ears to hear. We are not unlearned in these matters.' Abbot Ultán began to clear his throat angrily, and Abbot Ségdae suddenly rose.

'Enough!' he said sternly, holding his hands as if to cover his ears. 'Ard Macha may pursue what course it likes, Abbot Ultán. But, as there can be no agreement between us for the moment, let us end this argument now. The day after tomorrow is scheduled as a great occasion in our king's fortress of Cashel. The sister of our king is going to be married. Tomorrow morning, my steward and I ride for Cashel where I am to preside over the religious rites. It is a time for peace and jubilation. I am told that many kings, even those from the north, as well as the High King himself, will be attending. So come, dear brother in Christ, let us close this day as should true brothers in the Faith: in peace and fraternity. Let us put our differences aside and set out for Cashel together.'

Abbot Ultán scowled in response to the appeal.

'It was my intention to journey on to Cashel, but not to make merry,' he replied sourly.

Abbot Ségdae groaned inwardly. He said nothing; nor did he sit down again even when Abbot Ultán did not rise to join him. Ultán's three companions had all risen out of deference, for it was not seemly to remain seated when their host, an abbot and bishop himself, was on his feet. Eventually, with reluctance and marked ill manners, Abbot Ultán rose as well.

'I shall be journeying to Cashel to lodge a protest at this marriage,' he explained when no one spoke.

For the first time, a look of surprise crossed Abbot Ségdae's face. 'A protest? About what?'

'A protest that a sister of the Faith should be marrying at all, let alone marrying a foreigner, a Saxon brother who, of his own volition, should adhere to the decisions of the Council at Witebia and follow the course of the rules laid down by Rome.'

Abbot Ségdae was frowning. 'Why would you protest against the marriage of the lady Fidelma?'

'The lady Fidelma?' There was a sneer in his voice. 'As I recall, she took vows to serve the Faith in Cill Dara. We believe that it is wrong for the religious to marry. It is a sacred teaching that we can only hope to serve our Lord through chastity.'

Abbot Ségdae shook his head quickly.

'That is your interpretation and belief. Not even all those who follow the rules of Rome agree with you. True, there are some who are influential in arguing the path of celibacy, but the concept is not yet universal. Even at Rome celibacy is not a rule. The house of Ard Macha itself, which you claim as your superior, is a mixed house.'

'It will not be for long,' Abbot Ultán assured him. 'The *archiepiscopus* has decided to follow the ruling of the Council of Nicaea, where such marriages were condemned.'

'Condemned but not outlawed,' Brother Madagan pointed out.

'You quibble over words,' snapped Abbot Ultán. 'I will make my protest known in Cashel.' He turned suddenly, without the courtesy of a reconciliatory farewell, and left the chamber, followed by his small entourage.

Abbot Ségdae stood for a moment looking after him as if deep in thought. The others stood round him waiting nervously. He sighed, and then dismissed the scholars. After they had left, he said softly to Brother Madagan: 'Make sure that Abbot Ultán and his companions are treated with the utmost respect while they are our guests and, indeed, if they journey to Cashel with us tomorrow, that they continue to be treated with courtesy. I regret that Abbot Ultán is not the most diplomatic envoy that Ard Macha has sent us.'

Brother Madagan's expression was anxious. 'I do not like this. I have a feeling that all will not be well at Cashel. I feel it like a chill within me. I feel it and I do fear it.'

Abbot Ségdae shook his head with a smile. 'Abbot Ultán threatens wrath and damnation. Yet he is of the Faith and would not dare make physical threats. There is no need to fear him.'

Brother Madagan remained unhappy. 'I feel like a sailor who stands aboard his ship on a quiet sea and is aware of the lack of wind, the silence in the air, and the dark clouds gathering on the horizon. The sailor knows that something destructive is approaching. I know it. Is it not right to fear it? Storm clouds are gathering. I pray they will pass over Cashel without breaking.'

\*   \*   \*

The same wind that moaned round the grey buildings of the abbey of Imleach was blowing over the great limestone peak of Cashel, an outcrop of rock which dominated the plains around it and whose tall fortress walls enclosed the many buildings which composed the palace of the ancient kings of Muman. Sharing the rock was the church, the *cathedra* or seat of the bishop of Cashel, a tall circular building with connecting corridors to the palace. There was a system of stables, outhouses, hostels for visitors and quarters for the bodyguard of the kings as well as a monastic cloister for the religious who served the cathedral. Below the rock, sheltered in its shadow, was the market town that had grown under its protection to be the hub of the largest and most south-westerly kingdom of Éireann.

The wind was bringing icy showers of sleet with it, cold and hard like little darts, painful to the exposed flesh of the face. The elderly Brother Conchobhar, sheltering as best he could from the treacherous blasts, knew that snow had lain on the distant mountains since that afternoon and a thin layer had draped itself over Cashel and the surrounding plain. The sleet would soon drive the snow layer away, but the old man preferred snow to sleet.

The religieux shivered and pressed back against the wall as he gazed with narrowed eyes into the darkness of the sky above. He was an astrologer as well as the apothecary at the palace and did not need a clear sky to know the position of the heavenly bodies above him. He knew that the moon was waxing gibbous; that it was in the house of *an Partán*, the sign of the Crab, and it was opposing the warlike planet of *an Cosnaighe*, the Defender. Brother Conchobhar shook his head sadly.

'Ah, Fidelma, Fidelma,' he whispered. 'Did I not teach you better than this? Did I not show you the ancient art of *nemgnacht*, the study of the heavens? Why did you agree to marry on this feast of Imbolc when a few days later the new moon would rise and the evil signs diminish?' He paused and drew his cloak more firmly round his bent shoulders. 'There is some evil in the air, I swear it. Have a care, Fidelma of Cashel. Have a care.'

# CHAPTER TWO

Although it was nearly noon, the day was dark and cold. The low clouds were sooty grey, and here and there scudding patches came even closer to the ground indicating that rain was imminent. Brother Eadulf stirred uncomfortably in the saddle of his plodding horse and glanced anxiously upwards to the heavens. As he rode uneasily beside Caol, commander of the bodyguard of Colgú, king of Muman, he noticed that already some of the winter flowers, which should have been displaying their pale colours, were closing their leaves to protect them against the coming onslaught. He examined the sky again with a shiver and identified one or two of the anvil-headed clouds – thunderheads – that were the harbingers of storm.

'Is it much farther?' he called to the youthful guide who was riding just ahead of Caol and himself.

At his side, Caol glanced at him with a sympathetic smile. He knew that Eadulf was not fond of riding and would rather any other means of transportation than horseback. But determination was the Saxon's strength. He had managed the journey without complaint since leaving Cashel just after first light, although Caol would have preferred to canter the horses along the easier stretches of track that led westward across the swollen river of the Siúr via the Ass's Ford, and across the lesser rivers Fidgachta and Ara, towards the great glen beyond.

'Not far now,' confirmed their young guide. 'The river Eatharlaí runs beyond that forest and you can see the rise in the trees that marks the hill. That is where we are making for. It is called the Little Height.'

Eadulf tried to gauge the distance. 'Is that where the chief of the Uí Cuileann dwells?'

'It is not,' came the prompt reply. 'His rath rises on the northern slopes at the beginning of the valley.'

Eadulf was puzzled. 'So why are we to meet him at this place . . . Ardane, you say it is? The Little Height?'

The young guide shrugged. 'I am but a messenger, Brother Eadulf. I am not privy to the thoughts of my chieftain. All I know is what I have already told you. Miach, the chief of the Uí Cuileann, sent me to Cashel to ask if you would come to meet him at Ardane at midday to advise him on a matter of importance.'

Eadulf was troubled. The request had filled him with many questions. It was only two days before the celebration in Cashel when he and Fidelma would finally be officially united. He knew that there were many against the union of a princess of Muman with a Saxon. At first, he had wondered whether this was some plot to lure him away. Yet Fidelma had vouched for the integrity of Miach, chief of the Uí Cuileann. His people were an important sept of the Eóghanacht Áine, closely related to her own house of the Eóghanacht of Cashel. The Uí Cuileann dwelt in the great glen through which the Eatharlaí flowed. The name meant the river between the two highlands, indicating mountains to the north and to the south. Fidelma knew the area well but it was not Fidelma that Miach had sent for.

Caol, Cashel's foremost warrior, had agreed to accompany Eadulf after Fidelma, unbeknown to Eadulf, had suggested it. The glen of Eatharlaí was not a long ride from Cashel, but at walking pace progress was necessarily slow and should a problem arise the summons might mean an overnight stay.

The young guide eventually led them off the track into a shady grove by a large pond-like spring, deep within the great oak forest that spread through the glen. The trees were ancient, with broad trunks pushing their massive crooked branches up to their spreading crowns. If the open track had been dark and oppressive because of the low clouds, the grove was even more so. It was almost like night. Eadulf could not suppress a shiver as the musty, cold air caught at his body. He was aware that the path was gently ascending now. So this was the Little Height.

A hoarse challenge suddenly rang out and their guide drew rein and answered immediately. A moment passed before a short, stocky man came striding through the trees accompanied by two others. All three wore the accoutrements of warriors. The leader was dark and wore his hair long with a full beard. He had stern but not displeasing features. From the way his guide and Caol dismounted and greeted him, Eadulf knew that this must be the chief of the Uí Cuileann.

Eadulf slid from his horse without grace or dignity but recovered to turn and face the now smiling chieftain as he approached with his hand held out.

'You are well come to this place, Brother Eadulf.'

'I presume that you are Miach?' Eadulf did not mean to sound surly, and the man took no offence.

'I know these are busy times for you, Eadulf, but I stand in need of good counsel.' He paused and added: 'I am, indeed, Miach, chieftain of the Uí Cuileann. It is I who sent to ask for your help.'

Eadulf tried to make up for his ungracious greeting. 'How can I advise you?'

The chief turned and gestured up the path. 'Come with me and I will show you.'

Leading their horses, the three travellers followed Miach and his men up the woodland track and into another, larger clearing where several wooden buildings stood. There were more warriors standing or seated in the clearing. Among them, Eadulf noticed three men in religious robes and an elderly man whose dress proclaimed him to be a foreigner. The group sat near a fire in the centre of the clearing at which one of the warriors was cooking something in a steaming cauldron.

Miach halted and Eadulf paused by his side, frowning and wondering what mystery was afoot.

'Do you recognise anyone?' Miach asked.

'Am I expected to?' Eadulf replied, frowning.

'Come forward, brother,' the chief called to one of the seated religious.

The man glanced up and rose. He was tall; a handsome man of middle years. As he approached, Eadulf felt he seemed curiously familiar. He glanced at Miach but the man's face was without expression. Eadulf turned back and saw that the religieux was smiling. His greeting was in Saxon.

'Eadulf? Brother Eadulf? By Woden's teeth! Is it you, Eadulf of Seaxmund's Ham?'

Memory came to Eadulf. He gave an answering smile.

'Is it you, Berrihert? What are you doing here?'

The religieux reached forward and seized Eadulf in an embrace. 'Much has happened since we last raised a mug of ale together, my friend.' He turned swiftly back to the other religious, who had risen uncertainly. 'Do you recall my young brothers, Pecanum and Naovan? And yonder sits my father, Ordwulf, who has journeyed here with us. But you would not know him.'

Eadulf regarded Brother Berrihert in slight bewilderment. 'I thought you were all in Northumbria. When was it that I last saw you?'

'At the great Council of Witebia.' The religieux smiled, turning and waving his brothers to come forward. Eadulf greeted them by name, shaking their hands. Only the old man continued to sit stiffly by himself, as if ignoring them.

'A fateful council,' added the youngest of the three, whose Latin name, Eadulf recalled, indicated someone without fault. It was at the Council of Witebia that King Oswy of Northumbria had decided in favour of the usages and teachings of the Roman Church as opposed to the rites and practices of the Irish who had originally converted the pagan Angles and Saxons to the new faith.

'A fateful council?' Eadulf repeated. He had been one of those who had supported the ideas from Rome, although these last few years, living in the land of Éireann, he had had second thoughts about that decision. 'So you disagreed with the ruling of Oswy?'

Brother Berrihert nodded.

'Is that what brought you here?'

'It is a long story.'

They had been speaking in Saxon and now Miach came forward.

'Do I presume that you recognise these Saxon brothers, Brother Eadulf?' he asked in his own language.

'Indeed I do.' Eadulf frowned. 'Is there something wrong?'

'You identify them as . . . ?'

19

'Why, this is Brother Berrihert of Northumbria and his two brothers – brothers by blood as well as in the faith – Pecanum and Naovan. I knew them when I was attending the great council at the abbey of Hilda.'

'And the elderly one?'

'I know him not. But Brother Berrihert tells me that it is his father.'

'My father's name is Ordwulf,' intervened Berrihert, obviously able to speak the language.

'Is there something wrong?' Eadulf repeated.

Miach waved his hand in dismissal. 'I wanted to be sure as to their identity. They claimed that they knew you so I took the liberty of seeking confirmation. They have come seeking *comairce* in my territory.'

'Asylum?'

Miach smiled briefly. 'They wish to dwell here in the great glen among my people, under my protection. Indeed, even to build their own church here. These have been difficult times. It seems but a short time ago that not far from here we fought the great battle of Cnoc Áine. I think you know well that outsiders must be accountable. I would have you hear their story. Let us move to the fire and refresh ourselves while Brother Berrihert tells it.'

The young guide took care of their horses, and as they moved forward to the fire Eadulf introduced Caol to the Saxon brothers. Eadulf was then introduced to Ordwulf, although the elderly man seemed unfriendly and uncommunicative, which Eadulf ascribed to his lack of knowledge of the language of Éireann. Berrihert explained that the old man had been a warrior in his youth, a thane of Deira. His sons had brought him with them, as there was no one else in the family to look after him. Once they had seated themselves round the fire and mugs of foaming mead were brought, Berrihert began his story.

'It is true, Brother Eadulf. We do seek permission to settle in this valley.' He smiled quickly and added, 'I now speak the language of this land, as do my brothers. Our father's knowledge is imperfect but I will tell the tale so that Miach, our host, and his men will know it is the same as I have already told them.'

He paused for a moment as if to gather his thoughts before continuing.

'When King Oswy announced that he would follow the teachings of Rome, there was great consternation among the congregations in Northumbria. Abbot Colmán of Lindisfarne, who had been the leading spokesman for those opposing the reforms, could not, in conscience, accept the decision, or remain as chief abbot to the king. It was against all his beliefs and teachings, as it was against those of many of us who had been raised in the ways of those who first brought the word of Christ to our kingdoms. Arguments raged in many abbeys and churches, even to the shedding of blood in the heat of such quarrels.'

Eadulf nodded slowly. 'I had heard that Oswy's decision was not popular among either the religious or the people. I did not realise that it had led to bloodshed.'

Berrihert grimaced wryly. 'To say that it was not a popular decision is an understatement, Eadulf. Abbot Colmán said he could no longer preside at Lindisfarne and serve Oswy's churches. He announced that he would return to his native land so that he could practise his faith in the way in which he had been raised. Many decided to follow him. Colmán asked Oswy to choose a successor at Lindisfarne. The king chose Tuda, who was from the kingdom of Laigin. Although the Blessed Aidan at Lindisfarne had trained him, Tuda espoused the reforms of Rome. When Tuda agreed to succeed him, Colmán withdrew from the kingdom. Many went with him, including some thirty of the faithful community from Lindisfarne.'

'I thought that Eata, the abbot of Melrose, became abbot of Lindisfarne?' said Eadulf.

'Tuda was dead within the year from the dreadful Yellow Plague and then Eata succeeded him. My brothers and I – indeed, my father and mother also – had joined Colmán. We first travelled north through Rheged and then west to Iona. From Colmcille's little island community, to which we owe so much, we sailed across the sea to this land. Colmán was from the kingdom of Connacht and he sought the permission of the local prince of the Uí Briúin to settle on Inis Bó Finne, the island of the white cow, to the west. Permission was given and we established our community there.'

'I have heard stories of that community. I was told that it prospered.'

Brother Berrihert shook his head sadly. 'For the first year we prospered, and then we received an emissary from Ard Macha.'

'Ard Macha?' Eadulf was surprised. He knew the abbey was in the northern kingdom of Ulaidh. 'What did Ard Macha seek in Connacht?'

'The emissary was an abbot who came to demand that Colmán, and our community, recognise Ard Macha as the centre of the Faith among all the kingdoms of this land. He had an arrogance of manner that reminded me of Wilfrid.'

'Wilfrid who was the main advocate of Rome at Witebia?'

'The same. I had known Wilfrid since he was a callow youth sent by Queen Eanflaed to Lindisfarne to be taught religion. Wilfrid was, and is, an ambitious man. He went to Rome and then to Canterbury and, I believe, he expected to become leader of all the churches of the Angles and the Saxons. He was angry when it was not so. Alas, his demeanour was dictatorial and he never allowed that there could be many paths in religion other than the one he advocated.'

'And you observed the same qualities in this abbot from Ard Macha?'

'He and Wilfrid might have been born from the same womb. The abbot, as I said, was an emissary from the abbot and bishop of Ard Macha. Colmán, having rejected the ideas of Rome once, was not averse to rejecting similar demands again. But this man was very cunning and, indeed, had persuasive arts. Once more there arose arguments and dissension among the brethren. Some decided to accept what this envoy from Ard Macha argued. They were led by a brother from the East Saxons named Gerald. There was no dwelling in harmony with him and those who had been persuaded to follow him. Finally, they left our island and went to found a new abbey on the mainland – a place called Maigh Éo . . .'

'The plain of yews? I know of it.'

'We, my brothers and I, became increasingly saddened by what was happening. We saw how this man had destroyed our united community and knew that he would continue to work against those who wanted to follow the original teachings. When he came again to our island, great unrest followed.' He paused and swallowed, pulling a grim face. 'In that unrest our mother, elderly like our father, was killed. That was when we decided to leave Colmán and our island community and come south, to somewhere away from the dissension.

Somewhere where we can dwell in peace and follow our religion without interference.'

Caol intervened for the first time. 'What made you choose this place?'

Berrihert smiled broadly and raised his hands in a gesture of surrender. 'God led our footsteps here.'

Miach, who had been patiently following the conversation even though he had heard the story before, was nodding slowly. 'And you, Eadulf, say that you know these Saxons?'

'That is so, Miach.'

'Then I am willing to allow them sanctuary in this valley, among my people.'

Brother Berrihert came to his feet and offered his hand to the chief. 'God will bless you for your generosity, Miach.'

The chieftain smiled grimly as he took the man's hand. 'It is my people who need the blessing, my Saxon friend. As Eadulf here will tell you, we have been at the forefront of raids by the Uí Fidgente, until a few years ago our king Colgú managed to defeat the army that they sent against us on the slopes of Cnoc Áine not far from here. My people have suffered much. But, thanks be to wise counsels, we seem to have emerged from that conflict and we now look forward to a time of peace. So blessings come at an appropriate time. Is it not so, Caol?'

Caol nodded enthusiastically.

'These Saxon friends of Eadulf have joined us at a most appropriate time,' he added. 'In two days, Eadulf and our lady Fidelma, sister to our king Colgú, renew and strengthen their marriage bonds in a great celebration at Cashel.'

Brother Berrihert turned to Eadulf. 'We have already heard tales of Fidelma and Eadulf and of their deeds. Was it the same Fidelma whom you helped in uncovering those responsible for the terrible murders at Witebia and averting a great war between the Saxon kingdoms?'

'It was the same Fidelma,' replied Eadulf solemnly, but not without pride in his voice.

Brother Berrihert clapped him on the shoulder. 'Then we must come along to this ceremony, if we are allowed, to bless this great occasion.'

Eadulf shrugged. 'I see no reason why you should not attend. Are you truly going to settle in the glen and build a church?'

Brother Berrihert was serious. 'That is truly our intention, Eadulf. What better place than this lovely oak-strewn valley, its tranquil passes and great salmon river? This is where our footsteps have been guided in our search for solitude. And now that we have the approval of Miach, we may look forward to a future without conflict. Without the constant *meum et tuum* of petty squabbles among the churchmen.'

'The what?' frowned Miach, who was no Latin speaker.

'Mine and thine,' interpreted Eadulf automatically. 'I wish you well in this endeavour, Berrihert. But do not think that conflicts over the Faith do not intrude in this part of the world. There are as many arguments here as anywhere. Perhaps scripture has foretold it? *Et ponam redemptionem inter populum meum, et inter populum tuum . . .*'

'And I shall put a division between my people and your people,' translated Brother Berrihert. He gestured to the woods around him. 'This will be our fortress of peace. Anyone who does not respect the views of another will be told that their disruptive influence is unwelcome here.'

'It is a good objective to aim for,' Miach agreed. 'You will be twice welcomed for maintaining that philosophy.' He stood up and held out his hand to Eadulf. 'I am sorry that you had such a long ride here, but I had to be sure that you knew these compatriots of yours. I thank you, Brother Eadulf. I give them these dwellings and this land to start their community. And now I must return to my rath.'

He bid them farewell, and then he and his warriors departed.

Caol was glancing up at the sky through the canopy of branches.

'If we left now, Brother Eadulf,' he said, 'we could be back just after dusk.'

'There is much I would like to discuss with you all,' Eadulf said reluctantly, encompassing Berrihert and his brothers with his glance. 'It is a long time since I was in my homeland, and even longer since you were. It would be good to talk and reflect on the changes that have come upon us.'

Brother Berrihert smiled his agreement. 'You have much to do in these coming days, Eadulf. But, God willing, we shall come to Cashel to mark your momentous day. Thereafter, you will always find us in this place.'

Caol fetched the horses and Eadulf shook hands with them all, including Ordwulf. The old man still seemed distant, and had taken no part in the conversation. He seemed to be dwelling in his own inner world.

'I am glad that I have been able to put Miach's mind at rest,' Eadulf assured Berrihert, at parting. 'And good to see countrymen of mine dwelling here. I pray things will work out for you all.'

'At least, from what I hear of this kingdom, you will not get an envoy from Ard Macha coming to demand your allegiance.'

'You might be right.' Eadulf laughed. 'Who was this abbot from Ard Macha who put you so out of sorts, Berrihert?'

'I remember his name well – he reminded me so much of Wilfrid and his arrogance. His name was Ultán. Abbot Ultán of Cill Ria.'


It was well after dark when Eadulf and Caol returned to Cashel, but night came early at this time of year. It had not been long after they had crossed the great swirling river Siúr, the 'sister' river, at the Ford of the Ass, that the dark clouds had begun to roll more menacingly and the rumble of distant thunder was heard. Then the deluge began. Both riders were soaked within moments.

'Do you want to seek shelter, Brother Eadulf?' yelled Caol, leaning across as he held his shying mount on a tight reign.

Eadulf shook his head. 'What point in that when we are drenched already? Let us press on. It is not far to Cashel.'

At that moment a bright bolt of lightning lit up the sky, illuminating the great plain before them, and in the distance they saw the spectacular mound of limestone on whose precipitous crown rose the fortress of the Eóghanacht kings of Muman. It was a natural stronghold, dominating the countryside in all directions.

Crouching low on their horses, they headed through the blustery, whipping rain, ignoring now the flashes of white lightning that every so often lit the countryside before the accompanying crash of thunder. It was not long, though it seemed an eternity to Eadulf, before they entered the township that had grown up at the foot of the limestone rock and passed through its almost deserted square, barely lit with a few dim swinging lanterns. The pleasant pungent odour of turf fires came to Eadulf's nostrils and he sighed in anticipation of a warm fire, a goblet of wine and even a hot bath. The Irish had their main wash, a full body wash, before their evening meal. It was a habit that Eadulf could never get used to – this daily ritual of washing, called *fothrucud*, in a large tub or vat called a *dabach*. Every hostel and guest house had to be provided with a bath house for visitors by law. In his native land, Eadulf reflected, a quick plunge in a river – and that not very often – was considered to discharge one's duty to cleanliness.

A sharp challenge brought his mind back from his reverie to the present. A watchful warrior emerged from a corner of the square and Caol responded. The man disappeared again.

They moved up the track from the town, winding their way up to the top of the rocky prominence where the great man-made stone walls merged with the limestone rock to form impregnable fortifications. The tall wooden gates were closed, but at a shout from Caol they swung open and the riders passed inside where the *gilla scuir*, stable lads, came running forward to help them down and take charge of their horses. Eadulf exchanged a brief word with Caol, and then he departed for the chambers that he shared with Fidelma.

Muirgen, their nurse, opened the door and surveyed his sodden form with disapproval.

'You need to be out of those rags, Brother Eadulf, before you catch a chill. I will get my man to prepare a bath.'

She had barely finished speaking when Fidelma came forward and smiled ruefully at his bedraggled appearance.

'Muirgen is right. Get out of those clothes immediately while she prepares a bath.'

Muirgen had hurried off to find her husband, Nessán, who for some months now had been devoted to the charge of taking care of them and their little boy, Alchú. Eadulf shuffled to the blazing fire while Fidelma went in search of a towel and a woollen cloak. Within a short time, Eadulf was seated by the fire wrapped in the cloak and sipping mulled wine, explaining to Fidelma the nature of the business that Miach of the Uí Cuileann had summoned him for.

Fidelma listened more or less in silence, only asking a question here and there for clarification's sake. When he had finished, Eadulf noticed that her face wore a thoughtful expression.

'You seem pensive,' he ventured.

'It just seems strange that these Saxons have arrived here at this particular time.'

'Strange? In what way?'

'They said that they had come south because of the problems in Abbot Colmán's community on Inis Bó Finne. That this abbot from Ard Macha had created dissension among them, causing some of the community to break away and start a new community on Maigh Éo, the plain of the yew?'

'That is so.'

'Did they tell you what made them come here, to the glen of Eatharlaí of all places, and at this time?'

Eadulf shook his head. 'To be truthful, I think Caol asked the question.'

'And their reply?'

'Only that God had guided their footsteps here.'

'Which is no reply at all. Are you sure Abbot Ultán was the name of this influential abbot from Ard Macha?'

Eadulf was puzzled by her questions.

'I may be guilty of many faults but my hearing is still good,' he replied testily. 'Ultán is such a simple name that I could not mistake it. Why do you ask?'

Fidelma sighed, deep in thought.

'This is either coincidence or something else,' she said finally.

Eadulf was still irritable. 'Perhaps I might agree if I knew what you were talking about.'

'There is only one Abbot Ultán linked with Ard Macha – Ultán of Cill Ria, who is also bishop of the Uí Thuirtrí. He acts as envoy to the Comarb of the Blessed Patrick, one of the two premier abbots of the five kingdoms. I have seen him once, at the council where it was agreed that I become part of the Cill Dara delegation to Witebia to offer advice on law. He is, as your Saxon friends described him, a man of arrogance, and somewhat overbearing.'

Eadulf shrugged. 'I still do not understand what you mean by a coincidence.'

'A rider from Imleach came here this afternoon and among the news he brought to my brother was that Abbot Ultán of Cill Ria had arrived at Imleach with a small delegation. He is demanding recognition for Ard Macha as the primatial seat of the Faith in all the five kingdoms. Furthermore, Abbot Ultán and his delegation are coming here – here to Cashel – to protest against our marriage.'

Eadulf stared at her in astonishment. 'Why?' he demanded. 'I mean, what is there to protest about?'

Fidelma lifted a shoulder and let it fall eloquently. 'He is of the small group that believes that there should be no marriage among the religious.'

Eadulf relaxed and chuckled. 'Well, I do not think the day will come when that will become a reality. Why does he think God created men and women?'

'Now do you see why I think it is odd, that, at the same time, these Saxons have arrived here?'

'*Quam saepe forte temere eveniut*,' quoted Eadulf. 'How often things occur by mere chance.'

'I had no idea that you had read Terence,' Fidelma exclaimed.

'I found a copy of *Phormio* in the library here,' he replied complacently.

'So how well do you know these Saxons?'

Eadulf was suddenly thoughtful. 'I cannot say that I can place my hand on my heart and declare that I truly know them. I met Berrihert when I was studying at Tuam Brecain – he was a pupil there too. In fact, he is not really a Saxon but an Angle from Deira, which is part of the kingdom of Northumbria,' he added with tribal fastidiousness, knowing full well that all Angles and Saxons were deemed Saxons in Irish eyes. 'Then when I was sent to Witebia to attend the great council, where I met you, I saw him again. He had returned to his homeland and converted his younger brothers. I have no reason to doubt their motives. After all, they did leave their homeland to follow Colmán to this country so that they might practise the Faith in the way that they had been taught.'

Fidelma did not seem reassured, but she shrugged. 'Perhaps I am being overly suspicious.'

'Because they are strangers in your land? I have heard a saying: "Cold is the wind that brings strangers."'

Fidelma shot him a glance of disapproval. 'Then learn the meaning. It is a saying used by some of our coastal peoples and refers to what they might expect when the sails of raiding ships are sighted.'

Eadulf heard the familiar sharpness in her voice and sighed. 'Then why be suspicious of these compatriots of mine? It is probably chance that brought them here at this time. After all, it is chance that rules men and not men chance.'

'So you have indicated before,' she observed. Then she smiled and shrugged. 'I am probably just restless. Something that old Brother Conchobhar mentioned . . .'

Eadulf smiled. 'What has that old soothsayer been up to? Looking at patterns in the night sky again and foretelling doom and gloom?'

Fidelma knew that Eadulf respected Brother Conchobhar in spite of the levity in his voice so she did not rise to the bait. 'He believes that we should have a care over the next few days, that is all.'

Eadulf saw the seriousness in her eyes and was serious himself for a moment before smiling again. 'Have no fear. There is little that can go wrong now. Caol has been telling me that even the High King is coming to acknowledge the ceremony. And with all the nobles and warriors come to pay their respects to you, what is there to fear?'

There was a tap on the door and Muirgen returned.

'The bath is ready,' she announced, 'and, lady, your brother the king wishes you both to attend the feasting tonight.'

Eadulf rose and drew his robe round him. 'Then I shall go and soak myself in the tub. I am even getting use to this daily bathing custom of yours,' he added with a grimace.

He left the room. Muirgen was about to follow when Fidelma stayed her with a gesture of her hand. The nurse closed the door after Eadulf and waited patiently.

'How is little Alchú?' Fidelma enquired.

The nurse's face softened. 'He is sleeping peacefully, lady.' She hesitated. 'Is something troubling you?'

Fidelma started to shake her head, and then admitted: 'I am just a little worried, that's all. Have the guests started to arrive?'

Muirgen nodded quickly. 'Some have, but I am told that tomorrow is when the majority of guests are expected. Prince Finguine is going to arrange the erection of tents on the plains below, for many are coming and the fortress cannot accommodate them all.' Finguine was the king's *tánaiste* or heir apparent. 'Are you nervous, lady? All five kingdoms are coming to rejoice for you.'

Fidelma hesitated. 'I am not worried about the ceremony. However, make sure that you and Nessán keep a careful eye on little Alchú during these next days.'

'As if he were our own, lady,' replied the woman immediately. 'You need have no fear that we will neglect our duties, especially after . . .'

Fidelma rose immediately and went to embrace the woman.

When little Alchú had been kidnapped, Uaman the Leper had given the baby to Muirgen and Nessán, then shepherds in the distant western mountains, to raise as their own. He had not told them who the child was, or that it had been kidnapped. Being childless, they had welcomed the 'gift'. When Eadulf had recovered Alchú and it was discovered that Muirgen and Nessán had played their part in innocence, Fidelma had asked Muirgen to be the child's nurse.

'I cast no aspersions, Muirgen. But I am fearful . . . old Conchobhar sees bad signs and I respect his ability in the art. He has been right before.'

Muirgen sniffed and nodded. 'Then lay aside your fears, lady, for I will guard the child with my life, as will my man.'

'All the same, I cannot shake this feeling of foreboding.'

She turned and went to the window, and drew aside the heavy curtain to peer out at the inclement evening. The storm was renewing itself with intensity beyond the distant round peaks of the Slieve Felim mountains. Only when the lightning flashed behind them did their hazy shadows show up through the sheeting rain. The thunder rumbled low and menacing. Its threatening force was even more disturbing to Fidelma than the outright rage of a tempest directly overhead. A shudder ran down her back and she pulled the curtain firmly back into place.

'This is silly,' she told herself firmly. And while she knew that it was so, nevertheless she could not rid herself of the vague feeling of apprehension that had come over her. It was not merely Brother Conchobhar's warning. She had felt this presentiment for some time and it was a feeling that she could not share with Eadulf.

# Chapter Three

The ominous clouds had departed overnight to the north and a pale blue sky canopied the great plain around Cashel. The sun had risen as a soft pale orb without warmth. To the west, there was what sailors called a 'mackerel sky', small cloud globules floating as if in ripples which indicated that there was still unsettled weather to come. The storm had left swollen rivers and areas of sticky mud in the low-lying areas.

Finguine, the *tánaiste*, had been up since dawn with bands of enthusiastic helpers who would be erecting the canvas pavilions in which those who could not be accommodated in the fortress or the town's inn and hostel would stay. King Colgú had proclaimed three days of festivities and many people were already pouring into Cashel for the marriage rituals, which would start the next morning. Finguine had ridden through the area, trying to choose high ground that had not been so muddied by the torrent of rain that had fallen on the previous day. He directed his men to mark a spot here and there as it caught his approving eye.

Fidelma and Eadulf had also risen early, spent some time with Alchú, and then breakfasted before going down to the great hall to greet the arriving guests. There were the Eóghanacht princes – Congal of Locha Léin, Fer Dá Lethe of Raithlin, and many others whose names simply passed above Eadulf's head; there was even Conrí, warlord of the Uí Fidgente, who had come with his prince, Donennach, the new chief of the former blood enemies of Cashel.

As he moved through the throng of distinguished visitors, Eadulf realised, perhaps for the first time, that he was essentially a shy man.

Yet here he was, the centre of attention and subject of scrutiny by what he felt to be the entire population of the five kingdoms of Éireann. For the first time, he wanted to escape from it all. He was but an hereditary *gerefa*, a magistrate of his own South Folk, the East Angles, who had only turned his back on the gods and goddesses of his people in his teen years. Since the fateful meeting at the great Council of Witebia he had come to realise that his life was inseparably linked with Fidelma of Cashel. However, it had taken some years for them to decide on a trial marriage. Under Irish law they had bound themselves together for a year and a day during which Fidelma had become his *ben charrthach*, the 'loved woman'. Eadulf had been happy to be her *fer comtha* with rights as husband for that period. During that time their son little Alchú, 'gentle hound', had been born. Now the trial period was over, and either of them could move on without recrimination or compensation. But they had decided to confirm their marriage vows.

Eadulf had thought it would be as simple and as unremarkable as it had been when exchanging the vows at the trial marriage. But this was becoming an uneasy experience for him. He had not fully taken into account that Fidelma was a princess of the Eóghanacht, the ruling house of Muman, whose brother Colgú was hailed by the *senachaí*, the hereditary genealogists, as the eightieth direct generation from Gaedheal Glas, eponymous father of the Gaels, and the fifty-ninth generation since Eibhear Fionn son of Golamh called Míldih, who had brought the children of the Gael to Éireann. Eadulf had heard the genealogies, the *forsundud* as the bards called them, sung a thousand times. But he had not realised that this official marriage of Fidelma would draw such crowds of kings and nobles and onlookers to Cashel. He felt unsettled. With a feeling of guilt, he made an excuse about going to the chapel for a morning prayer, and left the great hall.

Sitting in the quiet solitude of the chapel, Eadulf was startled to realise that he wanted no part of life in a palace. He frowned as he thought about it. He felt that he wanted to leave Cashel and make his way to some more peaceful spot, away from the crowds, away from the dignitaries and nobles, away from the hustle and bustle. A place of solitude. A place like the glen of Eatharlaí.

Brother Berrihert had the right idea. Solitude and peace in a wooded valley.

He suddenly felt pangs of guilt again.

Was he being selfish? Of course, there was no question that he wanted to share his life with Fidelma and little Alchú. He caught himself again. Share his life? That was looking at things from a one-sided viewpoint. Should he not also be thinking of sharing Fidelma's life, and wasn't that life part of Cashel and all it stood for? He shook his head in perplexity as he tried to reason things out. Was he simply apprehensive of this large festival? As soon as it was over, as soon as the marriage contracts were agreed, surely life would return to its normal ebb and flow.

When had there been a normal ebb and flow to his life? Ever since he had known Fidelma there had been one adventure after another, one mysterious killing after another to be investigated. He found himself chuckling aloud.

'You seem amused by something, my friend?'

The hollow voice came from behind him, and Eadulf turned to find the bright blue eyes of Brother Conchobhar regarding him quizzically.

'Amused?' Eadulf repeated.

'You were laughing to yourself.'

Eadulf grimaced.

'At myself,' he corrected with a sigh.

Brother Conchobhar smiled knowingly. 'Yet you do not find yourself an object of humour. There was a bitter quality in your laughter.'

'I shall not deny it.'

'You worry about tomorrow. We have an old saying – marry a woman out of the glen and you marry the whole glen.'

Eadulf was astonished.

'How did you know that I was thinking of that?'

Brother Conchobhar grimaced. 'It is my nature to know these things. It is difficult for you, Brother Saxon, for you are a stranger in this land. But take comfort, for many who are not would find the path that you are taking difficult. Did you think it would be easy to marry an Eóghanacht of Cashel?'

'I did not think of it. Certainly, I did not know what it meant.'

Brother Conchobhar inclined his head with a sad smile. 'Yet you must have learnt something from your trial marriage.'

'I suppose I did.'

'Have you lost the feelings that you had for the lady Fidelma?'

'Of course not!'

'Have you lost the feelings that you had for Alchú, you son?'

Again, Eadulf's reply was emphatic.

'Then,' smiled Brother Conchobhar, 'your malady seems a simple one. You are simply fearful of the responsibility that you will take on.'

Eadulf raised his chin pugnaciously. 'Fearful?'

'Exactly so. Perhaps you are not ready to be the husband of an Eóghanacht?'

Eadulf snorted indignantly. 'I have been so this last year.'

Brother Conchobhar pulled a wry face. 'Then what else can it be?' he mused. 'Unless . . .'

Eadulf's brows came together. 'Unless?' he demanded irritably.

'Unless . . . it is merely the pomp and circumstance that you are fearful of? The gathering crowd and the nobles and officials who are assembling to see the sister of Colgú wed? Do not forget that her father was the great Fáilbe Flann mac Aedo, one of the greatest kings of Muman. Fáilbe was a man respected among all the kingdoms of this island. And you are fearful of the honour that the people do to the lady Fidelma?'

Eadulf flushed.

'That is not the way of it,' he snapped. 'I am just a plain man and no noble.'

Brother Conchobhar grinned crookedly. 'You are no common man.'

'I am but a simple magistrate who decided to choose the way of the religious . . .'

'That is not what I meant. Whatever your birth, you are no common man. No common man would be the choice of the lady Fidelma. She has seen in you something uncommon, something complementary and necessary to her. So, my friend, is it not how she perceives you that is the most important thing? Not your fears of how others perceive you.'

Eadulf was silent as he pondered the old man's words.

'Do I judge the basis of your fears correctly, my Saxon friend?' Brother Conchobhar prompted.

Eadulf stirred uncomfortably.

'I think . . .' he began, but he was silenced by the blast of a trumpet outside the chapel.

'That sounds like another distinguished guest arriving,' sighed Brother Conchobhar, 'and an important one for a trumpet to be sounded. Let us go and see who it is.'

Unprotesting, Eadulf followed the old man to the doors of the chapel and they halted on the steps overlooking the courtyard.

Two riders followed by a wagon had entered through the gates. To both Brother Conchobhar and Eadulf's surprise, the wagon contained two religieuse with luggage, while seated on the riding box were two armed men in menial dress, not of the religious. One of them had a small trumpet on his lap and had clearly sounded the announcing blast. However, the two riders caused the observers an even bigger surprise.

The first rider was a tall, middle-aged man, fairly handsome in a dark and saturnine way, who carried himself with an arrogant manner. He was looking round with an expression of disdain. At his side, his companion was elderly and sharp-featured. What was astonishing was that they were clad in monastic robes. True, they were richly embellished, but nevertheless the men were clearly members of the religious.

Brother Conchobhar snorted in disgust.

'Since when have the religious given themselves airs and graces?' he muttered to Eadulf. 'I know not these strangers.'

Caol, the commander of Colgú's bodyguard, had come hurrying from the stables with Dego, one of his warriors, and halted before the newcomers. Eadulf noticed that Caol looked slightly bewildered and guessed that he had shared their expectation of the trumpet's announcing the arrival of some noble or even a minor king. He was apparently nonplussed at being confronted by religious.

'You are welcome to Cashel,' he said warily. 'Whom am I addressing?'

It was the elderly, sharp-featured man, who replied in a grand tone,

'You are in the presence of the abbot of Cill Ria, Bishop Ultán of
the Uí Thuirtrí, envoy from the *archiepiscopus* of Ard Macha.'

Caol continued to frown uncertainly. 'Dego will see you to your
chamber, Abbot Ultán, and then conduct your companions to the
hostels set aside for them. The hostel for females is within the fortress
but that for males is in the town below.'

The abbot did not move as Dego went forward but the elderly man
at his side, glancing uneasily at his master, raised his tone querulously.

'Does your king not come to the gate to welcome the envoy from
the *archiepiscopus* of Ard Macha?'

Caol had begun to return to the stables but now turned with surprise.

'My king does not even come to the gate to welcome the Comarb
of the Blessed Ailbe who brought the Faith to our kingdom, let alone
to welcome an abbot from the north who represents someone with a
title that I do not recognise,' he replied shortly.

Even from where he stood, Eadulf could see the saturnine abbot's
brows drawing together in anger. Beside Eadulf, Brother Conchobhar
was stifling a chuckle.

'Now,' Caol was continuing, 'should you wish to be received by
Colgú before the ceremonies commence, I will convey your greet-
ings to him. But he is, at this time, welcoming the High King, the
provincial kings and the princes of these lands in his private chambers.'

He nodded to Dego to continue and began to turn away again.

'Young man!'

Abbot Ultán's sharp tones cut through the courtyard, halting Caol,
who again turned questioningly to the newcomer.

'You are insolent, young man. Know you that I am . . .'

'An arrogant messenger from an arrogant abbot,' snapped a new
voice.

Eadulf saw another religieux enter the courtyard from one of the
buildings and come striding over to stand by Caol. He was broad-
shouldered and looked more like a warrior than a leading member
of the church, for as such his clothes and accoutrements proclaimed
him.

'That is Augaire, the abbot of Conga,' whispered Brother

Conchobhar. 'He's also one of the chief bishops to the king of Connacht.'

Abbot Ultán had turned a venomous gaze on the newcomer.

'So? You are here too?' He almost hissed the words.

Abbot Augaire smiled but it was a smile without humour.

'Oh yes. Everyone who matters is here,' he replied softly. 'Even some who do not matter are here.'

'Including the jumped-up Uí Fiachracha whom some call a king in Connacht?' sneered Abbot Ultán.

'Including Muirchertach Nár,' affirmed the other, calmly. 'Several of your old friends are gathered here.'

The way the abbot pronounced 'old friends' made it clear to Eadulf that the people referred to were anything but friends of Abbot Ultán. He wondered what this exchange really meant.

'Do not think that they will intimidate me. I shall speak the truth,' snapped Abbot Ultán.

Abbot Augaire's smile broadened but it was still without warmth.

'They would not wish to stop you if ever you decided to speak the truth,' he replied with acid in his voice.

Abbot Ultán blinked. His expression was suddenly dangerous. He was about to say something but then seemed to change his mind and turned back to Caol.

'Young man, tell your king that I demand to see him. In the meantime, I also demand that you send a warrior to stand guard at my chamber door to protect me from . . .' he glanced at Abbot Augaire, 'from anyone who might wish to harm a truth servant of the true Faith.'

Caol looked bewildered for a moment and then he shrugged.

'As I have said, Dego will take you to your quarters. I will convey your request to Colgú,' he said, and left.

Dego moved forward to oversee the unloading of the luggage from the wagon and to conduct the abbot to his quarters, while another attendant went to see to the rest of the party.

For a few moments, Abbot Augaire stood in the courtyard looking thoughtfully after Abbot Ultán even when he had vanished through one of the entrances to the main building. He was unaware that Eadulf and Brother Conchobhar were still watching him. The expression on the abbot's face was not a pleasant one. Then, with a shake of his head, he was gone.

Eadulf turned to Brother Conchobhar. 'Well, what is to be made of that?'

Brother Conchobhar pursed his lips thoughtfully. 'Have you not heard of Abbot Ultán?'

'I seem to have heard his name recently.' Eadulf frowned. 'Ah, he was coming to protest against our wedding.'

'I have never seen him before but I have heard many stories about him, none of them to his credit. He is not a man whom I would pronounce as fit for the company of saints.' For once Brother Conchobhar looked serious. 'Beware of Abbot Ultán. He is full of ambition, and pays homage to nothing save power.'

'Ultán? Who speaks of Ultán?'

Eadulf swung round and found Brother Berrihert on the steps behind them. He smiled in warm greeting.

'So you have come to join us? That is good. This is Brother Conchobhar.'

Brother Berrihert nodded curtly at the old man but his eyes did not leave Eadulf's face. 'The name of Ultán was spoken. Abbot Ultán of Cill Ria?'

'The same,' agreed Eadulf, worried at the intensity in the young Saxon's voice. Then he remembered that it was Berrihert who had first mentioned the name of the abbot to him.

'Is he here?'

'He is. I am told that he has come here to protest against my wedding.'

Berrihert drew in a deep breath as if facing some momentous decision. Then he let it out slowly.

'Then I give fair warning, Eadulf. Make sure that his path does not cross mine or that of my brothers, for I fear the worst.'

'I do not understand.'

'I fear that one of us might kill him,' replied the young man sharply. He turned and strode off, leaving Eadulf staring in surprise.

Brother Conchobhar stood looking thoughtfully after him.

'Alas, it seems that Bishop Ultán's circle of acquaintances ever widens,' he said.

'I do not understand it,' Eadulf replied with a shake of his head. 'While yesterday Brother Berrihert told me of how this Abbot Ultán split the community in which he and his brothers served on Inis Bó Finne, and how they came south for independence and peace, he mentioned nothing that would give rise to some mortal hatred of Ultán. Certainly he gave no indication of animosity to the extent that his death might be encompassed.'

'The emotions of mankind are strange, my Saxon friend. You should know that above all people. You have seen enough violence in your investigations with our lady Fidelma. What angers one person, amuses another. What causes harm to one, causes benefit to someone else. Whatever slight your friend believes he has suffered might not seem much to you but will mean the world to him.' Brother Conchobhar clapped Eadulf on the shoulder and chuckled. 'At least you may give thanks to the arrival of Abbot Ultán for one thing.'

Eadulf did not understand.

'His arrival has caused you to forget your personal concerns about your fitness to go through with the ceremony tomorrow. You will be too preoccupied with watching Abbot Ultán and waiting for the trouble that he will undoubtedly cause.'

# CHAPTER FOUR

It was a sombre group that gathered that evening in the private chamber of Colgú, king of Muman. The handsome, red-haired king sprawled moodily in his carved oak chair before the fire. Fidelma sat upright opposite him with Eadulf standing behind her, one hand resting on the back of her chair. Caol, the commander of the bodyguard, stood discreetly with his back to the door, as if on guard, while a chair had been brought for Abbot Ségdae, newly arrived from the abbey of Imleach, and another for Baithen, the brehon of Muman.

'It is upsetting, I know, lady,' Baithen finally said, voicing the consensus of the group.

Fidelma returned his concerned gaze with a smile. 'I had a premonition that the arrival of Abbot Ultán would not bring happiness to this place. Yet we have heard these arguments so many times before. Is that not so, Eadulf?'

The Saxon inclined his head in agreement.

'You will remember the violent opposition of the old Bishop Petrán to our trial marriage?' he said. 'So violent was the argument that when he died a natural death soon after, I was even accused of his murder.'

There was an uncomfortable silence. It had been the prejudice and incompetence of Dathal, the former brehon of Muman, that had caused the mistake that had almost convinced everyone at Cashel that Eadulf was to blame for the old bishop's death. The discovery of the truth had led to Dathal's enforced retirement from office and the appointment of Baithen as brehon in his place.

'We have weathered these objections before and doubtless will do so again,' observed Fidelma.

Abbot Ségdae sighed, and not for the first time during the conversation. 'Nevertheless, it is upsetting that Abbot Ultán arrives on the eve of your wedding to seize the opportunity to voice his arguments before the assembled kings of Éireann. It is obviously done deliberately because the opportunity to address such an audience at one time comes infrequently.'

'A pity that this agitator did not meet with some accident on his journey here,' muttered Colgú darkly. Then, seeing the look of disapproval from his legal and spiritual advisers, he shrugged apologetically. '*Quod avertat Deus* – which may God avert,' he added without conviction. 'However, the abbot tells me he is an envoy from the abbot and bishop Ségéne of Ard Macha. At least he has no authority here.'

'He has no authority,' agreed Brehon Baithen. 'Neither in the law of this land nor, so far as I know them, in the rules of the Faith. Not even Rome enforces celibacy among its religious.'

'Exactly,' Fidelma agreed emphatically. 'If we can ignore Ultán's prejudice then surely our guests can?'

Colgú glanced at Caol. 'And our guests have all arrived and are secure in their accommodations?'

The young warrior took a step forward.

'As you know, Sechnassach, the High King, and his retinue were the last to arrive, at midday,' he replied. 'Before him, there arrived Fianamail of Laigin, Blathmac of Ulaidh, and the king of Connacht, Muirchertach Nár. They, with their ladies, and their *tánaiste* and nobles, are all settled in their quarters.'

'I see Muirchertach Nár of Connacht is accompanied by Abbot Augaire of Conga.' Abbot Ségdae smiled grimly. 'Caol tells me that Abbot Augaire has already engaged in an angry discourse with Abbot Ultán.'

Colgú looked surprised and troubled. 'Arguments already? About his protest over Fidelma? Caol, what happened?'

'Not exactly an argument over anything, so far as I witnessed. It seemed that there was an underlying tension. Abbot Augaire's words were spoken in a civil tone though they were bitter. He did call Ultán an arrogant messenger from an arrogant bishop. But no voice was raised, no specific argument made. It seemed that they had met in the past and that there was still bitterness between them.'

Abbot Ségdae's features were sorrowful. 'I presume that the tension arises from the same argument that he had with me at Imleach. It is the claim of Ard Macha to be the primatial seat of the Faith in all the five kingdoms. Abbot Augaire of Conga is one of the many abbots and bishops who reject that claim.'

The king turned his worried gaze towards his brehon. 'Is there any way that we can exclude Abbot Ultán from the ceremony tomorrow? I fear that there are enough problems without Ultán making public protests.'

Brehon Baithen exchanged a quick glance with the Abbot Ségdae.

'There is no legal excuse,' he said. 'He is entitled to stand up and voice his objections to the marriage. We all acknowledge that he is, after all, the emissary from Ard Macha, which is very influential. Any discourtesy to Abbot Ultán may be interpreted as an insult to Blathmac, the king of Ulaidh, in whose kingdom Ard Macha is the chief religious house.'

Colgú drummed his fingers for a moment on the arm of his chair.

'This was to have been an occasion of unity and serenity,' he said, half to himself. 'Kings and nobles and many of distinction have all come as our guests to witness this ceremony. Even the Uí Fidgente. That alone is a great tribute to my sister's diplomacy in attempting to heal the wounds created at the battle of Cnoc Áine. That dissension sown by a firebrand prelate from outside this kingdom should now threaten the day . . .' He ended with a helpless shake of his head.

There was a pause before Brehon Baithen cleared his throat.

'I have a suggestion.'

They turned to him expectantly. The brehon grimaced as if a little undecided whether to continue.

'The objection of this Abbot Ultán is based solely on the fact that the lady Fidelma took vows to serve the Faith. Is that not so?'

'Obviously so,' agreed Abbot Ségdae. 'And, as we continually point out, not even Rome lays strictures on the marriage of the religious. The idea that all who serve the Faith must remain celibate is only argued by a particular school of philosophers.'

'It would end all argument if the lady Fidelma simply withdrew from those vows. You, Ségdae, as senior abbot and bishop of the kingdom, could pronounce on it. After all, since she left Cill Dara, Fidelma has not served in any religious house. There is no need for it. She follows her primary calling as an advocate of our laws.'

Fidelma leaned forward slightly from her chair. Her voice was sharp.

'That would be admitting the validity of Ultán's protests – that religious should not get married,' she pointed out. 'It is true that I only joined the house at Cill Dara at the suggestion of my cousin, Abbot Laisran. I have never been a religieuse in the strict sense. But, having said that, I will not withdraw when there is no need. When there is no rule that would force me to do so, why should I? No,' she continued decisively, 'since Abbot Ultán is determined to make an issue of this matter by interrupting the ceremony in the chapel, I think we should face his arguments rather than seek to avoid them.'

Abbot Ségdae was puzzled. 'If you would attempt to debate with Abbot Ultán in the middle of a marriage ceremony . . . why, that would be most unseemly. And I must point out that no mean scholar advises him. I mean his hawk-faced companion, Brother Drón. Ultán's fault is that he tends to bombast when his arguments are blocked by counter-arguments.'

'Such a debate must not take place in the middle of the marriage ceremony.' Colgú's voice was determined. 'I forbid it.'

Brehon Baithen rubbed his chin thoughtfully. 'Even if we could debate this matter in private, I doubt that any conclusion arrived at would prevent Ultán from standing up during the ceremony and voicing his objections again in public. You cannot forbid his protest.'

Colgú turned in resignation to Abbot Ségdae. 'You tell us that this Abbot Ultán is advised by Brother Drón who is no mean scholar. Can you inform us what scholarship he can use to argue his case against my sister's marriage tomorrow?'

'None that cannot be countered,' replied the abbot with firmness. 'As has been said many times, this matter of celibacy among those who serve the Faith is merely a matter of opinion. At the time when our Lord walked upon this earth, his apostles, such as Peter the Rock, on which it was said that the entire church was founded, were married men. All the religions that I have ever heard of contain aesthetes who believe that celibacy, among both male and female, somehow bring them closer to their gods. Our Christian aesthetes had their first victory three centuries ago at a council in Iberia, at a place called Elvira. That council agreed that a priest who slept with his wife the night before Mass could not perform the sacrament. A quarter of a century later, at Nicaea, it was decreed by the council that a priest should not marry after he had been ordained. Nevertheless fifty years later Siricius, the Bishop of Rome, who was married but deserted his wife, ordered that priests should no longer sleep with their wives – clearly demonstrating that they were still marrying.'

Fidelma gestured impatiently. 'Most priests and other religious throughout all the kingdoms of the world still marry. I have heard that this inclination towards celibacy seems to be part of a movement emanating from those who seek to denigrate the role of women in the world. We all know that at the Council of Laodicea, three centuries ago, it was agreed that women must no longer be ordained priests. Today there are few women priests to be found.'

Abbot Ségdae nodded. 'And it cannot be denied that for the last hundred years the bishops of Rome, who have been accepted by many as the premier bishops of Christendom, have tended to side with those who seek to enforce celibacy. Sons of former bishops and priests no longer take the throne of the Blessed Peter. Homidas, son of the Blessed Silverus, was the last son of a previous bishop of Rome to ascend to his father's place. Now there are those such as Gregory, who uttered the curious statement that all sexual desire is sinful in itself.'

Colgú was impatient. 'Arguments! Precedents! It is like chasing a will o' the wisp. Is there no law written down by which a judgement can be given and adhered to? Is there no rule given in your religious writings, Ségdae?'

Abbot Ségdae shook his head. 'I am afraid that the sexual ethics and views on marriage in the Faith have been neither uniform nor static enough to be considered law. The decrees of the various councils have never been universally accepted so far.'

Eadulf coughed nervously. He was well aware that he was a stranger in the kingdom and, according to the social customs and laws, had no right to speak in the presence of a king unless invited. Colgú, however, immediately understood his hesitation and gestured towards him.

'Do not stand on ceremony here, Eadulf. You have something to contribute to this discussion?'

Eadulf shot him a look of silent gratitude. 'My experience of those who put forward the argument for celibacy is that they often rely on the writings of Augustine of Hippo.'

Abbot Ségdae looked interested. 'I would not have considered Augustine to have much influence in this land, especially in the kingdom of Ulaidh, for his views are so contrary to our laws and way of life. He considered women inferior to men both in morals as well as in physical being.'

'That is true,' Eadulf agreed. 'He once wrote . . .' He shut his eyes to recite from memory. 'I fail to see what use women can be to man if one excludes the function of bearing children.' He opened his eyes again. 'In my estimation, Augustine was a silly, narrow and prejudiced person, and I find it strange others hold him in esteem as a great philosopher.'

'What arguments would Abbot Ultán put forward from this authority, Brother Eadulf?' asked Brehon Baithen.

'Augustine believed that Adam and Eve were innocent of sexual temptation or feelings when they lived in the Garden of Eden,' Eadulf began. 'Augustine wrote that prior to their fall and expulsion, their sexual impulses had been under conscious control. But because they rebelled against God, the genitals of their descendants rebelled against their will. Humans then became incapable of controlling either their sexual desires or the physical reactions of their gonads, so the only way to achieve a holy life and salvation was to abjure all form of dealings with women.'

'Is what you have said considered to be the main argument of those who advocate celibacy?' Colgú asked. 'That suppression of the natural role between the sexes is a path to religious perfection?'

'There is another argument which, I think, many of the higher priesthood in Rome find more congenial,' Eadulf replied.

'Which is?'

'It is the practical consideration. In these kingdoms you do not have the concept of absolute private ownership in the land, so the argument does not affect you so much. But elsewhere, especially in Rome, property is a great consideration. It is the economic idea that drives the arguments for an unmarried clergy.'

Fidelma regarded Eadulf with some surprise, and he smiled re-assuringly at her unasked question.

'When I was in Rome, I attended many debates and arguments,' he explained.

'What is this economic idea, then?' asked Abbot Ségdae.

'Married religious are too expensive to maintain. They have to be given housing, food and clothing, not only for themselves but also for their wives and children. And the children of priests can inherit their property, so that assets which the church wants to hold can be left away from it. The church's resources are therefore spent in catering to the wives and children of the married religious. What is more, in many lands you now find that sacerdotal dynasties are common – indeed, normal. Sons of abbots and bishops become abbots and bishops as well.'

'Little wrong in that,' agreed Abbot Ségdae. 'In the five kingdoms it has always been tradition that the priesthood passes down in certain families. At the abbeys of Cluain Mic Nois, at Lusca and Claine, the abbacy passes down within the family, the abbot being elected by the *derbhfine* just like the king.'

Eadulf knew this well enough.

'The difference is that your civil laws provide for this and counter any impropriety by the fact that the abbey is not the sole owner of the land it covers,' he pointed out. 'The land is granted to the abbey by the chieftain or king, and the local clan also elects a lay officer to ensure that the land and property are not alienated. This is not so in other cultures where the abbot's family can seize the property and make it personal to their families. This is what the *curia*, the papal court in Rome, is concerned with.'

Abbot Ségdae shook his head with an exasperated sigh. 'I have no understanding of this.'

Colgú shared his perplexity. 'No more do I, yet I understand that Eadulf is saying that the concerns of Rome have no relevance in this land. What it comes down to is this, and correct me if I am wrong:

Abbot Ultán's views are not supported by any law or rule that must be obeyed by all members of the Faith. Is that so?'

'That is so,' agreed Baithen.

'Then, should Abbot Ultán start protesting, he must be told in front of the assembly that his personal views, no matter who shares them, are not law in this land. He must desist from voicing his protest until some council of the church, which has jurisdiction to do so, makes it into a binding law on members of the Faith. Only when such an ecclesiastical rule is incorporated into our law system can such protests be validly made.'

Brehon Baithen smiled in satisfaction.

'An excellent summary of the situation,' he applauded.

Colgú glanced at his sister with a smile. 'Do you approve of this course of action?'

Fidelma's expression was solemn.

'It is the only course,' she agreed almost reluctantly. 'I would rather that Abbot Ultán would not raise the matter in the first place, but . . .' She ended with a shrug.

'Perhaps . . .' began Eadulf, and then paused.

'Perhaps?' prompted Colgú immediately, turning to him.

'I wondered if Abbot Ultán could be informed of the decision in this matter tonight, before the ceremony starts tomorrow, in an effort to persuade him to hold his peace?'

'A good suggestion,' agreed the king. 'Surely that could do no harm?' Colgú glanced round the company and his eyes came to rest on Abbot Ségdae. 'But who would speak with him? As senior churchman . . . ?'

Abbot Ségdae shook his head immediately. 'Not I. Our discussion at Imleach has made Ultán view me as his prime antagonist and I doubt whether he would listen to a word I said.'

'Advising on law and procedure is my role,' Brehon Baithen interposed. 'I will go to his chambers and have a word with this fiery prelate from the north. Perhaps the commander of the guard will attend me as the person who will have to enforce order in case our northern friend becomes too inflammatory in his protests?'

Caol smiled broadly and signified his agreement.

'Then we are satisfied as to this course?' asked Colgú, glancing round. There was a murmuring of assent and the king sighed and sat back. 'Remain with me, Fidelma, and you also, Eadulf.'

He waited until Abbot Ségdae, Brehon Baithen and Caol had departed, and then he rose to pour three goblets of wine, handing one each to his sister and Eadulf before taking the third for himself.

'To a peaceful day tomorrow,' he toasted. They drank dutifully.

There was a pause and then Eadulf commented: 'Abbot Ultán apart, it should be anything but peaceful, judging from the distinguished visitors that have flocked to Cashel and the festival that is being prepared in the town. All this for what is no more than a confirmation of our wedding vows. We have already been married a year.'

Colgú laughed with good nature. 'You may have lived as *ben charrthach* and *fer comtha* for a year and a day but this is the significant ceremony whereby my sister becomes your true *cétmuintir*. It is an important step.'

'Well, I had not expected a ceremony so elaborate as to bring the High King and his Chief Brehon here, not to mention the provincial kings, nobles and envoys from other lands,' Eadulf said, with a shake of his head.

Fidelma had been unusually subdued all evening and now she stirred.

'My brother will tell you why they are here,' she said softly.

Colgú smiled encouragingly at Eadulf. 'Forgive me. Sometimes I forget that you have not learnt everything there is to know about our family and our kingdom. The attendance of the High King and the others is out of respect to our family, the Eóghanacht. Our ancients tell us that when our ancestors first came to this island, so long ago that time has no meaning, two great warriors named Eibhear Fionn and Eremon led them. They were brothers, the sons of Golamh, the progenitor of our people who died on the voyage here. Having fought the ancient gods and goddesses who dwelt here, and driven them underground into the *sídhe*, the hills, Eremon was given the northern half of the island to rule while Eibhear Fionn was given the southern half. From Eibhear Fionn are descended the Eóghanacht, our family, while from Eremon are descended the Uí Néill, which is the family of the current High King Sechnassach. Only our two families – the descendants of Eremon and Eibhear Fionn – are allowed to contest for the High Kingship. We sing the praises of twenty-four of the Eóghanacht who have sat in the seat of the High King until the days of Duach Donn Dalta Deagha, who was the last of our family to hold that office. The point is that the kingdom of Muman is the largest in this island and its kings are second to none, not even to the High King, although we pay homage to the concept of his office. It is out of respect for our ancestry, our traditions of kingship and our current strength in this land, that the High King comes to visit on the occasion of my sister's wedding day. Likewise, that is why the other kings and nobles come to pay their respects at Cashel.' He paused, and then his serious expression dissolved into a mischievous grin that marked his relationship to Fidelma, for Eadulf had seen that same grin on her features many times. 'But I would like to think they also come out of respect for my sister as well, because her reputation as a *dálaigh*, an advocate of our law courts, is known in all the five kingdoms.'

Fidelma frowned and glanced quickly at Eadulf.

'A reputation that is inseparably linked to that of Eadulf, without whom many a riddle would have remained unsolved,' she added quickly.

'What . . . ?' Colgú seemed puzzled for the moment before he realised his implied offence. 'Of course, of course. It is a shame that none of your Saxon kinsmen will be attending, although I hear some compatriots of yours – exiled religious – seek to settle in this kingdom and will be present. I understand that Cerball, the bard, has spoken to you so that he might compose a *forsundud*, a praise-poem, about your own ancestry. A wedding is not seemly unless the genealogy of both parties can be recited before the company.'

Eadulf did not reply. He could not boast that he knew more than three or so generations of his family. That was nothing compared to the Eóghanacht who boasted fifty-nine generations between Colgú and Eibhear Fionn son of Golamh. In spite of Brother Conchobhar's assurances, an hereditary *gerefa* or magistrate of his people was hardly the equal to an Eóghanacht princess. Not for the first time did Eadulf experience a feeling of insecurity. He was very much a stranger in a strange land.

Colgú seemed to sense the air of tension that caused both Fidelma and Eadulf to fall quiet.

'How is little Alchú?' he asked, changing the subject.

'Your nephew is well,' answered Fidelma brightly. 'Muirgen, our nurse, has been a godsend. I have no fears of leaving the child with her and her husband Nessán when my duty as a lawyer bids me spend time away.'

'He is growing apace,' commented Colgú. 'You have a fine son there, Eadulf.'

'A fine son, indeed,' Eadulf agreed quietly.

'So all is ready for tomorrow?' pressed Fidelma's brother in a determined fashion.

'As far as we are concerned,' Fidelma agreed. 'I think you will forgive us for some trepidation,' she added. 'There is, as Eadulf has pointed out, such an illustrious audience for the ceremony. It makes us both very nervous.'

Colgú felt that she was making an excuse for Eadulf's reticence. He wondered if there was something wrong between them. How could he approach it? Could he ask Eadulf to leave and question his sister directly? While he was hesitating, Fidelma stood up and put her goblet on a side tablet.

'Brother, forgive us,' she said. 'But the hour grows late and we promised Abbot Laisran that we would speak to him before we prepare for tomorrow.'

'Of course.' Colgú sighed reluctantly. 'Meanwhile, let us hope Brehon Baithen has persuaded Abbot Ultán to see some sense about his protest.'

The meeting with Abbot Laisran was a genuine arrangement. Laisran was a distant cousin, an Eóghanacht, who was abbot of the great teaching monastery at Durrow – Darú, the abbey on the oak plain. It was he who had persuaded Fidelma, after she had qualified as an advocate at the law school of Brehon Morann, to enter the religious life at St Brigid's mixed house at Cill Dara. From the time she was a young girl, Fidelma had been advised and guided by the elderly abbot. Her father, Fáilbe Flann, who had been king of Muman, had died in the year of her birth and Laisran had taken his place.

The abbot was awaiting them in his chamber, seated before the fire and sipping at a goblet of mulled wine. It was a position which Fidelma always associated with him. Laisran rose awkwardly as they entered in answer to his invitation. He was a short, rotund, red-faced man. His face proclaimed a permanent state of jollity, for he had been born with a rare gift of humour and a sense that the world was there to provide enjoyment to those who inhabited it. When he smiled, it was no faint-hearted parting of the lips but an expression that welled from the depths of his being, bright and all-encouraging. And when he laughed it was as though the whole earth trembled in accompaniment.

'Fidelma! Eadulf! You are both welcome. Is all well? I received your request to speak to me before the momentous events that are due to take place tomorrow.'

Fidelma took a seat before the fire while Eadulf brought a spare chair and seated himself beside her. Laisran had resumed his seat and was offering them wine from the jug that sat by the glowing hearth. They both declined, much to his surprise, and he refilled his own goblet.

'Do you know Abbot Ultán?' Fidelma asked without preamble.

'Ultán of the Uí Thuirtrí?' Laisran chuckled sourly. 'I have met him once or twice at councils. He aspires to be a leader of the Faith – alas, he has no sense of humour and humour is one of the foundations on which saintliness must repose. I have heard strange tales about his life before he entered the religious. But it is not my place to spread rumour.'

'He has arrived in Cashel to protest at my wedding,' said Fidelma softly.

Abbot Laisran did not seem surprised. 'It is just the sort of thing he would do. He sees himself as a great reformer of our churches here in the five kingdoms. He has become a leading advocate of the Roman rules, of the introduction of the *Penitentials*, even arguing them to the exclusion of our native laws. He also seeks to get Ard Macha acknowledged as the primatial church in the five kingdoms. Particularly, he believes in celibacy among the religious and abstinence from wine and other intoxicating beverages. He has picked up strange ideas from the eastern churches concerning self-punishment, the use of a *flagellum* to suppress impure thoughts. Instead of preaching a word of joy, I fear that he would have the world descend into a sad, grey place.'

Eadulf could not suppress his smile at Abbot Laisran's vivid description of the man. 'It seems that you know him well enough, then.'

Abbot Laisran nodded solemnly. 'I shall be doing my best to avoid him while he is in Cashel. He would certainly disapprove of me.' He paused and looked at Fidelma thoughtfully. 'Surely you are not worried about Ultán? You have heard the arguments about celibacy a thousand times. You cannot let his prejudices ruin tomorrow. Spoken words vanish in the air.'

'Though there is no bone in the tongue, it has often broken a person's head,' she replied, using an old proverb.

Abbot Laisran grinned and shook his head. 'When Ultán stands up and speaks, he is recognised for what he is. One should feel sorrow for a person who is so unhappy that he needs must make others join him in that sad world.'

'There is something else I wish to speak of to you,' Fidelma said. 'Indeed, I have been giving it much thought.' She paused for a moment and Abbot Laisran waited politely for her to continue. 'As you know, when I left the school of Brehon Morann, I followed your advice to enter into the religious life. Do you recall the reasons why you gave me that advice?'

Abbot Laisran nodded thoughtfully.

'You wanted independence from your family,' he replied. 'Independence to practise law. In these days most of the professions can be found within the abbeys and ecclesiastical schools throughout the land, just as in the old days it was the Druids and their colleges who took over all the professional and intellectual functions of society. I advised that if you entered into the religious it would provide you with security and the base to practise law. I have been proved right.'

'I do not understand,' Eadulf said, leaning forward. 'Why would Fidelma lack security by not entering the religious? She is the daughter of a king and the sister of a king.'

'And she would have become reliant on the status of her family and, as I understood it, Fidelma wanted to rely on her own talent,' replied Abbot Laisran. 'Is that not so?'

Fidelma smiled quickly in response. 'To enter a religious house in order to pursue a career in law was but a stepping stone for me. I cannot say that I was really an advocate of the Faith.'

'So what troubles you now?'

'I find a conflict between my commitment to the law and what many people see as my lack of commitment to the institutions of the religious. In fact, the matter was underscored only a short while ago when Brehon Baithen suggested that a way of dealing with Abbot Ultán's protests would be to simply disclaim my vow to serve the Faith.'

Abbot Laisran's eyes widened in dismay. 'But that would mean that Eadulf also would have to disclaim his vow. Is that what you both want?'

Eadulf leaned forward.

'We have spoken about this, Fidelma and I,' he said quickly. 'We feel . . .'

'Would you advise me to withdraw from the religious?' Fidelma interrupted.

'Withdraw?' echoed Abbot Laisran as if he had not heard aright.

'Resign from the religious,' confirmed Fidelma. 'My profession is law, not the propagating of the Faith. There are many others who are better advocates in that field. I have no calling to do so, as you would say.'

Abbot Laisran glanced at Eadulf.

'And what do you say to this, *Brother* Eadulf?' he asked with a slight emphasis on the title *Bráthair*.

'It is a choice that Fidelma must make first. I am content as things are at present. There are many religious who live life as we do without being forced to make such decisions. Many an abbot, many a bishop as well, marry and raise children, and pursue their interests in areas where the question of whether they should resign their ecclesiastical offices never occurs.'

'This is entirely my own idea, Laisran,' Fidelma added. 'Even before Brehon Baithen suggested it tonight.'

'And how did you answer him?'

'I answered him that to withdraw from the religious simply to stop Abbot Ultán's protest would be wrong. I should withdraw because it was my wish, and Eadulf's wish, that I do so.'

Abbot Laisran pouted a little. His usually cherubic face saddened.

'We must all follow our own path. I do not see that you need take this final step. After all, your current position is more or less that of a lay person. It is well known that you have already left your mother house at Cill Dara and dissociated yourself from it.'

'Left it but not resigned from the religious,' Fidelma pointed out. 'Marriage and motherhood are difficult at the best of times. I am also a *dálaigh*, but to be a religieuse as well is too difficult. I need advice, Laisran.'

The Abbot Laisran gazed down at his feet and uttered a deep sigh as if faced by a hopeless situation.

'It is advice that your husband is now better able to give,' he said. 'Brother Eadulf, you have said it is a choice that Fidelma must make. But yours should be the voice that she listens to.'

Eadulf shrugged. 'My advice is to let things be. I have already said so. There is no reason why she should make any decision. During this last year, the months of our trial marriage and the birth of little Alchú, very few have remonstrated with us about our relationship, and those few are those whose views are not worth listening to.'

Abbot Laisran smiled quickly.

'And Abbot Ultán falls into that category,' he said, turning to Fidelma. 'Is it that you are really concerned about his protest?'

Fidelma shook her head. 'I have said it would be wrong to do something simply to avoid confrontation with such a person as Ultán. I simply think that I need to order my life.'

'Ah! To *order* your life?' Abbot Laisran sat back with eyes half closed. His inflection seemed to imply that he had understood a great deal by her remark. 'And you seek my advice? So, you feel that Eadulf's advice is not good enough?'

Fidelma looked disappointed.

'It sounds as if you agree with Eadulf,' she said truculently.

Abbot Laisran chuckled. 'And if I do, does that change your mind? If you feel Eadulf gives you such bad advice, then I fear for your future together.'

Fidelma coloured hotly. 'That is not what I meant. I fully appreciate what Eadulf's views are. But, forgive me, he is biased. You have given me good advice in the past, Laisran.'

'And I shall give it to you in the future,' assured the abbot. 'For now, even as you listen to him, also listen to your own heart. You might find that you are hearing the same thing.'

Brehon Baithen, with Caol, the youthful commander of the guard, at his side, was making his way towards the chambers set aside for Abbot Ultán. As befitted his rank, Ultán had been given one of the guest chambers in the palace. While religieux guests of lesser rank were assigned to quarters in the town, Abbot Ultán had created such an altercation that a chamber had been allocated to his steward, Brother Drón, nearby. The females of his entourage had been given places in the hostel set aside for them in another part of the palace.

Baithen himself was very aware that he was ultimately responsible for the security of the many distinguished guests who had gathered at Cashel. He had scarcely settled into his new position as brehon of Muman and he realised there were many who resented the fact that he had displaced the old brehon Dathal. But Dathal had needed to be forcibly retired for he had been making too many mistakes in his judgements. It had been hard to allow Dathal to remain in office after the unjustified accusation of the murder of Bisop Petrán against Brother Eadulf.

Bishop Petrán! Brehon Baithen sighed. He had been of the same ilk as Bishop Ultán; firmly set in his beliefs and narrow interpretations, asserting his authority and determined to make people conform without compromise. As a judge of the laws of the Fénechus, Baithen had often come into conflict with Petrán who had wanted to follow the foreign laws and rules of Rome. Baithen could not repress the thought that if he followed the same laws, then he could have had Abbot Ultán thrown out of Cashel immediately without consideration of his rights. The Roman rules, the *Penitentials* as they were called, which some bishops and abbots wanted to adopt, did not have the same liberality of attitude that the Fénechus law allowed.

It was with these thoughts that Brehon Baithen turned into the quarter where chambers had been assigned for the northern prelate.

As he and Caol entered the gloomy corridor, lit by smoky oil lanterns hanging at strategic points along it, the guard commander said: 'Abbot Ultán's chamber is the last one along here.' He indicated a door that was set in the corner where the corridor turned sharply at a right angle. Whilst the door was set in the corridor along which they were preceding, it actually faced towards that part of the corridor that was hidden from them.

It was at that moment that a figure backed out of the very door Caol was indicating. It was a tall man wrapped in a multi-coloured cloak. His hair was long, black and shoulder-length. There was tension in his stance as he took a step backward into the corridor. He seemed to be staring straight into the room from which he had exited. Then, without noticing Brehon Baithen and Caol, the man turned and disappeared into the other section of the corridor.

Baithen and Caol had halted in momentary surprise, exchanging glances. Then they hurried to the open door of Abbot Ultán's chamber.

A lamp lit the interior. The first impression was of a room that was neat and tidy. But the lamp lit the bed and on it sprawled a figure lying on its back, dressed in the robes of a rich religieux. They were darkly stained. The flesh of the face was white, the eyes wide and staring. The whole expression seemed one of comical surprise but there was nothing comical about the scene. The dark stains were blood and the man was dead. The body was that of Ultán, abbot of Cill Ria and bishop of the Uí Thuirtrí, the emissary from Ard Macha.

# CHAPTER FIVE

Fidelma had imagined that she had only just gone to sleep but here was Muirgen, her attendant, shaking her arm and urging her to wake immediately.

She blinked and yawned.

'Surely it is not time yet?' she protested. Then she realised that the room was still shrouded in darkness with only the flickering light of the lamp that Muirgen held at shoulder level to relieve the gloom. Suddenly, she was wide awake and registering the worried tone in Muirgen's voice. 'Is something wrong?'

'It is urgent, lady. Your brother wishes you to attend him at once.'

Fidelma sat up and stared at the woman.

This was to be her wedding day and she had been expecting to lie in until the first light of dawn before rising to toilet and break her fast and begin the rituals for the ceremony. She blinked again. The chill in the room coupled with the darkness told her that it was long before dawn.

'There is something wrong,' she said sharply, rising from her bed. 'What has happened?'

Muirgen shook her head quickly. 'I know not, lady, but something stirs. Your brother, the king, has sent to ask for your immediate attendance in his private chamber. I have no idea what this portends.'

'Is Eadulf all right?' was her next anxious question.

'He is still sound asleep in his chamber, lady,' was the reassuring response.

Fidelma was not one to waste time on further questions that could not be answered. She went to the side table and washed her face and hands in the bowl of cold water which already stood in a corner of the room. It was not the custom to bathe in the morning but to wash one's face and hands, aided by *sléic*, a soap, and dry them with a linen cloth. Fidelma hurried through this process, known as *indlut*, while Muirgen sorted out a dress and then came to hand her a *cíor* and the small *scáth-derc* or mirror. Fidelma did not usually use much in the way of make-up or personal ornaments, so her toilet was quickly accomplished.

Because of the cold of the early morning, Muirgen had wisely chosen an undergarment of linen over which was drawn a woollen dress of sober colouring. As Fidelma slipped into her shoes, Muirgen handed her a small *bratt* which fitted round the shoulders and came down to just below the waistline.

Fidelma left her chamber and hurried quickly along the corridor. She almost hesitated at the door of the room which had been assigned to Eadulf. It was true that during this last year they had been legally married and shared the same chambers but at this time there was a tradition to be upheld. Yesterday they had formerly separated. That marked the end of their trial marriage and they would not be intimately together again until their new formal contract was agreed under the laws of the *lánamnus*. She wondered if she should wake Eadulf but immediately decided against it. Whatever the problem that caused her brother to rouse her in the middle of the night, it was up to him to decide if it was Eadulf's concern or not.

She hurriedly made her way along the corridors to her brother's private apartments. Two warriors stood on guard in the antechamber, as was usual day and night, and, seeing her coming, one of them immediately went to an inner door and knocked once before opening it for her to pass through. The door was closed behind her.

In the chamber, Colgú came to greet her with a worried look. She glanced swiftly to where Brehon Baithen was struggling to rise from his seat and signalled him to remain seated.

'There has been a murder,' blurted Colgú as he waved her to a chair near the fire.

Fidelma composed her astonishment.

'Who has been murdered?' she asked quietly, as she seated herself.

'Abbot Ultán.'

A blink of the eyes was the only registration of the information. Fidelma was already working out the consequences. Abbot Ultán murdered; not only an emissary from the Comarb of the Blessed Patrick at Ard Macha but a guest from the northern kingdom of Ulaidh. These were matters of great concern.

Colgú turned to his brehon and gestured towards him. 'Tell her the details.'

Brehon Baithen made a helpless gesture with his hand. 'It is simple enough. A short time ago, Abbot Ultán was stabbed to death in his chamber.'

'And the perpetrator of this deed?' asked Fidelma, her voice calm. 'Is he or she known?'

Brehon Baithen sighed and nodded. 'As chance would have it, Caol and I were on our way to speak with Ultán, as had been agreed when we met here. Turning into the corridor that led to his chamber, we saw the culprit leaving it . . .' He paused dramatically.

Fidelma suppressed her impatience and waited.

Realising that she was not going to respond to his pause but was awaiting his announcement, Baithen continued: 'It was Muirchertach Nár of the Uí Fiachracha.'

At the name a troubled frown crossed Fidelma's brow.

'The king of Connacht? Are you sure?'

Brehon Baithen looked pained. 'My eyesight is not at fault. Neither is that of Caol. It was Muirchertach Nár without a doubt. And after we called old Brother Conchobhar, the apothecary, to come and examine the body, we went straightway to the chambers of the Connacht king.'

Fidelma's eyes widened a little. 'And?'

'We challenged him, said that we had seen him hurrying from the chamber and demanded to know his explanation.'

'What was his response?'

This time Brehon Baithen gave a hint of a shrug. 'As one would expect from such a noble. He said that he would make no statement nor comment other than that he was not responsible for the death of Abbot Ultán.'

'This does not bode well, Fidelma,' Colgú added, his handsome features drawn into a worried frown. 'An abbot, who is an emissary from Ard Macha, is slain; a king of Connacht is charged, and at the very time when the princes of the five kingdoms are gathered here to witness your wedding. There will be much suspicion among them until this matter is resolved.'

Fidelma did not have to be told why her brother was so concerned but she was not sure why he had summoned her in the middle of the night and said so.

Colgú looked even more uncomfortable. He glanced at Baithen as if imploring his help. The brehon of Muman cleared his throat.

'As you doubtless know, lady, a king has certain privileges . . .' He hesitated. 'Muirchertach has . . . he has demanded the right to choose his own counsel to prove his innocence.'

Fidelma's expression was suddenly grimly set. She guessed what was coming.

'Today is my wedding day,' she said coldly. She could not feel for the loss of Abbot Ultán; she had never met him, and after what she had heard about him she was not overly concerned about his demise. Her mind only concerned itself with the legal aspect of his death, and the disruption it was causing.

Colgú gestured with his open hands as if in apology. 'Unless the murder of Abbot Ultán is resolved before the ceremonies, I think our distinguished guests will depart in suspicion and anger. There may even be war among the kingdoms, for many will ask how Ultán came to be slain in Cashel. Why was he not protected by his host?'

Brehon Baithen looked uncomfortable. 'Caol has admitted that when Abbot Ultán arrived he demanded in front of witnesses that a warrior should be placed at his chamber door. It was not done.'

Fidelma was surprised at that. 'It is unlike Caol to be irresponsible.'

'Apparently, he initially asked Dego to fulfil this task, but with so many lords and princes in the fortress there was much to be done, and Dego was needed elsewhere. Besides, very few guests had retired for the night by then. That was why we were on our way to see Abbot Ultán. I have assured Caol that no blame attaches to him,' the brehon told her.

Colgú's features were woebegone. 'This failure of protection lies at my door. Questions will be raised. It will be asked, was there enmity because of my chief bishop, Abbot Ségdae of Imleach? There will be reference to the argument when he refused to comply with Ultán's demand for recognition of Ard Macha. Was there some conspiracy to silence Ultán because it was known he would raise objections to the wedding of my sister?'

'That is nonsense!' exploded Fidelma.

'You know it,' conceded Colgú. 'But will those in the northern kingdoms know it?'

Fidelma lowered her head as she thought through the implications. Colgú was right. Under the laws of hospitality, it was his duty to resolve the matter. All the guests who had come to Cashel, including Abbot Ultán, were under the protection of the king. The death of a guest was the crime of *díguin*, violation of protection. If the matter was not resolved and the culprit made known, then Colgú himself could lose his honour price, be removed as king and be forced into paying the appropriate fines and compensation. Restitution had to be made. Fidelma realised that the Eóghanacht – indeed, Cashel itself – could become *mallachtach* – accursed. Colgú must be seen to be beyond reproach in this matter.

'So Muirchertach has demanded that I should be his advocate?' she finally asked, her voice resigned. 'Where is he now?'

'A king has rights and he has the liberty of Cashel until the hearing is held. As king of Connacht he has given his parole' – Colgú used the term *gell*, meaning the 'word of honour' usually given by noble prisoners of war and hostages – 'that he will not leave before the hearing exonerates him, as he says. I am afraid that we are in no position to refuse his request for us to defend him.'

Fidelma smiled faintly at Colgú's attempt to shoulder responsibility with her by the use of the plural form. 'I understand. Who will sit in judgement when the hearing is convened?'

'Who else but Barrán, Chief Brehon of the Five Kingdoms? I have asked him to attend us and perhaps it is fortunate that he is here with the High King because none of the northern kings or princes will be able to argue with his decisions.'

Fidelma nodded slightly in agreement. 'If I am to defend the king of Connacht, who will prosecute him?'

At that moment, there was a tap on the door and it was swung open by one of the guards to allow a tall man of indiscernible age, clad in robes that denoted high rank, to pass into the chamber. The man halted in mid-chamber and inclined his head in token deference to Colgú. His bright eyes, unblinking, set close to his prominent nose, gave him a stern expression. But as they alighted on Fidelma, his thin lips parted in a smile of greeting.

'I have heard your reputation has much increased since our last meeting at Ferna, in the kingdom of Laigin, Fidelma of Cashel,' he said.

'A reputation that is undeserved, Barrán,' replied Fidelma. 'Only my few successes seem to be talked about and not my many failures.'

The Chief Brehon's smile broadened. 'Your success at Ferna and our previous encounter at Ros Alithir was a clear demonstration that your reputation is well deserved. However, I did not expect to meet you before I was due to congratulate you after your wedding.' He glanced to Colgú and Baithen, whom he had already encountered on his arrival. His mouth twisted into a grimace. 'Your messenger has informed me of the matter in hand.'

Colgú waved Barrán to a chair.

'Have you been told why I have asked you to join us?' he asked.

Barrán made an affirmative gesture. 'You wish me to preside at the hearing of Muirchertach Nár for the murder of Abbot Ultán of Cill Ria?'

'Exactly so.'

'I accept, of course. As Muirchertach Nár is king of the *cóicead* of Connacht it is, perhaps, lucky that I am here for reasons that have more to do with politics than with justice.'

Colgú smiled.

'An observation already made, Barrán,' he said. 'Muirchertach Nár has demanded his right to choose his advocate and he has chosen Fidelma.'

Barrán glanced quickly at her. 'Have you responded to this request?'

'I have agreed, although Muirchertach Nár is not yet informed of that decision,' Fidelma replied.

'Again, that is good from a political viewpoint so far as Connacht is concerned. It is also good for justice so far as Muirchertach Nár is personally concerned, for he is now assured of an able advocate. Now, who is to prosecute this matter?'

'I asked that same question before you arrived, Barrán,' Fidelma replied.

Baithen stirred uneasily. 'The crime was committed here in Cashel and in the palace of the king. Even though I am a witness, it behoves me to prosecute as brehon of Muman.'

Fidelma looked thoughtful.

'Would you not be excluded from one role or the other?' she asked mildly. 'I would have thought the *berrad airechta*, the law on persons excluded from giving evidence, would be the basis for challenging you on this.'

Baithen was surprised. 'Are you challenging my right to prosecute? On what point of law?'

'If you are a witness, it conflicts with your role as prosecutor, for as prosecutor it is to your advantage to secure a conviction. A man cannot give evidence if it could bring advantage to himself. That is the law.'

Baithen shrugged indifferently. 'Then I shall not stand as witness but rely on the testimony of Caol who saw exactly what I saw. No contradiction in that.'

Barrán sighed and shook his head. 'I have to rule on this, Baithen, and say that Fidelma's argument is sound in law. You cannot deny that you are a witness. What you have already seen cannot be unseen and therefore you are prejudiced. As she says, it is a prosecutor's function to secure a conviction. That may lead a witness to zealousness in his evidence.'

Baithen accepted the point with good grace.

'But there must be a prosecutor,' he pointed out. 'It should be someone of distinction and certainly not a judge from the retinue of the northern kingdoms.'

'That is agreed,' replied Barrán. 'I propose Brehon Ninnid, the new brehon of Laigin. He is of the Uí Dróna of the southern part of that kingdom. Laigin is the only independent voice in these matters. Ninnid has accompanied his king, Fianamail, here for the ceremony. That, again, is most fortunate.'

Fidelma was frowning.

'I presume that he is better qualified than Bishop Forbassach?' she asked cynically.

Barrán uttered a brittle laugh. 'Indeed. Thanks to your case against him at Ferna, Bishop Forbassach was stripped of his rank, retired to some small community and prohibited from the practice of law. King Fianamail had to choose a new brehon and in this matter he sought my advice. I can vouch that young Ninnid is talented and has made a name for himself as an assiduous prosecutor. It is true that with youth comes arrogance but he will grow out of that, I am sure. But now is the time to voice any objections to his appointment, before he is instructed.'

Baithen seemed indifferent while Colgú said: 'I have no knowledge to make an objection. If you recommend him, then I accept. What do you say, Fidelma?'

'A brehon of Laigin is a logical choice,' agreed Fidelma. 'Perhaps the only choice, for he represents neither the kingdom of the victim, the kingdom of the accused nor the kingdom in which it happened. Therefore, ideally, he will be an unbiased prosecutor.' She glanced through the window at the still dark sky and then rose from her seat. 'I'd better inform Eadulf that the wedding is now delayed. And, of course, I shall ask Eadulf for his assistance in my investigation, if you have no objection, Barrán.'

The Chief Brehon shook his head. 'I would expect no less. Brother Eadulf's work is known and his name is now inseparably linked to your own.'

'Then it is agreed.' Colgú sighed. 'There is nothing left but to announce this sad news to our guests. The ceremonies must be postponed until this matter is resolved.' Colgú paused and smiled in sympathy at Fidelma. 'Let us hope that it will be but a short delay.'

Barrán was sympathetic. 'This is hard on you, Fidelma, but I know that you will bring this matter to a quick conclusion. We cannot allow all these distinguished guests to linger in Cashel for more than a few days.'

'Law and justice move along in their own time,' Fidelma rebuked him softly. 'I, above all our distinguished guests, regret the delay, but

I am the first to argue that no man should be exonerated or condemned simply because it interferes with our plans.'

With a quick nod to encompass them all, Fidelma turned and left the chamber.

'I am beginning to believe that there is some truth in old Brother Conchobhar's prognostications,' Eadulf finally said, after Fidelma had explained everything. She had gone to his chamber and woken him, making sure he was fully awake before explaining the events of recent hours.

'He was claiming that the portents were not good for our marriage this day,' she agreed.

There was a silence between them and faintly came the sound of the chapel bell calling the religious to the first prayers of the day. Fidelma smiled wanly, glanced into a mirror and adjusted her hair with an automatic gesture.

'Well, from what we have heard about Abbot Ultán, it did not need any divination to know that there was going to be trouble in the offing.'

'True,' agreed Eadulf. 'It is a pity that Caol took Dego away from his sentinel duties. I can understand it but I hope it does not mean that Caol will be in trouble.'

'My brother has taken full responsibility.'

'I told you that Brother Berrihert uttered a threat against Ultán's life in front of Brother Conchobhar and me?'

'I have not forgotten. But do not forget that the murder happened after the gates of the fortress were closed for the night. That much Caol told me. Your Saxon friends have accommodation in one of the hostels in the town, so they would not have been admitted here after the gates were closed.'

There was another awkward pause.

'So everything is put into abeyance until the matter is resolved?'

Fidelma nodded, moving to the window and glancing down in the direction of the few lanterns and lights that could be seen in the town below.

'I feel sorry for the people who have gathered down there for the *aenach*,' she remarked.

'Surely the fair can go ahead?' Eadulf said. 'It could amuse people and will not interfere with us in the fortress.'

Fidelma shook her head. 'Abbot Ségdae would doubtless say that it would not be seemly while an abbot and bishop of the Faith lies murdered and that death remains unexplained.'

Eadulf pulled a face. 'I suppose so. Although it is not as if many here will mourn his passing. Everyone seemed to hate him.'

'Well, though I shall not hurry this matter, the sooner we begin the sooner we can come to an end,' she said.

Eadulf had finished dressing and asked: 'What do you mean to do first?'

'As always, we will start with the body and the cause of death. Brother Conchobhar was called to examine it. After that, we shall see what Muirchertach Nár has to say.' She paused at the door and frowned, glancing back to Eadulf. 'As Muirchertach Nár is a king . . .'

Eadulf interrupted, as if reading her thoughts.

'It would be better if you saw him alone. It might not be . . .' He spent a few moments trying to think of the right word and settled on *cubaid*. 'It might not be seemly if I were to be present unless he wished it.'

Fidelma cast him a smile of thanks for his perception and diplomacy.

It was still dark but there was a light burning in the apothecary shop as they crossed the cobbled courtyard. Fidelma tapped softly on the door before reaching to the handle and swinging it open. At once the pungent smell of herbs and dried flowers assailed her nostrils and she was hard pressed not to sneeze.

In the gloom, Brother Conchobhar glanced up from his workbench where he had been mixing something in a bowl by the light of a lantern and smiled a welcome.

'I was expecting you,' he said simply, as they entered. 'Do you prosecute or do you judge, lady?'

'Neither,' Fidelma responded. 'The Chief Brehon of the Five Kingdoms, Barrán himself, will be judge. But the accused has requested that I should defend him.'

'It is a difficult path, lady.' Brother Conchobhar pulled a comical face. 'Thank God I do not have to be involved in such deliberations.

Surely it is hard to defend someone when there are eyewitnesses to the deed?'

'My mentor Brehon Morann once said, do not give your judgement on hearing the first story until the other side is brought before you,' she replied.

'A good philosophy,' agreed the apothecary. He glanced at Eadulf. 'So, are you both working on this matter?'

'We are,' Eadulf replied. 'We are told that you were asked to examine the body of Abbot Ultán?'

Brother Conchobhar nodded absently. 'To play the *dálaigh*, I should strictly say that I was called upon to examine a body. I recognised it to be Abbot Ultán only when I saw it. I was not told who it was before then.'

Fidelma smiled faintly. 'You are developing a legal mind, my old friend. Where is the body now?'

'The body is still in the chamber where it happened. Brehon Baithen ordered it to remain so until you came to conduct your examination. Baithen is a careful judge, unlike . . .' Brother Conchobhar stopped short and glanced at Eadulf in embarrassment. No need to remind Eadulf how Baithen's predecessor was so careless that he had accused the Saxon of murder. 'And you doubtless want me to come and point out the salient features?' the apothecary went on hurriedly.

'Even so,' agreed Fidelma.

Brother Conchobhar put aside the mixture that he had been working on and wiped his hands on a linen cloth. 'Then come with me. I shall show you what I can.'

They followed him to the main guests' quarters of the palace. Enda, another of Caol's warriors, was standing outside the chamber that had been allotted to Abbot Ultán. He let them pass inside with a deferential nod of his head.

Inside the room, which was still lit by tallow candles, the body of the abbot lay sprawled on its back on the bed. The blood had soaked his clothing and the surrounding bedclothes, staining them. Fidelma glanced quickly round. Apart from the way the corpse lay, the bedchamber was fairly tidy. There were no signs of any disorder.

'Has anything been moved?' she asked.

Brother Conchobhar shook his head.

67

'The abbot was obviously an orderly man,' he said. 'The room was perfectly tidy when I came here. Baithen told me to leave everything exactly as I found it.'

'So, there was no indication of a struggle,' observed Fidelma.

'None,' agreed Brother Conchobhar.

'That means that he probably knew his killer,' Eadulf pointed out softly.

'And the body was found as we see it now?' Fidelma pressed the apothecary.

'Exactly as I have said. I had no cause to touch or move it. It was obvious what the cause of death was.'

Fidelma peered down distastefully at the congealing blood. 'Which appears to have been a sharp dagger.'

'Just so,' agreed the old man.

'Then we can also be assured that the abbot had no suspicion of the impending attack.' Eadulf was examining the position of the body.

'How so?' demanded Fidelma.

'From the way the body has fallen back on the bed. He was sitting on it at the time. The legs still dangle over the side of the bed touching the floor and one foot is bare . . . the sandal came off as he fell or was pushed backwards by the force of the attack. That means that the straps were loose. He was sitting on the edge of the bed with unloosed sandals, in a relaxed state. He did not seem the type of man, especially in his office of abbot, who would relax in such a manner in front of a stranger.'

Fidelma smiled approvingly. 'Excellently observed, Eadulf.'

She bent down and examined the man's feet. Then she glanced round and with a grunt of satisfaction reached forward under a side table. Indeed, one sandal had been hidden under it, reinforcing the idea that it had been kicked off while the other was still on the foot. Fidelma rose satisfied.

Eadulf was now looking at the wounds on the man's chest.

'I presume that you agree that he was stabbed to death?' he asked Brother Conchobhar.

The old apothecary nodded. 'I am reminded, Brother Eadulf, that you studied for a while in one of our great schools of medicine . . . Tuam Brecain, wasn't it?'

'It was.'

'Examining the stab wounds, can you deduce anything else?'

Eadulf peered at the wounds, frowning before straightening up. 'The abbot was stabbed half a dozen times.'

Fidelma raised her eyebrows momentarily in surprise. She moved to Eadulf's shoulder and glanced down at the body once more.

'Half a dozen?' There was so much blood staining the clothes and surrounding areas that she had not counted the wounds.

'You remark on that?' Brother Conchobhar's tone was approving. 'It is not my place to draw conclusions but, nevertheless, there is a conclusion to be drawn.'

'The conclusion that here is a killing that was filled with emotion?' Fidelma said at once.

'One of the stab wounds would be fatal in itself,' agreed Brother Conchobhar. 'That one entered the body between the ribs.' He indicated. 'The rest were more or less superficial wounds that caused much blood to flow. They seem to have been struck at haphazard as if someone had thrown himself on the abbot with sudden fury. Eadulf rightly says that he fell backwards upon the assault but once that one blow was struck there would have been no defence. You will perceive the superficial nature of those other wounds . . . you see that they were not struck deeply. That means the hand that delivered these blows did not have strength behind it . . . probably surprise more than anything caused the abbot to be thrown backwards on the bed.'

Fidelma was nodding slowly. 'In other words, you are saying that we should take notice that the killer was physically weak?'

Brother Conchobhar pursed his lips in a cynical expression. 'I am thinking that a strong man would not have struck so many blows which made superficial wounds.'

Eadulf grimaced. 'But emotion could explain the weakness,' he observed quickly. 'Rage can often reduce even the strongest men to momentary inability and render them weak with the emotion.'

'Has a knife been recovered?' Fidelma asked.

'Whoever killed the abbot took the weapon with him.'

Fidelma was examining the coverlet on the bed and she pointed at a spot near the body. 'Indeed, after having wiped the blade clean on the coverlet.'

It was true that there were signs that something broad and bloody had been wiped on the cloth by the side of the body.

'That contradicts the idea of an emotional killer, Fidelma,' Eadulf muttered. 'That shows the action of someone in control and thinking. Yet why the number of wounds?'

Fidelma did not reply immediately. She cast another look over the body. Then she moved forward and carefully lifted aside part of the abbot's robe.

'There seems to be a piece of paper under the robe . . .' she began, as she bent down and extracted a small piece of folded paper smudged with blood. She unfolded it, glanced at it and handed it to Eadulf. He took it, read it and then chuckled.

'Well, well, perhaps Abbot Ultán was not the unfeeling and arrogant person we hear about after all. This seems to be a piece of poetry. Love poetry at that.'

He scanned it once more, reading aloud.

> Cold the nights I cannot sleep,
> Thinking of my love, my dear one,
> Of the nights we spent together,
> Myself and my love from Cill Ria.

'It shows that Ultán was not without some softness if he could write such poetry,' offered Brother Conchobhar.

Fidelma refolded the paper and placed it in her *marsupium* before glancing back to the body. 'At least, we can rule out robbery for financial gain. He still wears his necklet of semi-precious stone, and his bishop's ring of gold.'

Brother Conchobhar pointed to a small chest standing on a table to one side. It was half open.

'It was open when I was here. The chest is full of precious baubles. Perhaps the bishop was going to dispense them as gifts.'

Fidelma glanced in the small chest for confirmation. It was certainly full of valuable stones. But she had heard the inflection in Brother Conchobhar's voice and turned to him.

'Do you imply another meaning?'

Brother Conchobhar shrugged indifferently. 'I had heard that the abbot's mission here was not merely to attend your wedding, lady, but to persuade others to support the claims of Ard Macha as primatial seat of Christendom in the five kingdoms. If argument could not do so, perhaps the abbot's thinking was that financial tokens might help change people's minds.'

'And where did this story come from?' queried Fidelma.

Brother Conchobhar hesitated and then said: 'Abbot Augaire of Conga. I was speaking to him last night. He was telling me that such financial tokens have been distributed to the prelates of some of the northern abbeys to get their support.'

'Tokens? The term is a bribe, old friend.' Fidelma used the term *duais do chionn chomaine*, which literally meant 'a gift in return for kindness' but generally carried the connotation of an enticement – something for something.

'Well, that is what he told me,' agreed Brother Conchobhar gravely.

'And is there anything else you noticed or heard in connection with the abbot's death?'

Brother Conchobhar paused for a moment. 'It is not up to me to form deductions. But if it is observations you want . . . well, I can say that Abbot Ultán liked comfort.'

'How do you mean?' asked Eadulf.

'For one thing, he wore silk next to his skin under the rough woollen robes of his calling.'

'Many do so who can afford it,' Eadulf pointed out.

'Yet I have heard it said of this Abbot Ultán, that he claimed to live according to rules of austerity, chastity and poverty of spirit. He advocated the rule of the *Penitentials*.'

'You hear a lot in your apothecary, my friend,' observed Eadulf wryly.

Brother Conchobhar was complacent.

'I do,' he acknowledged lightly. 'But then I am old and find myself predisposed to listen to gossip whereas younger people rush hither and thither lest they miss a moment of time. By doing so they often find that the important things in life have passed them by altogether.'

Fidelma sighed and gave a final glance around the room. 'I think we have seen enough. We will have to speak to the abbot's entourage later. There is no more to be done here. The body can be taken and prepared for burial after Brehon Ninnid makes his investigation.'

Brother Conchobhar inclined his head.

Outside, Fidelma paused to say to Enda, 'I do not want any member of the abbot's entourage to enter the room without my personal approval.'

'Very well, my lady.'

'What now?' asked Eadulf, as he followed her along the passage.

'Now I must discuss matters with Muirchertach Nár,' she replied. 'I would get some rest now, Eadulf, or break your fast. I will return and tell you all that Muirchertach has to say . . . that I promise.'

# CHAPTER SIX

Muirchertach Nár, king of Connacht, had been allowed to remain in his own chambers with his wife, the lady Aíbnat. Fidelma found only Gormán, another of her brother's bodyguard, standing as a solitary sentinel outside. She greeted him with a smile. He was the son of her friend Della who dwelt in the town below the fortress of Cashel. Gormán was a tall, handsome youth with dark hair. He raised his left hand in a half salute.

'I was told to expect you, lady,' he said, his voice low but expressing relief. 'I am sorry that this day has been marred for you. My mother was looking forward to it.'

It was only recently that Gormán had felt able to acknowledge Della as his mother for she had once been a *bé taide*, a prostitute, who had been shunned by many even after Fidelma had successfully represented her in a claim for compensation when she had been raped. More recently, suspicion had fallen on Della of being responsible for the abduction of Fidelma's own child, Alchú, a charge that Fidelma had rapidly dispensed with.

'Thank you. It is to be hoped that matters will not long be delayed.' She inclined her head towards the guest chamber. 'Is all quiet here?'

Gormán looked troubled. 'I have had no real bother, lady. In truth, I am glad that you have come. It is hard to act as jailer to a king. Even so, Muirchertach Nár has been a courteous prisoner as befits his nobility. However, his wife, the lady Aíbnat, more than makes up for his courtesy by her discourtesy. She has anger and resentment enough for both.'

Fidelma grimaced in sympathy. 'In the circumstances one should not expect sweet dispositions from everyone.'

She squared her shoulders slightly and faced the chamber door. Gormán moved forward and rapped quickly on it. A voice called out and the young warrior answered loudly: 'The lady Fidelma!' Almost at once the door swung open and Fidelma passed inside.

Muirchertach Nár of the Uí Fiachracha Aidne, king of Connacht, was a tall, slimly built man with dark hair and light eyes that seemed expressionless and unblinking. There were dark shadows under them and he had a pale, strangely sallow skin that stretched tightly over his bony face. As he came towards her with hand held out, he carried himself with the curious rolling gait of a seafarer which, indeed, matched his name, which meant 'skilled in seacraft'. In spite of his appearance, his grip was firm.

In the five years that Muirchertach had been king of Connacht, he had tried hard to acquire a reputation that would bring him out of the shadow of his father. But he had a lot to live up to. His father had been Guaire Aidne, king of Connacht, a man much celebrated as a paragon of generosity and hospitality. At least Muirchertach had achieved the addition to his name of the epithet Nár, which meant not only noble, but courteous, honest and knowledgeable. But there was something about Muirchertach that made Fidelma think of the other stories she had heard about his father Guaire. There were tales of his ambitious and wily nature and stories that he had instigated the murder of his rivals. One story had it that he had killed some who were guests attending a feast at his own fortress at Durlas. Fidelma was reminded that her own father had fought Guaire in battle and defeated him. Yet when Guaire had died, he had been taken to the great abbey of Cluain Mic Nois, with many lamentations among the abbots and bishops of the land, to be buried with all honour. Perhaps, in such circumstances, the stories of his evil were simply stories.

Muirchertach Nár's features, unfortunately, were moulded with a crafty expression which would make anyone wonder, as Fidelma had momentarily done, just how trustworthy he was. Well might Juvenal say that 'no reliance can be placed on appearance', but she had found that many a person could be condemned by their physical demeanour.

'I am told that you desire me to defend you against the charge of murdering Abbot Ultán.' Fidelma was direct.

'That is why you have been sent for!' The voice had a hectoring shrillness and it belonged to a woman who had emerged into the room from the adjoining bedchamber. Fidelma turned to regard her with a slightly raised eyebrow.

The woman was still attractive although her figure was matronly, with tell-tale little fleshy folds round her neck. Her hair was still red-gold, her eyes light blue, and the fair skin dashed with freckles, but the rounded features were spoiled by thin lips and harsh, disapproving lines at the corners of the mouth. Her body seemed to exude aggression. There was no disguising the belligerence in her manner.

Fidelma returned her gaze for a moment without expression. Then she turned back to Muirchertach with a look as if asking him a silent question.

The king coloured a little. 'This is my wife, the lady Aíbnat.'

Only then did Fidelma turn and incline her head slightly in acknowledgement.

'It would be pointless to bid you welcome to Cashel, lady,' she said softly, 'although in other circumstances it would have been my duty as sister to Colgú to do so. Nevertheless, let us hope we can resolve this matter quickly, so that I may offer you hospitality later.'

Aíbnat sniffed. It was an irritating habit that Fidelma was soon to become familiar with.

'I have come in obedience to my husband,' Aíbnat replied coldly, 'and not because of deference to the Eóghanacht. I am of the Uí Briúin Aí. We have nothing to do with the Eóghanacht, nor do we want anything of them.'

Fidelma smiled tightly. 'Then I hope to welcome you as part of the courtesy that your husband, the king, extends to us,' she replied waspishly, before returning her face to Muirchertach. 'And now perhaps we can get down to the matter that brings me here.'

Muirchertach looked unhappily towards his wife. She had taken a seat close to the fire and seemed to be ignoring them. Fidelma promptly crossed to the other comfortable seat by the fire and sat down. Aíbnat stiffened immediately.

'You are sitting in the presence of a king,' she protested. 'Not even the sister of a king of a *cóicead* may do that.'

Fidelma smiled thinly. 'You may know, lady, that I am a *dálaigh*, qualified to the level of *anruth*. Under our custom and law I may seat myself in the presence of a king of a *cóicead* without seeking permission. I may even sit in the presence of the High King if so invited by him. Perhaps you did not know this?'

Muirchertach coughed nervously, at the same time taking a less comfortable chair from the corner of the room and bringing it near the fire.

'I am sure my wife had overlooked that fact, Fidelma,' he said hurriedly. 'Let us to this business.'

There was a soft hissing sound as the breath whistled through Aíbnat's teeth but the woman said nothing further.

'Very well. Tell me what happened.'

Muirchertach looked disconcerted. 'You don't know?'

Fidelma frowned irritably. 'What I have been told is beside the point. If I am to defend you, I need to know from your own words how you perceive the matter.'

'How can he defend himself in detail, if he does not know the accusations?' Aíbnat broke in with a sarcastic tone.

Fidelma did not even bother to glance in her direction.

'I thought that you were aware that you have been charged with the murder of Abbot Ultán of Cill Ria, the bishop of the Uí Thuirtrí?' she said quietly.

'I am aware,' admitted Muirchertach.

'Then that is all you need to be aware of. If you are innocent of the matters charged, you do not need to know the details of the accusation. But a guilty man can often use the details given by his accusers to find a path out of their accusations. Tell me your story first.'

Muirchertach glanced swiftly at his wife and then nodded quickly.

'My story is simple. I went to Abbot Ultán's chambers . . .' He glanced towards the window and saw it was already dawn. 'It was last night. The door was closed. I knocked lightly on it but, receiving no answer, I tried the handle and found it unlocked. I went in and the first thing I saw was Ultán. He was sprawled on his back on his bed. I thought he was asleep even though he was fully clothed. I went to his side, calling to him to wake up. Then I noticed the dark stains on his robes, and that his eyes were wide and staring. I have seen too many men in death not to realise that he was dead – and not only that, but death had come to him with violence. Horrified, I turned and fled from the room. I think that panic overcame me. I came straight back here wondering what to do. That is all I know.'

Fidelma waited for a moment or two before commenting. Then she said: 'Realising the abbot's death was violent, you left the scene and came back here without informing anyone?'

'I told you, my mind was confused. I was wondering what to do.'

'And the lady Aíbnat was here when you returned?'

'Of course.' The reply came quickly.

'And did you tell her what had happened?'

'Of course.' Again it was a sharp response.

'So why didn't you raise the alarm then?'

Muirchertach flushed and glanced nervously at his wife. 'She said . . .'

'I said,' intervened Aíbnat sharply, 'that the matter was no concern of ours. Abbot Ultán's body would be found soon enough without our being involved.'

Fidelma pursed her lips in disapproval. 'A poor piece of advice, for it merely endorses the suspicion that your husband was involved in the matter. It was counsel, Muirchertach, that you would have done better to ignore. But the milk has been spilt and there is no mopping it up now. We must proceed. So you and the lady Aíbnat were here, hoping that someone else would find the body and raise the alarm and that you would not be involved.'

Lady Aíbnat's expression was one of malignant dislike but Fidelma simply ignored her.

'I do not understand?' Muirchertach frowned.

'No matter. What happened next?'

'Brehon Baithen and the commander of Colgú's guard came here soon after. Baithen told me that I had been seen fleeing from Abbot Ultán's chamber moments before they had discovered his body. He accused me of the murder and of fleeing from the scene.'

Fidelma's expression did not change. 'Did Baithen claim that he had witnessed the murder?'

Muirchertach gave her a hard look. 'How could he?' he demanded. 'I did not do it.'

'So you would argue that all he saw was you leaving the chamber?'

'I do not dispute that he saw me leave the abbot's chamber. What I do dispute is the claim that I killed Ultán.'

'And all you know of the circumstances of the death of Abbot Ultán is that you went to his chamber and found him dead and left?'

'That is all I know,' agreed Muirchertach.

Fidelma eyed him thoughtfully. 'There is surely something more to tell me?'

Muirchertach looked uncertain.

'The most important thing,' prompted Fidelma. 'Why did you go to see Abbot Ultán in his chamber at that time? It was close to midnight.'

'Why?' Muirchertach blinked as if he had not expected the question.

'You must have had a reason,' she pointed out.

Once again Fidelma saw the king glance helplessly towards his wife. It was as if he was seeking her permission to speak. Fidelma swung round to the woman, meeting her hostile gaze levelly.

'Was it a matter that concerned you, lady Aíbnat?' Her tone was abrupt.

Aíbnat's expression told her that her guess had hit home. Muirchertach's wife made no reply. The corners of her mouth tightened in defiance.

Fidelma heaved a sigh. 'This matter can be dealt between us in a sympathetic way now or it can be extracted in the legal proceedings before the Chief Brehon of the Five Kingdoms . . .'

Muirchertach frowned and broke in: 'What has Brehon Barrán to do with this matter?'

'Have you not been told?' Fidelma asked softly. 'When it comes to a hearing, then it is Brehon Barrán who will sit in judgement and the High King himself will sit with him.'

'*When* it comes to a hearing?' snapped Aíbnat. 'You mean *if*!'

Fidelma shook her head. 'Unless you can provide me with evidence of facts to counter the accusation, it is definitely *when*.'

Muirchertach looked confused for a moment or two before his shoulders slumped and he nodded.

'I suppose that is logical,' he commented in a low voice. Once more he gave his wife an almost pleading look.

Aíbnat suddenly said, 'Does that mean that there is a chance that it will not come to a public hearing?'

Fidelma glanced at her. 'There is always a chance in these matters. If I am told the truth and can persuade both the prosecutor and the Chief Brehon that this truth is such that the guilt must lie elsewhere, then there is no need for a hearing before the courts. It depends on your husband and yourself, as a witness to his defence, as to how I am to proceed.'

Aíbnat's thin lips compressed into a line for a moment before she turned to glance at Muirchertach and nodded slightly.

Her husband cleared his throat softly. 'I fear the truth will do me no good, Fidelma of Cashel.'

'Why is that?'

'Because I went to Ultán's chamber to kill him.'

Eadulf was too restless to go back to his chamber and rest and he was not hungry enough to enjoy the first meal of the day. Instead, he put on his cloak of beaver skins and went out on the walkway round the great walls of the fortress. Below he could see the town stirring, thin wisps of smoke from many fires rising into the turbulent air. He could hear the distant noise of people unaware of the drama of the night, making their preparations for the great fair and entertainment that was due to be held later that day. Surrounding the wood and stone structures of the town were many pavilions and tents that were housing the visitors who had come to witness and join the celebrations.

Eadulf walked slowly round the walls. The cloudy sky was lowering again and there was the promise of more rain in the air. The wind was cold but not as chilly as it had been in previous days. It seemed to be blowing from the south. There was a shimmer of white across the plain that showed a frost was still lying on the ground. He could see sheep flocks moving across the plain with their shepherds, dark shapes against the flat whiteness.

Along the walkway a sentinel raised a hand in greeting with a smile. Eadulf acknowledged the salutation and walked on, breathing deeply in the cold morning air. He found it helped to clear the fuzziness of his mind. Lack of sleep was debilitating, and when it reached the state when the mind was too tired to rest it caused an additional sense of frustration.

He suddenly became aware of another figure at the corner of the walkway: an elderly man in a short woollen cloak with rabbit fur trimming. The long hair was white and tied back with a leather thong. The figure seemed familiar, but it took a moment for Eadulf to recognise him.

'Give you a good day, Ordwulf,' he called, reverting to his Saxon speech.

The old man turned, startled, the eyes wide like those of someone caught at some illegal enterprise. Then he frowned as if trying to recall who Eadulf was. Eadulf realised that at their previous encounter Ordwulf had seemed to live in his own world, and he wondered whether the father of Berrihert was senile.

'I am Eadulf of Seaxmund's Ham, in the land of the South Folk,' he said gently. 'We met two days ago when . . .'

Ordwulf made a thrusting gesture with his hand. 'I know, I know. Do you take me for an imbecile?'

Eadulf was a little puzzled at the angry retort. 'Of course not.' Then a thought came to him. 'I understood that you and your sons had accommodation in the town? I did not realise that you were staying in the fortress.'

'We are in some place set aside for religious in the town,' muttered the old man. 'But I came here at first light, when they opened the gates. There was someone I wanted to see.' He turned back to gaze across the battlement towards the distant mountains in the north. 'It is a pleasant enough land, but it is not Deira,' he said.

Eadulf knew that Berrihert and his brothers had come from the southern area of Northumbria, the old independent kingdom of Deira which Athelfrith of Bernicia had conquered, uniting the two kingdoms as the land north of the River Humber – Northumbria. That had been within the living memory of some.

Ordwulf grimaced at the distant mountains. 'There is no sea coast here. My *tun*, my fortress, stood on the coast. I was once lord as far as I could see along the sea's low dim level. From north to south along the shoreline, I was lord. Now I am an exile in this strange land.'

'Are you homesick for Deira?' Eadulf enquired politely.

'Homesick?' The old man seemed to contemplate the question for a while. 'I do not long for places. I long for my dead wife and for comrades who once peopled those places.'

Eadulf stood feeling uncomfortable for a moment.

'*Tempori parendum*,' he muttered.

The old man cast a disapproving look at him. 'You have the gift to speak good Saxon. Speak it, for I am sick of foreign gibberish!'

'I said that one must yield to time,' explained Eadulf. 'As time changes so must we change with it.'

'Unctuous rubbish!' snapped Ordwulf. Eadulf blinked at the vehemence in his voice. 'Time is a thief. It took Aelgifu, my wife, from me and what did it leave me?'

'With three fine sons, at least,' Eadulf pointed out. 'Sons to be proud of.'

'Fine sons, you say?' The old Saxon warrior turned to him and seemed to take in his manner of dress as if for the first time, examining him from poll to feet. He scowled. 'I suppose your kind would say that?'

'What do you mean?' Eadulf was beginning to be irritated. He felt the insult in the man's words but did not understand the meaning of it.

'Three sons all entered into this New Faith of yours. All pious and holy and not one of them a warrior.'

'Why wish your sons to be warriors? Is it not better to serve God and help people live than to take up the sword and meet an early death?'

'Help people live? Had even one of them been a warrior, my wife might yet have lived, instead of dying in this strange land. May Hel be waiting at the gates of Nifheim, the place of mist, to receive him that caused her death.'

Eadulf shuddered a little as the old man called upon Hel, the ancient goddess of death. Eadulf had been raised with the old gods and goddesses of his people and even now he sometimes felt the power of the old deities – of Woden, Thunor, Tyr and Freya – and realised that he still feared them. But above all he feared Hel who ruled the land of the dead.

'Do you reject the New Faith?' he rebuked the old man.

Ordwulf gave a wheezy laugh. 'The old faith was good enough for my forefathers and me. When my time comes, let me have my battleaxe in my right hand and Woden's name on my lips so that I may enter Wael Halla and feast with the gods and heroes of my people.'

'Yet your sons . . .' Eadulf began to protest.

'My sons!' sneered the old man. 'They could not protect their own mother from the members of the very Faith they espoused. I curse them! I curse them as I rejoice that he who took my lady Aelgifu from me is now sped to suffer the tortures of the damned. May Hel eat his living flesh!'

The old man spat over the wall and then turned and hurried away, leaving Eadulf staring after him in horror.

Fidelma was regarding Muirchertach Nár in astonishment.

'Are you admitting that you went to Abbot Ultán's chamber to murder him?' she asked incredulously.

Muirchertach lowered his head with a deep sigh. 'I went with that intention but I did not do so. I did not do so for the simple reason that someone else had already killed him.'

Fidelma sat back in her chair and folded her hands in her lap, trying to re-form her features to keep the surprise out of her face. She stared long and hard at him.

'Can you tell me why you went with this intention?'

Muirchertach glanced at his wife. She appeared to shrug indifferently as if she had washed her hands of the matter.

'My wife has told you that she was of the Uí Briúin Aí. Have you heard of the poetess Searc of that clan?'

Fidelma was unfamiliar with the name and shook her head.

'Searc was the younger sister of my wife. She was a gentle, affectionate girl, as befitted her name,' Muirchertach explained. Fidelma was reminded that the name Searc actually meant 'love' or 'affection'.

'I presume that she is dead since you speak in the past tense,' Fidelma commented.

'She is. Had she lived, she would have become one of the greatest of our poets.'

'Go on,' Fidelma prompted, after he had paused again.

'Searc had the ability to become as great a poetess as Líadan or Íta. Five years and more have passed since Connacht acknowledged her as among the foremost of its *banfilidh*, or female poets. So she went on her first circuit to the centres of the five kingdoms to recite her poetry at the great festivals. She attended a gathering at Ard Macha and it was there that she met a young poet called Senach.'

He paused and Fidelma waited patiently for him to gather his thoughts. She glanced at Aíbnat, who sat staring into the fire. The woman had a controlled expression on her features and it was as if she was not really hearing what was being said.

'They fell in love with each other,' he continued. 'Senach was a member of the abbey of Cill Ria and when he returned there after the poetry festival in Ard Macha, Searc followed him.'

This time when he paused, Fidelma said: 'I presume that Ultán was abbot of Cill Ria by this time?'

'Ultán was abbot at the time,' Muirchertach confirmed.

'So, tell me what happened.'

'I think that you know by now of Abbot Ultán's attitudes. He is one of those reformers who now advocates celibacy among the religious. He made all the members of his abbey swear an oath that they would shun the company of the opposite sex. Cill Ria was once a mixed house, a *conhospitae*. He divided it into two separate communities. Apparently Senach approached Abbot Ultán wishing to be absolved from his oath to the abbey so that he might transfer to a *conhospitae* which did not adhere to the rules of celibacy. Ultán refused outright. He went further and had Senach locked in his cell, and when Searc came looking for the boy he had her driven from the locality by monks wielding birch sticks.'

'Such an act is unlawful,' protested Fidelma, in horror. 'No one can physically attack a woman with impunity.'

'Abbot Ultán claimed refuge in the *Penitentials*,' Muirchertach explained. 'It was not the first time that he ordered his followers to beat a woman whom he claimed had transgressed against the rules of the Faith . . . or his version of them, anyway. I have heard that there were even some who did not recover from the beatings that he had ordered.'

Fidelma grimaced in disapproval. 'If this is true, then how could this man survive among his fellow religious? Indeed, how could he become an emissary of the Comarb of Patrick?'

'He had friends in high places. A friend can be more powerful than an army in some respects. He has been protected.'

'Are we to yield our law to these foreign ideas from Rome without protest?' muttered Aíbnat.

'We do not know exactly what happened,' went on Muirchertach, not answering her protest. 'According to one story, Abbot Ultán had Senach escorted against his will to a pilgrim ship which set out for Abbot Ronan's monastery at Mazerolles in Gaul. The ship never reached Gaul and there was talk of its having been attacked by Frankish pirates and those on board killed. Such stories reached Searc, who believed them and . . . He glanced at Aíbnat.

'My sister killed herself,' Aíbnat's voice was harsh.

Muirchertach compressed his lips for a moment.

'In her desperation, she threw herself from a cliff,' he added.

'If this action was caused by Abbot Ultán, did you not take action through the law?' asked Fidelma, trying to examine the matter logically. 'Your brehon would surely have advised you on that account.'

Aíbnat laughed harshly. 'How can one bring another before the law when only one of them recognises it? Ultán prated about the laws of God and quoted strange texts that we had no knowledge of.'

'But you did try to claim compensation from Abbot Ultán?'

'As we have said,' Muirchertach answered, 'my emissary and my brehon made the proper applications but Abbot Ultán took refuge in the *Penitentials*. We protested to the Comarb of Patrick, the abbot and bishop of Armagh. But he would do nothing for he, too, supports the ideas that Abbot Ultán propagates.'

Fidelma remained silent for a while, then finally said: 'So last night you went to see Abbot Ultán with the intention of killing him?'

Muirchertach shrugged eloquently.

'I suppose that was my intention,' he admitted. 'Having discovered that Abbot Ultán was here, I went in anger to his chamber, determined to make him pay for what he had done. He had destroyed the lives of two young people.'

Fidelma looked thoughtfully at Aíbnat. 'Did you know what your husband intended when he left this chamber last night?'

'My actions have nothing to do with Aíbnat,' Muirchertach said hurriedly.

Fidelma ignored him.

'Did you know that your husband was going to see Ultán and that he went in anger to seek recompense for the death of your sister?' she insisted again.

The wife of Muirchertach returned her scrutiny with the old belligerent fire in her eyes. 'My husband is king of Connacht. He should have led a raid against the Uí Thuirtrí and burnt down Abbot Ultán's abbey many months ago.'

Fidelma smiled tightly. 'I will take it that you have answered in the affirmative. Were you and Muirchertach here together in the hour or so before he left to see Abbot Ultán?'

Aíbnat frowned. 'I suppose so. Why?'

'I need to understand exactly what happened. You were both here and presumably talking over the fact that Abbot Ultán was here also. How did you find out that he was present?'

'Abbot Augaire of Conga told us.'

'Augaire?'

'He is my chief abbot and bishop.'

'I have heard that he exchanged some angry words with Ultán when he arrived.'

'So he told us,' Muirchertach agreed.

'Was Abbot Augaire here when you left to see Ultán?'

'He was not. He had retired to his chamber long before.'

Fidelma made a mental note to find out where all the guests' chambers were in relation to Abbot Ultán's room.

'So he left you and the lady Aíbnat alone and you talked of Ultán and your anger increased and you left to confront him?' she summed up.

'But I did not kill him. As God is my witness, I did not kill him – much as I would have liked to.'

Aíbnat suddenly laughed bitterly.

'My husband can scarcely kill a man in battle without swooning!' she sneered. 'Such a mighty king. All he cares for is his fine wine, good food, dancing and entertainment and women.'

Muirchertach flushed. 'I hardly think that . . .'

'You hardly think!' snapped Aíbnat. 'Return to your wine and leave the rulership of Connacht to your cousin. He is twice the man you will ever be.'

Fidelma knew that Muirchertach's *tánaiste* was Dúnchad Muirisci of the Uí Fiachracha Muaide. There certainly did not seem to be any love lost between Muirchertach and his wife. She coughed slightly to bring their attention back to the matter in hand.

'So, what you are saying, Muirchertach, is that you left here just before midnight and went to confront Abbot Ultán but found him dead. Is that so?'

She looked carefully into his eyes and he did not drop them before her bright quizzical gaze. His cheeks were flushed by his wife's insults.

'I did,' he replied firmly.

'But the only witnesses were those who saw you hurrying from his chamber?'

'You have the word of a king, even though he is but a poor specimen of one,' snapped Aíbnat. 'His word should take precedence over anyone else's.'

Fidelma could not help the pitying look that came to her features as she gazed at him.

Muirchertach shrugged defensively. 'My word is all I have.'

Fidelma turned slightly. 'Now, Aíbnat, did you remain here after Muirchertach had left?'

Aíbnat flushed.

'What are you implying?' she snapped.

'I never imply,' replied Fidelma waspishly. 'I am asking a question. I do it for your own sake. After all, Searc was your sister. You blamed Abbot Ultán for her death and that was the reason why your husband, presumably on your behalf, went to see Ultán with the intention of doing him harm, even if he did not do so. At the moment, her death provides a strong motivation for Abbot Ultán's killing. It could be argued that you both had an equal hand in this murder.'

'It could be as you say,' Aíbnat responded coldly after a few moments' thought. 'However, I was in this chamber the whole time. After my husband left, I did not stir.'

Fidelma sat in silence thinking over things for a few moments. Then she sighed.

'I have to say, although the evidence is circumstantial, it is good enough to create real problems. It is evidence that will have to be answered before the Chief Brehon.'

Aíbnat stared at her in barely controlled irritation. 'So you do not believe us?'

Fidelma looked sadly at her. 'My first impression is that if Muirchertach had been guilty as he is accused, he could have made up a far better story than one which actually hands his accusers a motive for the slaughter.'

She rose suddenly to her feet and Muirchertach rose with her. He looked anxiously at her.

'Will you undertake my defence?' His tone was almost pleading.

'I am always prepared to defend the innocent against a false accusation, Muirchertach,' she said quietly. 'Let me continue my investigation. It may well be in future that I will want Eadulf of Seaxmund's Ham to assist me. Do you have any objection to his presence?'

'A Saxon?' snapped Aíbnat querulously.

'Soon to be my official husband,' she replied. 'You may be aware that he has helped me on many investigations in the past.'

'Of course,' Muirchertach said at once. 'Is that not the reason we came to Cashel, to witness the ceremony? I have no objection to speaking in front of Eadulf.'

'That is good. We will speak again later.'

# CHAPTER SEVEN

Fidelma encountered Eadulf as she was crossing one of the smaller courtyards. He was coming down the steps from the walkway round the fortress walls. When he asked what she had discovered, she drew him aside and quickly told him of her conversations with Muirchertach and his wife Aíbnat. Eadulf rubbed his chin thoughtfully.

'This Muirchertach is either innocent or clever,' he finally said.

Fidelma followed his train of thought. 'You think that his willingness to confess to a motive, even to an intention of killing Abbot Ultán, and claiming someone else did it before he had a chance, is a sign of cleverness?'

'It could well be,' Eadulf replied. 'To tell a story which so obviously points to his guilt has the effect of making one believe him innocent.'

'That is devious thinking.'

'It is surely so. And who knows better than you what lengths people may go to in order to mislead? If he knew that the story of his wife's sister would be revealed, then best to confess it so that one could say that he was honest to his own detriment. Therefore, being so, he could not possible have committed the crime.'

'I will bear it in mind,' Fidelma acknowledged. 'But if Muirchertach is truly innocent? What then?'

'There are already enough suspects at Cashel.' Eadulf smiled thinly.

'You mean Abbot Augaire?'

'Also Berrihert and his brothers.'

'I had forgotten them,' she confessed.

'I met old Ordwulf on the walls just a short while ago. But I think we might discount them.'

'Why so?'

'Because they were in the hostel in the town last night and no one is admitted here without good reason once the fortress gates are closed for the night. None of them could have entered to do the deed. Ordwulf said that he entered only when the gates were opened at first light. From what he said, I think he came to see the abbot and was then told that he was dead. He does not disguise the fact that he is now rejoicing in that death.'

'Perhaps we should keep an eye on your Saxon friends. Abbot Ultán appears to have upset many people.'

'We must find out more about him,' Eadulf said. 'We could seek information about him from the king of Ulaidh.'

Fidelma shook her head quickly. 'No need to bother Blathmac just yet. I think we should first question the members of Abbot Ultán's entourage.'

Eadulf had forgotten the group who was travelling with Abbot Ultán.

'Who shall we begin with?'

A short while later they were in the library which Fidelma had requested they be allowed to use for examining the witnesses. Eadulf sat at a small table with a *tabhall lorga*, a wooden frame filled with wax on which he could record notes by the use of a *graib* or sharp pointed stylus of metal. Fidelma sat by his side, and in front of her sat the thin, elderly scribe of Ultán's household: a man with sharp features who peered at them with his pale blue eyes, his head moving in a curious birdlike, darting movement.

'Your name is Drón?' Fidelma began.

The head darted up and down. 'I am Brother Drón of Cill Ria. I am told that you are the *dálaigh* named Sister Fidelma?' His face was not happy as he peered from her to Eadulf. 'And you, scribe, who are you?'

'I am Eadulf of Seaxmund's Ham in the land of the South Folk,' Eadulf replied, falling into the form of introduction that he had grown used to using in the land of Éireann.

'Ah, ah, of course.' Brother Drón nodded. 'Of course. This is a terrible thing, terrible. That an abbot should be murdered while under the protection and hospitality of a king . . .'

'I understand that you were Abbot Ultán's scribe?' Fidelma cut in when the man appeared to be launching a complaint.

The elderly man lifted his chin a little pugnaciously. 'Not just scribe but his steward and adviser. I have served him at the abbey of Cill Ria for four years.'

'But you are not of the Uí Thuirtrí,' Fidelma said quickly, having listened to the man's accent. 'You do not even speak with the accent of the northern people.'

Brother Drón smiled thinly. 'You have a good ear, Sister,' he admitted. 'I am of the Uí Dróna of Laigin – hence my name. We are the descendants of Breasal Bélach, who ruled Laigin . . .'

'And are now a small sept dwelling to the north-west of Ferna,' Fidelma pointed out sharply when a note of pride entered his voice.

Brother Drón blinked. 'You seem to know much about my humble clan,' he muttered.

'I dwelt at Cill Dara for a time and it would be remiss of me not to know something of the clans of Laigin.'

There was a pause. When Brother Drón made no further comment she went on: 'So, tell us, how did you become adviser and scribe to the abbot? Cill Ria in the land of the Uí Thuirtrí is a long way from Ferna.'

'I left Laigin when I was at the age of maturity and entered the religious. I received my training at Ard Macha.'

'Why in Ulaidh?' intervened Eadulf. 'Laigin has many great ecclesiastical universities – Sléibhte, in your own clan territory, or the mixed house at Cill Dara, both of which are closer to your homeland than Ard Macha.'

Brother Drón turned to him with a thinly veiled sneer. 'Surely, Saxon, you would be better serving in your own land than here in the five kingdoms of Éireann?'

Eadulf flushed. 'That does not answer my question,' he snapped.

'I am sorry that you do not think so. Not all birds have to live their lives in the nest in which they were born. Ard Macha is the foundation of our great patron, the Blessed Patrick. Why shouldn't one want to go there and tread on the hallowed soil where he founded the greatest church in these lands?'

'So, how did you become scribe and adviser to Bishop Ultán?' repeated Fidelma.

'Abbot Ultán was a close friend and colleague of the Comarb of Patrick, the *archiepiscopus* Ségéne, and a frequent visitor at Ard Macha. I had become a scribe at Ard Macha and one day, acknowledging my abilities, he asked me if I would join him at his abbey of Cill Ria in the land of the Uí Thuirtrí. I did so and have served him to the best of those abilities for these last four years.'

'And we presume that you shared the abbot's view that Ard Macha should be recognised as the primatial seat of the Faith in the five kingdoms?' Fidelma spoke gently.

'Of course. Not only that but I provided him with all the salient arguments in support of the contention.' Brother Drón did not lack pride.

'And it was as a matter of course, as his adviser, that you accompanied Abbot Ultán when he embarked on this embassy to the southern kingdoms? Tell us how that came about.'

Brother Drón shrugged quickly. 'It was at the request of the Comarb of the Blessed Patrick . . .'

'Abbot Ségéne?'

'The *archiepiscopus*,' corrected Brother Drón heavily. 'He sought an emissary to visit the southern abbeys and churches to argue the case for the recognition of Ard Macha. As it was something that I . . . that Abbot Ultán had long argued, he undertook the mission with great joy.'

'As well as Abbot Ultán and yourself, who else is in this embassy?'

'Two of our religieuse: Sister Marga and Sister Sétach. We were accompanied by two attendants to look after our wagon and horses.'

'What is the role of your two religieuse companions?'

'They were record keepers and had care of the documents we were presenting in argument.'

'I see,' Fidelma acknowledged. 'And having worked with Abbot Ultán for four years, you must have had a good knowledge of him?'

Brother Drón frowned. 'A knowledge of him?'

'Of what kind of man he was, what his hopes and fears were, and whose enmity he aroused,' Fidelma explained.

Brother Drón sat back with his thin smile and folded his hands in front of him. 'I would have said that he was a man without faults, unless a passion for his cause be called a fault.'

'To some that may very well be a fault,' Eadulf pointed out, looking up from his notes. 'A man may believe so much in his cause that he becomes intolerant and despotic towards others.'

Brother Drón appeared shocked. 'You are speaking of the Abbot Ultán, brother.'

'But a man like any other man,' Eadulf replied calmly. 'Being an abbot does not make a man any more or less human, with all the faults that humans have.'

'I will admit that Abbot Ultán was resolute in his faith and turned a harsh face and a firm hand to those who were enemies to it.'

Eadulf smiled without humour.

'*Fortiter in re, suaviter in modo* . . .' he commented softly. Resolutely in action, gently in manner.

'Apart from these views,' Fidelma cut in hurriedly, 'which you have described as "resolute", would Abbot Ultán have garnered enemies?'

Brother Drón shrugged. 'His enemies were the enemies of the Faith. Perhaps there are many such enemies still in this land. Abbot Ultán, to my mind, was a great leader of men. Stern and forceful. He was much admired by *archiepiscopus* Ségéne.'

Fidelma was about to snap that no one outside Ard Macha recognised this new title *archiepiscopus*, for in the five kingdoms the Comarb of Patrick and the Comarb of Ailbe stood in equal status in matters of ecclesiastical respect. No bishop was superior to another. Then she shrugged. Let Brother Drón call Ségéne of Ard Macha what he may, it did not make it a reality.

'Sometimes the qualities that you boast of sit ill on a man of religious calling,' she mused.

Brother Drón frowned, not quite understanding.

'Firm and forceful, stern and harsh,' she pointed out. 'These are not the qualities of someone bringing a message of joy, of peace and love among humankind.'

'Sister, our movement – the Faith – is like an army on the march,' Brother Drón argued earnestly. 'We must conquer souls for Christ. Abbot Ultán was a great general in the crusade to convert the heathen to the one true faith.'

'Conquer souls?' Fidelma shook her head immediately. 'It is not a concept I could ascribe to. It means that you have vanquished the soul, subjugated it and become its master.' Eadulf nodded supportively as she made the variations of meaning on the old word *buad*. 'Is it not better to persuade, by reason and logic, to come to an understanding, than to simply conquer?'

Brother Drón grimaced angrily. 'It matters not how people come to submit themselves to the true religion. They have to bend their necks before the master.'

'Submit? Master? Bend their necks? These are words that fit ill in our tongue, Brother Drón. Not even the old gods and goddesses would claim that they were masters, or that we had to bend the knee or submit to them. Nor do I think Christ ever taught that we should. If God gave people free will then we have the will to choose and choice should be made freely – not by conquest, fear or force.'

Brother Drón was tight lipped with ill-concealed anger. 'I need no lessons in theology from you, Fidelma of Cashel. Abbot Ultán was right to come here to protest against your marriage. You are not deserving of a place in the ranks of the religious. Stick to your law and leave matters of faith to those who are qualified to speak of it.'

Fidelma blinked at the vehemence in the man's voice. Then her voice grew brittle.

'Very well, Brother Drón. I will speak to you of the law. I am a *dálaigh* and you are a *fíadu*, a witness. As such you have certain obligations, not just of honesty but of respect for the law and its officers. If you do not meet such obligations, then you must bear in mind that you will be liable to certain strictures and fines. Do you understand this?'

Brother Drón seemed abashed at being addressed in such a manner. He swallowed audibly.

'At Cill Ria no woman would dare speak in such a fashion. We are governed by the *Penitentials* and . . .'

'You are not at Cill Ria,' snapped Fidelma. 'The law of this land is, and has been from time immemorial, the law of the Fénechus. That is the law you will now answer to. If you refuse to do so, I will call one of my brother's guards to take you to a place where you may reflect on your position. Now, where were you last night?' She shot the question at him before he had time to recover his poise.

'Where was I?' Brother Drón sounded as if he could not believe his ears at being asked.

'I think that you heard the question,' she snapped.

'I was in the chamber which the good abbot had acquired for me. Originally, I was going to be placed in some dormitory with the other religious, but Abbot Ultán protested to your steward that I needed to be within call, being his scribe and adviser.'

'And where was this chamber?'

'My chamber? The abbot's room was in a corner where two corridors formed a right angle. My chamber was ten metres along the corridor from which one could see the door to his chamber.'

'Were you there at the time of the abbot's death?' pressed Fidelma.

'I retired early as it is my custom to be up several hours before dawn to pray and prepare myself for the day.'

'And when were you told of Abbot Ultán's death?'

'I had arisen and gone to the chapel and was at prayer when other brothers entered and spoke of the event. Horrified, I went immediately to Abbot Ultán's chamber but was not allowed to enter by some officious young warrior. I was told – no, ordered – to go back to my chamber and await a summons from the *dálaigh* in charge. I said I would protest at this treatment and went to see Blathmac mac Mael Coba, who is staying here.'

'I presume King Blathmac of Ulaidh instructed you as to your position under the law?' Fidelma said almost sweetly.

Brother Drón grimaced in annoyance. 'He told me that I had to wait until the *dálaigh* summoned me.'

'A wise king,' muttered Eadulf, staring at the ceiling.

Fidelma looked carefully at Brother Drón. It was certainly hard to deflate the man's ego.

'Did you go to find Sister Marga or Sister Sétach to tell them the news?'

'I had no time.'

'You slept well during the night? You were not disturbed at all?'

'I would have mentioned that,' snapped the religieux.

'Not even when the body was discovered and there would have been many people in the corridor or going into the abbot's chamber?'

'I slept soundly.'

'Very well. And, once again, you know of no particular enemies that Abbot Ultán had?'

Brother Drón sniffed. 'I did not say that. I said that his only enemies were the enemies of the Faith. When I heard that Muirchertach of Connacht was being spoken of as the culprit, I was not surprised.'

Fidelma lifted her head quickly.

'Really? Not surprised?' she asked.

'For some years he has been threatening Abbot Ultán.'

'Threatening? In what form were these threats made?'

'He demanded compensation on behalf of his wife's family. The honour price for his wife's sister. Ten *seds*, he claimed, because she was a poet.'

Fidelma's eyes narrowed slightly. 'Was the demand for this sum made through a brehon?'

For a moment Brother Drón looked bewildered.

'Of course,' he said hesitantly.

'A demand for compensation made through a brehon is hardly a threat. But you said that he had been threatening. Why was this claim, which had to go through the law, seen as a threat? Explain the matter.'

The scribe looked annoyed. 'It was the whole manner of the approach. The sister of Muirchertach's wife was a girl named Searc. She was a poetess, supposedly of the class of a *cli*. Therefore her honour price was ten *seds*. The situation was simple. We had, in the abbey of Cill Ria, a young religieux who was also a poet. Bishop Ultán had allowed him to take part in a gathering of bards at Ard Macha. It was there he met this Connacht woman. The woman, Searc, tried to ensnare him with feminine wiles and when he returned to Cill Ria she followed, like a siren, trying to lure him to his doom.'

Fidelma sat without expression as Brother Drón gave his account.

'Abbot Ultán decided to send the boy, whose name was Senach, to safety. He arranged passage for him to Gaul. There was a religious house looking for young members to help in the task of converting the Franks. As it happened, the ship did not arrive and there were stories that it had been attacked by Frankish pirates who had killed those on board or carried them off into slavery.'

Fidelma nodded slowly. It was a story not so different from Muirchetach's own version. The differences were simply in the motivations ascribed to the protagonists.

'So that was the end of the story, so far as Abbot Ultán was concerned?'

Brother Drón shook his head. 'After a while, we received a formal messenger from Muirchertach of Connacht. It was then that we discovered that this same Searc was the sister to Muirchertach's wife.'

'I see. You did not know before? What then?'

'This messenger . . .'

'Do you recall the name of the messenger?' interrupted Eadulf suddenly.

'Of course. It was the religieux who is now Abbot Augaire.'

'Augaire?' queried Eadulf. 'How do you mean, "who is now Abbot Augaire"?'

Brother Drón sniffed. 'He was Brother Augaire at the time. He received his office through the influence he secured with Muirchertach by representing him.'

'So Augaire came to the Abbey of Cill Ria? Presumably he accompanied the brehon?'

'He did, but it was Augaire who made the demands. He said that the girl had committed suicide and that he had been a witness to it. Well, Abbot Ultán said that proved the evil that was in the girl, to become guilty of kin-slaying, for which there is no forgiveness in this world.'

'But hopefully there is in the next,' muttered Eadulf.

Brother Drón glanced angrily at him but Fidelma quickly intervened.

'What exactly did Augaire tell you?'

'That he had discovered from Muirchertach that the girl, Searc, had heard the news of Senach's death and killed herself, a crime that is heinous in law,' he added in defiance, looking at Eadulf.

Fidelma grimaced. It was true that suicide was classed in law as kin-slaying and was regarded as a terrible crime.

'But was it explained why Muirchertach blamed Abbot Ultán for the girl's death?' she pressed.

'Augaire, speaking on his behalf, said the king of Connacht deemed Abbot Ultán responsible for separating Brother Senach and this woman Searc, thus bringing about Senach's death and, consequently, Searc's suicide. He demanded the compensation and, of course, Abbot Ultán refused to even consider the matter.'

'On what grounds did the abbot refuse to go to the arbitration of a brehon?'

Brother Drón looked angry for the moment and then abruptly smiled, but without humour.

'The abbey of Cill Ria, as I have explained, operates under the rules we have accepted from Rome, the chief church of Christendom. The *Penitentials*, which I am sure you know well, are the rules that have been blessed and approved by the *archiepiscopus* at Ard Macha.'

'And these forbade Senach and Searc to be together?'

'Of course.'

'There is no "of course" about it. Rome does not forbid marriage among the religious.'

'Had Bishop Ultán lived he would have brought the truth to you,' snapped Brother Drón.

'I do not doubt that he would have tried to put forward his views,' replied Fidelma calmly. 'But those views are not shared by everyone. By the way, are you saying that Senach did not respond to the feelings expressed by Searc?'

Brother Drón hesitated, his tongue passing swiftly over his lips.

Fidelma smiled thinly before he could reply. 'So he did respond?'

Again anger formed on Brother Drón's features. 'He had taken an oath to obey the rules of the community of Cill Ria. The woman was a siren who twisted his mind and seduced him away from his oath.'

'Is it true, then, that he asked if he could be absolved from his oath?'

'Once taken, such an oath is impossible to withdraw from.'

'Impossible? A formula of words in these circumstances is not made of chains and locks. Many have asked to be released from the oaths they took. An oath freely given may be ended if both sides freely consent.'

'And Abbot Ultán did not freely consent, for if you have made a promise to serve God you cannot break that promise.'

'As I understand it, Senach was not breaking the promise but asking that he be released from holding to it. And Abbot Ultán refused to consider his request and sent him off on this ship in which he was killed.'

'It was for the boy's own good.'

'Hardly good when it resulted in the death of both the boy and the girl.'

'That was God's will. It was obviously God's punishment on them both.'

Fidelma raised her eyebrows in distaste. 'It seems that God gets blamed for many things,' she said quietly.

Eadulf cleared his throat. 'I am unclear. If Muirchertach summoned Abbot Ultán through a brehon to seek compensation in the courts, how could Abbot Ultán legally refuse to answer the courts of this land, even if his own abbey is ruled by the *Penitentials*?'

'I have told you, in this the *archiepiscopus* supported him.'

'But the king of Ulaidh knows full well that the Fénechus law is the law of all five kingdoms and the *Penitentials* are rules within the confines of certain abbeys that have adopted them. It was the king's duty to obey the law and he should have compelled Ultán to come to account before the brehon,' Eadulf pointed out.

'A Saxon telling the king of Ulaidh how to obey his own law?' sneered Brother Drón.

'A *dálaigh* asking why the law was not obeyed,' intervened Fidelma irritably.

'That is something that the king of Ulaidh may answer and not I. In many places the *Penitentials* are displacing the old law and bringing our people into a true relationship with God's holy ordinances.'

Eadulf looked nervously at Fidelma, knowing her fierce commitment to the law. But she said nothing for a moment or two. Then she asked: 'Just to clarify this matter, Abbot Augaire made various representations to Abbot Ultán on behalf of the king of Connacht? When was the last representation made?'

'Several years ago. And he was, as I have said, simply Brother Augaire at that time.'

'And so the matter was forgotten?'

'So far as we at Cill Ria were concerned.'

'And is this argument the cause of the animosity shown yesterday between Abbot Augaire and Abbot Ultán?'

'Being on different sides in an argument did not endear them to one another. Abbot Ultán considered that Augaire used his witnessing of the girl's death to ingratiate himself with Muirchertach and his wife. Because of this matter he rose to the position of abbot at Conga. Abbot Ultán had two enemies here – Augaire and Muirchertach.'

Fidelma stood up slowly. 'That will be all for the time being, Brother Drón. I shall probably want to see you later. I may also want to see Sister Marga and Sister Sétach.'

'Why would you want to see them?' demanded Brother Drón belligerently.

'Why would you ask questions of a *dálaigh* conducting an investigation?' snapped Fidelma. 'This is not the first time that I must reprimand you on your attitude. You are in Cashel and we do not operate under your *Penitentials*.'

Once again Brother Drón swallowed and hesitated, and then he shrugged. After he had gone there was a silence for a few moments and then Fidelma glanced at her companion and smiled.

'You are exceptionally quiet, Eadulf.'

Eadulf returned her smile and indicated with his head towards the closed door. 'He is a vain, narrow and prejudiced little man. It is hard to hold a dialogue with such people.'

'You are doubtless right, Eadulf. But at least we begin to build up a picture of this doughty prelate. It would seem that Brother Drón confirms that he was a bigot who could attract hate.'

'I still do not understand how Abbot Ultán refused to answer the summons of a brehon. Surely the *Penitentials* cannot take any preference over the law of the five kingdoms?'

'You remember what happened to you in Laigin?' asked Fidelma softly.

Eadulf shuddered and nodded.

'More and more we find some local chiefs and even provincial kings giving in to abbots who take it on themselves to adopt an alien system of laws that come in from the dregs of what was once the empire of Rome. They are harsh, with often physical punishments. I believe this is what is happening in the northern kingdoms of the island. Certainly, at some time, I will ask to speak to Blathmac of Ulaidh about it.'

She paused for a while, her fingers drumming on the armrest of her chair.

'What now?' prompted Eadulf.

'Now?' Fidelma paused and regarded him as if with some surprise. 'I think a word with Abbot Augaire. He seems a central figure in the cause of this conflict between Muirchertach and Ultán.'

Eadulf raised his eyebrows for a moment as she moved towards the door. 'You don't want him sent for?'

Fidelma glanced back. 'He is an abbot and is entitled to a little more dignity in treatment than Brother Drón.'

# CHAPTER EIGHT

As they left the library to find Abbot Augaire, they were halted in the corridor by an earnest-looking young man. He was well dressed, of average height, with carefully groomed sandy hair and features that, while not of themselves unpleasant to look upon, were formed into an expression which forced the word 'conceit' to come to Fidelma's mind.

'I believe that you are Sister Fidelma?' he demanded, the voice inquisitorial as if he were interrogating her.

Fidelma faced him with a grave smile. 'I am Fidelma of Cashel,' she said gently, reminding him of her other rank. It was a trick of hers that she only used when she felt someone was trying to be over-bearing with her. 'And this is Eadulf of Seaxmund's Ham.'

Even had the stranger been sensitive to this warning sign, he chose to ignore it.

'Just so. When will you be ready with your defence? We cannot delay long and keep the Chief Brehon and the High King waiting.'

Fidelma's eyebrows arched a little in her surprise at the question and she glanced at Eadulf. He grimaced at her to indicate his amusement at the man's officiousness. She turned back to him.

'And you are?' she asked with icy sweetness and a slight smile.

The man blinked as if astonished that the question should be asked of him. 'I am Ninnid, of course.'

Fidelma's smiled broadened.

'Of course,' she replied gravely.

'No need to apologise,' went on the man in a confident tone.

'I was not . . .'

Ninnid waved his hand in dismissal. 'We have not met, of course, so I suppose you would not recognise me.'

Eadulf had turned away to hide his face. He seemed to be trying to stifle a cough. Then he turned back, frowning as though trying to remember something.

'Ninnid? Ninnid? I seem to have heard the name before.'

Fidelma was also trying to keep her face straight.

'There was a Ninnid Lámhderg who was one of the disciples of the Blessed Finnian of Clonard,' she suggested.

'But this young man is not old enough to have known Finnian, for surely he has been dead a century or more?' replied Eadulf gravely.

Ninnid was clearly someone without humour for his face was irritated.

'I am Ninnid the brehon of Laigin,' he explained.

'Oh.' Eadulf put on a patronising smile. 'You are surely young to be a brehon, even of Laigin.'

The young man looked uncertain yet he seemed not to know that he was being humorously rebuked for his arrogance. Fidelma realised that if he did not understand that, then it was pointless continuing the exercise.

'What is it you wish, Ninnid?' she asked seriously.

'I am ready to prosecute Muirchertach,' the brehon replied. 'Are you prepared to defend him?'

'I shall be ready to do so, but only after I have investigated the circumstances fully.'

'No need. I have already done so. There is a case for Muirchertach to answer. The facts are clear and there are eyewitnesses. All you have to do is relay to the court what reason in mitigation Muirchertach has to offer.'

Fidelma swallowed hard. 'Are you telling me what I, as a *dálaigh*, should do?'

Ninnid did not seem to recognise the warning tone in her voice.

'I am sure that you would appreciate some advice from someone with experience of these matters,' he replied calmly.

'Really?' Fidelma retained her temper with an obvious effort. 'With due respect, no witness saw Muirchertach actually stab Abbot Ultán.'

Ninnid made a curious cutting gesture with his hand as if dismissing the protest. 'The law accepts circumstantial evidence.'

Eadulf frowned at the unfamiliar term. To him the basic word *imthoicell* was an act of encompassing or encircling. It took him some moments, putting it with the word for evidence, to arrive at the idea of what 'encircling evidence' meant.

Ninnid was continuing. 'If the suspect is seen acting in a manner that appears to incriminate him, this evidence may be acknowledged. Muirchertach was seen fleeing from Abbot Ultán's room . . .'

'Fleeing?' snapped Fidelma.

'That is what the eyewitnesses saw and we have another witness who will say that for many years Muirchertach was in enmity with Abbot Ultán because . . .'

Fidelma held up her hand. 'We know the circumstances.'

Ninnid smiled condescendingly. 'Then I admire you for agreeing to make a defence. Naturally, should Muirchertach plead provocation, I will consider his arguments. However, I have to tell you that it may be difficult due to the circumstances of the crime. It is clear that Abbot Ultán was violently attacked as he prepared for bed.'

'There is no reason to suppose that Muirchertach will plead anything but total innocence,' replied Fidelma firmly.

Ninnid actually chuckled. 'When you have had more experience in these matters you will come to know that it is sometimes better to make a bargain over one's degree of guilt. I would suggest as much to Muirchertach if I were in your place.'

'Thank you for the benefit of your advice,' Fidelma said coldly.

'I am always willing to advise,' replied the other obliviously.

'It has been instructive speaking to you, Ninnid,' Eadulf intervened hastily, seeing the fiery glint in Fidelma's eyes. 'But you will excuse us . . .'

They began to move off but Ninnid stayed them again.

'You have not answered my question,' he protested mildly.

Fidelma turned back sharply. 'What question was that?'

'Why, when I can instruct the Chief Brehon Barrán to start the trial proceedings.'

Fidelma was quiet for a moment but Eadulf made an inarticulate sound that he again covered by a fit of coughing. Then she spoke quietly.

'You'll forgive us, Ninnid, but we have many things to do. Have no fear, when I am ready I shall let Barrán be advised and then *he* can instruct *you* as to when he will start the proceedings.'

They hurried down the corridor. Eadulf was still chuckling.

'*Beati pauperes spiritu*,' he laughed, quoting the Gospel of Matthew. Blessed are the poor in spirit.

Fidelma indulged in a mischievous grin.

'Our friend Ninnid is not so blessed,' she replied. 'I doubt if I have ever met such a colossal ego.'

'Perhaps the defence of Muirchertach will not be so difficult after all with such a pompous idiot prosecuting,' Eadulf suggested.

'Do not build your sty until the litter is born,' she replied, quoting an old proverb.

Eadulf shrugged. 'You think that there is some talent hidden in that pomposity?'

'You do not become brehon, even of Laigin, without some talent for law and good sense. Remember that Barrán himself recommended Ninnid because of his success as a prosecutor. Perhaps Ninnid merely dons the cloak of someone without humility to force his opponents into a false sense of superiority and then, when they are in such a vulnerable state, he will strike.'

'Could he be that clever?'

'We should never take things for granted. That is what I am saying. There is an old saying – things do not always end as we expect.'

From Caol, still looking chagrined at the belief that it was his failure to supply a guard which had led to the murder, they discovered where the guest chamber of Abbot Augaire was situated and made their way there.

The abbot himself opened the door to their discreet knock.

'Abbot Augaire, I trust we do not disturb you?'

Abbot Augaire greeted them with a smiling countenance. In many ways, he reminded Fidelma of her cousin and mentor Abbot Laisran except that Augaire was physically the opposite of the abbot of Durrow. He was a sturdy man, well muscled, with a tan that bespoke an outdoor life rather than one lived in the shadows of the cloisters. He had deep blue eyes that reminded her of the sea. His hair was of a sand colour, though not exactly golden. His smile was no mere superficial movement of the facial muscles but an expression that seemed to come from deep within him. The hand he held out to greet Fidelma and Eadulf was firm and strong.

'Fidelma – I have looked forward to our meeting.' He grimaced wryly. 'Though perhaps I was not expecting the current reason for it.'

He waved them into his small chamber and was not above pulling forward seats for them both.

'I have heard of the departure of Abbot Ultán, perhaps to a better world,' he said, smiling, as he sat on the edge of his bed after they had been seated in the only available wooden chairs.

Fidelma frowned.

'You speak with some levity, Abbot Augaire,' she said, making the words sound not a reproof but merely a question.

Again, Abbot Augaire grimaced with the corner of his mouth, and he glanced at Eadulf.

'Surely you must know from your companion that Ultán and I were not on the best of terms? I think I saw Brother Eadulf witnessing my last meeting with the northern cleric?'

Eadulf stirred a little.

'Was that the last time you saw Ultán?' he asked quickly.

'It was to speak to. I am not over-burdened with sorrow by that fact, nor, in all honesty, can I say that I mourn deeply, although he was a brother in Christ. Ultán of Cilla Ria was not a man who contributed to making this world a place of joy.'

'You are honest, Abbot Augaire,' Fidelma observed.

'*Probitas laudatur et alget*,' replied the abbot.

'You read Juvenal?' Fidelma recognised the quotation: honesty is often praised but ignored by most people.

'I admire his *Satires*.'

'Well, I not only praise honesty but will not neglect it in my considerations. But since it is obvious that you did not like the late Abbot Ultán, perhaps we should begin by clarifying where you were last night around midnight?'

Abbot Augaire actually chuckled. 'I have heard that you are an honest *dálaigh*, Fidelma of Cashel. That is why it would be pointless for me to pretend that I felt other than I did about Ultán. As to where I was . . . I was playing a game of *brandubh* with Dúnchad Muirisci of the Uí Fiachracha Muaide until close to midnight.'

'Dúnchad Muirisci, the heir apparent to Muirchertach Nár?'

Abbot Augaire nodded absently. 'Then I came directly here to my chamber and fell asleep almost immediately. And,' he added with a smile, 'I regret to say that no one saw me do so. So I can only prove my whereabouts until the moment I left Dúnchad Muirisci. Oh, I tell a lie. I passed one of your brother's bodyguards on my way from Dúnchad Muirisci's chamber to my one. I bade him a peaceful night and he answered me.'

'Dúnchad Muirisci's chamber was a short distance along the corridor from Abbot Ultán's chamber. In which direction were you heading?' Eadulf asked.

'My way did not pass Ultán's chamber, even though you could see the door to it from Dúnchad Muirisci's doorway.'

Eadulf frowned. 'How did you know which was Ultán's chamber?'

Abbot Augaire stared at him for a moment and then his features relaxed in a smile.

'Simply because, when I was making my way to Dúnchad Muirisci's chamber, where we had agreed to meet and have our game of *brandubh*, I saw Ultán entering a door in the corner of the corridor where it turns at a right angle. I gather that was his chamber. That was the last time I saw him as opposed to speaking to him.'

'And when was that?' asked Eadulf.

'Sometime after the evening meal. He had barely entered his room when one of his party brushed by me hurriedly in the corridor in the same direction as I was going. I didn't hear them before they pushed by. They went straight to his door and entered without knocking. Even as the door was closing, I heard Ultán's voice raised in a hectoring tone.'

'Which member of his party? Brother Drón?'

Abbot Augaire shook his head. 'One of the two women in his party.'

'You did not recognise her, I suppose? Can you describe her?'

'I do not know any of his party except Brother Drón. As for describing her, all I saw was her back as she brushed by. She wore a long cloak with the *cabhal* pulled up over her head. I recall the odour of some scent. I am not sure what. I am not good on such matters. It was strong. Perhaps honeysuckle. That was early in the evening. I thought Ultán was killed around midnight and I am told that Muirchertach was seen fleeing from his chamber.'

Fidelma sighed. 'Much use is made of this word "fleeing". It is a word that conjures guilt and prevents us from investigating a murder.'

'So far as I am concerned, the person who killed Ultán did a public service,' Abbot Augaire said firmly.

'Nevertheless, Ultán was murdered, and there is a law to be answered.'

Abbot Augaire grimaced dismissively. 'The irony is that Ultán refused to obey the law when he lived. Now that he is dead, others have to answer to a law that he ignored.'

Fidelma regarded the man carefully. 'I would like you to tell me what you know of Ultán and how you came by your views of him.'

'Not much to tell. But let me put this to you. If Muirchertach Nár is to be prosecuted, I would not want my words used to condemn him. If you are gathering evidence against him . . .'

Fidelma shook her head. 'Muirchertach Nár has asked me to stand in his defence. He claims that he is innocent. It is the Brehon Ninnid who prosecutes.'

Abbot Augaire seemed to relax a little more and he smiled confidently. 'Then I will tell you plainly what I know of Muirchertach and Ultán. I was sent as Muirchertach's representative to demand compensation from Ultán for the death of the sister of Muirchertach's wife. That was the beginning of our animosity.'

'I have heard that you had a more personal interest in the matter?'

'Personal?' the response came sharply.

'You saw the girl kill herself.'

'I do not deny it.'

'Tell us how that came about.'

Abbot Augaire sat back. 'It was about three or four years ago. I was a member of a community on the shores of the southern borders of Connacht. It was a place not far from Muirchertach's stronghold of Durlas. I was fishing on a small headland when this girl came along. The next thing I knew she had leapt to her death on the rocks. She was a very beautiful young woman. I could not imagine how such a one, so beautiful, so youthful, with so much life in her and before her, could be forced into such a terrible act.'

'You did not know who she was?' asked Eadulf.

'Not then. I started to make inquiries and these led me to the fortress of our king at Durlas. I found out that the girl's name was Searc and that she was the younger sister of the king's wife Aíbnat. I remembered her ethereal beauty that day on the foreshore. To explain my feelings, I suppose that I was moved by her image – the youth, beauty and femininity that she represented, you understand? I pledged my service to that image, to Aíbnat and Muirchertach, swearing that I would discover the reason for her death and punish those responsible.'

Fidelma was aware that there was a faint mistiness in his eyes as if he were holding back tears.

'It sounds as if this girl, in death, had touched something in you,' she said.

The abbot seemed to pull himself together. 'Her image still does. How many nights have I not been able to sleep as I run the events of that day through my mind, saying "if only". If only I had not been so blind as to fail to see the tragedy that was about to unfold; if only I . . . Ah, well. *Sic erat in fatis*, to quote Juvenal again.'

'So it was fated,' Eadulf repeated. 'So you blamed yourself for her death and that is why you took such trouble. Was her involvement with the religieux from Cill Ria known at that time?'

'It was. She was a poetess. I found out about the gathering at Ard Macha from some who had attended. I began to make inquiries about this boy, Senach, with whom she had fallen in love, and traced him to Cill Ria. I then found out what had happened to the boy.'

Eadulf was approving. 'It sounds as though you would make a good investigator, Augaire. So it was you who discovered the details. Searc had not told her sister, or Muirchertach?'

'It seems not.'

'Having discovered this information, what then?' asked Fidelma.

He replied with quiet vehemence: 'I swore vengeance on those who had prevented that young girl from achieving happiness, and in her grief had compelled her to her death . . .'

'But what did you do in practical terms?'

Abbot Augaire seemed to shake himself and resume his normal demeanour. 'I went to Muirchertach and Aíbnat and told them what I had discovered. Muirchertach was pleased . . .'

'Pleased? That is an odd way to react to this tragic tale.'

Abbot Augaire thought for a moment. 'Perhaps I have used the wrong word? He was pleased by the revelation of the truth about Searc. I had resolved the mystery as to why she had killed herself.'

'Was Aíbnat also, er, pleased?'

Abbot Augaire suddenly grimaced. 'Aíbnat is a fine noble lady of the Uí Briúin but her main emotions are irritation and anger and those she has in abundance. She made no comment, not even gratitude for the resolution of this mystery. She is a dour, sombre soul.'

'Perhaps with reason?' queried Fidelma. 'Her young sister killed herself. That is reason enough to be sombre.'

Abbot Augaire leaned forward as if confiding something. 'Truth to tell, Fidelma of Cashel, I do not think that she was overly upset by the death of her sister. I heard rumours during my . . . er, investigations. It was said that there was no love lost between them. Indeed, I heard that Aíbnat showed some jealousy at her sister's beauty.'

'But she was angry enough to start this demand for compensation against Ultán of Cill Ria?' Eadulf pointed out.

Abbot Augaire glanced at him and then shook his head. 'That was Muirchertach's idea. He said it would please his wife. But the idea was put to me without consultation with Aíbnat. I found out later that she was against the idea.'

'How did that come about?' asked Fidelma.

'Well, at first, as I said, Muirchertach was pleased with what I had done. He wanted to reward me. He had the power to make me abbot in one of the kingdom's abbeys.'

Fidelma nodded. It was not an unusual matter for kings who had great influence in their territories to offer ecclesiastical rewards.

'Only a few months before, the Blessed Féchin, the abbot of Conga, just north of Loch Corrib, had succumbed to the Yellow Plague. These events, you understand, happened, in fact, about the same time of the great council at Witebia.'

'I had heard that Abbot Féchin had fallen sick and died of the Yellow Plague,' Fidelma affirmed.

'To be offered such an abbey was a great thing for a poor monk such as I. Truly was the Blessed Féchin and his work renowned through the five kingdoms. Muirchertach's senior bishop was summoned and I was ordained both bishop and abbot of Conga.'

'And was this reward because you discovered the reason why Searc took her own life?' demanded Eadulf cynically.

Abbot Augaire gave a lopsided grin. 'I think politics played a part.'

'Politics?'

'You know that the lady Aíbnat was the daughter of Rogallach mac Uatach of the Uí Briúin Aí, who are rivals to the Uí Fiachracha for the kingship of Connacht?'

Eadulf looked helpless.

'Rogallach was king of Connacht and died nearly twenty years ago,' Fidelma explained quickly. 'But when he died, through the influence of Féchin and other leading churchmen, it was first Laidgnén and then his brother Guaire Aidne of the Uí Fiachracha who became kings. Guaire was Muirchertach's father.'

Abbot Augaire was nodding. 'Muirchertach wanted to keep the abbey of Conga in the hands of someone who owed him a debt and therefore allegiance.'

'Which you do?' queried Fidelma.

'I make no secret of it. My father was a huntsman, a tracker. From a humble beginning, now, as abbot and bishop, I control lands that make Ultán's miserable house at Cill Ria look poverty-stricken. From the river of the Uí Briúin northward to Sliabh Neimhtheann and from the Ford of the Sanctuary west to the great sea coast, these are the lands of the abbey of Conga.'

Abbot Augaire sounded as if he were boasting. Fidelma was looking disapproving.

'And what did you have to give in return for this?'

'Loyalty and service to Muirchertach,' he replied simply.

'Which included being his envoy to Ultán?'

'That, indeed, has been the extent of my service. I made the trip to Cill Ria seven times during two years. I was accompanied by a brehon to add to my authority. After which, these last two years, I have not been called upon for any service. I was glad when my journeys to Cill Ria ended. Each trip to Ultán made me want to forget that we both served God and were brothers in Christ. His refusal to concede any wrongdoing and even any involvement in the deaths of Senach and Searc made me, frankly, want to lay hands on him in a physical sense.'

'When compensation was demanded, he refused?'

Abbot Augaire grimaced irritably. 'Did that slimy little scribe Drón tell you that? He was usually at our meetings and bleating on about the *Penitentials* overriding the rule of our law. It became monotonous.'

'To sum up,' Fidelma said, 'Ultán refused to accept judgement by a brehon under our law.'

'Saying that he ruled by the *Penitentials* and would hear no more of the laws of the brehons in his abbey,' agreed Augaire.

Fidelma sat back thoughtfully and folded her hands.

'There is one thing that puzzles me,' she said softly.

'Which is?'

'The law is plain. There is a course that could have been taken to pressurise Ultán into submitting to the justice of a brehon.'

'Which is?'

'If a defendant is of the *nemed* rank, that is a privileged person or noble – and Ultán certainly came into the class of privilege – then the plaintiff could, if willing, proceed to the *troscud*, the ritual fast to ensure the defendant accepts judgement. Several times this has been used against the *óes ecalso* – churchmen of rank – to ensure they accept civil judgement.'

Abbot Augaire smiled sadly. 'Such a ritual fast was discussed and even attempted.'

'The *apad* was properly made?' Fidelma asked. 'The notification to all concerned parties?'

'So far as I know, it was.'

'Who undertook the *troscud*? Muirchertach was not blood kin and therefore he was excluded. So was it Aíbnat?'

'She was not concerned in the matter at all.'

'Then who?'

'Muirchertach persuaded a cousin of Searc, a youth named Cathal, to undertake the *troscud* on behalf of the blood kindred.'

'So what happened?'

'An evil sleight of hand, so far as I could see, and this is why I came to hate Ultán so much.'

'You'd best explain.'

'Cathal and his brehon went to a small chapel within sight of the walls of Cill Ria. The notices were given and the fast began. You will correct me on the law, Fidelma, but I have been told that if the plaintiff, that is Cathal, persists in his fast even though the defendant, Ultán, has offered to settle the case, the case automatically lapses. The defendant is exonerated and no further action can be taken.'

Fidelma looked thoughtful. 'This is true. But are you saying that Ultán offered to settle the matter and this was refused by Cathal who continued the ritual fast?'

Abbot Augaire leaned forward. 'What I am saying is that was how it was represented.'

'But the witnesses? There have to been witnesses to the offer and its refusal?'

Abbot Augaire shrugged. 'Oh yes. The brehon of Ulaidh had been invited to Cill Ria. Ultán said he would pay compensation as a token of goodwill to Muirchertach and his wife even though he still felt he was not responsible. The brehon of Ulaidh agreed that this was a noble thing. So the offer was inscribed on hazel wands and given to Brother Drón to take to the chapel where Cathal was fasting. What happened then is a matter of argument.'

'What happened according to Cathal and his brehon?'

'Cathal said that Drón had not come to the chapel. Three days later, as was the required time, the brehon of Ulaidh and Brother Drón came to the chapel and found Cathal still engaged in his *troscud* and denounced him, claiming that he had refused to give up his ritual fast even when compensation was offered. Therefore, according to law, he no longer had a claim.

'Cathal protested that no one had come to him with this offer. Then Brother Drón came forward and swore that he had done so. He said that he had found Cathal alone, and pressed the offer into his hands.'

'What did Cathal's brehon say?' queried Fidelma. 'As witness, he could not leave the one engaged in the *troscud* alone so he must have seen what happened.'

'Under fierce questioning from Brother Drón it was discovered that at dusk on the day Drón claimed to have delivered the offer, the brehon had been persuaded to go to the aid of a girl who had come tearfully to the chapel pleading for help with a sick mother who had collapsed. There was, of course, no sick mother and the girl had disappeared. I suspect it was one of the females at Cill Ria.'

'That in itself could have been legally challenged as an enticement to pervert the law.'

'True, but the brehon of Ulaidh – again it seems prompted by Drón – caused the chapel to be searched . . .'

'And the hazel wands were found in Cathal's belongings?' guessed Fidelma.

'Just so.'

Eadulf, who had been quiet for some time, snorted. 'It is possible that Brother Drón came that day, waited until Cathal's witness was lured elsewhere, then placed the hazel wands in the chapel and disappeared back to his master with this tale of having delivered the notice. But how can one prove it?'

Abbot Augaire nodded. 'That is how I would see it. Moreover, I am sure that it was at the specific behest of Ultán, who was not going to pay compensation in any form.'

'And Cathal? Did he challenge this?'

'There was no evidence against Drón or Ultán. The girl could not be found. Ultán magnanimously' – he sneered the word – 'suggested that Cathal be allowed to return to Connacht and no more need be said. Cathal came back, a broken young man.'

'So no one has prospered?'

'Except Ultán.'

'I do not think he prospered much last night.'

Abbot Augaire shrugged. 'It was not before time that his sins caught up with him.'

'Even so . . .' protested Eadulf. 'An abbot has been murdered.'

'You condemn me for not following the teaching of our Faith and forgiving and loving Ultán?' the abbot asked in amusement.

'It is not my place to condemn you,' replied Eadulf, 'but isn't it the cornerstone of our Faith to love one's enemies? . . . *diligite inimicos vestros benefacite his qui vos oderunt . . .*'

'I am well acquainted with the words of Luke,' snapped Abbot Augaire.

'Reporting the instructions of Christ,' Eadulf reminded him.

'Sometimes I am led to wonder whether his words were reported and translated correctly.'

Fidelma raised an eyebrow slightly. 'You doubt it?'

'When men like Ultán rise up and we are told we must all respect and obey him, then I believe we should rebel at such a teaching. When we are oppressed, it is our duty to deal with the oppressor. Was that not the faith of our forefathers?'

'That was before the Word reached us and told us to tread a different path.'

'*Beati pauperes spiritu quoniam ipsorum est regnum caelorum,*' Abbot Augaire quoted, unconsciously echoing Eadulf. Blessed are the poor in spirit, for theirs is the kingdom of heaven.

'It sounds as if you do not believe in those words,' Fidelma pointed out.

'I am no longer young and idealistic,' replied Abbot Augaire. 'I have seen man's evil nature. Why should poverty of spirit be the great virtue of the Faith? Indeed, I doubt it is a virtue at all. I believe poverty of spirit is a crime.'

Eadulf exhaled deeply. This was an argument against all that he had been taught of the Faith.

Fidelma was considering the abbot thoughtfully. 'A crime? Perhaps you will explain that reasoning.'

'When people are poor in spirit, do not the proud and haughty in spirit emerge to dominate them and oppress them? If you do not resist evil, if you do not resist wrong, then you encourage further evil and injury at the hands of those who have the other cheek turned to them. *Ego autem dico vobis non resistere malo sed so quis te percusserit in dextera maxilla tua praebe illi et alteram.* As Matthew reports the words of Christ – "I say to you, resist not evil and who strikes you on the right cheek, offer him the other." But to do what? To strike you a second time? Better, should he strike you on the right cheek, that you firmly prevent him from being able to inflict that hurt a second time.'

Fidelma was quiet for a moment and then she sighed. 'Perhaps you are right in what you are saying, Abbot Augaire. I remember the words of my mentor, the Brehon Morann. He would often point out an ancient saying: "He who encourages the oppressor shares the crime." I can understand your fear that poverty of spirit can lead people into bondage. But the New Faith makes demands and we must do the best we can.'

Abbot Augaire smiled wanly. 'You are a logical person, Fidelma. I have heard of your reputation. You understand the arguments and are not afraid to engage in them. I rushed to the Faith because of my emotions and now my emotions have become numb and logic has taken over. As an abbot and bishop, I find myself plagued with guilt. But I shall not add to my guilt by pretending that I can love and forgive someone who is evil.'

Fidelma nodded slowly.

'We thank you for your time, Abbot Augaire,' she said, rising as if she would end the discussion.

Abbot Augaire rose with them but he seemed preoccupied for a moment. 'Can it be that Muirchertach may well be guilty of this deed?'

'Do you doubt his innocence?' Fidelma demanded. 'I thought that you did not want to say a word against him lest it harm his defence.'

Abbot Augaire considered for a moment and then shook his head slowly.

'I would not like to see Muirchertach or anyone blamed for ridding us of a man like Ultán,' he said. 'If you would know more of Ultán, speak to Fergus Fanat, a warrior prince of the Uí Néill, who is with the entourage of Blathmac, the king of Ulaidh. As for Muirchertach, he is a man who has secrets. I have observed that there is little love between his wife and himself. So I wonder why he should go to such extremes to seek compensation for the death of his wife's sister?'

'And have you come to a conclusion?' asked Eadulf.

'It remains a mystery, Brother Eadulf.' The abbot smiled. 'It is like some itch that I need to scratch but can't locate the source of.'

# CHAPTER NINE

Fidelma and Eadulf walked back to their own apartments in silence. To their surprise, there was no atmosphere of gloom in the halls and corridors of the fortress in spite of the fact that most people had heard the news of Abbot Ultán's death. Few people seemed to mourn the passing of the abbot. Attendants were moving quickly here and there to serve the wants of the many guests. Most of them greeted Fidelma and Eadulf with a cheerful countenance. Some guests actually commiserated on the delay in the ceremony in a manner that implied that it should not have been deferred simply because of the abbot's death. A few warriors of the bodyguard, however, saluted them with doleful expressions as they went by.

The door of their chamber was opened by Muirgen, who cast a disapproving look at Eadulf.

'Lady, the ceremony has not yet taken place and it is not fitting for . . .' she jerked her head towards Eadulf, 'for himself to come to the chamber yet.'

Fidelma smiled broadly. 'Alas, Muirgen, the ceremony may well be delayed quite a while. So we shall return to what the situation was before until this matter of the abbot's death is resolved. This murder takes precedence over our affairs.'

Muirgen sniffed in dissatisfaction. 'Nothing should spoil your great day, lady.'

Fidelma patted her on the arm. 'It is, we hope, but a short delay. How is little Alchú?'

'As quiet as a lamb.' She nodded to a corner where, on a rug, the baby was playing happily with some furry toys. Fidelma crossed to the baby, who glanced up at her with a gurgling smile and held out his chubby arms towards her. She bent down and swept him up, giving him a hug and a kiss and making some uncharacteristic cooing sounds. Peering across her shoulder, Alchú waved a baby fist towards Eadulf and uttered a series of chuckling noises. Eadulf crossed to join her and, reaching forward, chucked the child under the chin with perhaps a little air of self-consciousness and muttered 'there, baby, there.'

As Fidelma turned back, with Alchú in her arms, towards Muirgen, the nurse observed: 'You look very tired, lady.'

Fidelma realised that she had only had an hour or so of sleep during the night. She glanced at Eadulf. He, too, seemed tired.

'I think that we both need a short rest,' she said. 'But first, something to eat and drink. I have not yet broken my fast.

'Nor I,' added Eadulf. 'I did not feel like eating earlier but I could do with something now.'

Muirgen made a clucking sound, like a mother hen rounding up her young chicks. 'Sit you both by the fire and I will bring something. Then I can take little Alchú into my chamber while you rest.'

She took Alchú from them, replaced him in his play area and left. Fidelma slumped into a chair. Eadulf, yawning, followed her example and then remarked: 'Abbot Augaire is a curious man.'

Fidelma pursed her lips thoughtfully. 'More curious than Brother Drón? It seems to me that most people have curiosities in character. We all have our eccentricities.'

'True, but for an abbot and bishop to openly wish a fellow bishop dead, and then say that he did not accept one of the basic teachings of our Lord Christ, is surely a matter for some surprise.'

'When it comes down to it, abbots and bishops are human. They are filled with the same qualities that most people have. They can hate and love in equal measure.'

'And commit murder?' Eadulf muttered.

'And commit murder,' confirmed Fidelma calmly.

'So he is a suspect?'

'There is so much more that I want to find out before I even start saying that this or that person is a suspect.'

'We need to have a word with this noble from the north whom Augaire mentioned. What was his name – Fergus Fanat? You have already said that the more we can learn about Ultán, the more it might point to his killer.'

'True enough. We must also confirm Abbot Augaire's story that he was playing *brandubh* with Dúnchad Muirisci.'

'You doubt it?'

'Not at all. But a good *dálaigh* never assumes anything. Also, it might help us with the time that Ultán went to his chamber and was seen by Augaire arguing with one of the two religieuse in his party.'

'Do we know that it was an argument?' Eadulf said. 'The abbot said that when the woman entered, he simply heard Ultán's voice raised in a hectoring tone. It takes two for an argument.'

Fidelma yawned and nodded.

'I am tired,' she said, as if by way of apology for her oversight.

Muirgen returned carrying a large tray laden with bowls of steaming broth, freshly baked bread and a dish of fruit. She set it down on a table and beamed at them both.

'Get that down, and then get some rest,' she advised, turning to scoop Alchú up in her broad arms. The child twisted and gurgled happily. Then, with a quick nod at them, Muirgen left them to their meal and rest.

It was two hours later when Muirgen entered to wake them and tell them that Colgú was waiting outside. They straightened their clothes, rubbed the sleep from their eyes and asked Muirgen to show him in. She did so and then diplomatically withdrew.

Colgú looked anxious but was apologetic for disturbing them.

'I know that you have not had much sleep, but I wondered how things are progressing?' he said.

'We need far more time to investigate, brother,' Fidelma said, while Eadulf poured cider for each of them.

'Do you believe Muirchertach is innocent or guilty?'

'I am prepared to defend him,' she replied cautiously. 'We both agree that if he is guilty then he is either a fool or extremely clever. Somehow, I do not think he is either. And as for Abbot Ultán, he certainly seems to have created more than his fair share of enemies and many of them are guests here. There is nothing for it but to postpone the ceremony for as long as it takes.'

Colgú looked unhappy. 'I know you have a hard task. I know it is your wedding, Fidelma. However, I also have to think of the guests. The High King, the kings of the *cóicead* and their nobles. They cannot stay here indefinitely.'

'I cannot force the pace of this inquiry,' replied Fidelma testily. 'In spite of the pressure from Brehon Ninnid.'

'I know that,' replied her brother. 'But I must think of distracting the High King and nobles for a while. I have an idea. The weather has been brightening and tomorrow morning at first light I thought that I would entertain our noble guests to a hunt.'

Eadulf looked up in surprise from his mug of cider. 'A hunt?'

'A wild boar hunt,' confirmed the king. 'There have been reports that a herd of boar are creating havoc in the fields of a farmer about five kilometres east of here. What better way to give some entertainment than to allow our guests to hunt the creatures?'

Fidelma considered the matter. 'I certainly do not expect the matter to be resolved by tomorrow. Whom do you expect to attend this hunt?'

'The High King is keen on the idea. In fact, it was he who suggested that something is done to entertain the nobles and their ladies while we wait for a resolution.'

Fidelma pursed her lips.

'I am sorry that Sechnassach finds this matter of law so tedious,' she said icily.

'You cannot ask everyone to be so patient,' protested Colgú. 'If you could even give an indication when you might complete this investigation . . . ?'

Fidelma sighed irritably. She could understand her brother's predicament but it was too early to form opinions. There was no denying her instinct that Muirchertach was innocent of the murder of Ultán, but that feeling was countered by a further suspicion that he was not being entirely truthful with her. There was something that he was holding back.

'You know that is impossible, Colgú.'

'Ninnid tells me that he is ready to prosecute and the Chief Brehon says he is prepared to sit in judgement. They simply await your word.'

'Well, I am not ready. There is more to this than Ninnid will argue.'

'Ninnid seems a pompous ass,' muttered Eadulf.

Colgú glanced at him. 'Pompous he may be, my friend, but I am told that he has an astute legal mind.'

'Even with this pressure, we need more time,' insisted Fidelma.

'If you delay beyond a reasonable period, Ninnid is within his rights to prosecute without further loss of time.' Colgú reminded her of the law she knew well. 'Barrán waits only because of who Muirchertach is and out of courtesy to you. If it had been any lesser person than the king of Connacht accused of this crime, then the trial would have been over by now.'

'Trial?' Fidelma retorted. 'And what sort of trial would that be? Is it unreasonable to allow sufficient time for truth to emerge before a person is rushed to judgement.'

Her brother gave an eloquent shrug.

'*Verbum sat sapienti*,' he said simply. 'A word to the wise. Barrán and the High King will not wait for ever.'

'I will not take for ever, brother. But I will not be rushed to trial before I have discovered the truth.'

Colgú sighed softly. 'Anyway, I presume that you have no objection to my distracting our guests?'

'None,' she replied, 'if the guests want to be distracted. Do they include Blathmac, the king of Ulaidh? I would have thought that he at least, among the nobles, would want to mourn one of his kingdom's abbots.'

'I do not think Ultán had any friends to mourn him outside his entourage who came here with him. Even Blathmac seemed to share the common dislike of the abbot. And Muirchertach has offered to extend his parole, his *gell*, so that he may accompany the hunt. I see no objection to that. I shall go ahead with it. The thought of the sport will at least occupy our guests for another day.'

'Muirchertach wants to join the hunt?' Fidelma was astonished. 'He seems very confident in my ability to exonerate him. Ah well, entertain the guests by all means, brother, but in spite of Muirchertach's parole, I would advise that you keep a close watch on him.'

'So you do suspect Muirchertach?' Colgú said quickly.

'Not at all. But there may be some who do and wish him harm. It would be foolish to let our guests wander too freely.'

Colgú grinned. 'We can hardly make the High King a suspect.'

'I would just prefer that a sharp eye was kept on this hunt . . .' She glanced suddenly at Eadulf, who jerked his head up in dismay. 'I need to remain here to continue the investigation . . .'

'I would prefer . . .' he began to protest.

Colgú caught her thought and clapped Eadulf on the shoulder with a chuckle.

'An excellent idea. I do not think that you have taken part in one of our boar hunts, have you, Eadulf? You will find it an excellent education.'

Eadulf's expression was positively woebegone. 'I am not a good horseman . . .'

'Nonsense,' interrupted Colgú. 'Anyway, the huntsmen lead the way on foot with their dogs. Only the nobles, who are the spearmen, follow on horse. Then behind them come the ladies on horseback. So you have a choice. You can go on foot with the huntsmen, of course.'

Fidelma took pity on Eadulf's alarmed expression.

'Let young Gormán ride with you to assist you in the task. He can also explain what is happening during the hunt. But keep close to Muirchertach.'

Eadulf was resigned. 'What will you be doing?' he asked moodily.

'We will not be able to speak to everyone today. There are several people that I still need to question, such as the two young religious who accompanied Ultán. They might be able to give more details of the man and his enemies. I also want to speak with Fergus Fanat of Ulaidh and Dúnchad Muirisci before the end of today.'

Colgú was surprised. 'What is their involvement?' he demanded.

'Perhaps none, but their word is needed as witnesses in clarifying some matters.'

'Then be as diplomatic as you can, sister,' Colgú advised her. 'These are nobles with much power.'

'And you are not?' she asked mockingly.

Colgú shook his head. 'The art of kingship is to maintain the peace but not to stir up antagonisms.'

'Do not fear, my brother. My intention is merely to search for the truth.'

Colgú grimaced wryly. 'There was a line in that play by Terence that was performed here last year – *The Girl from Andros* – what was it now?'

'*Veritas odium parit*,' muttered Eadulf.

'Exactly. Truth breeds hate. Be careful when you search for truth that you do not stir up hate.'

'While I am asked to function as a *dálaigh*, I cannot be stopped from that search,' Fidelma said firmly.

Colgú turned for the door, saying over his shoulder: 'I will go to draw up the list of those who will attend the hunt tomorrow. I'll let you have it later.'

Fidelma had decided that they should first follow up the intriguing reference that Abbot Augaire had made to Fergus Fanat of Ulaidh but, by chance, they encountered Dúnchad Muirisci, the *tánaiste* to the king of Connacht, as they were crossing one of the courtyards. He was young, sandy-haired and handsome, with a ready smile and large blue eyes. He carried himself with the bearing of a warrior.

'Abbot Augaire? Indeed he was with me last evening for some time. He left late. We were playing *brandubh*. He is a very determined player. Eventually I had to accept the loss of the High King.'

*Brandubh*, black raven, was one of the most popular board games in the five kingdoms. The board was divided into forty-nine squares, the centre square symbolising Tara, the centre of the cosmos, and the four squares round it the capitals of the provincial kings. Here the four defending kings had to keep the invading force at bay without leaving the High King on the centre square unprotected. Eadulf found it too slow and cerebral for his taste.

'So Abbot Augaire won the game?' he said. 'Do you know, roughly, when the abbot came to your chambers?'

'Not long after the evening meal. Many of the nobles continued to drink and listen to the bards and storytellers. But Augaire and I had agreed to match our minds across the gaming board. Indeed, we had a wager on it, and' – he shrugged ruefully – 'I confess I lost and he has my silver piece to prove it.'

'When did he leave?' asked Fidelma.

'Towards midnight, I think. I know that I had retired to bed some-time after he left but was disturbed by shouting in the corridor. I had already been disturbed once that evening so I ignored it. It was only this morning that I realised that it must have been when the body of Ultán was discovered.'

'What did you think when your king, Muirchertach, was accused?'

'Shall I be honest?'

Fidelma gazed at him with steely eyes.

'That is the purpose of my questioning,' she said sharply.

'I was excited. I am his heir apparent and if he were to be guilty of this murder, then I would automatically succeed and be king of Connacht.'

'That is being honest indeed,' muttered Eadulf.

Dúnchad Muirisci laughed as if it were a joke.

'You cannot make emotions illegal,' he said.

Fidelma's lips thinned for a moment. 'So long as they remain emotions and hidden rather than being given physical substance.'

Dúnchad Muirisci continued to smile. 'Come, lady, you do not suspect that I slunk into Abbot Ultán's chamber to kill him, then put the blame on Muirchertach in order that I could succeed as king?'

'Stranger things have happened,' Fidelma pointed out. 'In this case, I do not suspect that. However, how well did you know Abbot Ultán?'

'Not at all.'

Fidelma raised her eyebrows. 'With all the intercourse between the court of Muirchertach and the abbey of Ultán on behalf of the queen's sister, Searc, that comes as a surprise.'

'Yet it is true. The business was between Muirchertach and Aíbnat and later involved Cathal of the Uí Briúin Aí. But I never once laid eyes on Ultán and would have passed him by in the corridor without knowing him. It was Augaire and one of our brehons who conducted the intercourse with Cill Ria.'

'So what did you think of Muirchertach's attempt to seek compen-sation for his wife, Aíbnat, over this matter?'

Dúnchad Muirisci considered for a moment. 'I will admit that I found it strange. Aíbnat was never really close to her young sister and, in truth, I did not think she was much affected by the poor girl's death. But the fact that she pressed the claim against Ultán . . .'

'Aíbnat did not insist on seeking compensation, according to Augaire. It was your cousin Muirchertach who was the instigator of the claim.'

Dúnchad Muirisci's eyes suddenly widened. 'Muirchertach?' he demanded sharply.

'You did not know?'

'I did not. I assumed it was Aíbnat for she was the next of kin.'

'How well did you know Searc?'

'Not well at all. I met her only a few times at Durlas. She was a dreamy, romantic young girl. I was not surprised when people started to acclaim her poetry. It was of the *dántaigecht grádh* variety, love poetry. That is not really my style. You know the sort of thing?' He screwed up his face and recited in a falsetto voice:

*Cold are the nights I cannot sleep,*
*Thinking of you, my love, my dear . . .*

'How well is not well?' interrupted Fidelma with some irritability in her tone.

'When she came to stay with her sister Aíbnat at Muirchertach's fortress at Durlas, I saw her more . . . that was in the weeks before her death.'

'Did she give any indication that she would take her own life when she came back from Cill Ria having found that her love had been sent to his death at sea?'

Dúnchad Muirisci shook his head. 'In fact, while she was upset, she did not really believe that this lad – what was his name? Senach? – she did not believe that he was really dead. She was determined to pursue him.'

Fidelma exchanged a sharp look with Eadulf. 'What do you mean?' she demanded.

'When she came back she talked about finding a ship to go to Gaul and to the abbey to which the lad had been sent. She even knew the name of it. She believed that he would be waiting there for her.'

Fidelma leaned forward in surprise. 'How long was this before she took her life?'

'I saw her about three days before it happened. Augaire witnessed the event, you know. He didn't know who it was – it took him a day or so to discover it and so come to Durlas. Muirchertach was called upon to identify the body.' He paused and rubbed his chin reflectively. 'It is strange, now I think of it. She was talking about sailing after Senach and then, shortly after, she tosses herself from a cliff.'

'Strange, indeed,' muttered Eadulf.

'Did she tell anyone else about the voyage to Gaul she was planning?'

'I would have presumed that she told her sister Aíbnat as well as Muirchertach.'

'It seems strange that it was not mentioned,' Fidelma said thoughtfully. 'I will see what Muirchertach and his wife have to say later.'

Dúnchad Muirisci smiled knowingly.

'I am not sure that the truth will come out,' he said. 'Muirchertach never did like people knowing what was in his mind. Not even me.'

'But you are his *tánaiste* – his heir apparent. Who runs the kingdom if he will not discuss the affairs of the day with you?' inquired Eadulf.

'The truth? The tribes of Connacht are descended into anarchy. Muirchertach has brought the line of Fiachra into disrespect. Thank God that I am only a cousin, for I am of the tribe of Muaide.'

'If this is so, has no one recourse to the law, to declare Muirchertach incapable of his office?' Fidelma asked.

Dúnchad Muirisci shrugged. 'The time will come. He has few friends now, not even his own wife.'

'That is why I am interested in the reason he pursued this affair of compensation with Ultán,' Fidelma replied.

'Well, if Aíbnat did not press for it, then I cannot say. Maybe he wanted to impress her by doing so in order to win back her regard?'

'Perhaps. Yet if Aíbnat was not close to her young sister, as we have been told, it does not appear to be a sufficient reason.'

Dúnchad Muirisci shook his head. 'That is a matter that you'd best pursue with Muirchertach.'

'And I shall do so.'

The *tánaiste* suddenly looked seriously at Fidelma. 'I said that I would be honest. There is no love lost between Muirchertach and myself. I even avoided him as a child. He had a spiteful nature and later he had a reputation among women. I was surprised when Aíbnat and he were married, but then Aíbnat was of the Uí Briúin Aí and ambitious.' He stopped speaking when he caught sight of a woman crossing the courtyard. 'Ah, the lady Fína. You will excuse me? I have promised to go riding with her this afternoon while the light is still with us.' He hurried after the figure that was disappearing towards the stables.

Fidelma turned to Eadulf with a long face. 'This is irritating,' she said. 'There is something here which does not seem right.'

'You have said that before,' commented Eadulf.

'And I say it again now. Alas, I think we still have much to learn.'

'And much to do. We'd better go in search of Fergus Fanat.'

It was the commander of the guard who told them that Fergus Fanat was in the town below the fortress playing *immán*, or driving, with two groups that had been formed from the more active guests. Caol seemed more cheerful now that he had been assured by Colgú that he was not being blamed for removing the guard from Ultán's chamber.

Although the day continued to be cloudy, at least it was dry and Fidelma suggested they walked down to the playing field, the *faithche*, a level grassy meadow just beyond the last buildings in the town that was set aside for such games. Eadulf made no objection, so they walked down into the town, aware of some stares as people recognised them. Most were aware that this should be the day of their official wedding and some seemed to wish to commiserate while others were embarrassed as to how to acknowledge them. Fidelma seemed oblivious of the little huddled groups that formed in their wake, the whispered conversations and the looks of sympathy, as if it were some funeral cortège that had passed.

They could hear the game long before they passed the last of the houses and came on the open meadow. The shouts and cheers of the people gathered around the *faithche* were noisy enough, and the pair moved forward to a point where they could see the action on the field. There were two teams, and the aim was to drive the ball into the opponents' goal, or *berna*, with a wooden stick.

Eadulf found the game exciting, for the swinging ash clubs could easily inflict not just bruises and cuts but serious injuries. For the players it was warfare by another means. The shouts of instruction and curses when a strategy went wrong came thick and fast as the young men pushed sometimes one way and sometimes the other. To Eadulf it looked like a mad uproar with few rules, but when he mentioned this to Fidelma she shook her head.

'Our laws are strict about this game, Eadulf. See, there is Brehon Baithen observing the game to see they are obeyed. To strike a deliberate blow against another player, for example, is punishable by a fine.'

'There are other laws to protect spectators and, indeed, even to protect the field itself,' a voice echoed behind them.

They glanced round and found Abbot Augaire standing there, looking amused. 'I did not think you would have time to watch this diversion,' he observed.

Fidelma's chin came up a little. 'It is not for diversion that we are here, Abbot Augaire,' she told him. 'You suggested that we should speak with Fergus Fanat, who is apparently among the players.'

Abbot Augaire smiled. 'Ah, just so. I should have realised that you would not be attracted to this entertainment when there was an abbot's murder to be resolved.'

'Which of the players is Fergus Fanat?' pressed Fidelma, ignoring his cynical tone.

'You see the short, muscular man with the long raven-coloured hair? The one now out in front striking at the ball? That is Fergus Fanat. He leads the team from the northern kingdoms against the locals.'

Fidelma realised that her cousin Finguine mac Cathal, Colgú's heir apparent or *tánaiste*, was the leader of the second team.

'How long until the end of the game?' she demanded.

'Not long,' replied Augaire. 'Three times more must the bowl fill with water.'

He nodded to where Brehon Baithen was standing, another man was sitting before a water clock with which he was timing the progress of the game. The bowl to which Augaire had referred was placed on the surface of a tub of water. It had a small hole in its base so that it gradually filled and sank, after which it was taken out and emptied and the process was repeated. The bowl had to sink a prescribed number of times to measure the length of the game.

Fidelma's wandering gaze was suddenly attracted by a figure in the crowd behind Brehon Baithen, a slight female figure wearing a religious robe. The girl looked attractive. Her gaze seemed to be fixed on the players on the field as though she was fascinated by the game. For a moment, Fidelma wondered who she was.

Just then there was a shout of protest from the field. The players suddenly bunched into a group, shouting at each other. Brehon Baithen quickly hurried on to the *faithche*.

'What is it?' demanded Eadulf, frowning.

'One of the players is protesting a foul. He says that two opposing players jostled him before he had possession of the ball.'

The argument seemed short. Brehon Baithen had made some decision and the game recommenced.

Abbot Augaire gave a grunt of satisfaction. 'Do you realise, my Saxon friend,' he confided to Eadulf, 'that it was at the site of my own abbey of Conga, on the plain of Maigh Éo, where it is said the very first recorded game of *immán* was played?'

'I knew it was an ancient game,' Eadulf replied unenthusiastically, anticipating a lecture.

'It is said that when the Fir Bolg were waging war against the Tuatha Dé Danann it was agreed to settle their differences by playing such a game.'

'There are many such old tales about the game,' Fidelma put in quickly. 'Setanta was said to be the greatest player of his day. Wasn't it with his ball and stick that he slew the hound of Culann so that he had to offer to replace it and thus earned his new name: Cúchulainn – the hound of Culann?'

There was suddenly a great cheering. The game was apparently over and it became obvious that it was the team from Cashel who had won it.

With a curt nod to Abbot Augaire, Fidelma led the way through the milling crowd to where she had last seen Fergus Fanat. They found him seated with some colleagues, wiping his face on a linen cloth and taking swallows from a goblet of cider. In spite of their defeat, there was good humour among the northern team and much talk of how this or that point should have been played.

Fidelma was aware again of the young female religieuse, who appeared to be waiting on the edge of the group of players. She saw that Eadulf was also examining her with curiosity.

'Do you recognise her?' she whispered.

'I can't be sure. I think it is one of the two religieuse who accompanied Ultán. I saw them briefly when they arrived.'

While it was not unusual to find a woman so fascinated by the game and with the players, Fidelma found it odd that a member of Ultán's entourage would have forsaken the mourning of her murdered superior to come down to watch the contest. Then she dismissed the matter from her mind.

Fergus Fanat looked up as Fidelma and Eadulf approached. He rose to his feet, apparently recognising her.

'I am surprised to see you here, lady.' He smiled uncertainly, handing his goblet to one of his fellow players.

'Do you know me, Fergus Fanat?' she asked.

'You were pointed out to me when we arrived at your brother's fortress yesterday.' He glanced at Eadulf. 'And you must be Eadulf of Seaxmund's Ham.'

There was something likeable in the open-featured, friendly scrutiny of the young man. Eadulf smiled back. 'I am.'

'I am sorry that the plans for this day have had to be delayed, lady.' The northern noble turned back to Fidelma. 'I have heard that Muirchertach Nár has demanded that you conduct his defence. It seems a selfish thing to do in the circumstances.'

Fidelma was thoughtful. 'Selfish?'

'Knowing that this was to be your wedding day, he could have chosen another to represent him in law.'

'It is his right to demand whom he pleases in his defence,' Fidelma pointed out. 'When a man, even a king, is accused of murder, then he is entitled to some degree of selfishness.'

Fergus Fanat chuckled. 'You are right, lady. I suppose that I am not overly concerned at the death of Ultán.'

'That is precisely why I have sought you out.'

A look of surprise crossed Fergus Fanat's features. 'To talk of my lack of concern?' He gestured around him. 'I think you will be hard pressed to find many who will mourn him.'

'To talk of the reasons why that is so. Why is there this unconcern over the murder of an abbot from your own territory?' She glanced at the man's fellow players, several of whom were standing within hearing of their conversation, and added: 'I am sorry. Perhaps you would like to walk with us awhile?'

Fergus Fanat put down his towel and nodded.

'I need to return to the fortress to bathe,' he said. 'The game was quite arduous. Let us go back.'

They fell in step, Fergus Fanat walking between Fidelma and Eadulf, as they crossed the field. The spectators were quickly vanishing but for a few people here and there engaged in talk. No one bothered them. Again Fidelma was aware of the young religieuse. The girl stood hesitantly and then, noticing that Fidelma had glanced at her, turned and hurried away after the crowd.

'I presume that you did not like Abbot Ultán?' Fidelma began.

'I did not kill him, if that is where your questions are leading, lady,' replied Fergus Fanat quickly and with assurance.

'They are not . . . as yet.' She smiled. 'Why didn't you like him?'

'He was not a likeable person.'

'Surely that depends on an individual's subjective view? Even the worst people are often liked, even loved, by someone,' Eadulf pointed out.

Fergus Fanat laughed with good humour. 'Forgive me, Brother Eadulf. I am no philosopher. I am a simple warrior.'

'In the service of Blathmac, king of Ulaidh?'

'In the service of my cousin,' confirmed the young man, laying slight emphasis on his relationship to the king.

'So can you be more specific as to why you disliked Ultán?'

The northern noble grimaced. 'Indeed I can. Perhaps I should start with a story told me by my father, who was Bressal, brother of Máel Coba, who was then king of Ulaidh. He knew of Ultán when he was a young man. Ultán was a wild, profane and wayward youth.'

Fidelma's brow rose slightly. 'This same Abbot Ultán who was emissary of the Comarb of Patrick at Ard Macha?' Her voice was slightly sceptical.

'The very same. In his younger days he was a godless man. He was a thief and murderer, a dissolute and a womaniser.'

'It is hard to believe,' said Eadulf. 'I thought he was one of the great reformers of the church – one who welcomes the strict rules of Rome.'

'I will tell you the story,' Fergus Fanat went on. 'In his youth, Ultán was named Uallgarg, the proud and fierce. That's what he was. He cared nothing for anyone and answered to no authority. He was caught several times by the king's bodyguard and brought before the brehons for judgement. He refused their justice and went on his way as before. Then he fell in with a beautiful young girl whom he debauched. He shamed her by making her pregnant and then abandoning her.'

'You are repeating the story told you by your father,' Fidelma pointed out. 'In law this is inadmissible. How do you know that this was a true account?'

Fergus Fanat glanced at her for a moment and then grimaced sadly.

'The girl in question was my aunt,' he said softly. 'Her child was stillborn and she never recovered. Her mind fled her body and she lived in a world of her own – I remember her. I was fifteen summers old. She became a simpleton and died before her time.' He sighed deeply. 'To be truthful, I let out a shout of joy when I heard that someone had killed Ultán. My only regret was that it was not I.'

# CHAPTER TEN

Fidelma and Eadulf both paused in mid-stride at the quiet vehemence in the young man's voice. Then they resumed their pacing alongside him.

'In view of what you have just said,' Fidelma said quietly, 'perhaps, before we continue further, it might be best to tell us what you were doing when Ultán was killed last night.'

Fergus Fanat was not offended. In fact, he gave a deep chuckle.

'If I had any sense I would have been in bed, for I am told it was around midnight that Ultán was killed in his chamber. However, I confess that I was drinking with some comrades of mine who serve in the Fianna of the High King.'

The Fianna were the High King's élite bodyguards, just as the kings of Cashel boasted their élite warriors, the Nasc Niadh. Each king of a *cóicead*, one of the five kingdoms, had his warrior élite.

'And these comrades can vouch for that?'

The dark-haired man grinned at her. 'If any were sober enough to remember. I barely made it back to my bed.'

'What puzzles me,' Eadulf intervened, 'is how this man, Uallgarg as you call him, could transform himself into Ultán, the pious abbot and bishop who was so trusted by the Comarb of Patrick at Ard Macha? Brother Drón sings his praises as a great church reformer.'

'That is easy to answer, my friend,' replied Fergus Fanat. 'As I said, Uallgarg was a godless and intemperate man who won himself many enemies. He pushed the brehons to the limits and finally to the farthest limit of all. They deemed that he was so incorrigible that nothing more could be done with him except that he be given to the judgement of the sea.'

Eadulf noticed that Fidelma actually shivered.

'The *cinad ó muir*?' she whispered.

'What is this judgement of the sea?' he queried, not having heard the term before.

'In extreme cases,' she explained, 'after continued breaking of the law in crimes involving death, the offender, after due hearing, is put into a boat with food and water for one day. Then he is towed out of sight of land and left to the judgement of the wind and the waves . . . in other words, to the judgement of the sea, or, as the Faith would say, that of God.'

Fergus Fanat nodded quickly in agreement. 'That was exactly how it was. Uallgarg was towed far out to sea and left.'

'And survived?' The answer to Eadulf's question was obvious.

'Three days later his boat was cast ashore on the coast not far from the spot where he had been towed out. He was alive,' confirmed Fergus Fanat.

'Surely, then, he could have been killed by those who found him?' Eadulf asked.

Fidelma shook her head. 'There were two ways in which he could have been treated. Because God had given His judgement, the culprit's kin could have taken him back into their family as a *duine dligthech*, a lawful person. But if they did not wish to do so, then he would have lost all rights and become a *fuidir*.'

Eadulf knew that this was the lowest class in society: 'non-freemen' who were usually criminals of the worst order, cowards who deserted their clan when needed, men who no longer had the right to bear arms or take any political part within the clan, who were restricted in their movements and had to redeem themselves by work.

'The *fuidir cinad ó muir*,' agreed Fergus Fanat.

'So what happened to Uallgarg?' demanded Fidelma.

'No one wanted him except the old abbot of Cill Ria, which is near the coast. The old man wanted a servant who would do all the really hard work of the abbey. He made Uallgarg an offer. The only offer – to be driven out to sea again or to enter the abbey and work. Uallgarg made his choice for life but then threw himself into the part with great piety. He claimed that he had seen a vision on the sea and henceforth was a changed man. He said that he was born again – renamed himself Ultán, which, as you may know, Brother Saxon, simply means a man of Ulaidh. For a few years he did all the tasks at Cill Ria that he was asked to perform. He was more pious than any of his fellows. The old abbot, who was also bishop of the Uí Thuirtrí, was convinced that a real change had come over him and not only accepted him as a member of the community but ordained him as a priest.'

Eadulf was shaking his head. 'It sounds improbable.'

'Nevertheless, there have been some examples of this happening before,' said Fidelma. 'There was another case in Ulaidh. That of a man named Mac Cuill.'

'You know of him?' Fergus Fanat seemed surprised. 'That was many, many years ago.' He glanced to the puzzled face of Eadulf and explained: 'He, too, was a thief and murderer who was likewise cast into the sea in a boat. The wind and tide washed him ashore in Ellan Vannin, the island of Manannán Mac Lir – the old god of the oceans – which is situated between this island and that of Britain. He, too, claimed that he had seen a vision and converted to the Faith and eventually became a bishop on the island, where they venerate him down to this day.'

'So Uallgarg, or Ultán, repented and became a devout Christian?' said Eadulf.

Fergus Fanat sniffed disparagingly. 'I did not say that.'

'But the Comarb of Patrick, the abbot of Ard Macha, placed him in a favoured position,' Fidelma pointed out. 'He was the emissary of Ard Macha.'

'Uallgarg or Ultán certainly did well for himself. From a humble *fuidir* working to save his life in the abbey of Cill Ria, in a few years he had become abbot. The old abbot wrote a fulsome letter of praise just before he died to Ard Macha about his prodigy.'

'Was there anything suspicious about the old abbot's death?' Eadulf queried sceptically.

The warrior grimaced. 'Some people seemed to think so.'

'Do you have any facts to establish that?' Fidelma asked quickly.

'It was just gossip at the time,' replied Fergus Fanat with a shake of his head. 'But given his past record, it fits in with his ambition and ruthlessness. A wolf in lamb's clothing is still a wolf,' he added, resorting to an old saying. 'There were many stories that he had not really departed from his old ways.'

'Are you claiming that Ultán – we will stick to the name by which he is now accepted – was still a thief and murderer?'

Fergus Fanat shrugged indifferently. 'Obviously, he did not need to be the type of thief that he once was. Cill Ria is a wealthy community. Once he had control of it he did not need to take to the highways. But as for the rest, his women and . . .'

'I thought he didn't believe in mixed houses, or relationships among the religious?' Fidelma said quickly. 'He was supposed to be a strict follower of the *Penitentials*.'

'That!' Fergus Fanat grimaced. 'What he says, he does for show. Cill Ria was a *conhospitae*. Then he divided it into separate buildings, a community for males and one for females a short distance away. He claims the community of Cill Ria is a community of celibates. I doubt it.'

Fidelma was looking troubled. 'These are very grave charges that you bring against Ultán. I have to ask you, are you alone in holding these views, or do they have some currency with your cousin the king, Blathmac? Presumably the abbot of Ard Macha does not believe in them, otherwise Ultán would not have been his emissary.'

'You will have to ask them,' Fergus Fanat said dismissively. 'I merely give my own views, which are based on what I know.'

'What you are saying is that Ultán was a fraud and liar. That these reforms and demands from the Comarb of Ard Macha meant nothing to him except as a means to reinforce his position of power.'

The northern warrior smiled quickly. 'I would say, lady, that is a fair summary. Now, if you will excuse me, the game has been hard and dirty and I would go and bathe.'

Fidelma made a little gesture that gave him permission to hurry on to the fortress, leaving them to follow at a more leisurely pace.

'I am more confused than ever,' complained Eadulf. 'It seems that many people had cause to hate Bishop Ultán. But when it comes down to it, Muirchertach was the only one who was seen leaving his chamber at the time he was found dead. He did not report the matter until Caol and Brehon Baithen went to question him. He alone had the opportunity and the motive.'

Fidelma grimaced wryly. 'I want to learn still more about Ultán. We must talk more to our northern friends and to Brother Drón. We must decide whether Ultán was saint or sinner of the worst order.'

'How can we judge?'

'*Ex pede Herculem*,' quoted Fidelma.

'I do not understand,' replied Eadulf, trying to figure out what 'From the foot, a Hercules' meant.

'From the sample of stories, we may judge the whole,' explained Fidelma.

'I have never heard that expression.'

'There was a Greek mathematician and philosopher named Pythagoras to whom the investigators of crime owe much. Knowing that a person's height is proportional to the length of their foot, he deduced the height of Hercules from the length of his foot.'

Eadulf frowned. 'How would he be able to know the length of Hercules' foot?' he demanded.

'He did it by measuring and comparing the length of several stadia in Greece. Since Hercules' stadium at Olympia was the longest of them all, Pythagoras argued that his foot was longer than those of lesser men.'

Eadulf pulled a sceptical face as he seriously considered the matter. 'That argument cannot be without flaws.'

Fidelma laughed and took Eadulf's arm. 'It is meant as a concept, not as a concrete fact. By a sample we can see the whole. Let us test a few more sample attitudes to Ultán. But first I think I would like to have another look at the chamber where Ultán was murdered.'

There was still a guard in the corridor outside Ultán's chamber. It was Enda again, of Colgú's bodyguard. He greeted them with a weary smile, and Fidelma took pity on him.

'I do not think that there will be any need for you to remain here after I have made this examination, Enda,' she told him.

'The Brehon Barrán told me that I should await your instruction, lady. However, there have been some who have tried to get access here.'

'Such as?'

'Two of the late Bishop Ultán's entourage. The man, Brother Drón, and one of the women who travel with him. Sister Sétach I think her name is.'

'Did they give a reason why they needed to enter?'

'Simply to take charge of his personal belongings.'

'And you refused them entry?'

'Of course, lady. Those were my instructions.' He sounded slightly offended at being asked the question.

'Of course,' she said approvingly.

'Abbot Augaire also came by. He said he was wondering if there was anything he could do. Curiosity was his motive, I think, more than anything else.'

Fidelma glanced at Eadulf but kept her expression impassive. 'Were there any others?'

'Brehon Ninnid, of course. Obviously, I allowed him entrance. But there was a strange Saxon . . . begging your pardon, Brother Eadulf. He said his name was Ord . . . Ordwool . . . ?'

'Ordwulf?' supplied Eadulf.

'That's it. Ordwulf, an elderly man. I think he is a little crazy.'

'What makes you say that?' demanded Eadulf.

'He was saying that he wanted to see where the tyrant died and to make sure that he would not rise again as he had from the sea. I didn't know what to make of it. I told him that the body had been removed and that Abbot Ultán was clearly dead.'

'What did he do then?'

'He wanted to know where the body was. I told him that Brother Conchobhar had removed it to the chapel and that it would be taken at midnight tonight and buried in the graveyard of ecclesiastics as was the custom here. The Saxon's behaviour was most curious. He did not speak our language well and was difficult to understand.'

Fidelma sighed. 'Perhaps you would wait here until we have finished, Enda. We will not be long.'

They entered the chamber, which was in darkness. The early dusk had already crept over Cashel and there was a curtain hanging across the window obscuring what little light might have seeped in. A faint, acrid scent came to Fidelma's nostrils which she could not momentarily identify. She saw the shadow of Eadulf feeling for a candle and reached out to seize his wrist, preventing him from action.

Eadulf too became aware of the pungent odour from smoke arising from a newly snuffed out candle. Then there was a slight movement, and a shadow moved towards the window.

Fidelma gave a backward kick at the door behind her so that the light from the corridor would throw some illumination into the chamber. At the same time, she shouted for Enda's help.

Eadulf, however, had thrown himself across the room at the shadow that seemed to be trying to escape through the window. He threw his arms round what he perceived to be the waist of the figure and heaved back with all his might. He realised that it was a slight female form even as his weight caused him and his captive to tumble back into the room, where he measured his length on the floor with the figure on top of him, scratching, kicking and sobbing.

Enda entered, drawn sword in one hand and a lantern from the corridor in the other.

'Stop or feel the point of my blade!' he shouted, moving forward.

The figure went limp and Eadulf extracted himself from it and rose to his feet. Enda held up his lamp. The figure rose to its knees. It was a woman in the robes of a religieuse.

'I've seen you before . . .' gasped Eadulf, recovering his breath.

'This is Sister Sétach,' Enda said. 'I denied her entry here only a short time ago.'

Fidelma came forward. 'She does not seem to have obeyed you, Enda,' she said softly.

Enda glanced at her. 'Lady, I swear she did not get by me. I told her that she was not allowed here and have been outside ever since.'

'I believe you,' Fidelma assured him. She turned to the girl, who was now on her feet, looking shaken but defiant. 'How did you get in here?'

The girl did not reply but raised her chin pugnaciously.

Fidelma glanced towards the window. She knew that there was a small ledge that ran round the fortress walls just under the windows of these chambers, no more than a footstep in width and with a drop of fifty metres below. She pursed her lips thoughtfully.

'You are either very brave or very foolish,' she commented as she pointed to a chair. 'Sit down.' She glanced at Enda. 'Leave the lantern with us and remain outside.'

Reluctantly, Enda sheathed his sword and put down the lantern. He took a candle and lit it from the lantern flame, and then, with an irritated glance at the now seated girl, he withdrew.

Eadulf went to stand by the window, pushing back the curtain and glancing out. Even though the darkness obscured most of the fall, he shuddered. He would not have ventured on to the little ledge unless forced.

Fidelma had taken a seat on the edge of the bed, facing the girl, and now examined her features closely. Initially, she thought that it was the same young girl she had seen at the game of *immán*, the one who had seemed so fascinated by the play. But this religieuse was less slightly built, with darker hair and features and perhaps some years older. There was an odour of scent about her, some fragrance that Fidelma was not familiar with.

'So, Sister Sétach, what was so important here that you must risk your life in such a perilous manner?'

The girl shrugged. 'You would not understand.'

'I cannot understand unless you attempt to tell me.'

This was met with silence.

'Would you like to tell me where you climbed out on to the ledge to make your way here so that the guard did not see you?'

'There is a window at the end of the corridor.'

Fidelma's eyes widened a little. 'You crawled along that ledge for a distance of ten metres?'

'There was room enough to move along the ledge without crawling, as you put it.'

'So, again I ask you, what was so valuable that you must gain access to this chamber by such a means?'

The girl was silent for a moment and Fidelma was about to press her authority on her when she said: 'I wanted to make sure that Abbot Ultán's possessions had not been taken.'

Fidelma was puzzled. 'Why would they be?'

The girl was silent again. Fidelma was exasperated.

'Do you know that I am a *dálaigh*, a representative of the courts, and that you have to answer my questions?'

The girl's chin rose defiantly. 'I know well who you are. You are Fidelma of Cashel, masquerading as a religieuse. You are defending the murderer who slaughtered Abbot Ultán.'

Fidelma heard the hostility in the girl's voice. 'You have been identified as Sister Sétach. Is that so?' she asked mildly.

The girl nodded.

'You have a companion who also served the late Abbot Ultán. What is her name?'

'Sister Marga.' The girl sounded reluctant in her response.

'Very well, Sister Sétach. I am, indeed, Fidelma of Cashel, and I am also *dálaigh*. Whatever else you think I am, remember that I am a representative of the law and as such you are duty bound to answer my questions. Do you understand?'

Once more there was silence.

'Do you know the phrase *qui tacet consentit* – those who remain silent consent? I will take it that your silence means that you do understand. Now, I understand that you came here in the company of Ultán.'

'Of Ultán, abbot of Cill Ria,' snapped the girl.

Fidelma smiled thinly. 'Exactly so. What was your task in that company?'

'I was a record keeper, as was my sister in Christ, Sister Marga.'

'You both served in the abbey of Cill Ria?'

The girl hesitated. 'The abbey is divided into two separate communities, one for males and the other for females.'

'So I understand,' agreed Fidelma. 'What sort of records were you keeping?'

The girl shifted uneasily on her seat. 'Brother Drón was the scribe to Abbot Ultán. He was our immediate superior.'

'We have spoken with Brother Drón. I would like to know from you about your own work.'

'Then you will know that Abbot Ultán was sent as envoy from the *archiepiscopus* of Ard Macha to bring order into the churches of the five kingdoms and secure the Blessed Patrick's church as the primacy. We were travelling through the kingdoms and discussing these matters with the bishops and abbots. It was my task – and that of Sister Marga – to make the records of these meetings so that we might, on our return to Ard Macha, present a full account of matters to the Comarb of Patrick.'

'I understand. And how did you regard Abbot Ultán?'

A frown crossed Sister Sétach's forehead. 'What do you mean?' she said defensively.

'You are from Cill Ria and you have travelled many miles with Abbot Ultán. Did you like him? What did you think of him?'

Sister Sétach hesitated. 'He was a wonderful and pious man,' she replied, but there was a hesitation in her voice which was not lost on either Fidelma or Eadulf.

'How long had you known him?'

'Since I entered the community of Cill Ria.'

'And when was that?'

'Three years ago.'

'Were you chosen by the abbot for this task, this keeping of records?'

Sister Sétach shook her head.

'So how did you join this embassy? Through Brother Drón?'

'It was Sister Marga who asked me to join her as her companion. The abbot had asked her to come along to keep the records and said she could choose a companion to help her. She asked me.'

'I see. But you were happy to come?'

The girl nodded emphatically. 'It was a wonderful way to see the world beyond the Sperrins.'

'The what?'

'They are mountains in the country of Cill Ria. I had never been south before.'

'And did you get on well with Abbot Ultán?'

Again there came the slight frown. 'I don't know what you mean.'

Fidelma sighed impatiently. 'Was Ultán a pleasant person to work for? Were you at ease in his company? Was he a demanding taskmaster?'

'He was demanding . . . yes,' said Sister Sétach. 'He was especially so with Brother Drón, who was his close adviser in the discussions. Sister Marga and I merely made the records of our travels.'

'In the time that you spent at Cill Ria did you ever hear any stories about Ultán, about the time before he entered the religious life?'

Again came that defensive lifting of the chin. 'There were stories,' the girl finally admitted.

'What did you think of them?'

'They were of no concern to me. What a person has done in the past remains in the past so long as, if they have done wrong, they have truly repented and sought forgiveness. Is that not the essence of the Faith, Fidelma of Cashel?'

'So you were happy with Ultán?'

'That is not the way I would view it. I served the Faith in Cill Ria and Abbot Ultán was the superior there. He was regarded by all as a man of piety and strength, a great leader and reformer, who, in his martyrdom, will soon become venerated throughout the five king-doms.'

Fidelma sat back and gazed thoughtfully at the girl.

'Martyrdom? Well, let us return to why you risked your life to get back into this room.'

Sister Sétach made a curious gesture with her shoulders as if in dismissal of the question. 'I did not believe that I was risking my life.'

Eadulf had been leaning by the window but his keen eyes had been searching the chamber in the flickering light of the lantern. He suddenly walked across the room to a chest in the corner.

'Did you find what you were searching for?' he asked mildly, looking down. Then he added, for Fidelma's benefit, 'This chest appears to be Ultán's personal box. It seems to have been opened and closed in a hurried fashion since I saw it this morning. There are some clothes poking out of the lid where they have not been put back carefully.'

Fidelma nodded, still looking at the girl. 'What were you looking for?'

'Nothing.'

'Ah, then there will be nothing on you if you are searched?'

'You would not dare search me?' the girl said, aghast.

'I am a *dálaigh*.' Fidelma smiled. 'It would be my duty to search you.'

'I have taken nothing. You will find nothing. Go ahead. Search!'

'Let us apply some logic, Sister Sétach,' said Fidelma. 'You came asking to see the chamber. The guard refused you entry. You then climbed out of a window on to a dangerous ledge, which even a mountain goat would not dare to climb, and, in spite of the peril to your life, you made your way along it to enter this chamber in order to search Ultán's belongings. Now what could inspire such foolhardy courage?'

There was a silence and then the girl sighed. 'If you must know, it was imperative to make sure all Abbot Ultán's belongings were safe. The records of the meetings, especially. Nature dictates that you will have to bury his mortal remains here. But we will take his belongings back to Cill Ria, where they will be regarded as relics of inestimable value.'

Eadulf was astounded. 'You came looking for mercenary wealth?'

'Not at all,' snapped Sister Sétach. 'The relics will be beyond worldly value. They will be the subject of pilgrimage to Cill Ria – for Ultán will be our first great martyred saint.' The girl's voice was full of fanatical enthusiasm.

Fidelma was shaking her head slightly. 'Very well, Sister Sétach. Return to your room. I have no more questions for the time being.'

Even Eadulf looked surprised. The girl stood up hesitantly, seeming unsure of herself.

'Can . . . can I take the chest?' she asked at length.

'Not until the matter has been resolved. The chest will remain here.'

The girl moved reluctantly to the door. Outside, the warrior Enda was barring the way and Fidelma called on him to let the girl pass.

After she had gone and Fidelma and Eadulf were alone in the chamber again, it was Eadulf who uttered the first words.

'You can't really believe what the girl said? Holy relics? That's ridiculous.'

Fidelma smiled without humour. 'We could have sat here until the next feast day of Imbolc and not extracted more information out of the girl. Of course, she was lying.'

'Then why didn't you search her?' protested Eadulf.

'Because she did not have anything on her. If she had, she would not have been so quick to challenge me to search her.'

'She could have been bluffing.'

PETER TREMAYNE

'I believe not. She had not found what she was looking for. We might have interrupted her before she discovered whatever it was she wanted. Let's have a look at this chest.'

Eadulf dragged forward the small travelling chest. It was not heavy. He opened the lid while Fidelma held the lantern.

'Items of clothing, robes,' Eadulf muttered as he lifted them out one by one.

Fidelma leaned forward. 'Some leather bags and underneath some papers. What's in the leather bags?'

Eadulf checked through them. 'Various coins and some nuggets of gold in this one, and in the other . . .' He took out a piece of exquisite jewellery. 'It seems that our abbot had good taste in necklaces,' he said, holding it up.

'It could be that you were right, Eadulf, when you asked the girl if she had come looking for mercenary wealth. I don't think that it was relics to be venerated that she was after.'

'You mean that she was after the jewels and money?'

'Unless it was the records that she and Sister Marga were making of the meetings.'

Eadulf started thumbing through the papers.

'You might be right,' he said ruefully. 'They appear to be reports on leading churchmen of the abbeys that Ultán has visited.' He pulled a face. 'Those who favour recognition of Ard Macha as primatial seat get good marks, those who don't are marked with disfavour. There is also a Latin book here . . . *Liber Angeli*, something to do with the history of Ard Macha.'

'Well, there is little else here which might indicate what Sister Sétach was looking for.'

'It would be a little ironic, if it were jewels that she was after. A thief stealing from a man who had been a famous thief.'

'And murderer,' added Fidelma. 'Don't forget that.'

'A connection between the two?'

Fidelma considered and then shook her head. '*Alis volat propriis*, as Publilius . . .'

'. . . Syrus said,' finished Eadulf, who knew of Fidelma's fondness for the *Maxims* of the former slave from Antioch. 'She flies by her own wings. So Sister Sétach is an independent thief?'

144

'We would do well to watch her, that is all I am saying.'

Eadulf replaced the papers in the box.

'We'll get Enda to take the box and lock it in my brother's strong-room,' Fidelma said. 'It will be safe there.'

They called Enda in and gave him the instruction. Then, taking a last look around the chamber in which Ultán had met his death, they left.

'What now?' asked Eadulf as they settled in chairs before their own hearth and stretched towards its warming glow.

'Now?' Fidelma smiled. 'Now it is time to bathe and prepare for the evening meal. This was to have been our marriage feast so I will expect we shall have to eat with our guests in lieu of it.'

Eadulf wrinkled his nose in distaste.

Fidelma stood up suddenly. 'I am going to call Muirgen to start preparing the baths. After the feasting there is another thing that we must do.'

Eadulf raised his head wearily. 'What is that?'

'We must attend the funeral of Abbot Ultán at midnight. It will be interesting to see who attends that ceremony and why.'

'Attend it?' Eadulf had not been expecting that. This Irish custom of committing the body into the grave at midnight was one he found curious. 'It will be late,' he protested, 'and don't I have to be up at dawn to go on this boar hunt?'

Fidelma grinned mischievously at him. 'Then it is lucky that dawn arrives late on a winter morning.'

# CHAPTER ELEVEN

A small crowd had gathered in the lantern-lit graveyard that was known as Relig na nGall, the graveyard of strangers, within the dark shadows of the towering rock of Cashel. It was where distinguished strangers who died in Cashel were laid to rest. Fidelma and Eadulf had accompanied Colgú to the place. The High King Sechnassach and the Chief Brehon, Barrán, were in attendance with the other nobles, among whom was Blathmac, the king of Ulaidh. It was obvious that most of them were attending out of diplomatic courtesy, although Muirchertach, king of Connacht, was not surprisingly absent. Also attending were Abbot Ségdae of Imleach, Abbot Laisran of Durrow, Abbot Augaire of Conga and several other members of the religious. Most of these had come out of duty rather than respect. The brehons Baithen and Ninnid also were present, and the chief mourners were Brother Drón and the two religieuse, Sisters Sétach and Marga.

In spite of the illustrious company, so far as Fidelma was aware, there had been no *fled cro lige* – the feast of the deathbed – performed. And although when a great man died the watching, the *aire*, would usually take several days and nights, while lamentations were sung round the corpse, Ultán's body had not even been watched over for a minimum full day and night. When Fidelma asked her brother why this was, Colgú had merely shrugged and said it had been the desire of Brother Drón acting on behalf of the community of Cill Ria.

As they stood in the gloom among the graves, ogham-inscribed pillar stones marking the more distinguished burials, there came the slow rhythmic toll of a handbell approaching down the hill. It was the *clog-estechtae*, the death bell. The bellringer, a young man in dark robes, preceded the shadowy forms of four pallbearers who carried the wooden *fuat* or bier on which the body was laid, wrapped in a *rochell* or winding sheet. The small group entered the graveyard to the ringing of the bell and came to a halt by the head of the dark hole in the ground. The grave had already been measured and dug.

There was a silence.

The bellringer looked round nervously. No one in the crowd was moving. He cleared his throat.

'Who is delivering the *écnaire*?' he asked, puzzled when no one came forward. 'Who will deliver the requiem and perform the services?'

There was an uncomfortable shuffling among the religious, and then Brother Drón stepped forward angrily.

'I will do so!' he snapped, glaring meaningfully at Abbot Ségdae. 'My abbot was a great man and deserves better than this.'

'Your abbot came here as a stranger among us,' replied Abbot Ségdae, his voice quiet but authoritative. 'There is no religious of rank here who knew him other than as a man of belligerence and argument. None is therefore fit to deliver the *écnaire* over his grave. So say what you will, Brother Drón, and we will not deny you.'

Brother Drón turned sharply to where the hawk-faced king of Ulaidh stood by, watching the proceedings with dark, bright eyes which sparkled in the lantern light.

'And you, king of Ulaidh, do you allow this insult to a churchman of your kingdom to go unnoticed?'

The unease among the people grew a little. Blathmac turned mildly to Brother Drón.

'I see and hear no insult, Brother Drón. I hear a logical reason why no one of this company is qualified to speak of Ultán's life and work save only yourself. If you do not wish to do so then let the *strophaiss* cover the bier and let it be placed in the ground, for the hour grows late.'

Brother Drón swallowed hard. He stared angrily round at the company and then stepped forward and clapped his hands several times in the traditional way of starting the ceremony.

'I lament for the departed soul of Ultán, pillar of the church and fist of the Faith, who . . .'

'Who was a thief, murderer and man of evil!' shouted a harsh voice.

A figure pushed itself through the crowd on the far side of the grave from where Fidelma and Eadulf were standing.

It was Brother Berrihert. There was a shocked silence at his intervention.

'Let the truth be known of the evil that this man has committed. And let no one rhapsodise his misbegotten life by claiming that he may be numbered among the saints.'

Brother Drón was speechless for the moment.

'How dare you,' he finally gasped. 'What Saxon sacrilege is this?'

'Truth is no sacrilege!' cried Brother Berrihert. 'Let these people hear the truth. He was evil. He was the murderer of my mother!'

One of the two sisters, Fidelma was not sure whether it was Sétach or Marga, let forth a wailing moan. She saw one of them turn and cling to the other as if for comfort. She glanced at Eadulf and met his astonished gaze. He shook his head as if to say that this was something unknown to him.

Brother Berrihert had advanced with an outstretched hand pointing to Brother Drón.

'You, too, Drón, have espoused and shared that evil creature's guilt. I come here to spit on this grave and to curse Ultán's soul on its journey into everlasting darkness. As for you, Drón, may the *fé* soon measure your own corpse!'

There was a gasp of horror from the assembly. By the time they had recovered from the shock of hearing the curse uttered aloud – for the aspen rod used to measure graves was believed by many to bring evil on any who touched it – Brother Berrihert seemed to have vanished in the darkness.

Eadulf bent towards Fidelma. 'That outburst might explain the strange encounter I had with Brother Berrihert's father, Ordwulf, this morning. I knew that the mother had died but I had not realised that the death was claimed as murder.'

Fidelma nodded thoughtfully.

'We must speak with Berrihert and Ordwulf,' she replied.

The assembly was now in disarray. Colgú stepped forward, taking control.

'Let the *fuat* be lowered into the grave,' he instructed sharply. 'Let those who wish to say a prayer for the repose of this man's soul do so. But there are many here who feel that there are questions that have to be asked and answered before we can praise or condemn this man. God will forgive us if we delay until that time.'

The High King Sechnassach had been speaking to Blathmac of Ulaidh and now turned, nodding approval.

'It is well ordered, Colgú,' he said loudly, so that Brother Drón could be left in no doubt of his approval. 'Let us retire.'

The crowd began to disperse with the exception of the pallbearers, Brother Drón, and his female companions, Marga and Sétach. Eadulf was about to move when Fidelma stayed him with her hand.

'It would be unseemly to leave,' she whispered.

Eadulf suddenly realised that the brehons were remaining too. It was their duty also to do so.

Fidelma waited while Brother Drón quickly intoned a series of prayers for the dead. She noticed that it was Sister Marga, who looked fairly young, who seemed to be sobbing uncontrollably. Sister Sétach had her arms round the slighter girl and was giving her what comfort she could, almost like a mother comforting a child. Finally, Brother Drón had finished and the pallbearers lowered the *fuat* into the ground. The traditional branches of birch and broom were laid over it before they began to fill in the earth.

Fidelma and Eadulf waited until Brother Drón and his party had left in the company of Brehon Ninnid. Then they moved across to join Barrán and Baithen and walk with them back up the hill to the fortress gates.

'I have attended many a funeral,' were Brehon Barrán's opening words, 'but this was the most bizarre.'

'If proof were needed that Abbot Ultán was not well liked, it has been amply demonstrated,' replied Fidelma mildly.

'Yet only Muirchertach was seen leaving his chamber,' chimed in Brehon Baithen, obviously thinking that Fidelma would use the almost universal feeling against the abbot in her defence of the Connacht king.

'It is true. Yet we cannot proceed without knowing all the facts about the enmities that Abbot Ultán stirred up.'

'No matter what anger he created,' Brehon Baithen said, 'it does not excuse his murder. We are dealing with law.'

'Let us also hope that we are also dealing with justice,' responded Fidelma sharply.

'Well, I shall ensure that after what we have witnessed, a guard is placed outside Brother Drón's chamber,' remarked Brehon Baithen. 'We would not want that curse to become reality. I thought this Saxon Brother Berrihert was a friend of yours, Eadulf? Does he not know that he has offended against our law of hospitality?'

'I never said he or his family were friends,' corrected Eadulf. 'I said that I knew them. I studied with Berrihert and later met his brothers at the great Council of Witebia.'

'Did you not persuade Miach of the Uí Cuileann to give them asylum in his territory?'

'I did not,' replied Eadulf with irritation. 'Miach made up his own mind.'

Fidelma made a clucking noise of disapproval.

'What are you implying, Baithen?' she admonished. 'Eadulf admits to knowing Berrihert but that does not make him responsible for his actions or those of his relatives. In our lives we rub shoulders with many who turn out to be beyond redemption. Does that mean that we ourselves are beyond redemption?'

Brehon Baithen took refuge in silence. Brehon Barrán's face was impassive in the gloom.

'You do not have long, Fidelma,' he reminded her. 'I have to return to Tara within the week.'

After they had bidden a good night to the brehons at the gates of the fortress, Eadulf asked: 'Shall I attempt to find Brother Berrihert and ask the meaning of that scene in the graveyard?'

Fidelma shook her head. 'The hour is late, the gates will be closed soon and, besides, you have the boar hunt to contend with first thing tomorrow.'

'I have been thinking,' Eadulf said slowly, 'there really is no need for me to attend it. I am sure Muirchertach will keep to his word of honour. Our time may be more usefully spent here questioning witnesses.'

'Many people will be attending the hunt tomorrow,' Fidelma replied patiently. 'Even the ladies will follow it. I want someone I can trust watching our guests.'

'Are you telling me all you know?' Eadulf asked accusingly.

Fidelma laughed. 'What I know is very little, unfortunately. What I suspect is beyond the counting. Now, let us retire, for you especially need to be refreshed for the morning.'

The day was bright. There were no clouds in the sky and a white veil of frost shrouded the landscape. The sun was already a pale golden slash over the eastern hills but it promised no future warmth. In the courtyard the gathered hunters with the pack of hunting hounds, and the spearmen on their horses, seemed to exist in a cloud of rising steam, but it was merely their collective breath vaporising as it encountered the cold morning air.

Eadulf came into the yard to find that Gormán, who was to ride with him, had already saddled his horse and was holding it ready. The hunters, holding the long leashes of a dozen yelping hounds, were already moving off through the gates. It had been explained to Eadulf that their function was to spread out through the dark forests to the east of the town and drive the wild pigs into open country beyond. It would take them an hour or so to reach the point where it was thought the herd was to be found, and then the mounted nobles would be waiting with their spears.

In the meanwhile, attendants were handing round goblets of *corma* to the gathered nobles as they waited for the hunters and their dogs to reach their positions. Eadulf reflected that a similar custom prevailed among his own people where the stirrup cup, what the Irish called *deog an dorais*, a drink for the gate, was enjoyed before the start of the hunt. Gormán was handing him a goblet. '*Milsem cacha corma a cétdeog*,' he said, grinning. It was a moment before Eadulf had translated the ancient proverb – the sweetest of all ales is the first drink.

He took a sip of the fiery spirit and glanced round. Colgú was chatting with Sechnassach, the High King, and there were many other nobles and chiefs about. He immediately spotted the king of Connacht, Muirchertach Nár, clad in a royal blue woollen hunting cloak, among the group. The king looked unconcerned and was speaking to Dúnchad Muirisci, his heir apparent. They seemed to be sharing a joke. Eadulf was surprised when another familiar figure joined them on horseback, also prepared for the hunt. It was Abbot Augaire. His surprise lasted but a few moments before he realised that there was no reason why Augaire or any other religious should not be attending. The Faith did not forbid its members to desist from the chase and he knew many prelates boasted of their prowess in the hunt.

At the far end of the courtyard Eadulf saw some of the wives of the nobles gathering ready to mount their horses. He scanned their faces quickly, recognising few of them. There was the lady Gormflaith, wife to the High King, surrounded by her entourage, and many other finely dressed ladies. As his gaze swept over them, he realised with momentary surprise, that Aíbnat, the wife of Muirchertach Nár, was among them. But then, if her husband was attending the hunt, why should Eadulf be surprised if she was there?

'The ladies will follow the hunt after we have moved off,' Gormán explained, as if guessing his thoughts. 'Have you been on a boar hunt before, brother?'

Eadulf shook his head. Herds of wild pigs roamed his own land but he was not particularly fond of hunting. It had to be done because people had to eat but he was prepared to leave it to others to bring the food to his table unless it became a necessity.

'I have heard that boars can be very aggressive and dangerous,' he ventured mildly.

Gormán chuckled. 'There is an old saying here that the boar can send you home in a handcart but it is only the stag who will despatch you to your home in a coffin. A tenacious boar can wound but you need to be unlucky or lacking skill to be killed by one. However, it does happen. A friend of mine was killed by a boar. They are very strong and possessed of great courage. When they are cornered they will put up an heroic defence, but that does not often happen for they are very mobile and you need great skill in the chase to trap them. They are as tall, fast and strong as any hunting hound.'

'So the idea is for those on foot with the hounds to drive them into an open space where they can be killed by the nobles with spears?'

Gormán gave an affirmative gesture. 'Today's chase should be a good one. We have heard stories of a *torc eochraide,* a tusked boar, which is damaging the crops of a farmer on hills beyond the forest to the east. Our hounds will drive it and its pride through the forest and into the open.'

One of the men abruptly raised a horn to his lips and blew a short blast. At once the attendants came forward to take the swiftly drained goblets and help the nobles to their horses. They were all mounting now, laughing, and several boasting that it would be they who would encounter the wild boar first. Attendants handed each hunter his spear, the special sharp-bladed hunting spear called a *bir*. Colgú, at the side of the High King Sechnassach, began to lead the column of riders out of the courtyard of the great fortress and down the slope towards the track that led eastward towards the wooded hills. Muirchertach Nár was mounted on a distinctive-looking piebald mare, its irregularly shaped black and white patterning singling him out from the mass of his fellow riders. At least, thought Eadulf, it would not be easy to lose sight of the man.

Eadulf swung up on his horse with an ease that surprised even himself.

'Come,' he told Gormán, 'I don't want to be too far away from Muirchertach Nár.'

Gormán joined him and they set off through the gate, attaching themselves to the end of the column of mounted spearmen.

'We'll keep our eyes on Muirchertach,' Gormán said, 'but I think we should stay behind the main body of spearmen. You have experience neither as a horseman nor as a hunter to be in the midst of a chase, Brother Eadulf.'

At another time, Eadulf might have been irritated, knowing that the young man was right. Now, however, he was merely determined not to lose sight of the king of Connacht.

Fidelma had gone out on to the balcony of her chamber to watch the departure of the hunters. She, too, had seen Muirchertach depart and observed with approval as Eadulf and Gormán rode off with the main hunt. Then, with swift instructions to Muirgen and a smile and a kiss to young Alchú, who was happily absorbed with his toys, she left her chamber and hurried to the first of her self-appointed tasks.

Her cousin Finguine, the *tánaiste*, told her that he had not seen anything of Brother Drón that morning and, in response to a second question, directed her to the dormitory where the female members of the Faith were staying. When Fidelma inquired of the hostel's stewardess for Sister Marga and Sister Sétach she was told that they might be found at prayer in the chapel. However, Fidelma found the chapel apparently deserted and was about to leave again when she saw a small familiar figure in a corner.

'Ah, Sister Sétach.'

The girl turned towards her. Even in the gloom of the chapel, a beam of light coming through the window showed her tense and fatigued features.

'You look exhausted, sister,' Fidelma observed. 'Did you not sleep well last night?'

Sister Sétach was defensive. 'I often suffer from an inability to sleep.'

'We have an apothecary, Brother Conchobhar, who is able to supply herbs that can help.'

'I have my own remedies,' replied the girl curtly. 'I suppose you have reported me for breaking into the abbot's chamber yesterday evening?' she added belligerently.

Fidelma was not put out. 'That is something between you and your superior, Brother Drón. At this time I am concerned with the death of the abbot and not about his personal belongings.' She glanced around. 'I was also looking for your companion, Sister Marga. Where is she?'

Sister Sétach looked uncertain. 'I don't know. Why do you seek her?'

'I need to speak to her as I need to speak to you. Why do you think so many people hated your abbot when Brother Drón and you have praised him so much?'

The girl sniffed irritably. 'They are jealous, small-minded people, who cannot understand greatness.'

'There are some who would quote Horace. *Naturam expelles furca tamen usque recurret.* Do you know what that means?'

Sister Sétach shook her head. 'I know the literal meaning but I am uncertain how you are applying it.'

'You may drive nature out with a pitchfork, but it will still return,' translated Fidelma. 'Some say that if Abbot Ultán was once a thief and a murderer and a great womaniser, then perhaps he remained one. Would you say that was incorrect?'

'It is untrue,' snapped the girl.

'However, they will say,' went on Fidelma, 'quoting Horace's *Epistles*, as I have said, that you cannot change a person's nature. Once a thief and murderer, always a thief and murderer.'

The girl coloured hotly. She stared defiantly at Fidelma.

'That is untrue,' she repeated. 'Was not Paul reformed after his experience on the road to Damascus? Do we say that because he was one of those who consented to the execution of the Blessed Stephen, the first to suffer martyrdom for our faith, and stood by as a witness, holding the coats of those who were stoning him to death, he was not able to change his heart and that his conversion and work for the Faith was but a sham?'

Fidelma was not only surprised at the girl's vehemence but also astonished at her logic.

'You argue well, Sétach, and from knowledge. That is good. What do you know about Brother Berrihert?'

The girl was silent for a moment or two. 'I know nothing.'

'Yet you saw the passion that was aroused in him last night at the grave. What of the curse he levelled at Brother Drón? Do you say that you know nothing about what prompted such an outburst at such a sacred moment?'

'I can only tell you what I know.'

'But you are willing to defend Ultán without that knowledge?'

'I have no knowledge of what the Saxon claimed. All I can say is that I know Ultán, who has been a good and saintly man during the time I have served him at Cill Ria. You will have to speak to Brother Drón if you seek an answer to the hatred that this Saxon Brother Berrihert displayed last night. He was with Ultán during his visit to Abbot Colmán's island.'

Fidelma paused, and then said suddenly: 'And what do you know of Brother Senach?'

The girl started and then said: 'That was before I went to Cill Ria.'

'Ah, but you have heard the story?'

'Rules were drawn up by the abbot for the governing of the abbey in accordance with the Faith now being espoused at Rome. Brother Senach sought to disobey them. He was therefore sent abroad to Gaul but died on his voyage there.' Sister Sétach said this without emotion, as if repeating a lesson. 'That is all I know or have heard.'

'And what of the poetess Searc?'

'I know nothing more about that story.'

'These rules that the abbot has drawn up to govern his community – does everyone at Cill Ria obey them?'

The girl looked curiously at her.

'Everyone,' she confirmed. 'Of course they do.'

'Including Ultán?'

For a moment the girl blinked and there was a slight red tinge to her cheek.

'Ultán is . . . *was* . . . the abbot,' she replied.

'That does not answer my question,' Fidelma pointed out.

'He would not write down rules for everyone to obey but him,' said the girl. 'I do not understand what you are trying to imply. Surely it is obvious who killed him and no defence of yours will change that.'

There was a sudden emotional note in the girl's voice which made Fidelma think that she was treading on some dangerous path.

'Guilt or innocence is a matter for a brehon to decide,' Fidelma admonished. 'At the moment, nothing is obvious . . . unless you have witnessed something which you are not disclosing.'

Sister Sétach's head jerked slightly. 'What do you mean?'

'Exactly what I say. Do you have information that might help in this matter?'

She shook her head quickly in denial. 'All I know is what everyone knows. That Abbot Ultán was killed and Muirchertach was seen leaving his chamber. Isn't it obvious who killed him?'

Fidelma smiled gently. 'Not at all.' She paused a moment and then asked: 'How did you come to join the abbey at Cill Ria? What persuaded you to become a member of that community?'

Sister Sétach was frowning. 'I write a fair hand. I have a flair for languages. But, alas, my family were not of the *flaith* or nobility, nor of the professional classes. They were simple *céile*, free clansmen, who worked their land, paid their taxes for the upkeep of the community and formed the warrior bands in time of war. They had no great wealth or connections. So, if I were to use my talents, there was little choice but to join a religious house. I am of the Uí Thuirtrí, who dwell by the shores of Loch nEchach, Eoghaidh's lake. That is why I chose to enter Cill Ria, which is close to my home.'

'The *céile* are the basis of our whole society, Sétach. Without them we would have no society,' Fidelma rebuked her mildly.

'You can say that, you who are a *flaith*. Even more than a *flaith* – the sister of a king. What do you know of working in the fields and herding cows, or sheep?' The girl sounded bitter.

'As a practical experience of survival, I have no knowledge. Although I have done such work,' Fidelma replied softly. 'I suppose that you knew the rules of Cill Ria before you entered it?'

'Not exactly. I entered and was then taught the rules propounded by Abbot Ultán.'

'I am told the women live separately from the men?'

'That is so. A stream runs between the two houses; on one side is the male community and on the other the female community. It is . . .' She suddenly stopped.

'What?' asked Fidelma quickly.

'It was just that when I came south I had not realised that most of the religious houses were, what is the word? Con . . . con . . . ?'

'*Conhospitae*?' supplied Fidelma. Then she frowned. 'Was this trip your first outside the abbey of Cill Ria?'

Sister Sétach nodded slowly. 'I had not realised that there were other interpretations of the rules of the Faith. We only were taught Abbot Ultán's rules.'

'What about Sister Marga? Did she, being chosen, as you told me yesterday, by Ultán to come on this journey, know of the controversies that rage beyond the walls of Cill Ria?'

'I don't know. I think that she had accompanied Abbot Ultán several times to Ard Macha. I was therefore pleased when she asked me to come with her here.'

Fidelma sighed softly. 'And you have no knowledge of where I might find Sister Marga now?'

'None,' the girl replied firmly.

Fidelma was unsatisfied. She felt that old sensation that there was something not quite right. On the one hand Sister Sétach was intelligent, resourceful and strong in her defence of Abbot Ultán and his views. Her attempt at entering the abbot's chamber during the previous evening showed her courage. On the other hand, when pressed, she seemed to display signs of a lack of knowledge that bordered on the naïve. Still, it was no use pressing her without knowing anything further.

Knowing! Fidelma thought that trying to get knowledge in these circumstances was like drawing teeth. She abruptly thanked the girl and left the chapel, Sister Sétach staring in perplexity after her.

Fidelma knew there were few places in her brother's fortress that Sister Marga could be. She made her way down the steps to the courtyard. Finguine was still among the group of warriors at the gates and as she approached he called out to her.

'Weren't you looking for those two companions of Brother Drón?'

'I have found Sister Sétach,' she said, as she came up. 'But I can't seem to find Sister Marga.'

'The younger one? The attractive little sister with fair hair and blue eyes?'

Fidelma smiled at her cousin's appreciative tone.

'That is probably Sister Marga,' she replied gravely, because it was certainly not a description of Sister Sétach.

'I only just remembered it after you had gone off to the dormitory in search of them,' said Finguine. 'She rode off with the ladies.'

Fidelma stood still. 'Rode off with the ladies?' she repeated in amazement.

'On the boar hunt,' confirmed her cousin. 'She seemed to have acquired a horse and went off in the company of the ladies after the hunt this morning.'

# chapter twelve

The squeal of a hunting horn came faintly through the gloom of the dark oak trees of the forest and the surrounding thick brush. Gormán bent forward in his saddle, listening for a moment.

'The dogs have made contact,' he announced in satisfaction.

They could hear the hounds taking up the cry and suddenly the noise was joined by the sound of several horns echoing through the forest. The short staccato blasts rose to a volume that left no one in any doubt that the quarry had been sighted.

In front of them, Colgú raised his *bir*, his hunting spear, and gave a cry, leading the way forward. From almost a standstill, the horses of the hunters sprang into a canter that was soon a gallop.

'Best take it easy,' cried Gormán but, undeterred, Eadulf dug his heels into his mount.

'I don't want to lose contact with Muirchertach,' he called.

Although he was the first to proclaim that he had little ability on horseback, he bent forward along his horse's neck, his thighs tightening against its flanks, hands gripping the reins close into the neck, trying not to yank on the leather leads or hold them so tightly that they restricted the nodding motion of the beast's great head as it moved forward after the others. He tried to focus on the piebald of Muirchertach but soon his own mount's flying mane obscured his vision. He clung on and hoped that the horse knew where it was going.

Now and then low branches, and even bushes growing along the side of the track, seemed to rush towards Eadulf as if to strike him from his mount, but the horse seemed to pass them by easily with

Eadulf clinging on firmly, almost lying on top of the animal's broad back. He could just hear the thunder of Gormán's mount behind him but he dared not raise his head to look back. He was trying to focus on the horses before him.

Soon the crowd of nobles began to draw ahead, in spite of the best efforts of Eadulf's horse, which seemed aware of its rider's limitations. At one point the track narrowed so much that the beast itself decided to slow the pace without any help from Eadulf. When it emerged into a clearing, with no sign of the riders ahead, Eadulf finally managed to halt it. Gormán came up behind him in a moment.

'I've lost them,' Eadulf said in disgust.

Gormán cocked his head to one side, listening. 'I think that they've split up. Some have gone down that path to your left, some to the right.'

There came the sound of staccato calls on the horn to the right. They sounded close by.

'That way!' cried Eadulf, turning his mount. It responded immediately, believing another canter was required of it. But this time Eadulf kept to a steady, controlled trot, Gormán at his side.

The trees soon began to thin out and they came to shrubland, then open fields crossing the hills where crops had been planted. Stone hedges bordered some of the fields. Not far ahead of them, he saw some of the hunters on horseback and nearby some of the dog handlers and their hounds. The yelping of the hounds combined with the cries of encouragement from the men. They seemed to be surrounding something.

Then the something suddenly shot out of their encirclement.

A big, dark shape began to race directly towards where Eadulf's horse was trotting forward. He caught sight of a great muscular animal with heavy shoulders, as tall as a large hound with four times the bulk. He saw sharp white tusks protruding from an open, snorting mouth, and sharp red pinpricks of eyes.

His horse reared back with a whinny of fright.

So suddenly did it happen that Eadulf found himself dislodged from his seat and tumbling back over the rump of his horse, hitting the ground with such force that the breath was knocked from him.

He heard shouts and cries of alarm from all sides.

He blinked, trying to recover his senses, and a strange feral smell assailed his nostrils. It was the fetid breath of a wild beast. He opened his eyes and was aware of the black bulk of something standing almost over him. He registered a red eye, pink gums, sharp yellow teeth and curved tusks.

He shut his eyes quickly and it seemed that his blood froze.

Then came a sound as if a hand was smacking flesh. An appalling squeal in his ear, and he felt the bulk shifting. It moved with astonishing agility. He could hear the grunting and squealing fading rapidly. He opened his eyes and it was gone. Then someone was pulling him upright into a sitting position. It was Gormán.

'Are you hurt, Brother Eadulf?'

Eadulf, still sitting, examined his extremities carefully before, with Gormán's help, he climbed slowly to his feet.

'Bruised and winded,' he replied in disgust.

He was aware of cries, yells and a band of riders galloping swiftly by. Behind them came running the men on foot with the hounds giving full cry. Then Eadulf and Gormán were alone again.

'What, by all that is holy, was that?' Eadulf asked, shaking his head.

Gormán grinned. 'You have just encountered a wild boar. It nearly did for you.'

Eadulf shuddered. 'What distracted it? I thought it had me.'

'I smacked it across the snout with my sword and it turned off. Then the hunters came up. They have chased it back into the forest. I suspect that if it keeps in the cover of the trees and undergrowth, it will elude them.'

Eadulf rubbed the back of his neck and turned his head this way and that to ensure there was no damage from his fall. Then he remembered what he was there for.

'Was Muirchertach with them?' he inquired anxiously.

'I didn't see him,' replied Gormán.

'Devil's teeth,' swore Eadulf, annoyed.

Gormán mounted his animal again and waited while Eadulf clambered back into the saddle of his own horse.

'Muirchertach may have gone off with the other group, when they divided back at the clearing,' he suggested.

'Let's go and find him, then.'

They retraced their path back to the clearing, and as they reached it they saw a horse and rider coming along the path. It was the slight figure of a woman. She suddenly tugged on the reins of her horse as she noticed them and then, as if wanting to avoid them, plunged off along an adjoining path and quickly vanished.

'One of the women following the hunt,' muttered Gormán, 'but I think she is going in the wrong direction. Shall I go after her?'

'She is moving pretty rapidly,' replied Eadulf, adding: 'Did you notice who she was?'

Gormán shook his head.

'That was Sister Marga, one of those who came with Abbot Ultán,' Eadulf said. 'I thought I recognised the horse . . . that is the same horse that Ultán arrived on.'

Gormán pulled a face, expressing his disapproval. 'Obviously, Sister Marga does not believe in following the proprieties. One would expect a time of mourning after her superior's death.'

He suddenly glanced up with a frown. There came the sound of laughing and chattering and a band of riders appeared along the track in front of them. They were proceeding at a sedate pace through the forest. It was the rest of the hunt followers and their escort. The attendants carried baskets of food and drink and the ladies rode in a relaxed manner, talking and laughing as if out on some innocent picnic.

One of the attendants called to Gormán and asked him which way the main band of huntsmen had gone, and Gormán pointed along the path where they had last seen them.

'My lord Colgú, the High King and their party were chasing a tusker in that direction only a short time ago,' he told them. 'Be careful, ladies, for the animal is large and strong.'

Little cries of excited horror came from them but it was all done with humour and laughter. The attendant thanked him as the party moved slowly off. Meanwhile, Eadulf had ridden a short distance along the second path to the left. Gormán quickly caught up with him.

'The ladies seem to think this is an amusement,' he commented sourly. 'They don't realise the dangers.'

'Nor did I,' Eadulf observed dryly. 'I'm sorry. I neglected to thank you for what you did back there. You saved my life.'

Gormán gestured indifferently. 'Smacking the animal across the snout? That was nothing. It was frightened and wild. It would probably have run off anyway. The hunters were close by.' He drew rein and looked around, then cursed softly. 'Begging your pardon, Brother Eadulf, but I think we may have lost the other party. I see no sign of a large body of horsemen passing along here. That is the trouble in these hunts – people often tend to scatter all over the place.'

'Do you think that we should turn back again?' Eadulf was beginning to when, once again, the sound of horses came to their ears, but muted this time by the rich tone of a man's laughter.

'*Hóigh!*' shouted Gormán to attract attention. '*Hóigh!*'

There came an answering call and a few moments later two horses emerged through the woods from their left. One of the riders was the smiling Abbot Augaire and behind him came the sharp-featured lady Aíbnat.

'Brother Eadulf,' the abbot said in jovial fashion. 'Are you lost?'

Gormán immediately answered for him. 'Not lost, but we have become separated from the main hunt.'

Abbot Augaire shook his head with a smile. 'Well, my friend, we are definitely lost. I think the main hunt went in that direction.' He pointed back the way they had come. 'We were actually thinking of returning to Cashel, if we can find the way.'

Gormán nodded. 'In that case, if you follow the path along here as far as a fairly large clearing back there and then turn to the west, that track brings you to the main road back to Cashel.'

Abbot Augaire and lady Aíbnat were about to move off when Eadulf stayed them with a sudden thought.

'Have you seen anything of your husband, lady?' he asked politely.

She frowned irritably at him. 'I presume that he is with the main body of the hunt.'

'I thought that he and another group had moved further that way.' Eadulf pointed to the direction from which the two had come.

Abbot Augaire shook his head. 'We have seen nothing of anyone there. But I was part of the body separated from the High King's

163

group. We tried to get round behind the boars but in the excitement we lost each other. I don't think you'll see anyone back there.'

Eadulf acknowledged the information and they separated, Abbot Augaire and the lady Aíbnat riding off towards the clearing.

Gormán looked after them with a puzzled expression. 'I find it strange,' he muttered.

'Strange?' queried Eadulf with a smile. 'What is strange, my friend?'

'That people no longer seem to take notice of conventionality in their behaviour.'

'You mean Sister Marga going on a hunt when her abbot has just been buried after being murdered? Even to the extent of using his horse?'

'That, and Muirchertach Nár and his wife Aíbnat being part of the hunt when he is charged with murder.'

'It is a distraction,' explained Eadulf. 'No one is going anywhere until this matter is cleared up so why not let them have their diversions? And a king is hardly likely to flee from justice in these circumstances.'

They rode on in silence for a while and then another cry cut through the still forest air.

'*Hóigh! Hóigh!*'

This time it sounded like a man shouting for help. Eadulf and Gormán drew rein immediately and peered through the trees, turning in the direction of the sound.

One of the dog handlers emerged from the trees. He was red-faced and breathless but when his eyes alighted on Gormán a look of relief crossed his features. He gave another shout and came running forward, speaking rapidly. Gormán moved towards him, bending down. The man spoke so quickly that Eadulf was unable to hear what was said. Gormán turned in his saddle and waved Eadulf forward. He seemed troubled.

'What is it?' Eadulf demanded.

'Something that I think requires your attention,' replied the young warrior. He turned to the man on foot. 'How far?'

The man gestured with his outstretched hand behind him.

'Not far, through the trees there. There is a clearing beyond called

Cúil Rathan – the brook of the ferns. I'll show you the way. You'll have to dismount and lead your horses along here for the path is overgrown. The branches are too low for riders.'

Eadulf and Gormán slid from their mounts and followed.

The man led them quickly along a narrow winding path through the dark forest of oaks, beeches and chestnuts, through a covert of broom, bramble and ferns dressed in the brown-white sheen of winter. Then they were in open shrubland. There was a small mound ahead and the man trotted up it and pointed downwards without speaking.

Eadulf and Gormán left their horses and scrambled up the mound to join him.

He was pointing down into the gully where the tall figure of a man was sprawled on his back, a rich blue embroidered cloak rumpled from his shoulders.

Eadulf's mouth went suddenly dry. The blue cloak was familiar.

He moved to the side of the man and knelt down. There was no mistaking the strangely sallow, now deathly pale features, the skin tightly stretching over the bony face, the long dark hair surrounding it. Two things registered with Eadulf immediately. The man was Muirchertach Nár, the king of Connacht, and he was dead.

Deep in thought, Fidelma walked down to the accommodation for male members of the religious that had been set up beyond the town square below the fortress. She found the hostel steward, the *brugaid*, supervising the delivery of some straw palliasses by two men in a cart. He greeted Fidelma with a sad smile.

'I am sorry that the ceremony has had to be delayed, lady.'

Fidelma stifled an inward sigh. Everyone was sorry. She was sorry most of all. She had a wild desire to take her horse and ride away across the plains, ride and forget all the sad faces and the anger and confusion.

'Can I help you, lady?'

She came back to the present quickly. 'I believe that you have a Saxon named Brother Berrihert lodging here?'

The *brugaid* nodded confirmation. 'He and his two brothers – blood brothers, not only brothers in the Faith – and his old father.'

'I would like to see Brother Berrihert.'

'Alas, lady, he is not there. He went out before dawn. I know not whither he has gone.'

Fidelma felt disappointed. She had wanted to clear up several things before Eadulf returned. She was about to turn away when the hostel steward went on: 'But his two brothers are inside, lady. They might know where he went.'

Fidelma turned back with a word of thanks and entered the large tent. There were only two men inside. They were fairly young and both had fair hair. They came to their feet as she entered and crossed to them. She noticed that they wore religious robes and had their hair cut in the tonsure of St John, shaved at the front to a line from ear to ear, with the hair worn long and flowing at the back.

'Are you the brothers of Berrihert?' she asked.

The young men exchanged glances and one of them inclined his head slightly.

'We are brothers in flesh as well as brothers in Christ, sister,' he said.

'I am Fidelma. What are your names?'

The younger of the two smiled. 'We recognise you, sister, for we saw you at the Council of Witebia. I am Naovan. My brother is Pecanum.'

'Those are not Saxon names.' She had decided to assume no prior knowledge as a means of clarifying the information she wanted.

Brother Naovan smiled. 'Since we left our own land to sojourn in foreign fields, lady, we have adopted names in the language of the chief city of the Faith.'

'Then let us be seated. I am told that your brother, Berrihert, is not here?'

Brother Pecanum shook his head as they sat on the camp beds. 'He left early this morning. We do not know where he went but he assured us that he would be back this evening. It was some . . . some pilgrimage to make reparation, he said.'

Fidelma was puzzled. 'A pilgrimage of reparation made within a day's travel from Cashel?'

'That is what he said,' affirmed Brother Naovan.

Fidelma shook her head as she thought of the sites around Cashel where one could make what could be described as a pilgrimage.

'And has your father also gone on this pilgrimage?'

'He is not of our faith, lady,' replied Brother Naovan. 'But he is not here. We are not sure where he has gone.'

She paused a moment and then asked: 'I presume that you are aware of what happened at the funeral ceremony of Abbot Ultán last night?'

The brothers glanced uneasily at each other.

'There have been many stories among the people here,' said Brother Naovan. 'Many have condemned the curse that our brother put on a fellow religious.'

'Can you explain why he did so?'

'Although we would have preferred our brother not to have given way to his anger, there was a reason. But reaction in anger can bring no resolution.'

'Wise words,' agreed Fidelma. 'So, if I have understood right, your mother died as the direct result of some action of Abbot Ultán?'

'Perhaps you should be speaking to Berrihert,' Brother Naovan replied hesitantly.

'You have been in this country since the great Council of Witebia, have you not? That is nearly four years or so.'

'That is so, Sister Fidelma.'

'Then you know of our laws, the laws of the Fénechus? You know that I am a *dálaigh*, qualified to the level of *anruth*. I have been charged to make an investigation. I require information and you are duty bound to answer my questions.'

The brothers were uncomfortable.

'We do not wish to go against the laws and customs of the land that has given us refuge, sister,' Brother Pecanum agreed. 'We will do our best to answer you.'

'So tell me exactly what happened to your mother.'

By some silent consent between the two of them it was Brother Naovan who told the story.

'You know that our family did not accept the decision of Oswy, made at the Council of Witebia, as binding on us? We decided to follow Abbot Colmán to this land and enter a religious community that he had established on Inis Bó Finne, a little island . . .'

Fidelma gestured impatiently with her hand. 'Eadulf has told me the story as he heard it from Berrihert. But he also told me, and you have just confirmed, that your father Ordwulf, who came with you, is not a Christian.'

For a moment the younger brothers' expressions shared sadness.

'It is true that our parents came with us, though not of our faith. It was because we were their only means of protection in their old age. We could not abandon them to their certain deaths when they were no longer able to fend for themselves.'

Fidelma was momentarily surprised but then remembered that the Angles and Saxons had different views on age from her own people. The law texts of the Fénechus were absolute. 'Old age is rewarded by the people.' When men and women became too elderly or infirm to take care of themselves, the law stipulated the rules by which they were to be taken care of. No elderly person was allowed to become destitute or in need. The legal text of the *Crith Gabhlach* decreed that a special officer called the *úaithne*, the name meant a pillar or support of the society, be appointed by every clan to ensure all the elderly were looked after. They were to receive proper allowances and care and were protected from any harm or insults. The *Senchus Mór* stated, of the elderly, that it was the duty of the clan to support every member.

When the head of a family became too old or infirm to manage his affairs, the laws allowed him to retire and hand over to his next of kin. He and his wife or widow was then to be maintained for the rest of their lives. They could live with their next of kin if that was their desire or, if they wished to live in a separate house, that house, called an *inchis*, was maintained for them. Even if they had no children or close relatives to help them, this was done under the supervision of the *úaithne*. The elderly, if infirm, had to be washed a minimum of once a week, especially their hair, and to have a full bath a minimum of every twenty days. Provisions and fuel allowances were also stipulated in law.

Fidelma, widely read and travelled as she was, was sometimes shocked at the lack of provision in other cultures for the sick, the elderly and the poor.

'So your parents would have had no help from their tribe once they became elderly or infirm?'

The two brothers shook their heads.

'No one respects age. What can the elderly contribute to the good of the people?'

Fidelma made a noise that signified irritation. 'One can argue that they have already contributed. However, it is surely their wisdom that is their greatest gift. When the old cock crows, the young ones learn,' she added, using an ancient expression of her people.

Brother Naovan shrugged.

'We could not abandon them,' he repeated. 'So we brought them with us. They were firmly set in their ways, in the ways of the Old Faith, and continued as such.'

'There are still many in the five kingdoms who have not wholly endorsed the New Faith,' Fidelma replied. 'It is of no great consequence.'

'The consequence was very great,' muttered Brother Pecanum darkly.

'As I say, we brought them with us,' his brother continued. 'When we settled in the community of Colmán, we built them a small house, the *inchis* you call it? Yes, we helped them with a small house nearby where they could live out their days in peace. All went well, until, as Berrihert told Brother Eadulf, this arrogant prelate from Cill Ria came to demand that our community recognise Ard Macha as the primatial seat of the churches. What did we Angles and Saxons know of this? Nothing. But Abbot Colmán argued against such recognition, as did most of those men of your country who were in our community. But others argued in favour of the demands of this Abbot Ultán.

'The arguments were angry. Finally, Brother Gerald left our island and took his followers, who were mainly Saxons, to Maigh Éo on the mainland and formed a new community. That did not stop Abbot Ultán, who came again and provoked further arguments.'

Fidelma was puzzled. 'How did that affect either your father or your mother? They were not part of the community. They were not even part of the Faith.'

Brother Pecanum suddenly groaned in anguish and Naovan leaned forward and gripped him comfortingly by the arm. He turned to Fidelma. There was pain on his features.

'It happened when Abbot Ultán, who had been accompanied by

Brother Drón and a dozen men, warriors or mercenaries perhaps from his own land whom he had hired as bodyguards on his trip, was leaving our island. I believe he needed those bodyguards otherwise he would not long have been allowed the arrogance with which he conducted himself. They made their way down to the inlet where their boat was waiting to take them back to the mainland. The way lay past the house of our parents. My father was not there, for he was out fishing on the far side of the island.'

He paused for a moment, his hand still gripping his brother's arm. Pecanum's eyes were watering.

'My mother, Aelgifu, was outside, kneeling under a tree. There she had set up an altar to the old gods that she worshipped. Knowing that my father had gone out to sea fishing, she had sacrificed a hare to the goddess Ran, seeking her protection.'

'Ran?' queried Fidelma.

'In the old religion, Ran was wife to Aegir, the god of the sea. When seafarers drowned, she would take them to her palace beneath the waves where her nine daughters would look after them. Ran was protector of those who sacrificed to her.' The young man hesitated and coloured. 'That was what was taught in the old religion to which our parents clung steadfastly. There was no harm in them, for they were good people, but just a little old and set in their ways.'

'I understand,' Fidelma replied. 'Continue.'

'Abbot Ultán came walking by as she was making her sacrifice and demanded to know what she was doing. She did not speak your language well but one of the men with him, one of the warriors, who had been a mercenary among the Saxons, interpreted. Abbot Ultán was beside himself to learn that a foreign woman, in the shadow of a Christian monastery, was carrying out a pagan ceremony. He raged and stormed and told the warrior to beat my mother for her sacrilege.'

There was a silence. Brother Naovan raised his chin defiantly.

'He ordered an elderly woman to be beaten?' Fidelma was incredulous.

'God's curse on his soul,' muttered Brother Pecanum. 'He deserved his death.'

'What happened then?'

'They left my mother senseless and smashed her little altar under the tree. They left. We never saw Ultán or Drón again until we heard that they were here at Cashel.'

'How did you learn what had happened to your mother?'

'Someone came running to the community to say they had found her. Berrihert, Pecanum and I went down to her. She was still living but her life was ebbing fast with the shock. She told us what had happened as best as she could. She struggled to remain alive until evening so that she could say farewell to my father on his return, but before dusk descended her spirit had fled her body. May she rest with her own gods in peace.'

Fidelma sat regarding the two brothers carefully. 'Tell me, and tell me truthfully, did Berrihert, your father Ordwulf, and yourselves, come here with the intention of seeking vengeance on Ultán and Drón?'

Brother Pecanum raised his head and met her gaze. 'At first we did not know they were here. But when we found out, my father grew angry. Yesterday, at dawn, he went to the fortress, when the gates opened, and his intention was to seek out Ultán.'

'And kill him?' pressed Fidelma.

'And kill him,' confirmed Brother Pecanum.

Fidelma had been expecting a denial. She was surprised at the frankness of the young man.

'Since you have been so honest, let me ask you whether your family were involved in the death of Abbot Ultán?'

This time Brother Naovan replied.

'We were not. I speak only for Pecanum and me. I cannot say anything else. Our father raged against us for not being warriors, for not avenging our mother's death, but we are committed to the New Faith and vengeance is not ours to take. We did not know our father had gone up to the fortress until he returned to say that he had been thwarted and that Ultán was already slain by the hand of the king of Connacht.'

'So you are saying that Ordwulf and Berrihert were not involved in his death?'

'We heard that it was the king of Connacht who killed him. Why do you question us in this fashion?'

'Because I do not believe that the king of Connacht did kill the abbot.'

The brother exchanged a glance of surprise. 'Then you suspect . . . ?' began Brother Naovan.

Fidelma interrupted with a sad shake of her head. 'Do not think that I have no sympathy for you in this tragic tale. However, I must attend to the law. You will have to remain within this town until such time as the matter has been resolved.'

'We understand, sister. But it is hard for us to carry suspicion in our hearts against our brother and our father. God grant that they are not involved, and that you are wrong in your belief that the king of Connacht did not strike down Ultán.'

'There is going to be a price to pay for this!'

Gormán was peering over Eadulf's shoulder and was shaking his head in disbelief.

Eadulf made no comment. He was examining the king's body for the cause of death. In fact, it was fairly obvious. The killing blow had left a wound just above the heart, although Eadulf had noticed three more such wounds in the neck: deep, plunging, tearing cuts which, of themselves, would not have caused death. These wounds could have been made by sword or knife or . . .

He was about to rise when he noticed a piece of paper tucked into a fold of Muirchertach Nár's hunting cloak. He reached forward, extracted it and then unfolded it. He drew his breath sharply as he saw what it was. A poem. He knew the words.

> Cold the nights I cannot sleep,
> Thinking of my love, my dear one . . .

He did not know what it could mean but he folded it and put it in his purse. Then he rose to his feet and glanced round.

A short distance away he saw a discarded hunting spear, Muirchertach's *bir*. He moved towards it and looked down at the sharp honed point. It was blood-stained. He picked it up and returned to the body. Then he bent down again and let out a sigh as he measured the wound with the point of the spear.

'He has been stabbed with his own hunting spear,' he announced. Then, straightening, he added: 'There is no sign of his horse.'

Gormán beckoned the dog handler to come forward. 'Was there any sign of Muirchertach's horse when you came here?'

'There was not.'

Eadulf turned to the man. 'How did you make this discovery . . . what is your name?'

'My name is Rónán. I am one of the trackers at Cashel.'

'So, tell me how you came here.'

'We were driving the boars through the forest. I was on the far left of the line. One of the hounds, again to my left, starting giving cry and so I moved towards it through the forest, thinking it had a boar at bay. I was still in the forest when I heard the sound of a frightened horse, then the thud of hooves at a gallop. By the time I came through the undergrowth just there, there was no sign of anything. No horse and no hound.' The man paused and Eadulf waited patiently. 'I came to the mound here, it being high ground, to see if I could see anything.'

'And that is when you saw the body?' Gormán cut in.

'I did so.'

'Then what?'

'Recognising the body as that of Muirchertach Nár, I knew I had to tell someone immediately. I ran back to the main track hoping that someone would be passing and, thanks be, I saw you both immediately. That is all I know.'

'You say that you heard the sound of a horse?' Gormán asked. 'The ground is soft here. There should be tracks.'

'There are,' replied the man. 'Come with me.'

They followed him to a place beyond the body.

'Can you read the signs?' Eadulf asked.

The man crouched down to point at the hoofprints.

'So far as I can see, two riders came to this spot here by different paths.' He frowned suddenly. 'A third horse was here, with a split shoe. It went off in that direction.' He pointed. 'The other two horses followed it, but neither appears to have had a rider. The one with the split shoe seems to be the only one that was ridden away.'

Eadulf smiled a little sceptically. 'Is that guesswork?'

Rónán was not offended.

'It is observation, Brother Eadulf. I am a tracker. I can see when horses bear the weight of riders and when they don't. The hooves do not sink so deeply into the mud as when they have the added weight of their riders. Therefore, you can see those horses were carrying less weight when they left than when they came.' He shrugged and added: 'A hunter has to be observant. It is often a matter of eating or starving or, indeed, of life or death.'

Eadulf inclined his head in apology. 'So Muirchertach rode to this spot. Why? This was on the far left of the hunt. And how did he come to be on his own?'

Rónán shrugged slightly. 'Perhaps they wanted to circle the main body of the hunt, thinking that the boars would break through the undergrowth in this direction.'

'It can happen,' agreed Gormán. 'The boar is a clever animal. With the hunt moving over there, to the right, and the drivers and their hounds trying to push the boars towards the spears, a clever tusker can decide to break left and escape the encirclement. It has been known many times.'

'Say that you are right. Muirchertach has decided to move in this direction to outsmart the boar. Then he meets someone else, riding from which direction?'

Rónán pointed back to the forest. 'Muirchertach came through the forest more or less in the direction from which we came. The other rider – presumably his killer – came from the far left, round the edge of the forest,' he said. 'The horse with the split shoe seems to have been following the second horse, but the tracks are rather muddled there and it is difficult to tell.'

Eadulf was puzzled. 'From the left? Not from the right where the main body of hunters were?'

Rónán shook his head.

'Then we are developing a mystery,' Eadulf sighed.

It was Gormán's turn to frown. 'A mystery?'

'How did the person who met Muirchertach Nár know that he would be here?'

'A chance meeting?'

'Perhaps. But why would Muirchertach allow this stranger to take his hunting spear and kill him?'

'A fight? Perhaps he was overpowered?' suggested Gormán.

'There is no sign of that. If he had been knocked down from his horse, or set upon and disarmed with physical violence, there would have been some evidence of it. Bruises, torn or disarranged clothing. Look at the way he lies. It is as if he just fell back, arms slightly outstretched. Also,' he instructed, 'examine the expression on his face.'

'People in their death throes often show distortions of the face,' Gormán pointed out.

'That is true. Yet very rarely is the expression fixed as one of apparent surprise or even shock. That seems to be the last reaction he registered in life. And then there is the mystery of the third horse.'

There was something reminiscent of Abbot Ultán about the manner of the king's death. Eadulf turned to Rónán who was standing awaiting instruction.

'You'd better find some others and have the king's body removed to Cashel. Take it to Brother Conchobhar the apothecary. Wait!' he called as the other turned. 'Get some cloth and make sure the body is covered before you transport it. The more discreetly it is done the better.'

'It shall be as you say, Brother Eadulf.'

Eadulf turned to Gormán. 'We shall try to follow the horses' tracks and see where they lead.'

'The one with the rider should not be hard to follow,' Rónán called, overhearing. 'Look for an imprint of an uneven shoe. I think the metal was badly cast and has split. The left foreleg will be the one to look for.'

Eadulf raised his hand in acknowledgement, and then turned to where Gormán was examining the hoofprints.

'They seem to be leading through those woods to the north-west,' the warrior called, mounting his horse.

'That would bring them back to Cashel, surely.' Eadulf frowned as he climbed back on his mount.

'Unless whoever it is turns off the track.'

'I don't think they will do so,' Eadulf replied. 'I have a feeling we shall find that whoever killed Muirchertach Nár is heading back to Cashel.'

\*     \*     \*

175

Fidelma had left the two brothers in the hostel and returned to the main gates of the fortress in search of her cousin Finguine. He was crossing the courtyard to the stables when she caught up with him.

'Apart from the nobles, do you know who else went out on the hunt this morning?' she asked without preamble.

Finguine shrugged. 'Practically everyone who is anyone,' he replied, then added with a grin: 'With the exception of myself.'

Fidelma was in no mood for his humour. 'I was thinking of Brother Berrihert?'

Finguine considered for a moment before shaking his head. 'Apart from Eadulf, the only religious on the hunt were Abbot Augaire, Sister Marga and Brother Drón.'

'Brother Drón?' snapped Fidelma in surprise. 'He went on this hunt?'

'Brother Drón,' confirmed Finguine. 'That unpleasant man who came with Abbot Ultán.'

'I know Brother Drón well enough,' she said irritably. 'Did he and Sister Marga ride off together?'

'They did not. Sister Marga, as I told you earlier, went off with the ladies. It was some time after that that Brother Drón went after them . . . I don't think he intended to go on the hunt at first.'

'Why do you say that?'

'Well, he came hurrying to the gate with his horse and asked one of the warriors where some place was and how long would it take him to get there. The guard told me afterwards. I forget where it was, a ride to the south, anyway. He kept looking at some paper in his hand. Then, as he was mounting his horse, the other girl who was in his party came hurrying up. She said something and pointed eastward. That was the direction in which the hunt had gone. I was told that Brother Drón looked really angry, mounted his horse and rode off in that direction at a gallop. Unseemly for a religious,' her cousin added.

A guard at the gates suddenly called a challenge to someone outside and then a solitary rider came through into the courtyard. Fidelma recognised him as Dúnchad Muirisci, the heir apparent to Muirchertach, King of Connacht.

Finguine had called an order and a *gilla scuir*, a stable boy, hurried forward to help the man from his horse. Fidelma moved leisurely to greet him.

'You are back early from the hunt, Dúnchad Muirisci.'

The noble glanced moodily at her. His features showed none of the humour they had displayed when she had questioned him the previous day.

'You are perceptive, lady,' he replied sarcastically, automatically reaching with his left hand to hold his right. Fidelma saw that the latter was splashed with blood.

'I am sorry. You are hurt, Dúnchad Muirisci.'

The man grimaced in annoyance. 'It is nothing, just a scratch.'

'A scratch does not bleed with such profusion,' she reproved him. 'You had best let someone see it. Brother Conchobhar's shop is just behind that building there. He is our best apothecary.'

Dúnchad Muirisci grunted and began to move off, holding his arm.

She fell in step with him. 'What happened?' she asked.

'A stupid accident. A boar charged my horse and it moved to avoid it. It pushed into a thorn bush and I reached out my hand to protect myself and the thorns scratched it. That is all.'

'You rode back alone, bleeding?'

'There was no one else about. I was on my own and the boar came out of nowhere.'

'Then you were lucky that a worse injury did not befall you, Dúnchad Muirisci. Do you know how the rest of the hunt is faring?'

The *tánaiste* shook his head. 'I told you that I was on my own. I became separated from the main body once the hue and cry was raised.'

Finguine caught them up. 'There is no sign of your *bir*, Dúnchad Muirisci.'

'I dropped it when the thorns dug into my flesh. It hurt so much that I forgot to pick it up. It must be still lying where it fell.'

'The boy tells me that one of your horse's shoes seems to have been badly miscast and has cracked. He will take it to our blacksmith's forge and get it replaced for you.'

Dúnchad Muirisci frowned and seemed about to refuse, and then nodded. 'I should be grateful for it.'

He turned and hurried off towards the apothecary. Fidelma and Finguine did not bother to follow.

'He seems slightly agitated,' remarked Fidelma.

Finguine smiled knowingly. 'He has good reason to be so. The heir presumptive of Connacht is out hunting and he winds up in a thorn bush, cuts his hand badly on the thorns, loses his hunting spear, and, in addition, one of the shoes on his horse cracks . . . wouldn't you be agitated in his place? Imagine what a satirist would do with that information. It is a question of protecting one's honour.'

Fidelma laughed. 'Thankfully I do not have to protect this strange male honour that you speak of, Finguine.'

Her cousin chuckled. 'Even so, it is enough to put Dúnchad Muirisci in a bad humour.'

Fidelma glanced up at the sky. It was nearly midday. 'I suppose the hunt should be returning soon?'

Finguine pursed his lips. 'If it has gone well,' he replied. 'At least it was a distraction for the guests while they are waiting for a resolution.' He glanced quickly at Fidelma. 'I presume your inquiry has not gone well this morning?'

'You are correct in your presumption,' Fidelma admitted. 'I should have drawn up a list of those I wanted to see and ensured that they remained here in the fortress. But that would have given them warning of the intended interrogation. I'd much sooner question people when they are taken off guard.'

Finguine looked thoughtful. 'Then you have other suspects for the slaying of Abbot Ultán, and not only the king of Connacht?'

'Suspects?' Fidelma gave a wry smile. 'That is the one thing I am not short of, cousin, for it seems that everyone hated the man and everyone wished him dead.'

# chapter thirteen

Eadulf and Gormán had been trying to follow the trail but had eventually given up. They had come to a stretch of stony ground where the tracks had disappeared and even though Gormán had circled the area several times he had been unable to pick them up again.

'Let's continue to head in the direction of Cashel,' suggested Eadulf. 'If our suspicion is right and the killer is heading back there, we should soon be able to pick up some signs again. The split horse-shoe is easy to spot where the ground is soft.'

Gormán agreed and they turned their horses along the track. They had travelled but a short distance, traversing a copse of beech and aspen ringed round with clumps of thorn bushes and broom, and moving across a small hillock, when Gormán gave a stifled gasp. Eadulf followed his extended hand.

A little distance in front of them and slightly below, as the hill inclined into a small valley, was a single rider, leading a second horse by the reins. Eadulf recognised the piebald. It was the animal that he had last seen being ridden by Muirchertach Nár.

Gormán had already given a grunt of satisfaction and was digging his heels into his mount, sending it cantering forward down the slope. Eadulf gave an inward groan and followed the warrior's example.

Ahead of them, the rider must have heard the sound of their approach because he turned in the saddle to look back. The thought crossed Eadulf's mind that their quarry might fly but the figure drew rein, rested in the saddle, and in an unperturbed fashion watched their approach.

It was a few moments before Eadulf realised who the rider was.

He gasped in surprise. It was Brother Drón. And now that they drew close, Eadulf knew there was no doubt that the horse he was leading was the animal that Muirchertach Nár had been riding.

They reined in as they came abreast of him.

'You have a lot of explaining to do,' was Eadulf's greeting.

Brother Drón stared at him as if he were insane. 'Explaining? For what?' he demanded.

'Where did you get that horse?' Eadulf said, gesturing to the piebald.

Brother Drón's lip curled in disdain. 'What business is it of yours, Saxon?' he demanded. 'You have no authority to demand answers of me.'

Gormán was leaning forward on his saddlebow. 'But I do, brother.' He raised his hand to touch the golden necklet round his throat with a significant gesture. The necklet signified that he was of the Nasc Niadh, the élite warrior guard of the king of Muman.

'If you must know, I am taking it back to the fortress,' snapped Brother Drón

'That is not what I asked,' replied Eadulf coldly. 'I asked where you found the animal, not where you are taking it.'

Brother Drón looked as though he was going to refuse but Gormán said: 'It would be better if you answered.'

The man hesitated, frowning in annoyance. 'I was riding by the woods back there and saw it standing with its reins caught in a thorn bush. It probably tossed its rider and then got caught up. I am taking it back to . . .'

'You have said that,' Eadulf interrupted irritably. 'Are you telling us that you simply found the horse riderless?'

'I thought that was precisely what I said.'

'What are you doing out here, brother?' demanded Gormán. 'You were not with the main hunting party when we left the fortress this morning.'

Brother Drón shrugged. 'I do not see how that concerns you, even if you are a member of the king of Muman's bodyguard,' he countered.

Gormán's mouth tightened and he clapped a hand on the hilt of his sword. Brother Drón did not miss the gesture. His eyes narrowed.

'If it means so much to you,' he said tightly, 'I was not with the hunt. I came riding on my own. Satisfied?'

'For what purpose?' demanded Eadulf. 'Why did you come riding here on your own?'

'I was looking for someone.'

'Who?'

'Really . . .' began Brother Drón.

'Who were you looking for?' Eadulf's voice was a sharp crack, making Brother Drón blink.

'I was looking for one of my charges, if you must know. One who scandalously rode off to follow the hunt without permission. A shameful act. An affront to the abbey she serves since her superior, the abbot, is only newly dead.'

'Are you saying that you were looking for one of the two sisters who accompanied Abbot Ultán?' asked Eadulf, exchanging a glance with Gormán. He recalled that they had seen Sister Marga riding through the forest not so long before.

'I am, for it is the truth.'

'Who was it?'

'If you will have it, I was looking for Sister Marga. I was told that she had ridden out with the others, and on Abbot Ultán's very own horse. She will be punished for such an affront to his sacred memory.'

Eadulf was silent for a moment.

'Do you have any idea whose horse *that* is?' Gormán asked quietly. 'Whose horse it is that you claim to have found?'

'Should I?'

'Oh, indeed you should.' Eadulf smiled thinly. 'That is the horse of Muirchertach Nár.'

Brother Drón's eyes widened a fraction.

'And Muirchertach Nár now lies dead,' added Gormán.

Whatever reaction they were expecting, neither man hid their surprise when Brother Drón threw back his head and laughed.

'That is God's justice,' he chuckled. 'God's punishment for his killing of Abbot Ultán.'

Fidelma was about to leave her cousin at the gates of Cashel when there came a shout from one of the guards.

'Looks as if the rest of the hunters are beginning to return!' Finguine observed.

In fact, it was only Abbot Augaire in the company of Aíbnat, the wife of Muirchertach Nár. Fidelma's eyes narrowed in disapproval at the sight of the latter. The woman had not endeared herself to Fidelma. In fact, Fidelma was surprised to see the usually sour-faced Aíbnat smiling and apparently sharing a joke with the abbot of Conga. It did not seem appropriate for the wife of a man who had been charged with the heinous crime of murder.

As the abbot dismounted, he caught sight of Fidelma, and hailed her with a smile. 'What news, lady? Have you gathered all your evidence in defence of Muirchertach Nár?'

Fidelma ignored his question and answered with one of her own. 'I presume that the hunting was good?'

Abbot Augaire shrugged indifferently. 'I'm afraid that I was separated from the main party early on. I was lost in your forest. Then, by chance, I encountered the lady Aíbnat who was in a similar plight and, thankfully, we fell in with Brother Eadulf and a warrior who put us on the right path back to Cashel.'

Attendants had helped Aíbnat dismount and the horses were being led away.

'So you became lost as well?' Fidelma said to her. 'I understood attendants were supposed to ride with the ladies to ensure that you all kept together to prevent such misadventures.'

The woman was disparaging. 'The attendants who were supposed to be looking after the ladies allowed them all to scatter like sheep when the threat of the boars came close. In trying to find my companions, I became lost. Either your attendants need better training or your brother stands in need of knowing how to choose better servants.'

Abbot Augaire came forward to act as a peacemaker. 'It is easy to get lost in these dark woods of Muman. People are often scattered in the best controlled of boar hunts.'

Aíbnat's features were unforgiving. She looked round in disapproval. 'Has my husband returned?'

Fidelma shook her head. 'Dúnchad Muirisci was the first to return. No one else has as yet.'

'Where is Dúnchad Muirisci?' demanded Aíbnat. Fidelma tried to ignore the arrogance in her voice.

'Across the courtyard and beyond that arched doorway you will find Brother Conchobhar's apothecary. He is being treated there.'

'Treated?' snapped Aíbnat. 'What ails the fellow?'

'A slight misfortune. He is bleeding a little.'

Aíbnat frowned and mumbled something before turning and hurrying in the direction Fidelma had indicated.

Abbot Augaire stood for a moment, looking after her, before glancing at Fidelma.

'What was the nature of the misfortune?' he asked quickly.

Fidelma grimaced indifferently. 'He says that he fell into a thorn bush, that's all.'

Once again a call from the guard at the gate told her that others were returning from the hunt. She recognised the short, dark figure of Fergus Fanat immediately. He was carrying his *bir* loosely in one hand, and Fidelma saw that the point of it had been bloodied. His companion was none other than Sister Marga. For the first time, she could observe the girl carefully. Her assessment of her when she had espied her at the game of *immán* on the previous day had been correct. She was attractive. Her robe and headdress, the *cabhal*, had been thrown back, and the form that was revealed was young and pleasing to the eye. The girl had fair skin and dark hair, and the features in the heart-shaped face were moulded into a happy expression. The smile had transformed her from the sombre maiden of the previous day. As she watched them ride through the gates into the courtyard, Fidelma had the impression of closeness between the two young people, almost of a courting couple.

Abbot Augaire watched them in disapproval before turning and following in Aíbnat's steps towards Brother Conchobhar's apothecary shop.

'Good hunting, Fergus Fanat?' called Fidelma as the pair halted and attendants came forward.

'A good chase but, alas, I cannot claim a victory,' replied the northern warrior cheerfully as he slid from his horse.

'Yet I see your spear point is bloodied,' Fidelma observed.

'Ah, indeed. The boar received a sharp prick as it sped by me, but that is about all. After that quick thrust, I never saw hide nor hair of it again. By the time I had finished looking for it, the hunt had moved on. It is a hunter's saying that you are allowed only one shot at taking the prize. I heard the cry further through the woods but I decided that I had had my chance and should return. It was fortunate that I did, for I was able to help a lady in distress.' He half bowed courteously to Sister Marga, who had also dismounted, and now blushed but stood without speaking while their horses were led away.

Fidelma looked quizzically at the girl. 'You were in distress?'

'I became separated from the other ladies and was lost in the wood for a while until Fergus . . .' She hesitated, blushing.

'Fergus Fanat in the train of Blathmac of Ulaidh,' said the young warrior quickly.

Fidelma frowned. Was the northern noble trying to cover up the fact that Sister Marga already knew his name? She addressed the girl.

'You may know that I am Fidelma of Cashel. You surprise me, sister. I have already noticed that you are interested in *immán* . . .' Sister Marga coloured hotly. The point had been scored, 'but I had not expected you to be interested in following the hunt. I was looking for you earlier. Even Sister Sétach had not realised that you had gone.'

The girl hesitated a moment and then tried to regain her composure.

'Sétach would have disapproved,' she said quietly. 'I could not resist the temptation of following the hunt, for my father was a hunter. He was one of the trackers of the Uí MacUais. I suddenly felt that I needed just one more time of freedom, of riding with the hounds and the sound of the hunters' horns. A good horse under me and . . .'

'Even Abbot Ultán's horse?' Fidelma observed quietly.

'The beast is not responsible for the rider,' she replied. Then a worried look came to her face. 'Does Brother Drón know that I took the abbot's horse?'

'I think so. The stable lads knew that you had requested a saddle to be put on the beast. In fact, I was informed that Brother Drón rode off after the hunt as well.'

Fergus Fanat was laughing uproariously. 'Well, if Brother Drón can seek solace in the hunt, you are surely not going to condemn Sister Marga for doing so? As for Ultán's horse, she only borrowed it for a few hours.'

'It is no concern of mine if she borrows Ultán's horse,' Fidelma agreed. 'She has now explained to me why she went on the hunt. However, I still would like a word with you, Marga . . . alone.'

The girl looked a little defensive. 'What about?'

'I want to speak to you about Abbot Ultán.'

A shadow seemed to cross Sister Marga's features, casting them as in grey stone. 'I have nothing to say.'

Fergus Fanat was still smiling. 'Come now, everyone within the vicinity of the lands of the Uí Thuirtrí has something to say about Ultán. Usually nothing good, though.'

Fidelma cast him a disapproving glance.

'Obviously now is not the time to discuss this,' she said to the girl. 'I will come to see you later on. Make yourself available for me and do not leave the fortress unless I say so.'

'You have no right . . .' protested the girl.

'I have every right,' Fidelma assured her grimly. She glanced at Fergus Fanat. 'I am sure that you will be able to instruct Sister Marga about the powers of a *dálaigh*?'

Fergus Fanat's expression changed to one of seriousness.

'The lady Fidelma is right. You'd best do as she says,' he advised.

The girl hesitated before agreeing. They moved away across the courtyard just as one of the guards in the gate tower blew a blast on a horn, signifying that the High King and his retinue were returning.

Finguine came hurrying over to join her.

'The hunt returns, your brother and the High King,' he announced unnecessarily. 'The attendants are carrying three boars, so the hunt has been good.'

Eadulf and Gormán were staring in disbelief at Brother Drón as he sat on his horse chuckling to himself at the news of Muirchertach Nár's death.

'God's justice,' he repeated. 'God's punishment for his slaughter of Abbot Ultán.'

'God had little to do with it,' Eadulf replied grimly, 'unless you are claiming to be the hand of God.'

The coldness in his voice caused Brother Drón to pause uncertainly.

'What do you mean by that?' he demanded.

'Muirchertach Nár was murdered, killed with his own hunting spear. The killer, according to the tracker who found him, rode off with his horse. We have found you riding with Muirchertach Nár's horse.'

Brother Drón stared at him for a moment and then swallowed.

'I did not kill him,' he said quietly.

'You want us to believe this story you tell about finding the horse?' Eadulf replied sarcastically.

'It is the truth.'

'You have blamed Muirchertach Nár for the death of Bishop Ultán. You wanted revenge and now here you are – the king dead and you riding with his horse.' Eadulf smiled grimly. 'It seems the facts are unequivocal.'

Gormán's hand was resting gently on the hilt of his sword.

'It is obvious, Brother Drón,' he said. 'We will return to Cashel and put this matter before the brehons.'

'I swear by the holy . . .'

'Save your protestations for the brehons,' Gormán replied sternly. 'There will be time enough to plead your case.'

Brother Drón looked visibly shaken and Eadulf had a moment of unease. The man was either a very good actor or he was telling the truth. Then Eadulf decided that the circumstances could bear no other interpretation.

'I'll ride in front,' he told Gormán. 'Brother Drón will follow me and you can bring up the rear to ensure that he does not attempt to flee.'

But Brother Drón was hunched in his saddle, looking shocked. From the arrogant, confident person of a few moments ago, the change was marked.

'He will not flee,' Gormán assured Eadulf grimly, hand still on the hilt of his sword.


'How can this have happened?' Brehon Ninnid demanded, his face flushed.

They had gathered in Colgú's private chamber – Colgú, Sechnassach, Brehon Barrán, Brehon Baithen, Brehon Ninnid and Fidelma. Most people had now returned from the hunt and the body of Muirchertach Nár had been quietly returned to the fortress under cover of blankets so that no one would recognise the body. It had been taken directly to Brother Conchobhar's apothecary.

Fidelma regarded the young brehon of Laigin coldly.

'That is what we have to discover,' she said.

Brehon Ninnid's features were formed into a cynical expression. 'I thought that Brother Eadulf had gone along on the hunt to see that no accident befell Muirchertach Nár?'

Fidelma coloured a little at the jibe. Her eyes narrowed slightly.

'Eadulf went along and was nearly killed when his horse threw him during a wild boar charge. At least he and Gormán were able to apprehend a suspect.'

'Brother Drón? I do not believe it,' Brehon Ninnid snapped. 'A religious of his background could never do such a thing.'

The High King Sechnassach looked worried. 'If Brother Drón has done this in retaliation for the killing of Ultán for which you were defending Muirchertach Nár, then I foresee dangers ahead.'

The High King's Chief Brehon, Barrán, explained:

'First, Ultán was a leading churchman, an emissary of Ard Macha. Blathmac, the king of Ulaidh, in whose kingdom Ard Macha lies, was able to assure me that he could control any protest that Ard Macha might make against the killing of their emissary, providing that he could assure Ségéne, the Comarb of Patrick, that the killer had been caught and punishment pronounced. But now that' – he glanced at Fidelma – 'the suspect has himself been slaughtered, things have changed. At the moment, we are told that Brother Drón of Cill Ria is the likely killer of the king of Connacht. Connacht may want retribution from Ard Macha. Before we tell Muirchertach's heir apparent, Dúnchad Muirisci, we need to give him some assurances. Remember that kings are answerable to their people. It is the people who are powerful in these matters because it is the people who ordain the king. The king does not ordain the people.'

Brehon Ninnid thrust out his chest arrogantly. 'Then the sooner I speak to Brother Drón the faster this matter will be resolved. I cannot believe a religious would contemplate a revenge killing of Muirchertach Nár.'

'You can see him whenever you wish,' Fidelma said.

'Good. We cannot wait for ever for a solution. Perhaps if we had prosecuted Muirchertach Nár immediately there would not have been any revenge killing.'

Brehon Barrán glanced at Fidelma. She was shaking her head in annoyance.

'You disagree?'

'It is all too easy,' she muttered.

The High King sat back and regarded her thoughtfully. 'I have great respect for you, Fidelma of Cashel. Indeed, I might not be High King if it were not for your ability to solve conundrums. I remember how you solved the riddle of the sacred sword of office. So I owe you much. I am prepared to give you more time to resolve this matter, but why do you say that the obvious path is too easy? Surely, it is a painful path that admits a king has killed an abbot and that a churchman has killed a king in vengeance?'

'If that is what happened, Sechnassach,' replied Fidelma softly.

Brehon Ninnid began to say something, but the High King waved him to silence.

'You have an alternative view?' he asked.

'I have no view at this time. If we have learnt anything during the countless centuries that our brehons have devised and developed our law code, it is that truth is more important than law. Are we not taught that truth is the highest power, the ultimate cause of all being? So, therefore, we must discover the truth in order that justice might prevail.'

Brehon Ninnid smiled in a superior fashion. 'When is the prosecution of the law contradicted by truth?'

'When a judge chooses expediency in favour of a slow, deliberate investigation,' Fidelma replied sharply. 'Do you not recall the old story of the gold cup of Cormac Mac Art?'

'Pagan fiddlesticks!' Brehon Ninnid replied in a tone of dismissal.

'To those who only see the story and fail to realise its symbolism. The story is that Cormac came to possess a gold cup that fell asunder into three sections if three lies were told and would come together again if three truths were told. The act of truth made the cup whole.'

'What are you saying, Fidelma?' demanded the High King.

'I am reminding you of the words of my mentor; of Morann's

advice to the princes of these kingdoms. Let them magnify truth, it will magnify them. Let them strengthen truth, it will strengthen them. Let them preserve truth, it will preserve them . . .'

The Chief Brehon Barrán made an impatient gesture with his hand. 'His words are well known, Fidelma.'

'Then, in justice, the High King must not rush to judgement, pursuing law and expediency rather than truth.'

Sechnassach sighed deeply. 'You have made your case. I have said that you will receive more time to hear the evidence, Fidelma. But that time is not unlimited.'

'*Tempus omnia revelat*,' Fidelma reminded him. Time reveals all things.

'That is so,' agreed the High King. 'But for mortals such as we, time is not infinite. Our decisions must be measured in days, not left to eternity. I will speak to Dúnchad Muirisci and also to Blathmac. They are civilised people. But once news of what has happened here is voiced through their kingdoms, they may have difficulty controlling the hotheads who will cry vengeance. Time may not grace us with solutions.'

Fidelma rose and inclined her head towards Sechnassach.

'I will bear that in mind,' she said quietly. 'But I will attempt to present the solution in days and not wait until eternity.'

She found Eadulf waiting with Gormán in the corridor outside her brother's chamber.

'Has any word of Muirchertach Nár's death been leaked?' she asked Eadulf anxiously.

'We think not. Only Rónán the tracker and two others who helped cover the body and bring it here know of its identity and they have sworn to keep silence until word is released. But it cannot be long before the news spreads. Someone will notice that Muirchertach is missing.'

Fidelma nodded thoughtfully. 'First, we must tell Aíbnat. Then we should see Dúnchad Muirisci, for he is now heir assumptive to Muirchertach's throne.'

'What about Brother Drón?'

'What has been done with him?'

'We handed him over to Caol, who has taken him to one of the chambers and stands guard over him,' Gormán said quickly. 'I am told that he is still protesting his innocence. Quite volubly.'

'We will not keep him waiting longer than we have to,' Fidelma replied. 'You may tell Caol that Brehon Ninnid is allowed to see him. Eadulf and I first have to speak with the lady Aíbnat.'

Aíbnat met them at the door of her chamber. She stared with open hostility at Fidelma before glancing at Eadulf with an expression that left him in no doubt what she thought of him.

'What do you want now? My husband has not returned from the hunt,' she demanded, her voice brittle.

'We have some bad news for you, lady,' Fidelma said softly.

Aíbnat stiffened slightly. 'Bad news?'

'It is your husband. He has . . . been hurt.'

Aíbnat's expression was controlled. Then, as Fidelma hesitated, she recognised something in her expression.

'He is dead?' she whispered.

Fidelma tried to express sympathy towards this arrogant woman. 'I am afraid he is,' was all that she could say.

Aíbnat turned quickly away and stood with her back to them, her shoulders slightly hunched. Fidelma followed her into the room, Eadulf at her side. He closed the door gently and they waited awkwardly for a moment.

'Who killed him?' Aíbnat asked after a while, turning back to them.

Eadulf exchanged a glance of surprise with Fidelma.

'What makes you think that someone killed him, lady,' he said, 'and that it was not an accident in the hunt?'

Aíbnat swung her gaze round to Eadulf, her features under perfect control. There was now no hint of moisture in her eyes.

'I know my husband's abilities. He was a good horseman. Also, it was obvious from the threat that his life was in danger.'

'The threat? Danger?' queried Fidelma in surprise. 'Has he been threatened?'

'A raven's feather was found on the pillow of our bed last night when we returned from the evening meal.'

Fidelma's eyes widened a little. 'Did you report this to the guard? I was not told.'

Aíbnat shook her head. 'Muirchertach dismissed it, thinking it was just a silly gesture from one of Ultán's followers. That man Drón has been muttering dark curses of vengeance. But we thought we were well protected by your warriors. You have failed us. You failed to protect us, just as you failed to protect Ultán.'

'You should have reported this,' Fidelma said, ignoring her anger.

'Whether we did or not, there can be no excuse for not protecting Muirchertach,' she snapped.

Eadulf was frowning. 'What is the relevance of this raven's feather?' he asked Fidelma.

'It is a symbol of death and battles,' she said quickly. 'The goddess of death often appears in the form of a raven. Where is the feather now?'

Aíbnat shrugged. 'My husband had it.'

The woman seemed to be emotionally bearing up quite well, but then Fidelma remembered that she had not seemed particularly close to her husband when she had interviewed them on the previous day.

'Your husband's body has been taken to the apothecary of Brother Conchobhar here, lady. It will be washed and prepared, and taken to the chapel where the High King wishes it to receive all honour while you and Muirchertach's *tánaiste* decide its fate.'

'Its fate?'

'As king of Connacht, it is his right that his remains be taken back to his kingdom in pomp and state.'

Aíbnat nodded slowly. 'That will be up to Dúnchad to decide. Muirchertach's father lies in the abbey of Cluain Mic Nois with many other kings of Connacht.' She paused and added: 'Has the man who killed Muirchertach been captured?'

'Man?' queried Fidelma softly.

Aíbnat's face was without emotion. 'I presume whoever killed Muirchertach was a man.'

'We are investigating.'

'Well, all you have to do is look among Ultán's followers. There is only one among them capable of the deed of vengeance. However, I shall have my attendants prepare for my leaving here tomorrow. There is no need for me to remain. Dúnchad Muirisci will doubtless take care of the obsequies and the disposal of Muirchertach's body.'

Fidelma stared at her thoughtfully for a moment. 'I am afraid, lady, you will have to remain here until there is a resolution of this matter,' she said quietly. 'You will leave only when I say so.'

Aíbnat blinked in surprise at being contradicted. 'Do you know to whom you speak? You may be sister to the king of Muman but I am wife to the king of Connacht.'

Fidelma smiled coldly. 'You are now the widow of the king of Connacht who lies murdered and unburied in our chapel. I am the *dálaigh* given to his defence in the matter of the crimes he was accused of and therefore now the investigator of his murder. You stand before the law equal as all others are in this case.'

Aíbnat's eyes narrowed. 'I will see Sechnassach, the High King, and tell him of your impertinence.'

'Excellent. Sechnassach is well acquainted with the law and how things must be governed. In the meantime, should you wish it, a guard will continue at your door . . . for your protection. You may also speak to the Chief Brehon Barrán.'

Aíbnat stared at her as if not believing her ears. 'I will certainly speak to him,' she snapped. 'You may send the Abbot Augaire to me. I have need of some religious solace.'

Fidelma did not reply but merely turned and, followed by Eadulf, left the room.

Outside, Eadulf noticed that she was trembling slightly in anger.

In answer to his glance she shrugged. 'There are few people who have such an effect on me, Eadulf. The woman is so arrogant and cold that I feel I would like to strike her on the cheek.'

Eadulf reached out and squeezed her arm. 'That is unlike you. However, I have to say that she did not leave a favourable impression on me. In fact, her coldness at the news of her husband's death was surprising.'

'I do not think there was much love lost between them,' Fidelma agreed.

'She is right about vengeance, though. Brother Drón's story is so weak that it is laughable. When we came upon him leading Muirchertach's horse it all fell into place. By the way, why didn't you tell her that we are holding Drón for the murder?'

'We have to be certain of everything in this matter, Eadulf.'

'But it all fits together,' protested Eadulf. 'And now we hear that a raven's feather, the symbol of death, was left on their pillow last night. A threat of vengeance for Ultán's killing.'

Fidelma regarded him seriously. 'That is the one thing that doesn't fit.'

'Why not?'

'If anything, it rather precludes Brother Drón from involvement as it is a token of the Old Faith and not the new one. Why would one of the New Faith send a symbol of the goddess of death and battles?'

Eadulf thought for a moment. 'Old ways die hard. Maybe he put the feather there to mislead whoever took on the investigation – or maybe it was someone else entirely who put it there – someone unconnected with the killing.'

'Perhaps,' conceded Fidelma. 'Does a raven's feather have the same meaning among the pagan Saxons as it does here?'

Eadulf considered. 'The women Woden sends to gather the corpses of the slain are accompanied by ravens, so the raven is always a bird of ill-omen.'

'Then there is no need to explain the symbolism. We'd better have a word with Dúnchad Muirisci now that we have told Aíbnat.' She halted suddenly with a frown. 'You mentioned Rónán the tracker. I have known him since I was a little girl here. He is a good huntsman, so we must respect what he has to say. I presume that you have checked all he told you?'

'We were able to follow the tracks he pointed out quite well for a while before we lost them on the stony ground,' said Eadulf. 'Anyway, the fact that we caught Brother Drón with Muirchertach's horse seemed certain enough to me.'

'Rónán specifically mentioned to you that the horse ridden by the person who met Muirchertach in the wood, and who appears to be his attacker, had a particular identifying mark,' Fidelma pointed out patiently.

Eadulf stared at her for a moment and then gave a groan.

'I meant to check that as soon as we came back to the fortress,' he said. 'That would be an argument that Drón could not deny.'

'Then you'd better check it now,' Fidelma instructed. 'We should do that before going to break the news to Dúnchad Muirisci and certainly before we go to question Brother Drón further. I'll meet you at Brother Conchobhar's apothecary.'

Eadulf hurried away, rebuking himself for overlooking the point that could so easily have confirmed Brother's Drón's guilt. He had recounted everything to Fidelma: the finding of the body, Rónán's observations on the tracks, and the overtaking of Drón. To her credit, Fidelma had not pointed out the obvious but had diplomatically pushed Eadulf into a realisation of what was needed.

Eadulf crossed the courtyard to the stables and found the *gilla scuir*, the head stable lad. He asked to examine the horse that Brother Drón had ridden. The man looked curiously at him but nodded assent, taking a lantern and leading the way to the stalls.

'I want to examine its shoes,' Eadulf explained. 'I am not very good with horses. How do I go about it?'

The *gilla scuir*'s expression became somewhat pitying but he said nothing. Fidelma was an expert horsewoman but the stable lad knew all about Eadulf's unease with horses.

'Hold the lantern, then, Brother Eadulf,' he instructed. 'Which hoof did you want to see?'

'Front left.'

The stable lad entered the stall, talking softly to the animal, touching its muzzle so that the beast would recognise him, before bending forward and picking up the foreleg, so that the underside of the hoof could be seen.

'Come into the stall with the lantern,' he said. 'Gently now, and hold it so that you can see what you need. What were you looking for? A loose shoe?'

Eadulf shook his head. He peered at the hoof. There was nothing wrong with the horseshoe, no crack, no uneven quality. His mouth compressed to hide his disappointment while he considered the matter.

'Let's look at the others,' he said, just in case Rónán had been mistaken as to which leg it was.

It took a very short time to ascertain that there were no distinguishing marks on any of the shoes of the animal that Brother Drón had ridden.

Outside the stall Eadulf stood thinking carefully. The only

conclusion he could come to was that Brother Drón was not the rider who had led Muirchertach's horse from the scene of the slaying. Did this mean he was not the killer? He came back to the present to find the *gilla scuir* looking at him expectantly.

'What were you looking for, Brother Eadulf?' he asked.

'I was looking for a horse with a cracked or broken shoe.'

The lad's features broke into a smile. 'In that case, brother, you were looking at the wrong beast.' He pointed to another stall. 'That one came in this evening with the shoe cracked in two. A bad casting of the metal. It happens sometimes. I'm happy to say it wasn't cast here. One of those northern smiths did that.'

'Where was the cracked shoe?' demanded Eadulf.

'On the left foreleg. Oh, our smith has replaced it now,' he called as Eadulf made towards the stall. 'But there's no doubt about it. The left foreleg. I helped replace it myself.'

Eadulf turned back eagerly. 'But whose horse is it?'

The stable lad rubbed his chin. 'Dúnchad Muirisci is his name. The noble prince from Connacht.'

# chapter fourteen

Fidelma looked thoughtful as Eadulf finished telling her what he had discovered. Gormán had diplomatically left them together in the corner of old Brother Conchobhar's apothecary to discuss matters in the light of this information.

'There is no question that Brother Drón's horse did not have a cracked shoe?' she asked gently.

'None,' replied Eadulf, somewhat bitterly. 'I should have checked immediately. All four shoes were in good condition. Rónán told us that the horse that was ridden from the scene of the killing had a split horseshoe on his left foreleg. That is a description of Dúnchad Muirisci's horse.'

'Well, as I have said, we may trust Rónán. So from what we now know, the story that Brother Drón told you, that of simply finding Muirchertach's horse, could be true.'

Eadulf was irritated. '*Could* be true, yes. But it seems odd that the killer should leave the scene of the crime riding his horse and leading Muirchertach's for quite a way before deciding to abandon it.'

'I mean it as no insult when I say that you are not much of a horseman, Eadulf.'

'It is true, I'll not deny it,' Eadulf said stiffly. 'So what have I missed?'

'That Muirchertach's horse probably followed the killer's mount of its own volition. Horses do not have to be led. When the killer found that the king's horse was trailing him, which would have been a sure accusation, he dismounted and looped the reins into a bush so that the beast was tethered. Then he rode away.'

'I see the logic of that,' agreed Eadulf reluctantly. 'I wouldn't have thought that a horse would follow a strange animal, though.'

Fidelma smiled. 'That's just it. It probably would not. But it would follow a horse that it was familiar with.'

Eadulf's eyebrows rose in enlightenment. 'Dúnchad Muirisci's horse and the one belonging to Muirchertach were both out of the same stable. I see. Still, I feel angry that I did not spot the business of the split shoe before.'

'I share the responsibility. When you told me, I could have said who the beast belonged to. I was in the courtyard when Dúnchad Muirisci returned from the hunt. The *gilla scuir* mentioned the split shoe on the *tánaiste*'s horse. Furthermore, his hand was bloody from falling into a thorn bush, or so he said. And he said that he had lost his hunting spear.'

'Then he is our man! It is obvious!'

Fidelma grimaced wryly.

'Just as the guilt of Brother Drón was obvious?' she asked sceptically, shaking her head. 'Patience. We must go carefully, Eadulf. Especially now that Dúnchad Muirisci succeeds Muirchertach Nár as king of Connacht. We are dealing with men of power in this affair, so we must be sure of our accusations.'

'But just as Brother Drón had a motive to kill Muirchertach Nár, Dúnchad Muirisci had an equally good motive: that he would succeed to the kingship of Connacht.'

'But what motive had Dúnchad to kill Abbot Ultán?'

'Well . . . none.'

'Then you are saying that we have two killers here – the one who killed Ultán and the one who killed Muirchertach Nár.'

'Why not? Muirchertach could have killed Ultán and Dúnchad could have killed Muirchertach. Two separate murders.'

'I am not satisfied that Muirchertach Nár killed Ultán. If he had been nursing thoughts of vengeance against the man all these years then he would have invented a better story. He would have had a better plan than he did. The very fact that there was no love lost between Muirchertach and his wife makes me wonder, and not for the first time, why Muirchertach would pursue the matter on behalf of a wife who did not care. There is something here that continues to irritate me.'

'What should we do now? Release Brother Drón?'

'We will have to withdraw the guard and release him from confinement,' Fidelma said after a moment's reflection. 'But, for the time being, he is only free within the bounds of the fortress. We must now find out what story Dúnchad Muirisci has to tell us.'

Dúnchad Muirisci, his hand newly bandaged, greeted them with some surprise.

'I have told you all I can about Abbot Ultán's death. There is nothing more I can say.' He seemed slightly flustered and evasive.

'It is not his death that we have to speak of,' Fidelma replied. 'May we enter?'

The *tánaiste* of Connacht stood indecisively, which allowed the determined Fidelma to brush him aside and enter. She halted abruptly and, for a moment, even she was surprised.

Standing in the chamber looking nervous was Sister Sétach.

'I am surprised to see you here, sister,' Fidelma said calmly.

The girl made no reply, seeming to look at Dúnchad Muirisci for some guidance.

Eadulf had followed behind Fidelma and was equally surprised when he saw who the girl was.

Dúnchad Muirisci coughed, his face red with embarrassment. 'Sister Sétach came to see me to discuss the death of Abbot Ultán.'

Fidelma raised a cynical eyebrow. 'What aspect of the death?' she asked, looking at Sister Sétach.

'About the death of the girl that this whole matter is supposed to be about. About the death of Searc.'

'That is interesting,' Fidelma said pointedly, as if waiting for an explanation.

The two were silent for a moment.

'We were trying to see, now that Abbot Ultán is dead . . .' Sister Sétach was red in the face and she hunched her shoulders as she spoke.

'Trying to see whether some peace could be declared on this matter between Connacht and Cill Ria,' ended Dúnchad Muirisci hurriedly.

Fidelma glanced quickly at Eadulf.

'So you think that you are now in a position to make such a declaration?' she asked Dúnchad Muirisci softly.

The heir apparent smiled deprecatingly. 'It is clear that Sister Sétach could not approach Muirchertach in the current circumstances. As I am *tánaiste* it is obvious that she would first speak to me. Anyway, the matter is of no consequence. Sister Sétach and I will discuss it later.' He glanced to the girl with a nod as of dismissal and she took it as such.

Eadulf wondered whether Fidelma was going to hold her back but she allowed the girl to hasten from the room.

'Now,' Dúnchad Muirisci said, drawing himself together and trying to regain control of the situation. 'I have told you all I know about the death of Ultán.'

'As I have said, it is not his death we came to speak of. This morning, on the boar hunt, Muirchertach Nár was killed.'

If Dúnchad Muirisci was feigning astonishment he was very good, thought Eadulf.

'But he was a good horseman, an excellent spearshot,' muttered the *tánaiste*. 'How did the boar get him?' Then he paused. 'And why has no word of this reached me before now?'

'You seem to think he was killed in a hunting accident, Dúnchad Muirisci. He was not,' she replied.

'He was not?' The noble looked bemused. 'Then how?'

'He was attacked and murdered with his own spear.'

Dúnchad Muirisci took a step back and sat down quickly in a chair.

'Murdered? Who?' His eyes cleared. 'A vengeance killing?'

'We are investigating that.'

'That weasel, Brother Drón! Where was he at the time?'

'As I say, we are investigating.'

Dúnchad Muirisci frowned as a thought suddenly occurred to him.

Fidelma smiled thinly. 'That means that you are the new king of Connacht, provided your *derbhfine* is willing.' The *derbhfine* was the electoral college of the family, usually consisting of three generations from its last head, who would chose his successor.

'Of course, of course,' Dúnchad Muirisci muttered.

'It also makes you a prime suspect,' Eadulf added dryly.

'A suspect?' Dúnchad Muirisci stared at him stupidly for a moment and then anger began to form on his face.

Before he could frame a rejoinder, Fidelma added: 'That is

absolutely true, Dúnchad Muirisci. So perhaps you could begin by telling us how you came by that wound on your hand.'

Eadulf wondered why Fidelma was not going straight to the damning evidence of the split horseshoe but decided not to interfere.

Dúnchad Muirisci hesitated. 'I told you when I arrived. Down in the courtyard.'

'Tell me again.'

'My horse stumbled and I was pushed into a thorn bush. That's where I scratched my hand.'

'And you, by all accounts, an excellent rider and hunter,' murmured Fidelma.

The Connacht noble controlled his obvious resentment at her gentle sarcasm. 'The truth is that I was caught unawares. The boar came out of nowhere and startled my horse. And if you must know the total truth, my mount reared up and I was taken by surprise and fell off, into a thorn bush. By the time I was on my feet, the horse had galloped off.' He looked defiant. 'It can happen to anyone easily enough.'

Eadulf looked uncomfortable. He knew exactly how easily it could happen.

'So now you say that you fell into a thorn bush and found yourself without your horse,' Fidelma prompted. 'What then?'

'The boar had vanished. I was left on foot. I cursed myself for a fool. I knew that if the others learned of my misfortune, I would be shamed. That is why I did not tell you before. I, Dúnchad Muirisci of the Uí Fiachracha Muaide, whose bloodline is that of the great High King, Niall Noigiallach! If it was known that I had been unhorsed in a mere hunt, then the satirists of the five kingdoms would claim that Muirchertach Nár had been succeeded by Dúnchad Náire.'

Despite his concentration on the matter in hand, Eadulf's attention was caught. He knew that the word *nár*, which had been the epithet appended to Muirchertach's name, meant noble, honourable and generous, but now it seemed that a similar word, born of the same root, had come to mean disgraced and shamed.

'I decided, then, that if I recovered my horse, I would pretend that I had never lost it, in order to preserve my reputation.' Honour and reputation meant a great deal to the nobles and warriors of Éireann.

Dúnchad Muirisci sat back. 'That's the truth of it,' he said simply. 'I am not proud of it.'

'But you found your horse again and gave out the story as you told it to me and Finguine when you returned to the fortress,' Fidelma concluded.

Dúnchad Muirisci looked uncomfortable. He hesitated before replying and Fidelma leaned forward.

'So you did *not* recover your horse immediately? You lied. So what is the truth? I want the whole truth now.'

'The truth?' he asked. 'Is it so important? I found the horse again – what does time matter?'

'The truth is always important,' she assured him.

'I did not find my horse for a long time,' he confessed. 'I was on foot for what seemed ages. In fact, my long *bir* became an encumbrance. I finally tossed it aside in the bushes, to be the better able to travel on foot. I wandered about for a long time trying to find the animal. I had almost given up and decided that I would have to face the shame of the loss and come back to Cashel on foot.'

'But you did find it,' Fidelma pressed. 'How was that?'

'That is curious,' Dúnchad said. 'I came through the forest to a place where there was a hilly mound.'

Eadulf now leaned forward eagerly. 'Describe it,' he insisted.

The Connacht noble looked surprised at his intervention but then shrugged and gave a quick description.

'But did you not go up to the mound and look down in the gully beyond?' Eadulf asked.

Dúnchad Muirisci shook his head. 'Is it important?'

'It is important, because that is where Muirchertach Nár was killed,' explained Eadulf. 'His body lay in the gully beyond that mound.'

The Connacht noble appeared shocked. 'I did not know. I had come to the foot of the mound when I heard the sound of horses nearby.'

'Horses?'

'Having given up on saving my reputation, I gave a shout and hurried towards them, thinking that I might be able to get a ride behind one of the other members of the hunt. Distinctly, I heard horses. I thought that I had not been heard. The track these riders had taken led back in the direction of Cashel and so I felt there was nothing for it but to set my footsteps along that path. I had not gone more than a short distance when I came to an area where the path turned rocky and just then I saw my own mount. It was waiting docilely there.'

'You said this was curious,' Fidelma said. 'In what fashion was it so?'

'My horse was tethered to a bush.'

'The reins were not simply entangled?'

Dúnchad Muirisci shook his head quickly. 'I know the difference between entanglement and the way reins are wrapped over a branch so that the animal does not wander.'

'There was no one about? Not another horse tethered there?'

'No one about and no other horse.'

'So what did you do?'

'I decided to keep to my initial story. I mounted and returned to the fortress. Oh, I forgot. I noticed the horse was limping slightly, so checked and found it had cracked a shoe. It may have been on the rocky area. It was re-shod on my return. Now,' he looked from Fidelma to Eadulf and back again, 'tell me what this is about. You think that I killed my king?'

'Tell me, what was your relationship to Muirchertach? I don't mean your blood relationship.'

'I am . . . was . . . his *tánaiste*,' replied Dúnchad Muirisci hesitantly.

'So you were close to him? He was a good friend?'

Dúnchad shook his head immediately. 'He was of the Uí Fiachracha Aidni. I am of the Uí Fiachracha Muaide. I am five generations in descent from Náth Í, of the senior line, while Muirchertach Nár was eight generations from the second son of Náth Í. We were not even close as cousins, let alone as friends.'

'But, presumably, you were friendly enough for you to be in accordance in governing the kingdom?'

'We had an agreement that I would govern the western territories of Connacht and Muirchertach would spend his time in the eastern territories, and it worked well. He was, to be truthful, not a man who was assiduous in his pursuit of government. He preferred the pleasures of kingship to its duties.'

'Now that he is dead, what will happen to the lady Aíbnat? I believe that she is not grief-stricken at his demise?'

Dúnchad shrugged indifferently. 'Doubtless she will be disappointed that she no longer has a position of power. But then her family is of the Uí Briúin Aí. Their word is law in northern Connacht and we have little say in the government of their territories. They have long claimed the right to be regarded as kings of Connacht. They descend from Bríon the brother of Niall Noigiallach but only Aíbnat's father ever became king, and he held the throne for twenty-five years. Aíbnat always thought that her brother Cellach should have been *tánaiste* if not king. She will doubtless support him when the assembly meets to choose my *tánaiste*.'

'Was her position all that she cared about?' asked Fidelma. 'I certainly received the impression that she did not think highly of her husband.'

'I doubt if she felt highly about anyone except herself,' Dúnchad confirmed. 'My cousin's rule was short and not altogether spectacular. His father, Guaire, eclipsed him in deeds and valour and in bestowing lands to the church so that they might flourish. He worked hard to buy people's loyalty and praise rather than earn it.'

Fidelma looked carefully at Dúnchad. 'You sound as if you disapproved of him.'

'Disapproved? A good word. I'll be honest with you, even if it does endorse your obvious suspicion that I had a role in his death. I did not like my cousin. He was a vain man and he had acquired a reputation. But, on the other hand, I did not hate him to the point that I would kill him.'

'A reputation?' Fidelma smiled. 'A moment ago you were all for reputations and protecting them.'

'Not the sort of reputation that my cousin had acquired. He had a reputation as a *clúanaire*.'

Eadulf recognised the word as being concerned with deceit, but he had not come across its use in this fashion before. He asked Fidelma to explain.

'It means someone who beguiles another, usually a seducer of women.'

Dúnchad nodded in confirmation. 'That is exact what his reputation was. They said that no noble's lady was safe in his company.'

'What did the lady Aíbnat think of that?'

'I don't think she was concerned if it didn't threaten her position at court. She was content to let Muirchertach Nár get on with his own life, provided it did not interfere with hers.'

'I see. And what were your thoughts on that?'

'I thought that so long as he did not jeopardise the safety of the kingdom, there was no harm to it.'

'I presume that none of the ladies involved ever complained?'

'Not to my knowledge. If they did, he would simply have paid them and their husbands, if husbands there were, whatever their price was for silence.'

'And yet one would have thought that he was possessed of high morals. He went to such lengths to bring Abbot Ultán to justice over what he considered to be a slight to his wife's younger sister,' Eadulf pointed out.

'A man can have double standards,' said Dúnchad. 'Or set standards for others that he did not live up to himself. His double standards were somewhat peculiar in respect to the death of Aíbnat's sister, for the story was that he was attracted to her himself.'

'Did Aíbnat know that?'

Dúnchad Muirisci raised a shoulder and let it fall as an eloquent comment. 'It was common knowledge for a while. It was after she had come back from Cill Ria, shocked by the death of the boy with whom she had apparently fallen in love. I think Muirchertach tried to press his attentions on Searc, if you know what I mean. There was a problem and Aíbnat was angry for a time. But then the girl committed suicide and that was that. She obviously cared too much for the boy who was drowned, or killed, or whatever it was that happened to him.'

'But then Muirchertach sent Brother Augaire to Abbot Ultán for recompense over the suicide?'

'That is true,' conceded Dúnchad. 'Augaire had actually witnessed the suicide, traced the girl's identity and come to report it to Muirchertach and Aíbnat. Augaire was incensed at her death – a passionate man, Augaire. He saw himself as a vengeful spirit setting out to exact recompense. Muirchertach went along with it. Even appointed him as abbot of Conga. As I said, Muirchertach was full of double standards.'

'So what you are saying is that both Aíbnat and Muirchertach Nár had their individual faults but that they were compatible enough?' said Fidelma.

'Of course. We all have our faults.'

'But Muirchertach Nár's faults did not warrant his death,' Eadulf remarked.

Dúnchad Muirisci blinked and shook his head. 'It is obvious why he was killed. I said so at the start, as soon as you told me he had been murdered.'

'Vengeance?'

'Of course vengeance!' Dúnchad Muirisci was emphatic. 'That man, Brother Drón . . . he was Abbot Ultán's comrade, not just a travelling companion. He was steward at Cill Ria. And what of the others Abbot Ultán brought with him? Any one of them could have killed him. Come to think of it, wasn't Sister Marga riding on the hunt? That is scandalous enough in itself, but maybe it has a deeper significance too.'

Fidelma stood up abruptly. 'We will finish for the time being, Dúnchad Muirisci, but you, like everyone else, will remain now within these walls until we have done with this investigation.' Something had been worrying her for some time and now she finally dredged the question from the back of her mind. 'On the night that Abbot Ultán was killed, you told me that Abbot Augaire and you were playing *brandubh*.'

'We were.'

'Abbot Augaire left you close to midnight?'

'He did.'

'Then you said that after you went to bed shouting in the corridor disturbed you. You did not investigate because you had been disturbed already that night. What was the cause of your first disturbance?'

Dúnchad Muirisci appeared puzzled for a moment and then his face cleared. He smiled.

'I had almost forgotten. After Abbot Augaire had left, I was preparing for bed when there was a cry and the sound of someone falling outside my door. I went quickly to it and opened it. I found that weasel Brother Drón picking himself up.'

'How do you mean?'

'He had tripped and fallen outside my door.' Dúnchad smiled. 'I did not ask him how he came to fall but he sheepishly said he had been hurrying after someone and tripped. Easily done, I suppose. Anyway, it was nothing to do with me. That was why I did not respond to the second disturbance, which I later realised must have been the discovery of Ultán's murder.'

There was a silence, and then the Connacht noble rose hesitantly.

'So what of Muirchertach Nár?' he asked. 'What will happen now?'

'At the moment his body lies in the apothecary of Brother Conchobhar,' Fidelma replied. 'It will be washed and prepared ready for burial.'

'He should be taken to the great abbey of Cluain Mic Nois where his forefathers are buried, as are all legitimate kings of Connacht.'

'That may not be possible. Neither you nor Aíbnat, nor even your close personal attendants, may leave here with it until the investigation is over.'

'So you would keep the body here?' Dúnchad Muirisci was aghast.

'Let us hope that it will not be for long,' Fidelma replied gravely.

Eadulf grimaced wryly. 'We can be thankful that it is the depth of winter and the days are cold,' he added.

Outside in the corridor, he turned to Fidelma. 'It is an unlikely story that he is telling. I think it is not to be believed.'

'Unfortunately it is the unlikely stories that tend to be the truth,' Fidelma commented. 'However, I agree that we cannot take it at face value.'

'Especially the reason given as to why Sister Sétach was visiting. I don't think that promiscuity had anything to do with it.'

Fidelma smiled briefly. 'An interesting choice of word, Eadulf.'

'I merely meant that Sister Sétach would be immoderate in her behaviour if . . . well, you know. I believe that she could have only just met Dúnchad Muirisci.'

Fidelma suddenly smiled. 'Sometimes, Eadulf, you unconsciously put your finger on a point that eludes me.'

Eadulf looked bemused. 'Something about Sister Sétach? I don't see what.'

Fidelma shook her head. 'Something about Sister Marga. I now want a word with that young woman.'

They were walking to the hostel for the religieuse when, turning a corner, they nearly collided with Abbot Augaire. He halted and frowned at them.

'How does your investigation proceed, Sister Fidelma?' he inquired sharply. 'I have just come from Aíbnat. It is strange that you keep this matter so secret. Anyway, it means that Muirchertach Nár's body awaits disposal. Can you not conclude this matter so that we may accompany it to Connacht for burial?'

'Not yet,' Fidelma said calmly.

'Rumour has it that Brother Drón was caught with Muirchertach's horse.'

'Rumours spread quickly,' muttered Fidelma. 'But things must take their course, Augaire. You know that. However, speaking of Brother Drón, I did want to ask you a question. On the night of the murder of Abbot Ultán, did you see Brother Drón in the corridor when you left Dúnchad Muirisci's chamber?'

Abbot Augaire paused for a moment. 'Was he there?'

'I am asking you.'

'So far as I am aware, I left Dúnchad Muirisci, walked to my chamber without seeing anyone and was there for the rest of the night. I shouldn't think Brother Drón could have been lurking anywhere unless . . .' He paused.

'Unless?' pressed Fidelma.

Abbot Augaire grimaced dismissively. 'There is a sort of alcove there in the corridor. You must know it. There are several in the corridors here. I was going to say, unless he was lurking there . . . but then I walked past it and there was no one to be seen. Of course, he could have been standing on the ledge that runs outside the alcove window.' He chuckled. 'But I don't think Brother Drón is the sort to submit himself to such dangers. The ledge has several loose blocks along it.'

Eadulf smiled grimly.

'I think that we can discount Brother Drón's playing such acrobatics,' he said firmly.

Fidelma and Eadulf found Sister Marga in the women's hostel. The religieuse had just come from the bathing house, and there was the faint odour of some fragrance. Fidelma sniffed as she entered, for she could smell a combination of scents. She could identify *fedlend*, the soft smell of honeysuckle, but not the more powerful odour. Sister Sétach was fussing over her companion with some toiletry and looked up in annoyance as Fidelma came in.

'Are we never to be left alone?' she snapped.

Sister Marga glanced at her companion in surprise but Fidelma ignored the petulant tone.

'I am, as I have said, a *dálaigh*, Sister Sétach,' she said mildly, 'and must encroach on you as many times as is necessary for my investigation. However, it is Sister Marga that we have come to see, and I would appreciate it if you could leave us for a minute or two.'

Sister Sétach stood for a few moments, her jaw working slightly, as if she were considering this. Then she looked down at Sister Marga.

'Do you want me to go?' she demanded brusquely.

'I think it is better to do as Sister Fidelma asks,' Marga replied in an almost apologetic tone.

With a loud sniff of disapproval, Sister Sétach turned and left the room. Sister Marga looked after her with a frown before turning back to Fidelma and Eadulf.

'She does not sleep well and that makes her irritable. I think she believes it is her duty to protect me,' she said apologetically. 'She was at Cill Ria when I joined and considers herself my senior.'

'Yet it was you, so I understand, who asked her to come on this trip?'

Sister Marga looked startled for a moment. 'She told you that?'

'It is not true, then?'

'Oh, partially true, I suppose. I felt sorry for her, being so upset at not being chosen to accompany this embassy from the Comarb of Patrick. There was space for another one to help keep the records and she kept pressing me about it, so I asked Abbot Ultán if he would consider taking her as well. But Brother Drón, in fact, had already suggested that Sétach should be a member of the embassy and Abbot Ultán had agreed to it even before I asked.'

'Well, we will return to Sister Sétach in a moment. Let me start with you. You are from Cill Ria, of course. Are you of the Uí Thuirtrí?'

The girl shook her head. 'I am of the Ciannachta. My clan lands are to the north-west of their country. I went into the religious at Ard Stratha and that is where I learned to write a good hand and to read Latin, Greek and Hebrew. I was good at keeping records and copying texts. I was told that Cill Ria was looking for good scholars and so, a few years ago, I went to the abbey there. At first, the work was good. I was given texts to copy and to compile into books. But we are all allowed to make one mistake in life. The decision to go to Cill Ria was mine,' she ended ruefully.

'A mistake?' queried Fidelma. 'Did you know how the abbey was run before you went there?'

Sister Marga shook her head.

'Had you heard about Abbot Ultán?'

She gestured negatively again. 'I came to hate Cill Ria and the *Penitentials*. Moreover, I hated Ultán.'

'If you hated it all so much, why did you not leave?'

Sister Marga simply laughed. There was bitterness in her laugh but she made no reply.

'Your companion does not share your hate,' pointed out Fidelma.

'She is not my companion. She would like to be, if you know what I mean. I feel sorry for her. She is devoted to Cill Ria and appears to believe Abbot Ultán is . . . *was* some kind of saint.'

'You make it clear that you do not,' Fidelma observed.

'I not only believe but *know* he was not. There were two Ultáns. There was the false image of the pious abbot that he presented to the world. Oh, I know all about his miraculous conversion on the seas and what he was before that. However, I knew the second Ultán, the real Ultán.'

'You must explain.'

'Ultán had persuaded the Comarb of Patrick at Ard Macha that he was changed, as Paul had changed on the road to Damascus . . . that parable was always being spoken of in Cill Ria. Brother Drón was fond of using it to stifle any questions about the sincerity of the abbot.

Ultán enforced his *Penitentials* with such strictness simply to show how pious he was. That was the face he presented to the world. It was not the face I saw.'

'Which was?'

'Which was still the thief, the robber, who seized goods when he could maintain they were offerings that must be freely given to the church. He had individuals flogged for what he claimed to be sacrilege. He enjoyed inflicting physical punishment on people. At least one person a day was sentenced to a whipping for what he claimed were impure thoughts. He was even responsible for the death of several.'

'All this you saw in your time at Cill Ria?'

Sister Marga nodded grimly. 'And more.'

'More?'

'He used some of the girls from the women's house to satiate his lust.'

'Sister Sétach?'

'Never her, but perhaps that is not strange.'

'Did he use you?' Fidelma asked sharply.

Sister Marga coloured and then shrugged with a defiant gesture. 'How can the weak defend themselves from the strong? But all the time I remembered what my father used to say – there is no tide so strong that it doesn't ebb. I waited and prayed for any opportunity to escape.'

Eadulf leaned forward with a frown. 'Did you kill Abbot Ultán?'

The girl regarded him with a serious expression. 'I wish that I had possessed that courage. I did not.'

'Why did you come on this trip with him, if you so detested him?'

'Do you think that I had a choice? Besides, I thought there was a possibility that it might offer me an opportunity to escape. But Brother Drón was always keeping a watchful eye on me. And so was Sister Sétach.'

'You are saying that both Drón and Sétach are watching you?'

'I think Ultán became suspicious of my motives and ordered them to do so. They still do. This morning was the first time that I was able to escape from them. I think that they did not realise that I would dare seize the opportunity to leave with Ultán newly dead.

I managed to persuade the stable lad to saddle up Ultán's own horse so that I could ride out with the hunt. I had intended to ride east to Laigin.'

Fidelma saw the defiance in the girl's face. 'So you intended to flee Cashel entirely, not merely to go on the hunt?'

'My intention was to rid myself of Drón and Sétach for good, and certainly not return to the squalid halls of Cill Ria.'

'You managed to elude them this morning. Why did you return?'

The girl shrugged. 'I lost the opportunity. I was in the forest when I saw Brother Drón riding hard to catch up with me. I panicked and let the horse have its head. Drón chased me through the forest for a while but, thankfully, I proved the better rider. When I finally halted, I listened for his pursuit but could not hear it. I was unsure what to do next. Then Fergus Fanat came along . . . well, I found myself confessing all to him. He promised me that he would help me if I returned with him. That he would protect me. That is why I came back.'

She paused and Fidelma prompted her to continue but she shook her head. 'There is nothing more to be said.'

'I think there is. What made Brother Drón chase after you? How did he find out that you had fled?'

'I learned the story from Sétach. Brother Drón was looking for me. He found Sétach after I had left and said he had received a message that I was meeting a lover by the Well of Patrick. He had asked at the gate where this was and been told it was due south. Sétach is clever and she went first to the stable and discovered that I had taken Ultán's horse. She made inquiries, and the stable lads told her that I had gone off with the other ladies on the hunt. She found Drón in the courtyard about to set off to the Well of Patrick. Sétach advised him to follow the hunt, for she believed it was some ruse of mine to draw him in the wrong direction.'

'That is curious enough,' muttered Fidelma. 'Who gave this message to Drón?'

'I don't know. All I know is that it was certainly untrue.'

'That you were meeting a lover or that you had a lover?'

The girl flushed. 'That I was meeting anyone at this well or elsewhere.'

'Let us return to this meeting with Fergus Fanat,' Fidelma said. 'How long have you known him?'

The question seemed to throw Marga off guard for a moment.

'I presume that you met him in the land of the Uí Thuirtrí? Was that after you had entered Cill Ria?'

'How did you know that I had met him before?' she demanded.

'You were at the game of *immán* waiting for him, I think. Was your meeting during the hunt by design?'

'I have told you that it was not.'

'When you told him about your plan to flee, how did he persuade you to come back here?'

The girl looked unhappy.

'He is your lover, isn't he?' pressed Fidelma.

'For the love of God, do not tell Brother Drón nor Sister Sétach. They suspect me enough.'

'Then tell me how you met, and when.'

'As you say, it was just after I went to Cill Ria. I went to collect some manuscripts from Ard Stratha and it was on that journey that I met Fergus Fanat. He was young, a warrior, a cousin of the king of Ulaidh, and . . .'

Fidelma waved her hand in a swift dismissive gesture. 'I think you can spare us the description. Sufficient to say that you were attracted to him.'

'And he to me. We met several times after that. But then the clouds gathered at Cill Ria. I was sent to the bed of Ultán under threat of punishments. I was too ashamed to contact Fergus Fanat any more. He tried to get in touch with me several times without being too obvious and I do not think that either Ultán or Drón knew of my relationship with him. I had not seen him since. Not until we came here and I saw him on the playing field. I was going to speak to him then, but you forestalled me.'

'Why not contact him later?'

'Because I was watched closely. I was in despair. And at Ultán's funeral last night I saw him there with his cousin, the king of Ulaidh. I know he saw me. He saw Sister Sétach embracing me during the funeral. I think she did so on purpose because she saw him watching me and might have guessed there had been something between us.

But he made no attempt to contact me. I was in despair. That was when I decided to flee and strike out for Laigin.'

Fidelma sat back regarding her thoughtfully. 'And you still maintain that meeting Fergus Fanat on the hunt was an accident?'

'Aren't our lives full of coincidences?' the girl demanded. 'If the coincidence works against us we say "if only . . ." If only we had taken a certain path at a certain time we might have changed our lives. If only. When, however, we do take the path where there is a meeting, where our lives are changed, it is hailed as a suspicious act.'

'I will not disagree with your philosophy. But what I want to know is what Fergus Fanat could say to you, in these circumstances, to prevent your flight to Laigin?'

'It is what I told him. I told him everything. The truth about my life at Cill Ria, why I felt too ashamed to continue to see him, and my reason for accompanying Abbot Ultán on this embassy to Imleach and Cashel. And he accepted me as I am. We mean to marry. He told me to come here and stand up to Brother Drón and Sister Sétach and that he would support and protect me.'

'And have you stood up to them?' Fidelma asked.

Sister Marga shook her head. 'Not yet. We shall see them together. Then I shall travel back with Fergus Fanat to Ulaidh and be his wife.'

There was no mistaking the happiness in the girl's features as she said this. Then she glanced nervously round. 'Do not say anything until Fergus and I have that meeting. We desire to stand up to them together.'

Fidelma was reassuring. 'Have no fear, I will not speak about this for the time being.'

Eadulf nodded his assent as he saw the girl's face turned imploringly towards him.

'When is this confrontation with Drón and Sétach to be?' he asked.

'This evening, after the meal.'

It was just before the evening meal when Fidelma and Eadulf received another summons to Colgú's private chamber. The High King, Sechnassach, sat in the chair usually occupied by Colgú. He wore a worried expression.

Colgú sat beside him, and also present in the chamber were the brehons Barrán, Baithen and Ninnid. As Fidelma and Eadulf entered the room, the High King himself bade Fidelma to be seated. Eadulf, as a foreigner of lower rank who was not entitled to sit in the presence of the High King, stood up in a position behind Fidelma's chair. Finguine, Colgú's *tánaiste*, and Caol, commander of Colgú's guard, stood at the door.

It was Brehon Barrán who spoke first.

'Brehon Ninnid informs us that you have released Brother Drón, thus apparently admitting that Ninnid was correct when he told you that a churchman could not have taken part in a vengeance killing. Further, he says that he has found that the obvious suspect is Muirchertach's heir apparent and that you know this but are delaying the charges to be heard against him.'

Fidelma remained impassive, although Eadulf sensed stiffening in her body.

'There is no evidence to bring charges,' she replied tersely.

'An abbot is murdered and now a king. In each case it seems that the evidence against one person is overwhelming and yet you seem to be delaying a hearing on both matters. We must bring things to a resolution and quickly,' Brehon Barrán insisted.

'We have already discussed this. I thought that it had been agreed that more time was needed,' Fidelma said, speaking directly to Sechnassach. The High King looked uncomfortable.

'Brehon Ninnid has asked for this meeting to make a plea that, after the unilateral release of Brother Drón and his discovery of the evidence against Dúnchad Muirisici, charges should be brought against Muirchertach's *tánaiste*.'

At this, Brehon Ninnid coughed nervously and rose from his seat.

'With due respect, I think Sister Fidelma is making this matter complicated when it is simple in its resolution,' he said. 'Abbot Ultán was slain by Muirchertach Nár.'

'For what reason?' demanded the High King.

'I think that the lady Fidelma will agree with me on the reason. I have learned that he blamed Ultán for the death of his wife's younger sister and had once sought compensation from him. The compensation was refused. Everything was done within the law, although

Muirchertach Nár claimed that it was not so. That gave him a cause for anger and resentment.'

Sechnassach glanced to where Fidelma was seated. Her face was impassive. 'Do you agree with this?'

'I agree that there was an enmity between Muirchertach Nár and Ultán over the death of this girl,' Fidelma replied.

Brehon Ninnid smiled triumphantly. 'There is the motive. That makes sense of those distinguished witnesses' – he inclined his head in swift succession to Brehon Baithen and Caol – 'who saw Muirchertach Nár flee from the bedchamber at the time of Ultán's murder.'

'It makes sense, but it does not prove beyond dispute that Muirchertach Nár was the killer,' Fidelma pointed out. 'And now Muirchertach Nár is slain himself and cannot make a proper defence.'

'He was slain by his heir in order to seize the throne of Connacht,' went on Brehon Ninnid. 'We have the evidence of Brother Eadulf there, who, with the warrior Gormán, having been called to the scene of the king of Connacht's death, followed the tracks of two horses from that very spot. One was the riderless mount of Muirchertach Nár found by Brother Drón. The other was the horse that had a split horsehoe and belonged to Dúnchad Muirisci. But now Sister Fidelma, having claimed that Muirchertach Nár was innocent and demanded time to investigate, has released Brother Drón from confinement. Yet she has not put forward charges against Dúnchad Muirisci. I say that she is delaying a hearing unnecessarily.'

'As a point of correction, tracks of three horses were observed by Rónán the tracker. We have not identified the third set of tracks.'

Sechnassach sighed. 'Even so, it seems very logical. There is much speculation and unrest among our people, Fidelma. A quick hearing of these facts could stop it.'

'Except,' Fidelma's voice cut in coldly as she rose from her seat, 'except that it would not be justice. Not justice to Bishop Ultán nor justice to Muirchertach Nár nor even justice to Dúnchad Muirisci or Brother Drón.'

Brehon Ninnid glanced at her, shrugged eloquently and sat down. 'You have contrary evidence then?' he said, almost with a smirk.

Fidelma hesitated.

'Well, Fidelma? Do you?' prompted Sechnassach gently.

'I have only inconsistencies to put forward at this time. However, such as they are they do cause concern.'

Sechnassach glanced at Brehon Barrán as if seeking help.

'We all are aware of Fidelma's reputation,' Brehon Barrán said. 'There is none here who does not respect her knowledge of law and the sharp penetration of her questions. I certainly would not dismiss her arguments lightly without some consideration of them.'

Fidelma bowed slightly towards him. 'If there is one thing that irritates me about this whole matter it is that we have circumstantial evidence pointing to two people. And in their defence, both of them – I am speaking of Muirchertach Nár and Dúnchad – have put forward curious tales, which seem to confirm some guilt. But, by his own weak tale, even Brother Drón is also a prime suspect.'

'Why does circumstantial evidence irritate you, Fidelma?' asked Brehon Barrán. 'It is still acceptable in law.'

'Because if any or all of them had really undertaken these acts of murder they would have prepared better stories to elude suspicion. They tell stories that are so impossible to believe that they actually speak of innocence.'

Brehon Ninnid laughed aloud in scepticism, but Brehon Barrán's face was grave.

'You have made a point that needs consideration, Fidelma, but it comes back to what the High King Sechnassach says. The people are growing restless. Two deaths in two days – an abbot and a king. We cannot keep everyone confined here for ever during this search for the truth.'

Fidelma's tone was unemotional. 'You'll recall that yesterday was meant to be my wedding celebration. If anyone is suffering by this delay, as Brehon Ninnid calls it, it is Eadulf and I.'

Sechnassach grimaced with a wry expression at Brehon Barrán, who gave a a ghost of a nod in the High King's direction.

'I am afraid that a decision has to be made, Fidelma. I thought earlier today that I could allow you what freedom you wanted. But the members of my council have made representations about the growing unrest. So I have decided. One further night and a day can pass. Then we shall meet again. The matter must then be pronounced capable of resolution. Is that clear?'

Brehon Ninnid stood up and both he and Fidelma bowed towards the High King in acquiescence.

Outside the chamber, Eadulf could see that Fidelma was unhappy.

'Justice is not served by pandering to people because they are rest-less or want to get home.' Her voice was quiet but angry as they walked back to their chamber.

'Or get married.' Eadulf grinned, trying to introduce some humour into the conversation.

Fidelma's face softened for a moment. 'Even brehons seem to forget the purpose of the law – *jus est ars boni et aequi*.'

'Law is the art of the good and the just,' Eadulf translated. 'I think our friend Ninnid believes it to be the art of gaining reputation. Anyway, what now? It is already dark. There is only this night and tomorrow in which to find a solution.'

'You go on to our chambers, check to see that all is well with little Alchú and Muirgen. Have something to eat. I will be along shortly. I want to have a word with Abbot Laisran.'

'Laisran? Why?'

Fidelma smiled. 'He is often a good counsel in times of stress.'

# CHAPTER FIFTEEN

Abbot Laisran's cherubic countenance was unusually glum as he welcomed his cousin. 'I am truly sorry that what should have been a time of happiness for you has been cursed, Fidelma.'

'Even these days will pass,' Fidelma said reassuringly. 'Indeed, by tomorrow evening, it seems that I must have a solution.'

Abbot Laisran waved her to a seat.

'And are you near one?' he asked hopefully.

'Not exactly. I have many questions but cannot find the right people to answer them. That is why I have come to you.'

Abbot Laisran sat back before the fire and folded his hands across his broad stomach. He smiled complacently.

'As you know, it is my privilege to be abbot at Durrow, whose students not only come from all the corners of the world but, after their training, return to those four corners. There is little gossip that does not eventually reach my ears. How might I be of help? You have doubtless discovered that Ultán of the Uí Thuirtrí was not always the pious religious that he pretended. That surely gives you some scope in your investigation?'

'It complicates things. I know that many hated him.'

'Just so. He was not a likeable person.'

'But that being so, it means that many desired to kill him.'

'And, from what I hear, many with justification,' agreed Abbot Laisran. 'Though I was not surprised when the finger of suspicion fell on Muirchertach Nár.'

Fidelma regarded him with interest. 'What do you know of Muirchertach Nár?'

'Ah, poor Muirchertach.' Laisran shook his head, his features in an expression of mock sorrow. 'I have heard that he is no longer of this earthly realm. They do say *de mortuis nihil nisi bonum* . . . of the dead speak nothing but good. But, in justice, when good and bad mingle, one should speak truthfully. He was a sad man. Overshadowed by his father, King Guaire. When he became king of Connacht, he tried his best to emulate him. I'll wager that you have no liking for his wife . . . his widow,' he corrected himself. 'The lady Aíbnat. Truly, she is a strange lady. There is a saying among her servants that if you put her in an empty chamber, she would pick a fight in it within seconds.'

Fidema chuckled appreciatively. 'I can agree with that.'

'I am not sure why she and Muirchertach married. She, of course, is of the Uí Briúin Aí – they are rival families for the kingship of Connacht. I do not think mutual feelings had anything to do with their relationship. Muirchertach found his carnal pleasures elsewhere, by all accounts. I think it was a marriage of convenience. The two families trying to patch up their quarrels. A marriage of politics.'

Fidelma had gathered that much from Dúnchad Muirisci.

'You have heard of Muirchertach's clash with Bishop Ultán over Aíbnat's younger sister Searc? Was that to do with a desire to pacify the Uí Briúin family rather than any regard for his wife?'

'I have heard about this matter,' agreed Abbot Laisran. 'It seems a little out of character for Muirchertach to pursue such a course unless he were doing it for politics rather than out of personal affection. That might make sense.' He rubbed his chin reflectively and seemed to fall into deep thought.

'Do you have another conclusion?' she prompted.

'I have heard that Searc was a beautiful girl and, as I say, Muirchertach was disposed to forming attachments to young women.'

Fidelma shook her head immediately. 'But Searc was in love with the young man named Senach of Cill Ria.'

'Just so. But there were stories that Muirchertach was attracted to her. I understand that she initially went to live at his fortress at Durlas to be companion to her sister Aíbnat.'

'Before she met Senach?'

'I don't know. However, there is certainly no question that the attraction was mutual. She rejected Muirchertach's advances. At least, that is what I have heard.'

Fidelma looked at the leaping flames in the fire for a few moments. 'Are you saying that Muirchertach tried to seduce Aíbnat's sister?'

Abbot Laisran's chubby face was not exactly serious. 'It would not be the first time that such a thing has happened. Whether of the nobility or the Faith, men are often led by their desires. Myself now, I am too old to desire anything more than a good jug of wine, a nicely cooked repast and perhaps the entertainment of a good horse race.'

Fidelma broke into a smile. 'I know your faults only too well, Laisran. You should add to them the fascination of the gaming board.'

'Ah.' The abbot nodded reflectively. 'I had not forgotten. I fail to mention that because I have learned never to challenge you to *brandubh* or *fidchell*, either board game would spell disaster for me against one of your wit.'

Fidelma suddenly frowned again. 'Are you saying that Muirchertach had a reputation with women and that his wife Aíbnat knew about it?'

'It is what I have heard. I cannot bear witness to it.'

'But where did you hear this? Durrow is a long way from Muirchertach's fortress at Durlas.'

'As Virgil said: *fama malum quo non aliud velocius ullum*,' Laisran replied with a wink.

'It is true that nothing travels faster than scandal,' Fidelma agreed, 'but one has to separate mere rumour and mischief-making.'

'Often there is truth in rumour,' the abbot replied. 'Tales told from different sources may be treated with less suspicion than a tale told by a single source. There were several religious arriving at Durrow and each told a similar tale.'

Fidelma grimaced disapprovingly. 'For Virgil I give you Horace – say nothing in case what you say hurt another or bring down on us an unfavourable act of the gods.'

The abbot smiled broadly. 'You cannot believe that,' he rebuked humorously. 'Otherwise, where would you be? You could not function if people obeyed the *favete linguis* that Horace suggested we obey. Without gossip, without speculation, without people talking to you, your investigations would hardly lead anywhere.'

Fidelma thought for a moment and shrugged. 'I agree that there is truth in that, Laisran. I suppose the secret is knowing where to look for the nuggets of truth among the silt of hearsay, calumny and defamation.'

'I am afraid that is your task in life, Fidelma. You chose your profession.'

'So,' Fidelma returned to a more practical issue, 'these rumours that religious wanderers from Connacht brought to you at Durrow had a consistency? They spoke of Muirchertach as a libertine, profligate in his behaviour to women?'

'They did.'

'Even in his behaviour to Searc, the sister of his wife Aíbnat?'

'It is so.'

'Even if this were just scandal without substantiation, something is strange,' she said with a shake of her head. Then she rose to her feet. Abbot Laisran looked up with a questioning expression.

'Have I been of help?'

'I think so,' she replied, after a moment's thought. 'At least you have prompted an interesting question in my mind. Unfortunately, there are many pieces that seem to form patterns but I am not sure whether they are the right patterns. I don't think, as yet, that I have all the pieces.'

'With both Ultán and Muirchertach dead, is there any reason to seek any more pieces?' queried Abbot Laisran. 'After all,' he waved a hand, an odd little gesture as though unsure of himself, 'it does make a resolution to the matter, doesn't it? Ultán killed and no great loss to anyone. Muirchertach was blamed and now Muirchertach dead, perhaps in revenge.'

'But who killed Muirchertach?' demanded Fidelma.

'Does it serve anyone to find out?'

'It serves justice and that is what we are about or we are about nothing at all in life.'

'I have heard that one learned brehon would prefer not to implicate anyone from Laigin,' he said softly. Fidelma gazed sharply at him. 'It is just a thought that I heard expressed.'

'I think I know where that thought came from. Sometimes I forget that the abbey of Durrow lies across the border in the kingdom of Laigin.'

'You have a sharp mind, Fidelma,' sighed Abbot Laisran. 'I always thought that you were a great lawyer.'

'When you see Brehon Ninnid of Laigin you might say that you heard that I was as determined to track down whoever killed Muirchertach as I was to clear Muirchertach Nár's name of the murder of Abbot Ultán by discovering who really killed him.'

'I shall tell Brehon Ninnid. Perhaps, if I were looking for Muirchertach's killer, I would be thinking of the type of man that Muirchertach Nár was. If the rumours that he was a libertine are true, who might be the one to suffer from his behaviour?'

'Aíbnat?' Fidelma grimaced dismissively. 'I should not think that she would care one way or another.'

'Yet with her own sister?'

Fidelma thought a moment and then inclined her head, turning for the door. 'I will bear in mind what you say, Laisran.'

Fidelma had just finished telling Eadulf the gist of her conversation with Laisran when there was a knocking on their chamber door. Muirgen the nurse hurried across the chamber to open the door, making a disapproving noise as she did so, glancing in young Alchú's crib as she passed by to ensure that he had not been disturbed. It was Caol, the commander of the guard, on the threshold, looking agitated. He glanced past Muirgen and caught site of Fidelma.

'Lady, a thousand apologies, but it is Fergus Fanat . . .' he called.

Fidelma rose and hastened to the door to join him, dismissing Muirgen with a motion of her head.

'What about Fergus Fanat?' she asked softly.

'He has been attacked.'

Eadulf now joined them.

'Is he dead?' he asked.

Caol shook his head. 'But he is barely alive.'

'Where is he?'

'He has been taken down to Brother Conchobhar's apothecary.'

'Where did the attack take place?' asked Fidelma, reaching for a cloak, for the hour was nearly midnight and the night was chilly.

'Outside the guest chambers given over to Blathmac, the king of Ulaidh, and his attendants.'

'Who was responsible?' demanded Eadulf, as, by common consent, they left Muirgen looking after the still sleeping baby, and followed Caol into the corridor.

'No one knows.'

'Were there no witnesses?'

Caol shook his head. 'None so far as is known.'

'Tell us what you do know, Caol,' said Fidelma.

'The servant of Blathmac, the king of Ulaidh, came to find me a short time ago. He told me that Fergus Fanat, the king's cousin, had been found badly injured.'

'Stabbed?' asked Eadulf quickly.

'I don't think so. Brother Conchobhar will know the extent of his injuries, for, having ascertained the man still lived, I had him removed to the care of the good apothecary.'

'Let us go and see Blathmac immediately, while the events are still fresh in his mind,' Fidelma suggested.

They found the ruler of Ulaidh in his chamber, looking a little careworn, seated with a flagon of *corma* at his side. His two personal attendants were standing in the room, wearing their short swords, while outside his chamber were two more warriors of Caol's guard. Blathmac greeted Fidelma with a wry smile.

'Until I know whether there is a design to kill me, I am taking no chances,' he explained, indicating his men. 'It seems that kings' and abbots' lives are not over-valued in Cashel.'

Fidelma did not seem to take offence.

'I think you may be assured that Fergus Fanat was not attacked in place of yourself, Blathmac,' she said, seating herself as was her right, while Eadulf stood behind her chair, as custom dictated.

Blathmac grimaced. 'A king has already been killed. One of my abbots also. How can I be sure that the design is not against me?'

'There is no surety in this world except that we all die at some time,' she returned. 'However, I would not lose sleep over fear that you were the intended victim. Can you tell me what happened?'

Blathmac shrugged indifferently. 'There is little enough to tell, lady. I was taking supper when I heard a noise outside my chamber door.'

'A noise?'

'I suppose you might call it a scuffle. Unsteady footsteps. A cry of pain abruptly cut off and the sound of what, in retrospect, would have been a body falling. Fergus's body. I grabbed my sword and went to the door and found Fergus lying there in front of the threshold. His head was covered in blood.'

'Who else was in the corridor?'

'No one.'

'No one? Had you heard the sound of any doors along the corridor being shut?'

Blathmac shook his head. 'Why?'

'Because it is a long corridor. How long was it from when you heard the sound of the body falling until you opened the door?'

'Only moments.'

'In those moments, the attacker had time to vanish. They would have had to go into another chamber.' Fidelma paused, suddenly struck by a thought. 'Unless . . .'

Blathmac looked at her expectantly. Abruptly, she changed the subject.

'What did you do next?'

'I called my servants and sent one of them to raise the commander of the guard. He came, found Fergus still living, thanks be to God, and had him removed to the care of an apothecary. That is all I know.'

'Fergus Fanat was unconscious all this time?'

'He was.'

Fidelma stood up.

'Will you search the corridors – I mean the rooms leading off?' asked Blathmac as she turned to the door.

Fidelma glanced back with a grimace. 'In retrospect, I do not think anyone eluded your scrutiny of the corridor by entering one of the chambers. Whoever it was had left by another means. Have no fear, Blathmac, this attacker means no harm to you. But if it makes you feel more secure, I am sure Caol will allow his warriors to maintain a watch for the rest of this night.'

Outside the chamber, Fidelma glanced down. There were blood-stains in front of the threshold. She looked up and down the corridor while Eadulf watched her in perplexity. Then she grunted and walked swiftly a short distance along the corridor to an alcove in which a window was set.

'Ah.' Eadulf suddenly understood what she was thinking. 'You believe that the culprit ran back here into the alcove?'

'Just so,' Fidelma muttered, peering at the window which was, of course, unglazed and open to the elements. 'Bring a lantern here.'

Eadulf turned back into the corridor and took down one of the lanterns that lit it.

'Hold it higher . . . here.'

He did so.

She sighed and pointed down at the sill of the window. Eadulf could see some blood smudges.

'The hand of our attacker as they climbed out of the window on to the ledge that runs just beneath. A short distance along, they turn the corner and are in a different corridor. It seems these outside ledges have been much in use.'

Eadulf was staring at the window and the bloodstain. His face suddenly cleared.

'Do you mean . . . ?' he began, but Fidelma had turned away.

'Put back the lantern and let us go to see how Fergus Fanat fares.'

Brother Conchobhar looked up from his workbench as Fidelma and Eadulf entered and smiled grimly.

'I thought it would not be long before you came along.'

'How is he?'

'At least he is not dead,' replied the elderly apothecary. 'However, he remains unconscious.'

'What are his injuries?' asked Eadulf, who knew something of the physician's art.

'I believe he was struck twice on the back of the head. There are two distinct wounds. The skin is split open but I do not think the bone of the skull is broken. We can only wait and see if he awakes from the darkness into which he has plunged.'

'Do you know when we are likely to be able to speak to him?' Fidelma sounded disappointed.

'Lady, there are limitations to my knowledge. He may wake soon or he may not wake at all. I have known such cases. Unless he wakes, he cannot take food or drink and he will die. That is how it sometimes happens with wounds that cause this lengthy loss of consciousness.'

Fidelma compressed her lips in a thin line for a moment. 'May we see him?'

'Little point, but you may,' the old man replied, sliding from his stool and taking them into the back of his apothecary, which served as a place to treat the wounded and to prepare the dead for burial. Fidelma was reminded that just hours before Muirchertach Nár had rested here, being prepared for his removal to the chapel of Cashel.

Fergus Fanat lay as if he were asleep, his shallow breathing making no noise. Brother Conchobhar had bound the wounds around his head but other than that there was no sign of injuries.

Fidelma stood looking down for a moment and then she shook her head. 'You are right, Brother Conchobhar. There is little to be done here except wait. But the waiting is for you and not for us. We have other things to do now.'

She turned, and was leaving the apothecary when she paused by his work bench and sniffed. 'That is a familiar scent. What is it?'

Brother Conchobhar glanced at the mortar and pestle on his bench.

'I am crushing lavender,' he said. He used the Irish term *lus na túis* – the incense herb.

'It has a comforting fragrance,' Fidelma observed.

Eadulf agreed. 'I believe it was brought to Britain by the Romans some centuries ago. They used the flowers to scent their baths, and hence we call it after their word *lavare*.'

Brother Conchobhar endorsed Eadulf's knowledge. 'I grow it in my *lúbgort*, my herb garden. Some people like to use it as a relaxant, or as *cumrae*, a fragrance, as the Romans once did. It is very aromatic.'

'So I notice,' replied Fidelma, thanking the old apothecary as they went out into the courtyard, where Caol was waiting for them.

'What news, lady?' he asked hopefully.

'None,' she replied. 'He is still unconscious. However, we may need you. Come with us.'

She led the way to the hostel for the religieuse. The place was in darkness and it seemed that everyone was asleep. However, as they drew near, the flinty-eyed *brusaid*, the hostel keeper, challenged her. Fidelma identified herself.

'I can let you in, lady, but not the men,' protested the old woman.

'That's all right,' Fidelma replied. 'They can wait here. I want to see the sisters Sétach and Marga.'

The old woman took a lantern and, while Eadulf and Caol waited outside, Fidelma followed her into the dormitory rooms.

Sister Sétach was in her bed but awake and sat up with a frown as they approached.

'What is this?' she demanded shrilly. 'Do you come to haunt me?'

Fidelma glanced at the neighbouring bed. It was empty.

'How long have you been here,' she asked brusquely.

'Since I came to bed after the communal meal ended.'

'You have not stirred?'

'Why should I?'

'Show me your hands,' demanded Fidelma.

'My hands?' Sister Sétach looked astonished.

'Show me!'

Reluctantly, the woman held out her hands to Fidelma. Fidelma glanced at them by the light of the lantern. It was obvious that they had been washed recently and in a hurry, for Fidelma noticed that some flecks of soap had dried on them unnoticed. Her features remained impassive.

'Where is Sister Marga?' She nodded to the empty bed.

Sister Sétach shrugged. 'I don't know.'

Fidelma felt that her ignorance was feigned. 'Yet you say that you have been here the whole time?'

'It is true,' Sétach insisted. 'I came here and she was preparing for bed. I fell asleep and awoke only moments before you came in. She was not here then.'

'So she left after you fell asleep? You seem to have slept well. I thought that you had difficulty sleeping?'

'I fell asleep,' snapped Sister Sétach.

Fidelma hesitated a moment. 'At what time was your meeting with Sister Marga, Fergus Fanat and Brother Drón this evening?'

This time, the expression of incomprehension on the woman's face did not seem to be feigned.

'Our meeting?' she repeated, puzzled.

'Did Sister Marga and Fergus Fanat meet you and Brother Drón this evening?' Fidelma said slowly.

Sister Sétach shook her head in bewilderment. 'We had no meeting.'

'Was such a meeting discussed?'

'What purpose could such a meeting have?' countered the woman.

Fidelma's breath came out in an exasperated sigh. 'Was such a meeting mentioned or arranged?'

'Of course not. Why should such a meeting be arranged?'

'Very well. If or when Sister Marga returns, the hostel keeper is to be informed and she must inform me. Is that understood?'

Fidelma hurried to rejoin Eadulf and Caol.

'I thought our attacker might have been Sétach,' she muttered, a little disappointed that her suspicion seemed to have been unfounded.

Eadulf was not surprised. 'Because of her ability to climb along narrow ledges? That occurred to me.'

'Her hands were unmarked. Yet there was a bloodstained hand print on the sill of the window where the attacker had climbed out. Of course, that is not conclusive. However, Marga is missing. Significantly, according to Sétach, neither she nor Fergus Fanat made any arrangement to see her and Brother Drón this evening. Sister Marga did not tell us the truth.'

'Sister Sétach could be lying,' Eadulf pointed out.

'She could,' agreed Fidelma. 'Alas, we cannot ask Fergus Fanat and get to the truth that way. But we can ask Brother Drón.'

They came to Brother Drón's chamber and knocked on the door. There was no answer, and, when a further knocking did not elicit a response, Fidelma impatiently opened it and entered. Caol came behind her holding the lantern high. The chamber was empty. The bed had not been slept in. There was no sign of Brother Drón.

'It still lacks a few hours until dawn,' Caol pointed out. 'Drón must be still in the fortress, for the gates will still be closed, and in any case, no one would go out into an unfamiliar countryside in the dead of night.'

'We must check,' replied Fidelma, leading the way down to the main courtyard.

The guard at the gate looked sheepish.

'Brother Drón, the hawk-faced man from Cill Ria? A boy came with a message for him and he took his horse and left about an hour ago. There was no instruction to detain him. He told me that he had to be at some place by first light. Some religious place, I think it was.'

'You let a stranger out into the countryside in the middle of the night?' thundered Caol.

'But I had no orders not to. I did seek the advice of the noble Finguine when one of the religieuse earlier sought permission to leave to go to visit someone in the township. But that was before the gates were closed for the night.'

Fidelma stared at him. 'A religieuse? Do you know her name?'

'She gave it as Sister Marga, lady,' replied the unhappy man.

Fidelma stifled a groan. 'Was she on horseback?'

'I don't think so, lady.'

Fidelma was already hurrying across the cobbled patch to the stables.

The *gilla scuir* was seated on a hay bale with another of the guards and a *fidchell* board between them. They rose guiltily as Fidelma entered.

'Is Abbot Ultán's horse still here?' she asked.

The stable lad nodded immediately and pointed.

'Still here, lady,' he confirmed.

'Is there any other horse missing?' demanded Fidelma.

'Any other horse?' The stable lad was bemused for a moment and then shook his head. 'They are all accounted for with the exception of Brother Drón's horse. He rode off on it some time ago. Is there something wrong?'

But Fidelma was frowning. 'So Marga is on foot and Drón on horseback.'

'Do you think it was Marga who attacked Fergus?' asked Eadulf. 'Do we go after them?'

Fidelma was about to reply when there was shouting from outside the gates. The guard said something in response, then swung the gate open a fraction to let a figure enter. To their surprise, Brother Berrihert pushed his way in, halted, saw them by the stables in the light of the lanterns and came hurrying across. He barely acknowledged Fidelma but let forth a flood of Saxon to Eadulf, speaking quickly and with emphasis. Fidelma had a working knowledge but could not follow all that was said by the intense, pale-faced religieux.

'Eadulf, I need your help. My father is missing.'

'Ordwulf?'

'I fear my father plans to kill Brother Drón. When I found him gone tonight I came here to warn you. The guard has just told me that Brother Drón has already left the fortress. I should have told you before that Ordwulf has thought of nothing else but vengeance killing. But he is my father, you understand. I cannot tell you the full story but he blamed Abbot Ultán and still blames Brother Drón for the death of my mother. I need your help, and . . .'

Fidelma interrupted. 'You mention Drón and death. What do you mean? My Saxon is not good enough to understand everything you say. Speak in Latin if it is more comfortable than Irish.'

Berrihert frowned in annoyance. 'We have no time . . .' he began.

'There is always time for a clear explanation,' snapped Fidelma.

Brother Berrihert took a deep breath. 'My father says that Ultán and Drón were responsible for my mother's death, his wife's death. It is . . .'

Fidelma made a gesture with her hand. 'I have heard the story from your brothers. I understand it. You say that your father is about to kill Drón? Where are they?'

Brother Berrihert lifted his arms helplessly. 'I do not know, lady. I had a feeling that my father had something planned yesterday, but it seemed that Drón went off with the hunt. I heard my father cursing to himself about Drón going in the wrong direction and thwarting him.'

'The wrong direction?' Fidelma frowned.

'I did not understand what he meant. But now I think that my father sent a message to Drón asking him to go to some spot where my father planned to kill him.'

Fidelma turned and beckoned the guard to join them. 'You said that Brother Drón mentioned some place where he was going? A religious place? Can you remember anything else?'

'I cannot remember, lady. It was some place of pilgrimage, I think.'

Fidelma closed her eyes and groaned. 'Fool!'

The guard looked shocked. She opened her eyes.

'Not you. Me!' She turned to Eadulf. 'It's the Well of Patrick, just south of here. Marga told me that Sétach had told her that Drón had received a message before he set out on the hunt, telling him that Marga was meeting her lover at this place. He was about to ride there when Sétach told him Marga was following the hunt in the other direction. That message came from Ordwulf, I'll wager it.' She turned to Brother Berrihert. 'Would your father know about the Well of Patrick?'

Brother Berrihert closed his eyes in agony. 'On our journey here, my brothers and I went there because it was blessed by the great apostle of the Faith. We went to sip the sacred water from the well and seek a blessing on our new life here in your land. We took our father.' He suddenly let out a low moan. 'My father seemed impressed by the isolation of the glade and apparently noted its location in his mind. He knows it is not far away from here.'

'The Well of Patrick,' muttered Fidelma. 'By the honey fields. An ideal spot for a murder. Once it was a sacred place for the Druids and then Patrick visited it when he baptised my ancestors here on the Rock of Cashel. Patrick went south to purify the well in the name of the New Faith.' She glanced at the sky. 'An hour or two before dawn. Get our horses ready, Caol. You will have to come with us.'

'I must come too,' declared Brother Berrihert.

Caol looked questioningly at Fidelma for guidance and she nodded. 'He can mount up behind you.'

Caol went off shouting instructions to the *gilla scuir* to saddle their horses.

In a short time, the four of them, on three horses, were heading south-east from Cashel along the road towards the field of honey, a small settlement that lay on the banks of the river Siúr. Initially, in the darkness, Caol led the way with a sure determination. It was not long before the grey of the oncoming day lit their path. It was fully light long before they skirted the western bank of the smaller river Mael and then crossed a marshy stream passing below a hill on which stood an ancient pillar stone, rising higher than any man on the hilltop.

Eadulf knew it was ancient and that local clerics had carved crosses on both its south and north faces to expunge any pagan spirits that remained there. But some of the ancient customs remained, for Fidelma had told him that it was the habit of the chief of the Déisi to bring his warriors to the spot before they embarked on any hosting against an enemy and to lead them sun-wise round the ancient stone.

Just south of this ancient landmark was the little vale that Fidelma had once told him of, a place where she used to play as a child, and where a spring rose, once sacred to the old religion, but converted by the Blessed Patrick to a Christian Holy Well.

They rode on in grim silence for a while, and when Fidelma judged that they were close enough to the glade she raised a hand and halted.

'Best to leave the horses here and go on on foot,' she said quietly. 'A path leads through those trees there and down into the small dale. Let us hope that Brother Drón is not here before us.'

They tethered their horses and moved off quietly, with Fidelma leading them for she knew the way well. They were just starting down the path into the small hollow when a plaintive cry came to their ears.

'For the love of God, stranger, spare me. It was not I. Not I!'

# CHAPTER SIXTEEN

Fidelma recognised Brother Drón's voice. Before she had time to consider what to do, Brother Berrihert had pushed by her and gone crashing down the path. She knew enough of the Saxon language to hear him shouting: 'Father! For God's sake. Put down your weapon!'

The response was immediate.

'Stop there, Berrihert! Come closer and this pig dies now.'

Following Berrihert, Fidelma and the others came into the small hollow at whose centre the sacred spring rose. The first thing that she noticed was the figure of Brother Drón tied against a tree trunk, face towards the trunk, arms spread round it as if in an embrace. Behind him, holding a double-edged battleaxe of the type she had been told Angles and Saxons used in warfare, was the old warrior, Ordwulf.

Brother Berrihert had halted at the bottom of the pathway and they came to a stop behind him. Ordwulf did not seem astonished to see them.

'So you have brought your Christian friends with you, my son?' he sneered. 'That is good. They can witness this act of retribution.'

Brother Drón gave another long moaning cry. 'Save me, save me, I beseech you.' His voice ended in a sob.

Ordwulf smiled grimly. 'Tell them what you told me, you unspeakable pig.'

'It was not I, I told you. It was Ultán who ordered it. Ultán.'

Brother Berrihert cleared his throat nervously.

'Father,' he said softly, 'we all know how our mother died. But Ultán is dead.'

'Aye, but not by my hand, more is the pity,' cried the old warrior. 'It should have been my hand that struck that vermin down. But now it is left to me to strike down his lackey.'

'Do you think our mother would want this revenge?' demanded Brother Berrihert.

'She was Aelgifu, daughter of Aelfric, a noblewoman of Deira who adhered to the old ways of our people. You would have done well to remember that, before you decided to go with these Christians.' Ordwulf was uncompromising.

'What good will killing this man do?'

'He and his evil master had Aelgifu beaten to death. They dared lay hands on my lady. I was not there to save her. But I am here to take vengeance as is the right and custom of our people. His master is dead and now he will die. It is a just retribution.'

Ordwulf took a pace forward, his battleaxe raised. Caol went to move, his hand going to his sword hilt.

'Tell your friends to stop where they are, or this pig's death will be that much quicker.'

Fidelma laid a restraining hand on Caol's arm.

'You would not make it across the clearing before the old man dealt the death blow,' she pointed out quietly.

'Father, it is not the way of the Faith,' Brother Berrihert cried desperately.

'Do not shame me, boy, with your faith which forgives evil.'

'You cannot do this!'

'By what right do you tell me . . . ? You whose faith made you stand by and forgive those who slew your mother? You are worse than a churl. You are not a man and not my son. Your faith peoples the earth with murderers and evildoers. You would have men go to hell while only slaves go to heaven. Well, it is not to be. I am Ordwulf, son of Frithuwulf Churlslayer! My faith is in Vali, archer son of Woden, god of vengeance! Stand back, foreigner, lest you taste my steel as well . . .'

This last was shouted at Caol who had taken another step forward, hand on his sword. The old man raised his double-edged battleaxe and brought it level with his chest, his eyes glinting with some mad fire. Fidelma again motioned Caol to halt. She wanted to end this confrontation without bloodshed.

'If you will not listen to your son, Ordwulf, then listen to me,' Eadulf said quietly, his hands held out in a non-threatening fashion.

'Listen to another betrayer of the manly faith of his people? Why should I listen to you, Eadulf, sometime of Seaxmund's Ham, sometime of the South Folk, who once followed the true path of Woden and the great gods of our people but who has turned to crawl after a god of weeping slaves.'

'I am not going to justify my faith to you, Ordwulf. Nor am I going to appeal to you to give up vengeance in the name of that faith, the same faith that your sons now follow. I will simply say, that vengeance taken in this fashion will not soothe your troubled spirit.'

'Neither will forgiveness, slave follower,' sneered Ordwulf.

'No, it will not,' Eadulf agreed, keeping his voice low and calm. 'We agree that vengeance is required. But let our vengeance be what we call justice. It is not only desirable but also necessary. The only thing we need to agree on is how this should be achieved. Killing a person is easy. Letting an evildoer live and bringing them to justice so that everyone can see that justice has been served is another matter and more rewarding.'

Ordwulf looked uncertain. 'I do not understand you . . . it sounds as though you have a honeyed tongue, Christian.'

'This land that you are exiled in is a country with laws and judges, where a man does not have to seek out vengeance for himself and his family. The laws and judges do that. The killing of your wife should have been brought before the judges so that those responsible could be punished. It was not. Time has passed on. Yet it is not too late and if this man' – he gestured to where Brother Drón was still bound to the tree – 'was responsible, let us take him back to Cashel, to the courts, and to the judges, where, if judged guilty, he will be pronounced so throughout the land . . . That is justice and that is proper vengeance.'

'And will I then be allowed to slay him?' demanded Ordwulf.

'There is no such punishment here but the punishment is worse.'

'What can be worse than being despatched into the arms of the goddess Hel, and taken to a world of eternal darkness and pain?'

'What is more painful than to live with your guilt proclaimed to all who know you, to live suffering in the knowledge of what you have done, and to spend every waking moment trying to compensate those whom you have injured?'

Ordwulf stood for a moment and shook his head slowly. 'That is no punishment for the likes of him. Yesterday we entered the month of Solmanath, sacred to our goddess of love Sjofn. It was the month that Aelgifu and I met and when we married. Yesterday, at first light, I took cakes to the foot of an oak near here and offered them to the gods. I swore that in a few days, when the feastday of Vali, the god of vengeance, was celebrated, that thing there' – he nodded to Brother Drón, now whimpering quietly against the oak – 'or I should be dead. That he be taken in the arms of Hel or I be feasting in the hall of heroes with Woden. No words, Saxon brother; no more words now.'

The old man's grip on his battleaxe tightened.

'Mark me, boy,' he called to Berrihert, 'mark me well, and see what a warrior should do when his mother is violated. This is for you, my love, my Aelgifu, this is for you . . .'

He raised the great battleaxe high over his head.

Brother Drón let out a wailing scream.

Everyone seemed unable to move, as if rooted to the spot by the terrible inevitability of the scene.

Then Ordwulf's eyes grew wide, as if in startled surprise. An expression of pain re-formed his features for a moment. He gasped and lurched forward a step and then dropped to his knees, the axe falling to the ground at his side.

No one, it seemed, could move as they stared at him, not under-standing what was happening.

A low shuddering breath came from the old man.

Eadulf took a pace forward as if to go to his aid.

The pain-stricken eyes flared at him.

'No!' came the old man's cry. His features had turned grey. He was on his knees, resting back on his heels, his chest rising and falling rapidly. The eyes turned to the young man at Eadulf's side. 'Berrihert . . . my son . . .'

The old man was fumbling blindly for the haft of his battleaxe, unable to make contact with it. His voice was pleading.

'My son . . .'

Brother Berrihert swallowed and then stepped forward to his father.

He bent down and picked up the axe and placed it in his father's trembling hands.

The old man looked up at him with misty eyes and, even in pain, he smiled.

'Thank you, my son.'

Berrihert nodded and stepped back to Eadulf, who was the only other who knew what was about to happen. Fidelma gazed at them uncertainly, wondering whether to order Caol to rush forward and seize the axe, but she saw Eadulf shake his head warningly at her.

Ordwulf, by some amazing feat, using the axe as a fulcrum, had struggled to his feet. He took several deep breaths.

'So soon?' the old man gasped. 'Yet it is time.'

Then, with a swift motion, fuelled by an inner strength that came they knew not whence, he raised the battleaxe once more over his head, a swift upward thrusting movement, his head going back, eyes staring at the heavens.

Ordwulf's voice rang out in the tiny glen, one last long, loud shout of defiance.

'Woden!'

Then he fell abruptly backwards, stretching out on the green grass by the tiny stream, the axe falling uselessly to his side.

Eadulf was hurrying forward even while the body was falling.

A moment's examination and then he looked up to Fidelma and shook his head. 'Some seizure, I think,' he muttered. 'He was elderly and the exertion . . . well, his heart was old.' He glanced to Brother Berrihert, who stood silently with bowed head, and smiled sadly. 'At least his death was one a warrior would wish. He has gone to his hall of heroes, standing on his feet, weapon in hand and the name of Woden on his lips. It would be as he would have wanted it, Brother Berrihert.'

The young man nodded sadly. 'I will light a candle for his soul and pray that God looks kindly on Woden's hall of heroes.'

Eadulf reached forward and laid a hand on the young man's arm. 'Who knows but that any god whose followers believe in truth, justice and doing good to one's fellows in this life, is but another manifestation of the one God we of the Faith believe in?'

He had been speaking in Saxon the while and now he turned, while

Berrihert bent down to his father's body, and swiftly explained matters to Fidelma and Caol.

Caol cut Brother Drón free.

Finding himself still alive and Ordwulf dead, it was surprising how swiftly Brother Drón recovered his arrogance.

'That foreigner was a maniac,' he shouted. 'I shall demand compensation for this indignity. I am a guest beneath the roof of your brother, lady, and it is your task to protect me as it was your task to protect the abbot. You have failed and I shall demand . . .'

Before anyone knew what was happening, Brother Berrihert had risen from his father's body, taken a few swift strides to the outraged Brother Drón and, with an open hand, smacked him hard across the right cheek, so that the man staggered a few paces and the cringing fear returned to his face. Caol moved forward to intervene but Brother Berrihert made no further aggressive movement.

'You are an unspeakable pig. My vows forbid me to do more, Drón, than to smite you and that I do willingly for my mother's memory and for my father. I did not agree with my father's concept of vengeance. We have moved on from the old ways, the old gods of Woden and Vali. But I will welcome the ways of the laws of this land and I will pursue you through those paths so that you will answer for the scourging of my mother which led to her death.'

Holding his stinging cheek, Brother Drón recovered his anger.

'Warrior, strike the foreigner!' he yelled at Caol. 'Strike him, I say, for the outrage he has committed!'

Caol glanced helplessly at Fidelma, who shook her head. 'You will compose yourself, Brother Drón,' she said.

'You would stand up for this foreigner?' snarled the northern cleric. 'Ah yes, I forget, you would support them.' He glanced in derision at Eadulf. 'You prefer to be with them rather than with your own kind?'

Fidelma coloured hotly. 'You are only compounding your transgressions, Brother Drón,' she replied quietly. 'I would take refuge in the teaching of the religion that you claim to represent.'

'What do you mean?' snapped the man.

A smile played on Fidelma's lips for a moment. 'Having been struck on the right cheek, turn to Brother Berrihert the left.'

Brother Drón took a quick pace back, his face angry. 'I shall bring your conduct before the Abbot Ségdae, before the High King and his Chief Brehon. You shall answer for this outrage.'

'We all have to answer for our actions sooner or later, Brother Drón, just as you will eventually answer for what happened at Colmán's island of Inis Bó Finne. I will make sure that the matter is investigated and the truth is known. Now, tell me where Sister Marga is.'

Brother Drón's anger increased. 'If I knew where she was, do you think I would have been chasing her into this cursed glade?' he demanded. 'I was told that she had come here to meet her lover.'

'Did you met Sister Marga and Fergus Fanat last night?' Fidelma asked.

'Fergus Fanat? Is that whom she ran off with?'

'You did not meet Fergus Fanat?'

'I did not.'

'Do you claim that you know nothing of the attack on Fergus Fanat?'

Brother Drón began to speak but then gazed at her incredulously. 'Attack?'

Fidelma sighed shortly. 'When did you last see Sister Marga?'

'At the meal last night. Then she and Sister Sétach left for their hostel.'

'So what brought you here?'

'Sister Sétach told me that Marga was missing sometime around midnight. For the second time a message had been brought to the fortress telling me that she was meeting a lover in this glade.'

'So you came here, and found the message was from Ordwulf. Why are you so anxious to pursue and keep control of Marga?'

'She took an oath to serve at Cill Ria. An oath is not lightly taken and she must maintain it.'

'Even as Senach did,' Fidelma observed.

Brother Drón blinked rapidly. Before he could respond she turned to Caol. 'Take Brother Drón back to Cashel and make sure that he does not leave the fortress again.'

'What of you, lady?' demanded Caol.

'We will follow on shortly. Brother Berrihert will ride the horse Ordwulf came here on.'

Caol acknowledged her instruction with a slight bow of his head and then turned and pointed up the narrow path out of the small glade. Angrily, Brother Drón preceded him, prompted by the way Caol's hand rested on the hilt of his sword.

Fidelma looked questioningly at Brother Berrihert. 'How do you wish to bury your father?' she asked gently.

'He was not a Christian,' Brother Berrihert replied. 'Therefore, I would like to send him to his hall of heroes in the traditional manner on a funeral pyre. It must be done tonight and it should be in some place apart that will not offend anyone. Would Miach give permission to have it raised on the hills near where we hope to dwell?'

'I'm sure he would,' Fidelma said at once. 'You will want your brothers to attend as well?'

'It is their right.'

'Very well. If you take the track from here which leads north-west, within twenty kilometres you will find yourself back in the great valley of Eatharlaí, which you have made your new home. Wait there at Ardane and I will send your brothers to you. To the south you will see the wooded mountains rising above you – Sleibhte na gCoillte, the mountains of the woods. Tell Miach that I have requested this. When you are ready, proceed up into them; you may build your pyre there. It is isolated up there and you will not offend anyone. Miach will tell you the best path. That will be a fitting place for your father. Eadulf and Gormán will bring your brothers to you at Ardane by this evening.'

Brother Berrihert impulsively reached forward and took her hand.

'Bless you, lady. For your understanding and for your trust.'

Fidelma smiled wryly. 'I do not think it will be displaced.'

'Yet I know that my father, indeed, myself and my brothers, could be suspect of killing Abbot Ultán just as my father attempted to kill his lackey Drón.'

'I do not think that you or your brothers had a hand in it,' replied Fidelma.

'You may rest assured, lady, that, having observed the obsequies for our father this night, we shall return to Cashel after dawn tomorrow, there to await your judgements on the matters of Abbot Ultán's death and my father's attack on Drón.'

Eadulf helped Brother Berrihert to carry the body of Ordwulf, with his battleaxe, up the path to where they had left their horses. He helped Berrihert secure the body on Ordwulf's horse and Berrihert mounted behind it. Fidelma pointed to the track he must follow which was easy enough as the great Mountains of the Woods were visible. They rose to the north-west and once round their most easterly end, the mouth of the valley of Eatharlaí opened up and Ardane was near.

They watched him set off along the track and then mounted their own horses. Fidelma was a little saddened.

'Let us pray that the blessed glade of Patrick's Well will extend its healing quality to the poor lost soul of Ordwulf.'

Eadulf grimaced sceptically. 'It seems to me that Brother Drón stands more in need of its healing and calming qualities than did Ordwulf.'

Fidelma was thoughtful. 'Drón and all his ilk are trouble,' she said as they turned their horses back towards Cashel. 'Eadulf, I am sorry to place this extra journey on you and Gormán when we return. While I trust the Saxons, I would prefer it if you both accompanied Berrihert's brothers to attend this funeral of Ordwulf.'

Eadulf gave her a quick glance. 'You expect some problem?'

'Not exactly. I want to ensure that there are no problems. Ninnid is always looking for easy solutions and there is a growing impatience among the guests at Cashel which might substitute expediency for justice.'

'You mean that some will blame Ordwulf for Ultán's death now that he has attempted the life of Drón? But then who killed Muirchertach? Dúnchad Muirisci?'

'As I say,' Fidelma replied, without answering his question, 'some at Cashel want quick solutions which will probably not be the right ones.'

They arrived back at Cashel by mid-morning and immediately Fidelma sought out Caol to ensure that he and his prisoner had arrived back safely.

The young warrior was rubbing down his horse in the stables.

'There were no problems on your journey back?'

Caol grinned crookedly. 'How did you guess that there would be problems, lady?'

'I did not think that Brother Drón was the type to be a docile companion and come here under your guidance without creating a problem.'

'Well, he did once try to elude me. But I would not be fit to be commander of your brother's bodyguard if I had allowed him to be successful.'

'What did you do?' asked Eadulf.

'I gently stroked him on the head with the blunt part of my sword, and while he was stunned I tied his hands with some cord.'

Fidelma grimaced. 'He will doubtless complain of ill treatment but you did the right thing. Where is he now?'

'Well, I know he is a guest here but, judging by his behaviour, he needed to be placed somewhere secure until you can decide what to do with him. I had him placed in the Duma na nGiall.'

At the back of the fortress was an area that was separated from the rest of the palace buildings by a high wall through which only someone with authority or special permission could enter. It was know by the ancient name Duma na nGiall – the mound of hostages. Nobles who had been taken prisoner in battle, who would not give their *gell*, their word of honour, not to escape, were imprisoned there. Until recently it was where the Uí Fidgente chieftains had been held until the peace with the new Uí Fidgente prince Donennach was concluded.

'Has my brother been informed of this?'

Caol nodded quickly. 'I explained the circumstances. The king said that he would inform Blathmac of Ulaidh because Drón was theoretically under his protection. Colgú does not want any arguments to arise . . .'

Fidelma held up her hand, nodding.

'. . . over such a sensitive matter,' she concluded. 'He is punctilious.'

'But Colgú agreed to allow Drón's incarceration until your return.'

'So Brother Drón is still incarcerated in the Duma na nGiall?'

'He is.'

'Good. I will see my brother before I have a long talk with Brother Drón.'

She turned to Eadulf as they began to walk back across the courtyard to the main buildings.

'Find Pecanum and Naovan in the hostel for the male religious in the town. Tell them gently what has happened to their father. Take Gormán and two spare horses with you and go to Ardane, as we have agreed. Explain to Miach that he should do all he can to help Brother Berrihert and his brothers with their burial of their father. They must be allowed to do it in the manner they think fit. Say it is my wish.'

'I will. But what of you? This means I shall not be back before tomorrow morning at the earliest. You promised the High King that you would tell him tonight who killed Ultán and Muirchertach.'

Fidelma gave him a reassuring look. 'I promised only to tell him whether I was in a position to have a hearing before the Chief Brehon. I think I can do that now. Don't worry, I shall not be bringing this matter to a conclusion before your return. We need all the suspects to be brought together here before that can happen. So make sure that you return safely with Brother Berrihert and his brothers.'

Colgú was actually with Blathmac when Fidelma was shown into her brother's chambers. The king of Ulaidh looked up with a frown.

'You are placing a heavy burden on me, lady,' he greeted her sourly.

Fidelma took a seat before the fire.

'What burden would that be, Blathmac?' she inquired innocently.

'The incarceration of Brother Drón of Cill Ria.'

'Why would that be a burden?' she asked as she warmed herself at the flames.

'Whatever has happened here, lady, and however Ultán and Drón have been regarded, they were still the emissaries of Ségéne, abbot of Ard Macha, and, moreover, the Comarb of the Blessed Patrick. It is to Ségéne that I have to justify these events. Even if the southern kingdoms do not regard him as the senior bishop in the five kingdoms, we in the northern kingdoms do so. Abbot Ségéne can be a powerful friend and a powerful enemy. Remember that I am king of Ulaidh and if I am not seen to be protecting the interests of my people

– all my people, the good and the bad – then my position will be questioned.'

Colgú was anxious to placate his fellow king. 'We understand that, Blathmac.' He glanced at his sister. 'Fidelma, is there a good reason to hold Brother Drón in such a manner?'

'I am afraid so. Caol has undoubtedly informed you of the facts?'

'He has, and I have explained them to Blathmac.'

'I simply require him to be held long enough for me to question him,' Fidelma explained.

'You are no longer suggesting that he killed Muirchertach?' inquired Blathmac.

'I have long ago learned to refrain from speculation until I know all the facts. I know that he has taken a curious interest in one of the Cill Ria group – Sister Marga. I want to know why, and until I have put these questions to him I cannot allow him to range across the country at will, which is what he is intent on doing. Do you know anything about him, Blathmac?'

The Ulaidh king made a negative gesture.

'I try to avoid having anything to do with the abbey of Cill Ria,' he confessed. 'You have doubtless talked to my cousin Fergus Fanat on that subject, since he had some interest there. But Abbot Ultán was not a person I favoured. God forbid, but I think the judgement of the wind and waves was wrong on the day that he was washed back to shore and claimed conversion to the Faith.'

'Did you believe that conversion was not genuine?'

'Whether I did or not, the Comarb of Patrick thought it was and welcomed Ultán into his circle of friends and senior clerics. And Drón, as you may know, was trained at Ard Macha and sent as a scribe to Ultán. What I am saying is that Abbot Ultán and Brother Drón have powerful friends at Ard Macha. So we must walk softly in their shadows. Even a king such as I has to be careful.'

'I understand,' Fidelma said. 'I will ensure that Drón is held no longer than is necessary. In fact, I came only to reinforce what Caol has told you before I go to question him.'

'You have my gratitude, lady,' Blathmac acknowledged. 'I hope this whole matter will come to a speedy conclusion.'

Fidelma left them and went to find Caol before making her way to the back of the palace complex and the gates of the area separated from the rest of the buildings by a high wall.

The same wiry little man that Fidelma had already encountered during the release of the Uí Fidgente prisoners was still the *giall-chométaide*, or chief jailer. Fidelma found that she still did not trust him but put it down to his unfortunate ferret features: the close-set eyes, thin lips and ready smile. However, it did not signify whether she liked the jailer or not, provided he was efficient in his job.

He unlocked the gate at their approach, smiling and bobbing his head in obeisance.

'Welcome, lady, welcome, commander. How may I serve you?'

'We have come to question Brother Drón whom you hold here,' Fidelma replied, trying to hide her irritation at the man's ingratiating behaviour.

'Brother Drón?' The man's smile suddenly seemed fixed and he echoed the name as if it had no meaning.

'I do not have much time,' she said tersely. 'Come, take me to him.'

The jailer looked at her and now dismay was registering on his face. 'But, lady, your brother the king ordered Brother Drón's release an hour ago.'

# CHAPTER SEVENTEEN

Fidelma's brows drew together in anger as she stared at the jailer's bewildered features. 'Don't be silly, man! I have just come from my brother, and am here to question the prisoner.'

The man's face was pale. 'But . . . but . . .'

Fidelma was impatient. 'Take me to the prisoner immediately.'

'But I tell you the truth, lady,' replied the dismayed jailer. 'I released Brother Drón over an hour ago. The Brehon Ninnid ordered his release in the name of King Colgú.'

Fidelma stared aghast at the man. 'Brehon Ninnid did *what*?'

'He ordered the immediate release of Brother Drón,' the man repeated helplessly.

Fidelma was already turning to Caol and issuing curt orders. 'Find out whether Brother Drón is still in the fortress. I suspect he is probably gone by now. Seek out Brehon Ninnid. If you find him, bring him to Colgú's chamber at once – bring him under duress if necessary. If you see the Brehon Barrán ask him to come there straight away. I have never . . .' She was shaking her head in disbelief even as Caol hurried off on his errands.

Fidelma erupted into her brother's chamber in the violence of anger. Colgú was alone and started up in surprise as his sister burst in.

'Brother Drón has been released in your name!' she thundered before he could speak.

Colgú looked at her in bemusement. 'But you know I did not order . . .' he began, but Fidelma interrupted.

'It was Ninnid. He dared to go to the jail and order Drón's release in your name.'

At that moment Chief Brehon Barrán entered behind her. 'What has happened?' he demanded. 'I was asked by the commander of your guard to come here with all despatch. Is something wrong?'

Colgú had realised the seriousness of the situation and assumed a steely glint in his eyes that matched his sister's.

'Brother Drón was being held in the jail here under my authority, with the knowledge of Blathmac of Ulaidh. My sister tells me that Brehon Ninnid of Laigin has ordered his release in my name without my knowledge nor permission. He must answer for this.'

Even Brehon Barrán appeared momentarily shocked at this news, but his surprise was tempered with curiosity. 'What had Brother Drón done to deserve being incarcerated in the first place?'

Fidelma swiftly sketched in why she had agreed to Caol's taking the unusual step of keeping Brother Drón secured. She had barely finished speaking when Caol himself entered.

'Brother Drón has, indeed, left the fortress,' he said quickly. 'So has Brehon Ninnid. Using the brehon's authority, they took their horses from the stables and rode off.'

'Is it known what direction they took?'

Caol shrugged eloquently. 'They were last seen riding down into the township. After that, who knows? I have sent men to see if they can find anyone who can tell us.'

Brehon Barrán's countenance was bleak. 'I have no understanding of Ninnid's actions, except they are of great affront to you, Colgú. First, we must try to repair the damage,' he said firmly, turning to Fidelma. 'Are you saying that Brother Drón is guilty of one or other of these murders?'

'He is an important witness,' Fidelma replied. 'Something links him to Sister Marga and that is the mystery I must elucidate. It is a mystery that apparently makes it imperative that he control her movements. What it is, I was hoping to find out by questioning him. I suspect that Marga's life is in danger now.'

'I was told that Sister Marga had fled during the night after there was an attack on the Ulaidh warrior, Fergus Fanat.'

'Another matter that needs clarification,' Fidelma said. 'Marga did leave here and Drón attempted to follow her. As it was, it was on a false trail.'

She quickly told the Chief Brehon what had happened at Patrick's Well. Brehon Barrán looked puzzled. 'It sounds a complicated story.'

'Due to Ninnid's intervention, Drón has eluded me. I think he will now try to track down Sister Marga.'

'Track?' Colgú turned abruptly to Caol. 'Who is the best tracker we have?' he asked.

Caol had no hesitation. 'Rónán.'

'Of course.' Colgú smiled briefly. 'Fetch him to me. The only thing we can do is attempt to trace Drón's tracks and see where he is heading.'

Caol was just leaving when one of his warriors halted him in the doorway and whispered something. The commander turned back with a grim smile.

'Brehon Ninnid has just returned to the fortress. My men have brought him hither protesting innocence of any wrongdoing.'

Colgú turned to Fidelma in grim satisfaction. 'Now, perhaps, we shall learn the answers to some of our questions.' He glanced at Barrán. 'As Chief Brehon of the Five Kingdoms, you must give authority to this matter.'

Brehon Barrán's features were stern. 'I will conduct the questioning myself, for Brehon Ninnid's actions are without support in law.'

Fidelma went to sit by her brother while Brehon Barrán took up a stance before the fireplace with his hands clasped behind his back. Colgú nodded to Caol, who stood aside and motioned to someone in the adjoining antechamber.

Brehon Ninnid entered the room, red-faced and angry, followed by Enda, whose hand was clasped on the hilt of his sword.

'You can fetch Rónán now,' Colgú told Caol, 'and wait with him in the adjoining chamber until we are ready.'

As the door closed, Brehon Ninnid took a pace forward. His features showed his hostility. Then his eyes widened with surprise when he saw the grim face of Brehon Barrán.

'I am glad you are here,' he said, recovering his poise. 'I have been treated with the utmost discourtesy. This warrior almost hauled me off my horse as I rode back from the township just now. He marched me here under threat of physical force. He dared to use me thus in spite of the fact that I am a brehon. This is outrageous!'

Brehon Barrán waited calmly until Ninnid stopped speaking.

'So you have no idea of any reason why you should be asked to come here?' he asked softly.

'None that demands such discourteous treatment,' snapped Ninnid.

Brehon Barrán raised an eyebrow. 'Not even that you abused your authority to help a prisoner to escape?' His voice was still gentle.

'Help a prisoner . . . ?' Brehon Ninnid began angrily, and then his expression changed slightly. 'Ridiculous. I presume that you refer to Brother Drón? He was unjustifiably incarcerated by a warrior and I merely released him.'

Brehon Barrán's expression did not change but his tone hardened. 'You are in the palace of Colgú, king of Muman, and the release of prisoners from the Duma na nGiall can only be made in his name. Did you tell the jailer that the release was ordered in the name of Colgú?'

Brehon Ninnid frowned. 'I probably implied it . . . but I am a brehon. It is my right and duty to correct injustice and it was obvious that the warrior had gone too far.'

'How do you know this, Brehon Ninnid? Who told you that Brother Drón had been jailed in the first place?'

'Someone saw him being marched there and I went to investigate. I demanded to speak to the prisoner in my capacity as a brehon.'

'So how did you learn the details of why Brother Drón was jailed and decide that it was an injustice?' pressed the Chief Brehon.

'It was simple enough to decide. Brother Drón told me.'

The Chief Brehon's expression became incredulous. 'And you believed him?'

'Why should I not? He is a religious man, a leading churchman of Ulaidh, and he . . . he is . . .' Brehon Ninnid was suddenly quiet.

'And he is originally from Laigin. Of the Uí Dróna, as are you, Ninnid,' Fidelma said softly.

Brehon Barrán frowned as he considered this. 'Of course. I had forgotten. Are you related to him?'

Brehon Ninnid raised his jaw defensively. 'I am of the Uí Dróna but that is irrelevant.'

'Is it? Drón told you that he was being wrongly imprisoned?'

'Of course. I saw at once that the commander had simply over-stepped his authority and made the jailer release him.'

'Further, you took him to the stables where you both took your horses and rode out of the fortress . . . what direction did he take?'

That something was seriously wrong had finally registered with the arrogant young brehon. He was beginning to look nervous.

'I wanted to see someone staying in a hostel in the township below. We rode to the town together. I stopped at the hostel and Brother Drón rode on. He told me that he was hoping to find Sister Marga, who had fled without his authority.'

'Where did he go? In what direction?' snapped Fidelma, unable to stay silent any longer.

Brehon Ninnid looked nervously at her, and when he hesitated Barrán added sharply: 'Answer the question.'

'I think he took the road that runs west to the great river, the Siúr.'

Fidelma sighed. 'That is of no help. We shall still need Rónán to track him.'

The Chief Brehon gazed sadly at the brehon of Laigin. 'Know that in your arrogance, Ninnid, you have transgressed the law. Even the fact of releasing a prisoner is as nothing compared to taking the authority of the king without his permission. Did it not occur to you that Drón would not tell you the truth? Did it not occur to you that the warrior was acting with authority and not on some whim of his own? You will be brought before a hearing, Ninnid, and if it is found that you acted out of nepotism because you are of the Uí Dróna you will never hold office again.'

Ninnid swallowed nervously. 'But it was not that . . .' he began.

Brehon Barrán raised a hand to silence him. 'Every brehon must bear the responsibility for any mistake he makes,' he said firmly. 'As I see it, you are already self-confessed of the mistake of *leth-tacrae*.'

It was the legal term used when a brehon gave a judgement after hearing only one side of a case. Such a judgement was considered an injustice against the king and the nobles of the kingdom. It was the most serious breach of duty for a judge and the punishment was that he not only be deprived of his office but also pay his honour-price.

Ninnid turned pale. 'I swear that I did not act out of kinship for Brother Drón. The fact that he was of my people might have influenced the way I felt about my decision, but not the way I came to it. I did believe that I was acting out of right.'

Fidelma suddenly found herself feeling almost sorry for the arrogant young man.

'I am not excusing the enormity of what Ninnid did,' she said. 'But perhaps *leth-tacrae* might be too strong a term for what was, after all, not a legal judgement but a mistaken opinion, an ignorance born of arrogance.'

The Chief Brehon regarded her in amusement. 'Are you entering a plea for Ninnid?'

Fidelma met his amused gaze and her eyes twinkled in answer. 'I was unaware that this was a duly constituted court but thought it merely a means of questioning Ninnid as to what prompted his actions. That those actions were wrong and without legal authority is in no doubt, but perhaps the lesson that we trust he will learn can be underscored by a fine. After all, is there not an often repeated maxim in the law books *cach brithemoin a báegul* . . . to every judge his error?'

Chief Brehon Barrán turned gravely to Colgú. 'As your sister points out, this is not a properly constituted court hearing of an accusation of misdeed against Ninnid. It is your right, as the injured party, to demand such a hearing before a court of three judges of equal stature to Ninnid. Do you wish to proceed legally against him?'

Colgú looked at his sister as if for guidance and then shrugged. 'If Ninnid is willing to admit his error, then I am content.'

Brehon Barrán turned back to the Laigin brehon whose arrogance had long since deserted him and who now stood with hunched shoulders and bowed head.

'The king and the lady Fidelma have been lenient in this matter. As Chief Brehon, I cannot be so lenient, so I will say that you will not only pay five ounces of silver, which would have been the pledge in support of your position of prosecutor of Muirchertach Nár had he lived, but a fine of a *cumal*, the value of three milch cows, which would have been your fee. Furthermore, you will have no further involvement in the case of either the death of Abbot Ultán or that of Muirchertach Nár. Nor can you be the chief brehon in Laigin but will return to the lower order of judges. Do you accept this ruling or do you wish to appeal?'

Ninnid's shoulders seemed to sink even lower.

'I accept,' he said softly.

When Ninnid had left the Chief Brehon relaxed a little. 'A vain and silly man. He is talented in his knowledge of law but his arrogance makes him defective in his judgement. Yet perhaps he will learn from this event.' He suddenly turned to Fidelma. 'Are you close to a solution to these matters now?'

'You may tell the High King that tomorrow at midday, either we will have the answers to these deaths or we may have to assume that the culprit has escaped us.'

'Ah, you mean Brother Drón?'

Fidelma would not comment but made her excuses and left. Colgú stood up, moved to a side table and waved the Chief Brehon to a chair near the fire.

'A goblet of wine, Barrán?'

The Chief Brehon smiled. '*Corma* would be better still,' he said.

Colgú poured the drinks and settled in a chair opposite Barrán. They both sipped appreciatively for a moment.

'I hope my sister will be able to sort out this puzzle,' Colgú finally commented. 'It is a bad business, with everyone ready to condemn Cashel if there is no resolution.'

'I have confidence in Fidelma.' The Chief Brehon was reassuring. 'Her reputation has not been won merely by luck. If I had influence with her, I would try to persuade her to separate entirely from the religious and become a brehon instead of just a *dálaigh*. She has the ability to make such sound judgements that she is often wasted in pleading cases before others . . . especially when they are so inferior in judgement as Ninnid.'

'I know that she has been considering her position in the religious,' Colgú confided. 'However, she feels uncomfortable about it because she places such reliance on our cousin's advice . . .'

'Abbot Laisran of Durrow?'

Colgú nodded. 'He was the one who persuaded her to enter the religious in the first place. He argued that it would make her independent of a reliance on her work in law. But monastic life was not to her taste. Her first interest and commitment is to the law and, as you know, for the last few years now she has been her own mistress. However, I know that she feels that any severance from the religious will be a betrayal of Laisran.'

'Do you think her marriage to the Saxon will alter her attitudes?'

'I think Eadulf is a good man. A stable man. I would, of course, have preferred her to wed one of our own, but he shares her enthusiasm for her work. He is not qualified in our laws, but he seems to have a natural aptitude in helping her to solve these conundrums. I have often suggested that he should study our law, for he was an hereditary . . . *gerefa*, I think is the word. It means a magistrate of his own people in the Saxon lands.'

Barrán sighed deeply. 'I share your view of Eadulf. A good man, even though he is a Saxon. Perhaps you are right, Colgú. Maybe he will help steer her away from the stormy waters that this new faith is bringing with it. The debates between our native forms and these foreign ways that emanate from Rome are becoming more vicious. Truly, I do fear for the future.'

Fergus Fanat was sitting up with a bandage round his head and looking rueful as Fidelma entered the little room where old Brother Conchobhar nursed his patients. Fidelma had been informed that the warrior had recovered consciousness as she was about to leave the fortress with Caol and Rónán. She told them to continue down to the town to begin the search for Brother Drón and that she would catch up with them later.

'How are you feeling?' she asked as she dropped into a seat beside his bed.

The warrior managed a brief smile. 'As if someone has hit me over the head with a cudgel.'

'At least they have not repressed your humour,' she commented. She paused and then went on: 'You know that Sister Marga has left the fortress? And Drón, in spite of our best efforts, has escaped and we think he is in pursuit of her.'

Fergus Fanat sighed deeply but said nothing.

'You do not appear surprised?'

He glanced up at her and then shrugged. 'I am not exactly surprised,' he said cautiously.

'Why didn't you tell me that you knew Sister Marga when I first questioned you after the game of *immán*?'

'You did not ask me,' he countered.

'That is true,' she agreed. 'But you did not volunteer the information even though she was standing on the field waiting to speak to you.'

'At that time, our last parting had not been in the best spirit. I wasn't sure whether I was going to speak to her anyway.'

'When did you first meet Sister Marga?'

Fergus Fanat frowned. The contraction of his muscles resonated on his injury and he winced, raising a hand to his bandaged forehead.

'She must have told you,' he said.

'I am asking you to tell me,' Fidelma said firmly.

He made a resigned gesture with his shoulders. 'I was visiting the abbey of Ard Stratha on behalf of Blathmac and Sister Marga had come there to investigate some old manuscripts . . . I cannot remember precisely. The story is not complicated. I fell in love; she said that she reciprocated my feelings. When she went back to her own abbey at Cill Ria, I contrived to meet her many times . . .'

'You *contrived*?' Fidelma emphasised the word.

'You will recall that I knew all about Abbot Ultán, his background and his pious prejudices. He had already separated what used to be a *conhospitae* into separate houses for the males and females. He did not sanction any fraternisation between the sexes and our meetings were very difficult to arrange. Then she stopped meeting me at all, and through an intermediary she told me that the relationship was over and that she no longer wanted to see me.'

Fidelma raised her head with interest. 'Who was the intermediary?'

'The same woman who is her companion now.'

'Sister Sétach?'

Fergus Fanat nodded. 'I was forced to accept it, though I could not understand it. I saw no more of Marga until the very day you mention, in the township here when I was playing *immán*.'

'And when was the first time that you spoke to her after that?'

'In the woods, during the hunt.'

'Tell me about that,' Fidelma said, sitting back.

Once more Fergus Fanat gave her a quick examination from under lowered brows. 'I suppose you know that she was running away from Cashel?'

'I do.'

'Well, we had encountered the boars, a whole pride of them with a large male tusker who had already caught one of the hounds and injured it badly. Then this boar espied us and did it run off? It did not, but came and charged our horses. Boars are fighting animals and do not scare easily – but to charge at the spearmen? Incredible. That was when I managed to prick it with my *bir*. Anyway, some of the horses were frightened. Some took off. I was separated in that charge and started looking for the main body. It was then that I came across Marga.'

Fidelma leaned forward. 'So your meeting was not prearranged?'

He shook his head quickly, confirming the story that Marga had told Fidelma. 'I knew that she was a good horsewoman. She told me her family bred horses up on the Sperrins. Those are the mountains in Uí Thuirtrí country. So I was not surprised when I found her.'

'You had not known that she was in the party of women following the hunt?'

'Not until then.'

'What then?'

'She halted and we exchanged a few awkward words. Then she began to cry and we dismounted and began to talk. She told me why she had decided that we should stop seeing each other.'

'Which was to do with the way she had been treated by Abbot Ultán?'

Fergus looked shocked. 'You know that?'

'She told me. Go on. What was your response?'

'The response of any man who loves a woman,' he replied vehemently. 'I said that it was of no consequence to me. I loved her still and wanted her to be my wife.'

'In spite of what she had been made to suffer?'

'In spite of it and because of it. It was not her fault. She told me that she was on her way to Laigin. She had wanted to escape from Ultán for a long time. She had come on this trip with Ultán only as a means of finding the right opportunity. She was afraid that even with Ultán dead, Brother Drón, who was Ultán's friend and the heir apparent to the abbacy, would force her to go back to Cill Ria.'

Fidelma had not realised that Drón would be the successor to Ultán, but she supposed it made sense. The heads of the abbeys and religious houses of Éireann were elected in the same way as the clan chiefs, nobles and kings: by the *derbhfine*. In the case of the abbeys and monastic houses, the *derbhfine* consisted of the *familia* or the religious.

'So why did you prevent her going to Laigin? Why bring her back? It seems illogical behaviour if you were concerned for her welfare.'

Fergus Fanat was silent for a moment. 'Not so illogical. I understood why she wanted to escape from Brother Drón and Cill Ria and she had seized the first opportunity. But I realised that it would do her no good in the long run.'

Fidelma put her head on one side thoughtfully. 'Why not?'

The young warrior smiled without humour. 'I do not need to tell you that.'

'I think you do. Whatever I know or can guess, I need you to tell me what thoughts are in your mind.'

'As I say, it is obvious. Ultán is murdered. Marga hated him and had every reason to hate him. She takes Ultán's own horse and flees from Cashel. It takes no great leap of the imagination to guess what people would think. They would believe that she was the killer and she would soon be overtaken and tried for his murder.'

'Two questions then,' Fidelma rejoined. 'First, how did you know it was Ultán's horse she was riding?'

Fergus Fanat smiled briefly. 'Simple enough. She told me.'

'Second, why would you think that once it was known that Marga had fled from Cashel a hue and cry would be raised and she would be soon overtaken and the murder of Ultán laid at her feet?'

'Because . . .' began Fergus Fanat confidently, and then he paused, staring at her.

'Exactly,' murmured Fidelma. 'So far as you would have known at the time you met her in the forest, Muirchertach was still alive and Muirchertach was the person charged with the murder of Ultán. Even though you knew I was defending him, there was no reason to think that Marga was under any suspicion.'

Fergus met her penetrating blue-green eyes with his black defiant ones.

'You were trying to be protective?' she suggested, when he failed to reply.

'Of course I was.'

'But only because you believed that she had killed Abbot Ultán. You believed that Marga had killed Ultán and that she was probably justified. But you feared that if she continued her flight to Laigin, then I – who did not believe Muirchertach Nár was guilty – would immediately be suspicious about her; that I would raise that hue and cry. That is why you persuaded her to come back to Cashel.'

Fergus thrust out his jaw pugnaciously.

'She had every right to kill that swine,' he said stubbornly. 'She is a poor frightened girl, trying desperately to survive. That beast has made her change from a beautiful, intelligent young woman into someone who can only act out of instinct and who thinks the entire world is against her.'

'Does she know that you believe she killed Ultán? When I spoke to her before she disappeared this time, she thought that you supported her.'

'I would have done so,' Fergus said, suddenly avoiding her eyes.

'Even though you believe she killed Ultán? What makes you so certain that she killed him?'

Fergus Fanat raised a hand slowly to his bandaged skull. 'Because on the night that Ultán was killed, I was passing along the corridor and saw Marga entering his chamber . . .'

'When was this?' pressed Fidelma quickly.

'Close to midnight, I suppose.'

'Think carefully, man,' snapped Fidelma. 'Describe the scene. Where were you?'

'I didn't see her face,' he admitted. 'I was coming up the corridor which faces Ultán's door. In fact, Brother Drón had just come out of his chamber a little way in front of me just as Marga came out of Ultán's chamber . . .'

'How did you know it was Ultán's chamber?'

'It was pointed out to me earlier. All the representatives of Ulaidh were placed in apartments close together.'

'Go on. Did Brother Drón say anything to you?'

'He did not see me. He was too busy looking at Marga and then he went back into his room. Marga did not glance in our direction but went directly along the other corridor. I went on to my own chamber which was close by that of Brother Drón.'

Fidelma shook her head. 'So you saw her leaving Ultán's chamber. I still do not understand what makes you so sure it was Marga who killed him.'

Fergus Fanat stared at her for a few moments and then shrugged with a sad expression.

'I am sure because . . . Marga tried to kill me,' he said simply.

The rain was cold and blustery but very fine as the group of horsemen approached the Lake of Pigs on their way to cross the river Siúr. It was a small lake standing just south of the Ford of the Ass which Eadulf knew well. Gormán, however, insisted that due south from this little lake was a shallow crossing which could be negotiated over the broad river and that would be a shorter route into the great glen which was their destination.

All four men had heavy woollen cloaks to protect them against the fine but penetrating rain. The route lay over the plains where there were numerous little homesteads and prosperous farming lands.

Gormán was leading the way confidently and setting a good pace. Eadulf came next and behind him the two Saxon brothers, Pecanum and Naovan.

'We should be at Ardane just after nightfall,' called Gormán. He pointed one hand to the sky. 'The clouds are breaking up in the west. The rain will cease soon. We can let the horses water at the lake.'

By the time they reached the Lake of Pigs, as Gormán had fore-told, the rain had stopped and a pale winter sun had even appeared between the drifting, dark clouds. But it was not warm enough to remove their heavy cloaks, and Gormán suggested they have a swallow of *corma* to keep out the chills.

The lake lay surrounded by oaks and yews that seemed to vie with one another for predominance.

They had let the horses water themselves, though not too much, and having taken their drink of fiery spirit were about to mount up when Eadulf saw a movement among the trees at the far end of the lake.

'Another traveller,' he observed to Gormán, nodding in the direction of the movement, as he mounted his horse.

Gormán, already seated in the saddle, squinted in the direction Eadulf had indicated. There was a glimpse of a rider moving swiftly through the trees.

'A religious,' Gormán observed. 'In a hurry . . . a female at that.'

The thought struck Eadulf immediately. Could it be Sister Marga? She had disappeared from Cashel before midnight. But she had been on foot, not on horseback – and had she had a horse she would have surely been able to travel farther than this? Nevertheless, some instinct pricked his curiosity.

'Can we catch up with her? It may be the missing woman from Cill Ria.'

'Keep straight on this path with the others, for this is the path she will join further along,' replied Gormán, pointing. 'I think I may be able to halt her long enough for you to catch up with her.' The young warrior turned, nudged his horse forward into the shallows of the lake and swam it across.

Eadulf waved his companions, Pecanum and Naovan, to follow him. He did not pretend to be a good horseman but he nudged his horse into a swift trot that soon became a canter. He hung on grimly, thankful that his mount seemed to sense, as intelligent horses do, what was wanted of it. He had no idea where Gormán was going, though he presumed that the young warrior knew a short cut over the small lake that would bring him round to cut off the figure in front. It was now that Eadulf began to have second thoughts. Why would the lonely figure be the missing Sister Marga? What made him think it was? The girl, if running away from Cashel, would surely not head in this direction but east towards Laigin as she had done before? Yet the instinct that made him act was strong.

He felt as if the canter would never end. In reality it was a short time indeed before he saw the figure of the religieuse on the road ahead, riding at a steady pace and apparently unaware of pursuit. The thudding of their hooves, however, eventually came to her ears and she glanced back. Even so, Eadulf was unable to identify her. Her action denoted panic for she turned and kicked her beast forward, but at that very moment Gormán appeared, bursting through the woods on to the track just in front of her.

Her horse, startled first by her vicious kick and then by the appearance of another horse and rider blocking its path, reared up. The slight figure fought to maintain her balance, lost hold and rolled off its back. Gormán grabbed the beast's reins and brought it under control just as Eadulf and the others came up.

Eadulf slid from his horse's back and bent down to the girl. She lay on her back winded.

He felt a strange combination of relief and concern.

It was Sister Marga.

Sister Fidelma's face was impassive as she regarded Fergus Fanat as he lay stretched on his bed.

'Tell me, Fergus, what happened when you were attacked?'

'I didn't see. I was hit from behind.'

'Yet you say that you are sure it was Sister Marga.'

'I am sure.'

'When was the last time you spoke to Marga before that?'

'After we came back I promised her that I would try to resolve the problem. It was some time before I came up with an idea. The resolution was simple. I would go to my cousin, Blathmac the king, who, like me, knew of Abbot Ultán's unsavoury reputation. I would tell him the story and ask for his intervention. At least he could prevent Marga's being sent back to Cill Ria.'

'There is one thing that puzzles me.'

'Which is?'

'If you thought Marga had killed Abbot Ultán, did you believe that she had also killed Muirchertach Nár?'

He hesitated and then nodded. 'When I asked her about

Muirchertach, she became very angry. She denied it, of course. But I wondered if she had killed him because Muirchertach had seen her on that night of Ultán's killing just as I had and was trying to use it as a weapon over her. He wanted a weapon against Cill Ria.'

'That sounds very far-fetched. From what I know, Marga would have been happy to join with anyone who wanted to bring Cill Ria into disrepute.'

'Marga is a woman who does not like to be forced into anything,' he said grimly. 'In the forest, when I asked her if she had seen Muirchertach during the hunt she denied it. I believe she killed him.'

Fidelma sat back for a moment with closed eyes.

'You do not sound as if your proclaimed love allowed you to trust her,' she commented sceptically.

An expression of anger crossed his face. 'My proclaimed love, as you call it, allowed me to put my honour at stake in standing by her over the murder of Abbot Ultán . . .'

'Which you believe she committed even though she denies it,' Fidelma said with emphasis.

'I was trying to help her.'

'Just so. And you proposed to go to Blathmac, proclaim that she was a murderess but that you loved her, and ask him to intercede so that . . . what? What exactly was Blathmac to do?'

'Let the truth be known that she had every good reason to kill Ultán. I was prepared to pay the fines and honour-price on her behalf.'

'What did Marga say to this plan?'

'When she realised that I was not pleading her innocence but mitigation in the belief that she was guilty, she turned on me angrily. She felt that I ought to be pleading her innocence. She felt I could not love her if I thought her guilty. I explained that she could not hope to get away with such a plea with the overwhelming evidence against her. I was pleading mitigation out of my love for her.'

'Would your love not accept that she was innocent?' queried Fidelma dryly.

Fergus Fanat once again raised his head defiantly. 'My love is tempered with logic.'

'So what then? Was this when she hit you?'

He shook his head. 'This conversation had taken place before the evening meal, at the side of the chapel. She went running off to the hostel. I spent some time walking round the walls of the fortress, trying to get things clear in my head. But my mind was made up. With or without her approval, I had to show that she had reason to kill Ultán, before she was found out and condemned. I decided to go ahead with my plan to tell Blathmac.'

'And then?'

'Then I went to Blathmac's chamber intending to discuss the matter with him. I remember that I entered the corridor that led to his guest chamber. It was empty and I started along it.' He paused, frowning suddenly.

'A thought has just occurred to you?'

'I had passed a small alcove in which there was a window . . .'

'I know the one.'

'I thought that it was empty. But now I recall that after I had passed it, I thought I heard a soft thump. I remember now, I glanced over my shoulder but there was nothing to account for it. Mind you, I could not see back into the alcove. I had almost reached the door when I heard a soft rustle of clothes behind me and before I could turn . . . well, I suppose I was hit, for the world seemed to explode into darkness. That was all I recall until I awoke with the old apothecary tending my wounds here.'

Fidelma was silent for a moment. 'But you told me a moment or so ago that it was Marga who attacked you. Now you are saying that you did not see who it was.'

Fergus Fanat shook his head firmly. 'I did not need to see her to know that it was her.'

'I don't follow.'

'There was the rustle of clothes, her dress, and, for a moment, I smelt perfume on the air. It was the same fragrance that I have noticed on her before.'

'What fragrance was this?'

'It is called *lus na túis* – lavender.'

Fidelma gazed at him thoughtfully for a moment. 'And that is how you knew it was Marga? By this fragrance?'

'It was. She is so silly to think that attacking me would hide her crime. But what it has done has been to show that she is either out of her mind or was just using me.'

'Where do you think Marga will go now? To Laigin?'

'She will know that would be the direction in which any search for her will be made. I suspect that she will go to earth.'

'Go to earth?' He had used the phrase in the manner in which a hunter spoke of a fox hiding in a burrow. 'That is an odd expression.'

'It was a phrase that she used when we were speaking during the boar hunt. I asked her what she would do if the alarm were raised before she could make her way to Laigin. It was a phrase that came naturally to her. I told you, she was a good horsewoman and hunted as well as any man I know.'

Fidelma was thinking that if she had been forced to go to earth near Cashel, waiting for the right moment to leave for Laigin, where would she have chosen? Uppermost in her mind now was the fact that she had to find Sister Marga before Brother Drón caught up with her.

Eadulf bent close to the recumbent form.

'Sister Marga, are you all right?'

The girl opened her eyes. She tried to focus but she gave up and closed them again. She took several deep breaths and tried again. This time she succeeded and said softly: 'I am merely winded, I think.'

Then she recognised Eadulf and her eyes widened in fear. She scrambled to a sitting position.

Eadulf put a restraining hand on her shoulder.

'Lie still!' he ordered. 'You might have broken something.'

She shook her head and replied: 'Why are you following me?'

Eadulf smiled grimly. 'It was purely coincidence that we saw you on this road. We were heading for the Glen of Eatharlaí when we saw you. Where were you going?'

She stuck out her lower lip pugnaciously. 'Away . . . away from Cashel . . . from everything.'

Eadulf smiled. He had seen no signs of pain from the girl, and now he helped her to her feet. It was true that she appeared none the worse for her fall.

'I am afraid, Marga, that you will have to come with us for the time being and tomorrow return with us to Cashel.'

'I will not!' the girl replied sharply.

Eadulf shrugged. 'You have no choice.'

'You are no brehon. You are a foreigner and cannot compel me.'

In this respect, the girl was speaking the truth. Eadulf glanced at Gormán, who had dismounted and was examining the horse she had been riding with a curious look. The warrior responded at once.

'I am afraid that Brother Eadulf is right, sister,' he said sharply, 'for I am of the Nasc Niadh, the bodyguard of the king of Muman, and can compel you to return to Cashel to face questioning.'

'Questioning about what?' demanded the girl angrily. 'I have already been questioned about Abbot Ultán's death.'

'About where you stole this horse from to start with.'

The girl flushed indignantly. 'I did not steal it.'

'Really? I know the horse well,' Gormán said sharply. 'I gave it to someone very dear to me as a present.'

Eadulf glanced at the warrior in surprise but decided to stick to the important matter in hand. 'And we have to ask you what knowledge you have of the attack on Fergus Fanat,' he added quietly.

The girl seemed to stagger a pace and went pale. 'An attack on . . . on Fergus?' she began.

'He was attacked last night, and he had not recovered consciousness when I left Cashel just after midday. All we know is that soon after that attack you left Cashel. This necessitates many questions.'

Sister Marga stared at him as if not understanding his words. Then, finally, she was able to say in a tremulous voice: 'Are you accusing me of attacking Fergus?'

'I am not accusing you of anything, Sister Marga. I am telling you what has happened and why you need to return to Cashel to clarify matters.'

'If I do, I shall be killed,' she suddenly sobbed.

'I presume that you fear Brother Drón?'

She nodded quickly.

'Then do not, for he has been taken under guard to Cashel this morning to answer questions also.' He quickly told the story of Ordwulf and Drón and the reason for their journey to the Glen of Eatharlaí.

She listened quietly.

'It must have been Brother Drón who attacked Fergus,' she commented at last. 'He is an evil man. If he tried to kill Fergus, then he will try to kill me.'

'We will protect you,' Eadulf assured her. 'Brother Drón is safe under lock and key in Cashel. He will not escape to harm you.'

# CHAPTER EIGHTEEN

Fidelma had caught up with Caol in the main square of the town-ship below the great rock of Cashel. He had selected four other warriors of Colgú's bodyguard and together with the tracker Rónán they had ridden from the fortress down into the town. Already Rónán had pointed out to them the hopelessness of his being able to pick up any tracks of Brother Drón's in or around the township. He had spent some time examining the stall where Drón's horse had been kept and discovered that there was nothing significant about the animal or its tracks. Caol had sent his men about the town to see if anyone had seen the religious from Cill Ria, but by the time Fidelma joined them he had had no success.

She found Caol standing morosely outside the main inn or *bruighean* speaking to the innkeeper.

'There are still many strangers in the township, lady,' he said in a resigned tone.

'It is true, lady,' added the innkeeper. 'People find it hard to tell one from another. I can't recall any northerner making such inquiries as you ask.' Fidelma was about to thank him when he added: 'Perhaps Della might know something. I know she gave shelter to a young female religieuse from the north last night. Perhaps, if she is still there, she would know the man you are looking for?'

'Della?' Fidelma was astonished at the mention of her friend, the mother of Gormán. 'Last night? Are you sure?'

The innkeeper answered in the affirmative. There was not much that happened in the township that he did not know about, he boasted.

Fidelma suggested that Caol's warriors wait for them at the inn while she and Caol went directly to seek out Della. If the innkeeper was so free with the information about a northern religieuse staying at Della's, then Drón would have probably been there before them.

Della was standing at her open door when Fidelma swung down from her horse. She was a woman of short stature, in her forties, but her maturity had not dimmed the youthfulness of her features or the golden abundance of her hair, or the trimness of her figure.

'You are welcome, lady.' She smiled. 'I was hoping that by now I would be at your wedding feast.'

'Alas, there are matters to be sorted out first,' responded Fidelma. 'You have heard of what has happened, of course?'

'My son . . .' she spoke the words with an added pride, as it had been only recently that she could admit in public that Gormán was her son, 'has told me some of the details.'

'I am told that you also had a visitor last night? Is she still here?'

Della's eyes widened and her hand crept to her throat.

'She left at midday. Surely, lady, she was not connected with the murders?'

Fidelma smiled reassuringly. 'Do you know her name?'

'Indeed. She told me that she was Sister Marga from Cill Ria.'

'How did she come to stay with you?'

'It was late last night. I was aroused by a noise in the little barn at the back where I keep my pigs and goat during the cold of winter. I know there are wolves about at this time of year and so I rose and lit a lamp and took my blackthorn stick and went to investigate. It was cold and the rain was falling so hard it was difficult to see one's hand in front of one's face. I went to my barn and there in a corner was this young, frightened girl.'

She paused and Fidelma waited patiently.

'She told me that she was fleeing from some man in her community who wished her harm. She was on foot and had come to the barn, driven there by the cold and rain and night. She had thought to go east to Laigin but felt the man would guess her intention so she was going to attempt the western road but was overcome with tiredness and the rain. She was also exhausted. Naturally, I offered her shelter and warmth in my house.'

'Did she give any further details?'

'Only that she kept on about this man, Brother Drón, who wanted to harm her and how she had tried to escape from him once, and fallen in with someone whom she thought she could trust to help her. I gathered it was some young man. She did not tell me his name. She told me that he had betrayed her because he did not believe in her and so she had decided to flee from Cashel. We talked awhile and then she slept. In fact, the poor girl was so exhausted that she slept almost until midday.'

'She left here at midday?'

'Shortly afterwards,' Della agreed.

'I don't suppose you noticed in which direction she went?'

'Is the girl in trouble?' Della demanded.

'She will be unless I reach her first and speak to her.'

Della hesitated a moment and then sighed. 'I put her on the road to the glen of Eatharlaí.'

Fidelma was surprised. 'Why there?'

'As I have said, she was fearful of going east to Laigin. I have a cousin among the Uí Cuileann who dwell in the glen. I told her to go to Rumann the smith. I loaned her my horse and told her to go there and that he would protect her. I promised that I would send word to her when all the guests had departed from Cashel.'

'Having just met the girl, you are very trusting, Della.'

The older woman smiled wanly. 'In my lifetime, with my experience, lady, I have come to know people. Not their outward appearances but their inward beings. I am sure there is no harm in that girl, only fear.'

'I hear you, Della,' replied Fidelma grimly. 'Nevertheless, I will have to send one of the warriors after her. The thing is, news of your guest was known by the innkeeper and if he was passed that news on . . .'

Della looked troubled. 'The innkeeper was passing the house just as the poor girl was leaving. I told him that she was a friend who was staying with me but he picked up on her northern accent. Send Gormán after her, lady. My son will treat her gently.'

Fidelma shook her head. 'Coincidence is a strange thing, Della, for not long after Sister Marga departed on that road, Gormán set out for the glen of Eatharlaí on an unrelated errand.'

The woman looked surprised but Fidelma was frowning as she considered matters.

'The main thing now is whether Brother Drón has discovered the road on which she was travelling.'

'He has not,' Della offered unexpectedly. 'A short time after the innkeeper left, this northern brother came here asking where Marga was going.'

Fidelma tried to hide her surprise. 'He came here?'

'The innkeeper is a blabbermouth. He had told someone and that someone told this Brother Drón. Well, he came here looking for her and I told him that she had gone. He wanted to know where.'

'But when was this?' Brother Drón had left the fortress in the early hours of the morning before dawn. Where had he been overnight?

'It was about an hour or so after Sister Marga left here. After midday.'

Fidelma groaned softly. 'That means he could catch up with her before she gets to the glen of Eatharlaí . . .'

She noticed that Della was smiling broadly. 'Unlike you, lady, with your religion and your law, I am not governed by a rule that I have to tell the truth.'

Fidelma glanced at her uncertainly. 'What did you tell him?'

'I sent him along the road south-east to Rath na Drínne. I said that she had mentioned something about meeting someone at Ferloga's inn there at nightfall.'

Fidelma stared at her for a moment and then her features moulded into her famous mischievous grin.

'Well done, Della. For the first time, I approve of an untruth. I have a feeling that it will not be long before you will be enjoying the wedding feast after all. I will despatch one of the warriors to Eatharlaí while Caol and the others can find Brother Drón at Ferloga's inn.'

For the first time in the last few days Fidelma felt relaxed and almost happy.

'That's Ardane!' Gormán pointed as he led the party of riders through the woods towards the surprisingly brightly lit settlement. There were many men moving around with lighted brand torches and they were challenged several times.

'What is happening?' Eadulf called to Gormán as he rode along-side the silent Sister Marga. She had not spoken since they had left the spot where they had encountered her and forced her to come with them.

'I have no idea,' Gormán replied. 'There seems to be a lot of activity.'

Miach, the chief of the Uí Cuileann, was the first to come forward to greet them.

'What is happening?' asked Eadulf again, as he dismounted.

'We heard that you were coming, Brother Eadulf. Brother Berrihert has explained everything. It is all arranged. We gave Ordwulf and his sons hospitality in our territory. With hospitality comes duty. Some of my men have already gone up into the mountain with Brother Berrihert to help him to build a funeral pyre.'

'You are very generous,' said Eadulf. 'You realise that Ordwulf was not a Christian?'

Miach grinned. 'Neither were my people a hundred years ago. What matter so long as a man lives a moral life and dies firm in his belief?'

Gormán nodded in approval. 'From what I saw, Ordwulf was a warrior and deserves to be saluted by fellow warriors,' he agreed.

'Fidelma told me to tell you that she approves of this action,' Eadulf added.

'She has a great heart.' Miach smiled, and turned to Pecanum and Naovan. 'I share your grief, sons of Ordwulf. Your father was a fine warrior and I salute his spirit. We have waited here to guide you up to where the funeral pyre is prepared for your father. I have suggested it be placed not so high up but on the summit of An Starraicin, the small peak on the south side of the valley. We can ride up there on horseback.'

'Before we do,' Eadulf interrupted, 'I would request a further favour. This is Sister Marga.' He motioned to the girl. 'She is our unwilling guest, for she is needed back in Cashel to answer ques-tions from Fidelma. She will not go of her own accord. Therefore, until we are ready to return, I would like her to stay here, for she has no place at the funeral of Ordwulf.'

Miach looked thoughtful. 'She will stay willingly or unwillingly?'

Eadulf looked at the girl, who raised her chin slightly but maintained a defiant silence. 'She will remain unwillingly.'

Miach sighed and motioned to one of his men to come forward. 'Then we shall ensure that she is here on our return.' He issued instructions and a couple of women were summoned from one of the buildings.

'Sister Marga, your safety will be ensured with these women until our return.'

Still saying nothing, Sister Marga was led away.

Half a dozen men with burning brand torches had now gathered on horseback. Everyone remounted and, with Miach leading the way, they set off across the valley floor before beginning to ascend the wood-covered mountains of Sleibhte na gCoillte. They followed one of the gushing streams that rose on the mountainside to tumble down into the river Eatharlaí, the path along the eastern side of this white water stretching up through the trees towards the bare higher slopes.

It was growing dark now. The low black clouds had descended on the mountain tops that rose in front of them. As Miach had said, An Starraicin, as its name indicated, was a small peak, almost a foothill, to the higher peaks behind. They left their horses at the edge of the wooded area and Miach, with his men holding their torches aloft, led the way out on to the bald, open summit of the hill, warning those following where to avoid the boggy ground round which they had to walk. It was a short distance, over the boulder-strewn landscape, to where there was a group of men also holding torches and standing round an already constructed funeral pyre of stacked logs.

To Eadulf, the scene was familiar. Many Saxon warriors had been sent to Wael Halla, the eternal hall of the heroes, to feast for ever with Woden, Thunor, Tiw and the other great warrior gods of his people. He swallowed nervously. The former gods of his people, he corrected himself.

Pecanum and Naovan went forward immediately to greet their brother Berrihert, to exchange embraces and talk for a moment of their father's death. Ordwulf's body now lay on top of the pyre, his weapons beside him. His double-edged battleaxe had been placed on top of his body, his lifeless hands clasping its shaft and the blade flat against his chest.

Eadulf and Gormán moved forward to stand beside the chief of
the Uí Cuileann while Pecanum and Naovan went forward to the pyre
and solemnly raised their hands in salute to their father. It was a traditional gesture of farewell. Then they both stepped back to stand either
side of their brother Berrihert.

He started to speak in the Saxon tongue. Eadulf found himself
automatically translating for the benefit of Miach and Gormán, so
that they could tell the others what was happening.

'We come not to make the funeral obsequies for a pagan but for
our father. He was Ordwulf son of Frithuwulf Churlslayer. He was a
noble warrior of his people. He lived and died as a warrior believing
in the gods of his childhood and of his people. He came to this land
because his sons wanted him to come; he came with his wife, our
mother, Aelgifu daughter of Aelfric. Even though he and his sons had
parted company in their religion, they had not parted company in
their common blood. He was our father. And he died seeking justice
against those who slew his wife, Aelgifu, our mother. We will promise
him one thing and this we swear by his funeral pyre this night. We
swear to achieve justice for our slain mother. We have adopted a new
faith, come to a new country and will follow the laws and customs
of this country. We will continue to follow these laws that are still
strange to us in order to pursue the justice that Ordwulf sought. We
swear to bring the punishment of those laws to those who slew his
wife, our mother. This we swear.'

Pecanum and Naovan echoed him: 'This we swear.'

Brother Berrihert turned his face to the darkened sky.

'Great God, Aelmihtig, you are known to men in many guises and
by many names. Our father knew you as Woden. If you are truly he,
then take our father into your eternal hall Wael Halla so that he might
reside for ever with the heroes he knew and let our mother, Aelgifu,
be there as young and beautiful as he knew her once, to serve his
mead and bring his meat, according to custom. Aelmihtig, if you are
not Woden, then, as we believe, you are more powerful. Soften your
stern eye, for being all-knowing, you know that our father was a good
man and that he and Aelgifu are deserving of their belief that they
may live for ever in whatever Wael Halla you decree for them.'

Berrihert paused, then, turning, he took up one of the burning brands in his right hand. His brothers, on either side of him, reached forward, so all three grasped the staff of the torch. All three raised their faces to the heavens and gave one long eerie cry. 'Aelmihtig!'

Across the mountains behind them first one lone wolf and then another and another took up an echo of that cry until the valleys echoed with their ghostly chorus. The three brothers had taken the steps forward to the pyre and thrust the burning torch into it. The dry twigs and fuel that had been placed there caught immediately and within moments great flames were leaping upwards to the sky.

# chapter nineteen

It was approaching midday when the sound of a sentinel horn caused Fidelma to look up with relief from the game of *brandubh* that she was playing with her cousin Abbot Laisran of Durrow. The chubby cleric noticed her expression and smiled across the wooden gaming board.

'I presume that is Brother Eadulf returning.'

Fidelma rose, with a studied leisurely poise, and crossed to the window of the chamber that overlooked the courtyard. She tried not to make her movements seem anxious or hurried. She glanced down and saw the cavalcade of horses entering the fortress courtyard and she tried to disguise her smile of satisfaction.

Eadulf and Gormán rode at the head, while behind them came Sister Marga alongside the warrior whom she had sent to Eatharlaí. Behind them came the three Saxon brothers, Berrihert, Pecanum and Naovan, and behind them rode Miach of the Uí Cuileann and two of his warriors.

She turned back to the abbot and seated herself once more at the *brandubh* board. He stared quizzically at her.

'It is Eadulf,' she confirmed, answering his unspoken question.

'Then we can finish this game later,' Laisran suggested.

Fidelma smiled confidently. 'I am not so distracted, my cousin, that I cannot win this game before I go down to greet them.'

Abbot Laisran chuckled in appreciation before glancing down at the board, examining the pieces. 'I am still in a strong position, Fidelma. I believe that it will take you some time to attempt to weaken me.'

'I make it three moves before my High King reaches safety from your attack,' she said.

Abbot Laisran frowned, peering forward. 'I don't see . . .'

'There is no advantage for you,' she said. 'Look, you have to begin your attack from here and I move there and then . . .'

He saw at once as she indicated the squares on the *brandubh* board. It was logical. But then she was always logical. He sighed, trying to remember the last time he had won a game from his young cousin. He raised his shoulders and let them fall in a gesture of resignation.

'Then I resign and acknowledge you have the game,' he said, his chubby face almost mournfully comic.

She hesitated, wondering whether she had not been diplomatic, but the abbot was suddenly smiling again.

'Does the arrival of Eadulf mean that you are now close to resolving this riddle?'

'I believe so,' she replied. 'Now we have all those concerned back at Cashel, I think that we will be able to resolve this by midday as I promised Brehon Barrán.'

Abbot Laisran's eyes widened a little. 'So you already know who killed Bishop Ultán and Muirchertach Nár?'

Fidelma rose again from her seat. 'I am sure I do, but to reveal the truth in such matters is very much like a game of *brandubh*.'

'I don't follow.'

She pointed to the board. 'Let us merely substitute the roles. We have the board, which is seven squares by seven squares – forty-nine squares in all. That is the board on which the murderer and suspects can move this way and that. The High King piece represents the murderer. The four protecting pieces are the false leads, those suspects who will eventually be cleared of wrongdoing. Our inquiries begin from the four corners of the board; the investigators are represented by the four attacking pieces. As you know, these attacking pieces can only move in logical lines whereas the defending pieces, our suspects, can move in any direction they choose. The murderer is at the centre of the board and can move in various directions but not as far as the suspects can. He can only move one square at a time. The murderer is slow and encumbered.'

Abbot Laisran looked at the board game, trying to follow her logic. 'Very well, I accept your symbolism. But then what?'

Fidelma bent over the board. 'The attacking pieces have to be relentless and corner each defender and eliminate it before moving on to the High King piece, finally trapping it. So, the investigators have to corner each suspect and eliminate them from the inquiry before moving on to trap the murderer.'

'I understand.' Abbot Laisran smiled. 'So where is your analogy leading?'

Fidelma straightened up. 'The *brandubh* board will now become the great hall here where all the players and pieces will be gathered. Before the Chief Brehon Barrán, I shall commence my attack, eliminating each suspect before cornering the murderer.' She turned for the door and then paused. 'But before I do that, I have a few things to sort out with Eadulf.'

An hour later, in their chambers, with Muirgen fussing over them, Fidelma and Eadulf had brought each other up to date on the developments since they had parted on the previous afternoon.

'Where is Sister Marga now?' demanded Fidelma.

'Because of her inclination to keep running away, I have had her placed in a locked chamber. Do you want to question her now?'

'Not at once.' She looked up to where Muirgen was playing with Alchú, and called to the nurse to go to the chamber where Sister Marga was held.

'After her journey from Eatharlaí, I fear that she must be in need of a bath. Provide all her wants, perfumes and the like, so that she may bathe. Tell her that, should she require it, Brother Conchobhar has many scents for her bath and she may ask for anything she desires. When she has done, I will come and question her. Is that clear?'

Muirgen was a simple soul and did not question Fidelma's instructions, but Eadulf was looking at her as if she had lost her reason. Fidelma merely returned his gaze with solemn features and did not answer his unasked question.

'And send an attendant to take care of Alchú while you are gone,' she added as Muirgen left.

'Now we will have a word, at long last, with Brother Drón,' she said when the attendant arrived. She explained how Caol and his warriors had picked up the surprised northern religious at the inn at Rath na Drínne on the previous evening and returned him to the fortress.

Brother Drón scowled as they entered the room where he was confined.

'You are a fool, Sister Fidelma! I have been chasing Marga because I know that she killed Abbot Ultán, as doubtless she also killed Muirchertach when he found out what she had done.'

Fidelma took a chair and said: 'You'd better tell me how you know that.'

Brother Drón scowled and looked as if he was about to argue, but Fidelma urged him to continue.

'Sister Marga was a temptress, a siren conjured to seduce that God-fearing man. She forced an unnatural liaison with the abbot.'

Fidelma looked solemn. 'Are you admitting that there was a sexual relationship between the abbot and Sister Marga?'

'The fault lay entirely with Sister Marga,' Brother Drón replied. 'Why else would he have succumbed had she not tempted him?'

'From what I have learned,' said Fidelma pointedly, 'I doubt whether he needed any temptation. Is your preamble necessary to the reason why you assert that Marga killed him?'

'Marga came to hate him. Probably because he finally rejected her advances. That's why she killed him.'

'A lot of people hated Abbot Ultán with more reason.'

'I was a witness that night. A witness to the killing.'

'A witness?' For the first time, Fidelma was genuinely surprised.

'I went to Bishop Ultán's chamber late that night . . .'

'For what reason?' demanded Eadulf.

Brother Drón blinked at the interruption. 'Why?' He hesitated. 'Because Abbot Ultán was preparing a protest against your wedding on the following day. He needed my advice.'

'Go on,' urged Fidelma.

'He asked me to go to his room about midnight to run through some of the arguments that he was going to put forward. I had just left my room when I saw Abbot Ultán's door open. His door faces the corridor where my room is. Then Sister Marga emerged. She did not see me and I pressed back into my room, for, at that time, I thought it unseemly that either Abbot Ultán or Sister Marga know that I shared their dark secret.'

'You display a curious sense of proprieties, Brother Drón,' Eadulf observed dryly. 'You knew about his penchant for women, you knew even darker secrets such as his taste for sadism, the beating to death of his victims . . . like the poor Saxon woman at Colmán's island. You ignored that. Yet you ask us to believe that you were concerned for his sensitivities or Marga's feelings? Come. What game were you playing?'

Brother Drón coloured hotly. 'I was not playing a game. I . . .'

'Perhaps you were thinking of how best to extort something from the situation?'

The barb seemed to strike home for the man flushed and was at a loss to reply.

'Carry on,' insisted Fidelma. 'You say that you saw Marga leave Ultán's chamber. What happened then?'

'I decided to remain where I was for a while in order to give Abbot Ultán a little time so that he could be assured that I had not seen anyone exit his room.'

'For how long?' At least, she thought, Drón's story corroborated that of Fergus Fanat.

'Not long. I doubt my candle had burned down by more than a *gráinne*.' He indicated the smallest Irish measurement, meaning the length of a wheat grain.

'And then you returned to Ultán's chamber?'

'The door was closed. I knocked. There was no answer. To my surprise, I found the door unbolted so I entered and saw Abbot Ultán lying on his back on the bed. It was clear what had happened. Sister Marga had stabbed him to death. I exited hastily from the room, closed the door, and started to hurry along the corridor after Sister Marga to confront her.'

'In your haste you tripped and fell,' put in Fidelma.

Drón looked at her in astonishment for a moment.

'How did you know . . . ?' he began. Then he nodded. 'Ah, from Dúnchad Muirisci. I fell outside his door and he opened it to find me picking myself up. I explained that I had tripped. The fall brought me to my senses. It was little use accusing Marga of Abbot Ultán's death. To what end?'

'Justice?' put in Eadulf cynically.

Brother Drón ignored him. 'I realised that we had to get her back to Cill Ria where her fellows in the abbey could be told of what she had done and inflict the punishment in accordance with our rules rather than allow her to go free with a simple fine under the laws of the brehons. So I went back to my chamber to consider the situation.'

'And when did you find out that Muirchertach Nár had been accused of Abbot Ultán's murder? Why did you not come forward with your information?'

'For the same reason. Sister Marga had to be taken back for punishment to Cill Ria.'

'When did you hear that Muirchertach was accused?'

'I heard a great fuss in the corridor and overheard a guard saying that Muirchertach Nár had been seen fleeing from Abbot Ultán's chamber just before he had been found murdered. I realised what had happened. After I had returned, Muirchertach Nár had gone to see Ultán and probably entered as I had. He likely found Ultán dead, turned and fled, but just as Brehon Baithen and one of the palace guards had come along the corridor. They had jumped to the natural conclusion.'

'So you could have proved Muirchertach Nár's innocence immediately?'

'Not without incriminating myself or revealing that Sister Marga was the killer.'

'When did you tell Sister Sétach about this?' asked Fidelma. 'When did you ask her to search the abbot's chamber?'

Once again, Brother Drón frowned at her apparent knowledge. Fidelma decided to explain.

'As you know, Sister Sétach came to Ultán's chamber the day after the murder was discovered. However, the guard refused her entry. She was so desperate in her search for something that she actually climbed on to the ledge that runs along the outside wall and made her way from the corridor window to the window in Ultán's chamber. I can only surmise that you must have told her about Ultán's death. What was she looking for?'

Brother Drón hesitated. 'The next day everyone knew about the murder and that Muirchertach Nár was suspect. That morning in the chapel, I took Sister Sétach aside and told her what I knew – that Sister Marga had killed Abbot Ultán. I told her that my intention was to get her back to Cill Ria as soon as it was possible to leave. As I say, in her own community, among her fellow religious, we could punish her under the full rigours of the *Penitentials*.'

'Leaving Muirchertach Nár to take the blame for the murder?' Fidelma was aghast at the admission.

Brother Drón shrugged. 'It was God's justice on the man. He was no friend to Cill Ria or to what we stand for. I rejoice at his death.'

'I find it hard to believe that you could ignore both the law and your self-proclaimed charity of the Faith. So what made Sister Sétach go to Abbot Ultán's chamber that evening?'

'Our duty was to ensure that there was no evidence left which would implicate Abbot Ultán with Sister Marga. I feared that there might be some incriminating evidence left in Ultán's belongings which, having been discovered, might lead to Sister Marga. Sister Sétach offered to go, but unfortunately she had barely begun her search when you and the Saxon brother entered. At first she did not know what to do but she thought that she had finally diverted your suspicions by telling you what was an approximation of the truth.'

Fidelma smiled thinly. 'In fact, she merely enhanced the suspicion. But, in all of this, Brother Drón, I find it hard to believe that you as a religieux would allow an innocent man to be blamed, that you would conspire to aid someone whom you thought was guilty of murder to escape the law . . .'

'Not escape the law,' intervened Brother Drón. 'To answer to a higher law, to suffer all the agonies that are due to a witch and murderess.'

Brother Drón's features were alight with fanatic zeal and Fidelma realised that he truly believed in his cause.

'Thank God it is not the *Penitentials* that rule this land, Brother Drón. At least you will now have to answer to the laws that do govern us,' Fidelma said firmly as she stood up.

Brother Drón was undaunted. 'You may shelter in your man-made rules, Sister Fidelma. Remember you will, yourself, finally have to answer to the rules of the Faith.'

'And what rules are they?' Fidelma asked sharply. 'These *Penitentials*? Who set them down? Are they not also man-made?'

'They are the law! The law of the Faith!' Brother Drón replied vehemently.

'I would have a care in your interpretation of the word "law".'

'Christ said that he came to fulfil the law, that the law was permanent and that people should obey it,' grated Brother Drón.

'And that law was Mosaic law, the ten commandments, not your *Penitentials* that have been devised to inflict suffering on mankind. Christ kept the commandments but he did not keep the law as made by men. Did he not set aside the understanding of his own people on issues like ritual cleansing, food laws and other matters – even the very understanding of the Sabbath day? Attend to your Scriptures and mark well, before you quote the words of Christ on law to me. If Scripture teaches anything, it is that it is not the appearance of law, the external appearance of purity and obedience, but its reality that should be obeyed. Christ's concern was for inner purity, for the ethic of the principle of truth rather than the ethic of rules for the sake of rules. You may claim to support the ethic of punishment of the transgressor in Cill Ria but I would hope that the true Faith teaches you the principle of charity.'

Brother Drón swallowed at her emotional rebuke. For the first time, he saw the anger and passion in her usually composed features and found no answer for her.

Fidelma paused at the door and glanced back at him. 'Does not Paul speak of the law written on the heart? Give me a pagan with a moral conscience rather than a man who proclaims the Faith in all outward appearances and yet denies that inner morality. The sooner that your type of faith is eliminated, Drón, the better will be the world.'

Silently, Fidelma and Eadulf made their way to the chamber where Sister Marga had been temporarily confined.

Enda was standing outside as they approached. He stood aside and rapped on the chamber door. Muirgen opened it.

'Sister Marga is bathed and dressed, lady,' she reported, with a salutation to Fidelma.

'Excellent. And you ensured that she lack for nothing in her toiletry?'

'I did everything as you asked, lady.'

'Then I shall not detain you any longer. You may return to little Alchú.'

Muirgen hurried off, and Fidelma and Eadulf entered the room. Sister Marga rose uncertainly.

'I shall not go back to Cill Ria, even if I am forced,' she declared fiercely.

Fidelma moved forward with a smile. 'No one will force you to go back,' she said. 'Be seated.' Then she sniffed the air. 'A nice fragrance,' she observed.

'I have just bathed. Your attendant was most helpful,' replied the girl stiffly.

'Excellent. You were able to ask for whatever perfumed *sleic* or fragrances our apothecaries could provide?'

'As a matter of fact, I have my own, which I always carry in my *cíorbholg.*'

Fidelma sniffed again and said approvingly: 'A good choice. Eadulf tells me that you were shocked to hear of the assault on Fergus Fanat?'

Sister Marga's face was set in stone. 'I did not attack him.'

'You have to admit that it was an unfortunate coincidence that you fled from Cashel at the time he was attacked?'

'It was nothing more than a coincidence. I had to get away, that is all. I did not know Fergus Fanat had been attacked.'

'Life is so full of coincidences,' Fidelma observed with a sigh. 'In fact, the one constant factor in all our lives is that when events do become intertwined there does seem to be a fated eventuality to them. We believe that coincidence is an unusual occurrence instead of its being a normal one.'

Sister Marga stared at her, trying to understand. 'Since you have brought me forcibly back here, I demand to be protected from Brother Drón. I demand sanctuary. I will not go back to the Abbey of Cill Ria.'

'Fergus Fanat offered you protection,' Fidelma pointed out. 'You did not appear to want that.'

The girl coloured hotly. 'I trusted Fergus . . .' she said brokenly. 'But he did not trust me. Now I cannot trust him further. After he told me that he had seen me come from Ultán's chamber that night, I told him that Ultán had summoned me there and why. But I also told him that I was innocent of his death. He was alive when I left the chamber. But I am sorry that he has been attacked. I am glad he is recovering. Muirgen told me,' she added. 'I wish him no harm at all. I believed that I loved him, but love means knowing and trusting someone and he showed that he neither knew nor trusted me. Even he thought me guilty of . . .'

Fidelma smiled sympathetically. 'Even the person you loved thought you guilty of murder. Well, the blindness of a lover often distorts things through the fear it arouses. It is easy to swing from love to jealousy and into a total distortion of reality.'

Sister Marga was trying to follow what Fidelma was saying. Then she repeated: 'My fear is of Brother Drón. I will kill myself rather than be taken back to Cill Ria.'

Fidelma was thoughtful. 'There is no need to fear Brother Drón. I can assure you that you will not be forced back to the Abbey of Cill Ria. We will meet again in a little while.'

Fidelma, followed by Eadulf, left the girl sitting with a bewildered expression on her features.

Outside, Eadulf was equally bewildered.

'Did you learn anything?' he demanded.

'Oh, I did.' Fidelma smiled. 'Now I must spend a short time with that trunk we found in Ultán's room. It is still under lock and key in my brother's strongroom.'

'But there was nothing of interest there. Clothes, papers, the records of Ultán's embassy on behalf of Ard Macha . . . just papers.'

'Exactly so,' Fidelma replied. 'Once I have seen those we can set up our *brandubh* board.'

Eadulf looked startled, not being privy to her discussion with Abbot Laisran. She chuckled and took his arm.

'The great hall is to become the *brandubh* board for this game in which we will find the centre piece. The centre piece is the murderer and we will now trap it.'

# CHAPTER TWENTY

The great hall of Cashel was not filled to capacity. It had been agreed that only the most distinguished guests and those directly involved in the matter would witness the resolution to the murders of Abbot Ultán and Muirchertach Nár. These were the kings, their leading nobles, their brehons and the leading churchmen. The princes and chiefs of the Eóghanacht, the Déisi and the Uí Fidgente were all gathered there. Barrán, the Chief Brehon of the Five Kingdoms, sat in judgement with the High King Sechnassach on his left side and Colgú, king of Muman, on his right. A chagrined and silent Brehon Ninnid had taken his place behind King Fianamail of Laigin, among the seated nobles and other dignitaries. Fidelma and Eadulf sat slightly to the right in front of the judges, and Caol, as guard commander, stood close by, having placed his men at strategic points about the hall.

Brother Drón was seated with Sister Sétach under guard. Sister Marga was seated with those who had been requested to attend in the role of witnesses, ranging from Aíbnat and Abbot Augaire and Dúnchad Muirisci, to Rónán the tracker, Della, Brother Berrihert with his two brothers, Brehon Baithen and Brother Conchobhar. Even so, the spacious hall was only half filled.

Colgú's steward, having been given a signal from the Brehon Barrán, moved forward and turned to the assembly. He banged his staff on the floor three times to call them to order. Then Brehon Barrán turned to Fidelma.

'Are you ready to present your resolution to the matters that have been placed before us?'

'I am,' she responded, rising from her seat.

'Proceed,' instructed the Chief Brehon.

'The matters before us are the murders of two men. First, the murder of Abbot Ultán of Cill Ria, the emissary of the Comarb of the Blessed Patrick. Second, the murder of King Muirchertach Nár of Connacht . . .'

'I would like to make a protest,' cut in a voice.

To her surprise it was Brehon Ninnid who had risen. Even Brehon Barrán seemed astonished.

'A protest? About what?' he demanded.

'The learned brehon presents the slaying of Ultán, an abbot, to be considered before the murder of a king, Muirchertach. That is not socially just.'

For a moment Fidelma did not understand the meaning of the intervention. Then she realised. There was no humour in her smile.

'I present these murders in order of their chronological precedence rather than that of their social precedence,' she replied dryly.

Brehon Barrán was frowning at Ninnid. He, too, had realised as Fidelma had that Ninnid, having been admonished by Barrán over the release of Brother Drón, was now trying to ingratiate himself by attempting to show off points of law. He was trying to present a good figure in front of his king.

'I will not accept frivolous interruptions in this court,' Brehon Barrán snapped and, flushing, the petulant Ninnid sat down.

'Let us begin, as we should,' Fidelma said with emphasis, 'with the first murder. It should not fall to a mere advocate such as I to judge a man when he is dead but the judgement is necessary to an understanding of this death. Everyone here had cause to dislike Abbot Ultán, even his close associates – or should I say *especially* his close associates? He was not a likeable man. He pretended to have been converted to the Faith even as the Apostle Paul had been when he saw the blinding light on the road to Damascus, as the Scriptures tell us. But I believe that Ultán's conversion was false. He used his rescue from the judgement of the sea, to which he had been condemned as an unrepentant criminal, in order to seize a path that would lead him to power. He was persuasive. He was even appointed by the Comarb of the Blessed Patrick as his emissary to attempt to persuade all the abbots and bishops of the five kingdoms that Ard Macha should be the primatial seat of the Faith in these lands.'

She paused and looked round the hall until her eyes alighted on Abbot Ségdae, who was seated with his steward, Brother Madagan.

'The Comarb of the Blessed Ailbe had cause to dislike the arrogance of Abbot Ultán when he arrived at the abbey of Imleach. Ultán attempted to make him acknowledge subservience to Ard Macha. And Abbot Ségdae was not alone in that dislike of this emissary. Many of the abbeys and churches of the five kingdoms had already stood up to Abbot Ultán's blustering and bullying.

'Hatred walked hand in hand with Ultán and that was the cause of his death. His murder was the ultimate act of vengeance. Muirchertach Nár had cause to dislike Ultán. Did his feelings reach the degree of hatred that was needed to kill him? Some thought so. But then Muirchertach Nár was killed. That, too, was an act of vengeance. The two murders were linked. But was it, as some thought, that Muirchertach Nár killed Ultán in vengeance and was then killed, also in vengeance, by someone who had admired Ultán?'

She paused and glanced to where Brother Berrihert and his brothers were seated.

'There was, of course, one person who came to Cashel with the open intention of killing not only Abbot Ultán but also Brother Drón. That was the Saxon warrior Ordwulf.'

Brother Berrihert rose quickly from his place. 'I protest. My father is dead and cannot defend himself. So I must answer in his place. I admit that he did try to kill the creature called Drón. But I know from his own lips that he did not kill Ultán. If he had, he would have been proud of the act and willingly acknowledged it. Such people as Ultán do not have the right to shelter under the name of the Faith. My father, indeed, my brothers and I, rejoice in Ultán's death. But we did not kill him.'

Brother Berrihert sat down abruptly. Fidelma continued as if ignoring the interruption.

'Ultán and Drón had gone to Inis Bó Finne to the community of Colmán the former abbot of Lindisfarne who, after Witebia, had brought his like-minded brethren to that place. Ultán demanded that

287

Colmán, so much respected for his adherence to the church of
Colmcille, make obeisance to Ard Macha. Colmán sent him away.
But as he was leaving the island, he saw the wife of Ordwulf, the
mother of those three brothers – Berrihert, Pecanum and Naovan –
making some token veneration to the old gods to whom both she and
Ordwulf had clung despite the conversion of their sons. Ultán had
this defenceless old woman scourged and whipped to death. The sons
of Ordwulf tried to forgive him as the New Faith teaches and came
south. But when Ordwulf heard that Ultán and Drón were here, the
old creed of blood vengeance stirred that old warrior.'

'He did not do it!' cried Brother Berrihert again.

Fidelma turned calmly to him.

'I did not say that he did. He wanted to, as you admit, but he had
no opportunity, for he could not enter the fortress that night and when
he entered the next morning he found the deed already done. He
admitted as much to Eadulf. However, he conspired to kill Drón. He
lured him to a spot not far from here in order to slay him, to complete
that vengeance. But his frail body failed him before that act of
vengeance and, as you see,' she pointed to where Brother Drón was
seated between the warriors Dega and Enda, 'Drón still lives, whereas
old Ordwulf now feasts with his gods.'

'So Ordwulf is in no way suspect of killing Abbot Ultán?'
demanded Brehon Barrán, bending forward from his chair in order
to clarify matters.

'Even had he been able to gain entrance to the fortress that night,
I would have to have eliminated him because the murders of
Muirchertach Nár and Ultán are inseparably linked. Ordwulf had no
opportunity to kill either. When the king of Connacht was murdered,
Ordwulf was waiting in vain for Drón at the Well of Patrick almost
in the opposite direction. That was the first time he had tried to lure
Drón there, but Drón was pursuing Sister Marga, who was at the
hunt.'

Brehon Barrán stirred a little impatiently.

'So we have eliminated Ordwulf. Do you point the accusation at
his sons? They would have equal cause for blood vengeance.'

'On Ultán and Drón but not on Muirchertach Nár. There was no
motive to kill the king of Connacht.' She paused for a moment. 'Let

us come back to Brother Drón, for it is Brother Drón's actions on the night of Abbot Ultán's death that are the most important.'

'Brother Drón?' Blathmac had stood up suddenly. 'It would be logical if he had killed Ultán. He would succeed as abbot, then. He is ambitious. It would follow.'

Brother Drón struggled to his feet but was held back by Dego and Enda.

'I see it! This has already been decided to salve your consciences. I refuse to be judged by you, for I am ordained in the Faith and answer to no man but only to my God. I will not recognise this court.'

'Sit down, Drón!' instructed the Chief Brehon. 'You will observe the law and respect it.'

Brother Drón took no notice of him. His voice rose in strident tones. 'Beware you who call yourselves kings or place yourself under their authority! There are two powers by which this world is ruled – the sacred authority of the priesthood and the authority of kings. But of these, the authority of the priest carries the most weight and is superior to that of the king. It is the priest who renders the accounts of kings before the tribunal of God. It is the priest who stands superior to the king for the priest intercedes with God on behalf of the king. So beware in judging me lest I judge you.'

Brother Drón turned to Fidelma with his anger and fanaticism still distorting his features. 'You beware, woman. Your days of lording it over men are numbered. I echo the words of Timothy and Titus. I permit no woman to teach or have authority over men. She is to keep silent. That is what is written in Scripture. So it is written, so let it be done!'

Fidelma sighed. 'I would advise you to return to the original text and amend your translation, Brother Drón. The word *epitrepsecin*, which means "not to permit", is used for a specific permission in a specific context. When translated correctly in Timothy and Titus, it means that Timothy is not presently allowing women to teach until they have studied and learned in silence.'

Brother Drón stared at her for a moment, trying to follow her argument. 'Then do you deny that our beloved Apostle Paul wrote to the Corinthians that women are not permitted to speak but should be subordinate, as the law says, to men. If there is anything they should desire to know, he says let them ask their husbands at home because it is shameful for a woman to speak in a church.'

Fidelma shook her head. 'I cannot believe that they have such poor Greek scholars in Rome as to misinterpret the nuances of these texts. Perhaps those that render these texts into the language by which others may teach are scared of women? Perhaps it is men who find misinterpretations an easy way of denying women their just role in life? What was once a normal practice has now become abnormal – women can no longer be allowed to be ordained and officiate over the divine offices. What sort of loving religion is it that teaches the subjugation of one sex by another? Is it the fault of the religion? Or is it the fault of the prejudiced men who have risen to high office in the services of that religion, seeking to protect their petty authority?'

There was silence. Even Eadulf was surprised, for Fidelma had never been so forthcoming on her thoughts about the role of women in the religious.

'Only man through his natural resemblance to Christ can express the sacramental role of Christ in the Eucharist,' cried Brother Drón.

'A weak argument and an insult to those women who have spread the Faith and have now been rendered as servants and foot-washers to men,' Fidelma observed dryly. 'Thank God that here, in the five kingdoms, we still have some degree of our ancient freedoms left.'

'Fidelma, much as we would like to hear more,' intervened Brehon Barrán firmly, 'this is not the place for a discussion on theology unless it is relevant to these murders. Do you charge Brother Drón?'

Fidelma shook her head. 'I do not charge Drón with either Ultán or Muirchertach's deaths. But an understanding of theology – that practised by Drón – was necessary before I could understand one of the mysteries that obscured the truth of their deaths for a long time. The mystery of why, when he was positive that it was Sister Marga who killed Abbot Ultán, he sought to cover it up and forcibly take her back to Cill Ria.'

'He believed Sister Marga killed Ultán?' echoed Brehon Barrán.

'Drón saw Sister Marga emerging from Ultán's chamber and a short time afterwards went there and found Ultán dead. This was before Muirchertach Nár was seen leaving that chamber and proof that the king of Connacht did not kill Ultán. But Drón kept that fact to himself, thus withholding evidence that would have proved Muirchertach's innocence.'

'So are you identifying Marga as the murderer?' Brehon Barrán queried.

Fergus Fanat, sitting close by Blathmac, groaned loudly and held his still bandaged head in his hands. Fidelma did not look to where Sister Marga was sitting, pale-faced but with composed features.

'Fergus Fanat also saw Sister Marga emerge from Ultán's chamber and leapt to the same conclusion as Drón. Sister Marga did have good reason to hate Abbot Ultán. Marga had gone to Cill Ria because of her abilities as a scribe and it was while she was on a visit to Ard Stratha that she met and fell in love with Fergus Fanat. Abbot Ultán intervened when she made a request to leave the community. In this case, he himself developed a sexual passion for Marga, a young attractive girl, and he forced her to satiate his needs under what manner of coercion I can leave to your imagination. Sister Marga ended the relationship with Fergus because she felt unclean.

'She came here hoping for an opportunity to escape Ultán's clutches. On the night of his death he had summoned her to his chamber and she had no option but to obey. When Fergus Fanat and Drón saw her leaving his chamber, Abbot Ultán was still alive. She did not learn of his death until the next morning. Later that day, she saw her old love, Fergus Fanat, but he made no effort to respond when she tried to speak to him and she thought the relationship was over. Later she went on the boar hunt. It was an attempt to escape to Laigin, away from Drón and his acolyte Sister Sétach to whom I shall return in a moment.

'As she was doing so, she fell in with Fergus Fanat, who professed that he still loved her. She told him what had happened but Fergus Fanat chose to believe that she was guilty, and not only guilty of Ultán's murder but later that of Muirchertach.'

'For what reason would she kill Muirchertach?' demanded Brehon Barrán.

'Fergus Fanat thought Muirchertach must have seen her leaving Ultán's chamber. That he tried to coerce her into helping him against Cill Ria and she had eventually killed him to silence him.'

'I tried to protect her in spite of her guilt,' cried Fergus Fanat.

'This was nonsense,' snapped Fidelma. 'Marga was innocent of both crimes. But Fergus Fanat's love was not sufficient for him to have faith in her. He wanted her, that is true. He announced that he was going to see Blathmac to tell him that she was the killer and ask Blathmac to protect her for his sake. This Fergus Fanat had the makings of a martyr! Can you imagine Marga's mortification, her feelings, at this pronouncement? A man claiming to love her but not believing in her innocence? What could she do?'

Fergus Fanat had risen angrily. 'What did she do?' he cried shrilly. 'You know well what she did. I went to see Blathmac and I was just outside his chamber door when she came up behind me and hit me over the head, trying to silence me. Then she fled from this fortress.'

'That is not so,' replied Fidelma calmly. 'You went down the corridor, passing one of the alcoves in which, you told me, you saw no one. It was after you passed by this alcove that you said you were struck over the head. Your assailant could only have been hiding on the ledge outside. You agree that you did not see the assailant?'

'I told you I heard the rustle of her clothes and I identified her by the perfume that I smelled as she came up behind me.'

'You told me that you detected the odour of lavender.' She took a vial from her *cíorbholg* and handed it to Caol. 'Let Fergus Fanat smell that.'

Reluctantly, Fergus did so.

'Was that the odour that you perceived?'

'It is not.'

'But that is the perfume that Marga always wears – and it is honeysuckle. I am afraid you must learn to distinguish your scents, Fergus Fanat.'

'I know the odour . . .'

'It is Sister Sétach who uses lavender and she does so for medicinal reasons. It was pointed out that she had difficulty sleeping and therefore used lavender as a means of relaxing into sleep. Brother Conchobhar will tell you of the medical properties in this connection. It was Sister Sétach who tried to stop you. She and Drón desperately wanted to take Marga back to Cill Ria.'

'Why?' demanded Brehon Barrán.

'When I put that question to Brother Drón, he put forward the feeble excuse that it was to have her punished under the *Penitentials*, as practised in Cill Ria, which would bring down harsher penalties than our law. If Fergus Fanat told Blathmac that he thought she was guilty of these murders then their plan would be upset.

'Marga had been so distressed that she told Sétach what Fergus Fanat was about to do. She then fled the fortress. Sétach told Brother Drón, who went after her. But this time he was misled by Ordwulf's attempt to entice him into an ambush. It was left to Sétach to prevent Fergus Fanat from telling Blathmac. But Fergus was mistaken in identifying Marga as his attacker just as he was wrong in accusing Marga of the murders. And just as Drón and Sétach were also wrong in believing that Marga had killed Ultán and Muirchertach.'

'This is a tangled skein, Fidelma,' Brehon Barrán said. 'You say that Brother Drón's reason for seeking to hide the fact that he thought Marga guilty of these murders and take her back to Cill Ria was simply to bring her into harsher punishment? I find that a very weak reason.'

'I also said that I found it feeble. It was the mystery that almost prevented me from looking for the real murderer.'

'How is it explained?'

Fidelma turned to where Sister Sétach was now quietly sobbing. 'Eadulf found the answer, perhaps unwittingly. Drón asked Sister Sétach to go to Ultán's room after his murder and retrieve something. When Eadulf and I found her there she claimed she was trying to retrieve his belongings as holy relics to return to Cill Ria. In fact, she wanted to remove the documents in his trunk. Records of Ultán's embassy to get the religious leaders of the five kingdoms to recognise Ard Macha as the primatial seat.'

Brother Drón had sunk in his chair with a despairing moan.

'Among the documents was a copy of a work in Latin – the *Liber Angeli* – which tells of the miraculous appearance to the Blessed Patrick of an angel announcing that Ard Macha should hold supreme authority over the churches and monasteries of the five kingdoms. That book was used to good effect in persuading some of the abbots and bishops to recognise the claims of Ard Macha.'

Fidelma glanced to Abbot Ségdae of Imleach. 'Tell Brehon Barrán what you told me before we entered the hall.'

Abbot Ségdae rose. 'Simple enough. Ultán and Drón, when they made their demands at Imleach, tried to use the *Liber Angeli*, the Book of the Angel, to persuade me to give Ard Macha recognition. But I had been in Ard Macha on a pilgrimage many years ago and this book was not then known. My steward, Brother Madagan, and I refused to let it sway our consideration.'

'And with just cause,' added Fidelma. 'The proof that this book was a forgery was in the papers in Abbot Ultán's box which Drón wanted so badly to get his hands on. This *Liber Angeli* was written but a short time ago. It did not exist when Abbot Ségdae was visiting Ard Macha, nor were stories handed down before that time of any visitation from the celestial world. The book is a collection of claims by various northern churchmen combining to argue that Ard Macha should be recognised as the central authority of the Faith in these kingdoms. The scribe who, under Abbot Ultán's authority, was forced to compile these stories was Sister Marga.'

Brehon Barrán turned to the girl.

'Is this true?' he asked sternly.

'I wrote merely what I was told,' Sister Marga confessed. 'Abbot Ultán knew I wrote a fair hand. I told Sister Fidelma as much. I did not realise the story was entirely untruth. I thought they were some old traditions that I was putting down.'

'So now we see why, if Ard Macha's campaign for recognition was to succeed, those documents and, indeed, Sister Marga had to be taken back to Cill Ria. I suggest that Blathmac take into care both Drón and Sétach and return them to Ard Macha, and through his brehon find out whether this was done with the abbot of Ard Macha's knowledge.'

When Brother Drón and Sister Sétach had been removed, Brehon Barrán turned with a bewildered expression to Fidelma.

'But this doesn't resolve the murders of Ultán and Muirchertach unless . . .' He turned a suspicious gaze to Dúnchad Muirisci. 'Well, Fidelma, you have led us down a complicated path and seem to have eliminated all the suspects except one. It appears that there is no logical choice of culprit left other than the man who stands to gain most by Muirchertach Nár's death.'

Dúnchad Muirisci began to rise indignantly.

'If you refer to the *tánaiste* of Connacht, then the business of his horse and the split shoe was compelling,' interrupted Fidelma. 'I considered it. But his story was weak, so weak that it had to be the truth. If he were lying then he would have worked out a stronger alibi. His mount did bolt when the wild boar charged and Dúnchad was thrown. Doubtless Muirchertach and his killer found the horse. After the killer had killed Muirchertach, he heard Dúnchad calling in the woods. He mounted Dúnchad's horse and led his own and Muirchertach's away. As soon as he had gone a short distance, he left Dúnchad's horse with its reins over a bush so that it would not wander. Then he left Muirchertach's horse loose, and went off to re-join the hunt on his own mount. Dúnchad finally caught up with his horse, the one with the split shoe, and rode back to Cashel. As had the real murderer.'

Brehon Barrán looked utterly bewildered. 'We already know that Drón had found Muirchertach's horse and was leading it back to Cashel. Drón is not guilty of killing Muirchertach. Now you say that Dúnchad is equally innocent. I confess, I am totally lost.'

Fidelma smiled grimly. 'I believed from the start that there were not two separate murderers and, moreover, that both murders had been committed for the same motive. It was vengeance, as I said at the beginning of this hearing. That was the link. But what person would have cause to want vengeance on both Ultán and Muirchertach Nár? What had they done in common to one person here that would warrant their death?' She swung round. 'Perhaps you will answer that question, Abbot Augaire?'

Abbot Augaire was startled for a moment. Her accusing eyes had glazed into an icy coldness, the green fire turning to a chilling blue-grey. Augaire read cold determination in her features. He accepted that the accusation was no mere guesswork. He sat back in resignation.

'How did you work it out?' His tone was almost genial as he asked the question.

'Let us come to the means first and then the motive, for the motive has been staring me in the face ever since our first meeting. The means only fell into place when we discussed how Brother Drón might have hidden himself in the alcove. You said that you had not seen him in the alcove. When it was mentioned that he might have stood out on the ledge that ran under the window along to Ultán's chamber, you replied: "But I don't think Brother Drón is the sort to submit himself to such dangers. The ledge has several loose blocks along it." How did you know that fact unless you had been along that same ledge yourself?'

Abbot Augaire winced in disgust as he acknowledged the slip.

'On the night of Ultán's death you were playing *brandubh* with Dúnchad Muirisci,' went on Fidelma. 'You left Dúnchad's chamber towards midnight. As you went down the corridor, you heard Ultán's door open. You saw Sister Marga come out. She was probably looking back into the chamber and did not see you. Why hadn't she then seen you when she turned into the corridor? We know that Drón and Fergus Fanat were in the corridor facing Ultán's door, so you were in the corridor along which Marga had to come. The answer was that you had slipped into the alcove and she passed by without seeing you. I think that the idea came to you on the spur of the moment. You noticed the ledge and realised that it ran all the way to Ultán's chamber. Knowing that he was alone, you took the decision to make use of it as a means of reaching his chamber unseen. No one would then observe you if they came along the corridor. You would be safe. You entered his room, surprising him, and you stabbed him to death in a frenzied fashion as befitted your great hatred for him. Then you slipped back along the ledge the way you had come.'

Abbot Augaire made no comment.

'You left Ultán's chamber not a moment too soon, for that was when Brother Drón entered. He did not tarry long, for he had also seen Marga leaving and came to the conclusion that she had killed him. Drón, as he had told us, had paused before going to Ultán's so as to save the abbot embarrassment. That pause was lucky for you in that it gave you the time and opportunity. Drón initially raced after Marga to accuse her but slipped and fell on the flagstone outside Dúnchad's room. He then came to his senses about challenging Marga. She could bring down the claims of Ard Macha. He decided to return to his chamber saying nothing. It did not occur to him until too late that he should have taken from Ultán's room the documents which showed that Marga had been the scribe of this so-called *Liber Angeli*.

'By the time he realised it, lo and behold, Muirchertach Nár had decided to speak to Ultán. He went to his chamber, saw the body and, aghast, backed from the scene only to be spotted by Brehon Baithen and Caol who came to the natural conclusion. He was accused of the murder.'

Abbot Augaire still sat quietly, not speaking.

'For a while, Augaire, you probably thought that you had the ideal situation. Your first victim was dead and the intended second victim was charged with the crime. When you heard that I was going to defend Muirchertach Nár, you did your best to emphasise Muirchertach's hatred of Ultán to me. However, you realised that I was developing a good case to defend him and you decided that you could not take the chance. You needed to complete your act of vengeance.

'The boar hunt was the ideal opportunity, especially when the hunting party became scattered. You were shadowing Muirchertach, though probably keeping out of his sight, and when he stumbled alone on a secluded spot you continued to sweep round and meet him face to face. You must have persuaded him to dismount and somehow got hold of his *bir*, the hunting spear. You killed him with that.

'Then coincidence came to your aid. Dúnchad's horse being loose was a godsend. You told me that your father was a hunter and tracker. You knew the skills involved and utilised your knowledge to lay a false trail. You took his horse and mounted it, taking Muirchertach's horse as well. You rode a short distance to stony ground, tied Dúnchad's horse to a gorse bush and probably slapped Muirchertach's piebald across the rump causing it to canter off to where Drón found it. You then re-mounted your own horse and rode off in time to find Muirchertach's wife Aíbnat to guide her away from the scene. As you were returning with her, you encountered Eadulf and Gormán. But you were now satisfied that your revenge was complete.'

Abbot Augaire was smiling now.

Brehon Barrán leaned forward with a puzzled frown.

'But revenge for what?' he asked, confused. 'I do not follow this at all.'

Fidelma was still looking expectantly at Abbot Augaire. 'Shall I continue?'

Abbot Augaire shrugged a shoulder in eloquent indifference. Fidelma turned back to Barrán.

'Revenge for the death of Searc, the poetess.'

'But Augaire did not know Searc the poetess,' Dúnchad Muirisci interrupted. 'He was only a witness to her death. That is how he became involved with Muirchertach and was appointed emissary to demand compensation from Ultán. There was no personal relationship there.'

Fidelma smiled. 'Augaire was a member of a small community near Rinn Carna in Connacht. He was fishing one day when he witnessed the distracted girl Searc plunge to her death. It was suicide . . .'

'To which she was driven,' snapped Abbot Augaire fiercely, speaking for the first time since Fidelma had begun her peroration.

'Just so,' agreed Fidelma. 'As we know, Searc had fallen passionately in love with a young religieux of Cill Ria. Ultán forbade the relationship and sent the boy Senach overseas and he was killed on the voyage. Searc was full of grief.'

'I can see why Ultán could be held to account for having a part in driving the poor girl to her death,' Brehon Barrán agreed. 'But why should anyone want to exact revenge on Muirchertach Nár? Surely Searc was his wife's younger sister and Muirchertach made lawful representations for compensation for her loss?'

'It was not hard to discover that Muirchertach Nár had a reputation as a philanderer and womaniser. Aíbnat knew it and disliked him. Dúnchad Muirisci knew it and hinted of things that were subsequently repeated in stories that reached even the ears of Abbot Laisran at Durrow. I asked myself this question – why, when Augaire was painting a black picture to persuade me of Muirchertach's guilt of slaying Ultán, did he not dwell more on this very point? The point that Muirchertach Nár forced his attentions on Searc when she arrived at his fortress in shock and grieving for the loss of Senach. Muirchertach raped her and she, deep in shock and shame, fled to the coast and threw herself from the cliffs. It was Muirchertach's act that caused her suicide. But Augaire was too much in love with Searc to have her reputation besmirched by revealing it.'

Brehon Barrán sat back looking even more confused. 'But we have heard that Augaire did not know this girl before. Why would he be in love with her?'

'Because he fell in love with an image,' replied Fidelma sadly. 'It is hard to explain the feelings that motivate a man or woman to this emotion we call love. He saw Searc once in life and then in death and could not get that image from his mind. He did not know who she was. But the image obsessed him. He tracked her identity down and it became a fixation to discover the reasons for her suicide. Ultán's part in it was fairly clear. But at some stage he learned the reputation of Muirchertach Nár . . .'

'I told him.' It was Aíbnat who spoke. Her voice was quiet and unemotional. 'Before we set out here, I told Augaire. I knew my husband's reputation and one night, in a burst of anger towards me, he boasted what he had done with my sister. I told Augaire, knowing that, eventually, retribution would catch up with him.'

Fidelma turned towards Brehon Barrán and held out her arms in a gesture to show that she could bring no further proof. 'I have finished except to say that I started to suspect Augaire when he could not refrain from putting a clear sign on each corpse that this was done to avenge Searc.'

'A clear sign?' The Brehon frowned. 'What sign? What have we missed?'

'The verse of a love poem written by Searc. It was a symbol of the reason why they died.'

Brehon Barrán turned to Abbot Augaire. 'Do you plead a defence? You may choose to be heard with a *dálaigh* to defend you.'

Abbot Augaire shook his head.

'Have you nothing to say?' pressed the Chief Brehon. When Augaire still said nothing, he ordered Caol to take him to a secure room and keep him there until Barrán could speak with him and explain his rights under the law. As Caol was guiding Augaire past where Fidelma was sitting, the abbot paused and smiled down at her.

'Muirchertach Nár thought he had bought me off.' His voice was quiet, almost a whisper. 'He offered me the abbacy of Conga as a

299

means of keeping me silent. I took it because I needed time to work out that vengeance. I waited my chance and when it came I took it. I have no regrets.'

Colgú was sprawled in his chair before the fire, regarding his sister over the rim of a goblet of mulled wine with a quizzical smile.

'I don't know how you do it, Fidelma. How can you enter the labyrinth of people's distorted minds and see beyond their lies and deceptions?'

Fidelma smiled in amusement. 'I thought that you excelled at *brandubh*, brother.'

'This is not exactly *brandubh*, Fidelma.'

'It is the same principle. You have to have a dexterity of the mind. Identify the problem and gather the information and then analyse it. However, I will say this – of all the cases that I have encountered, this one was most frustrating in that there were too many people who had cause to hate Ultán. At first that blinded me.'

'At first?'

'It was only after Muirchertach Nár was killed that I started to see some light. That is not good. I should have been able to solve the first murder without waiting for the second. And then there was the confusion caused by the intrigues of Brother Drón to protect his embassy. I should have seen through that earlier. I had thought that it was Drón tried to mislead everyone with that pagan symbol of the raven's feather. Of course, it was Augaire who had placed it on Muirchertach's pillow to make the King look elsewhere for the threat.'

Colgú shook his head. 'You are always too hard on yourself. You have heard that Abbot Augaire has escaped and fled from Cashel?'

'I heard,' she replied calmly.

'It is believed that he is heading for the coast. Probably to the harbour at Ard Mór.'

'He will doubtless take ship for Gaul or Iberia, and vanish into one of the religious communities there. Ah well, maybe it is for the best.'

'I suppose so,' agreed Colgú. 'Certainly, Dúnchad Muirsici saw him as an embarrassment. There is already unrest between his family, the Uí Fiachracha, and lady Aíbnat's Uí Briúin Aí. They are now contesting the kingship of Connacht.' He was silent for a while and then said, changing the subject: 'I noticed that your friend Della seems to have taken Sister Marga in hand.'

Fidelma inclined her head thoughtfully. 'I feel sorry for Sister Marga. She is a real victim in all this. I don't think she will be able to forgive Fergus Fanat for not believing her and she certainly cannot return to the abbey of Cill Ria.'

'Sister Marga has my full permission to stay here,' Colgú replied. 'Either here or at Imleach. Both Cashel and Imleach need someone of her talent, able to write a good hand, to copy and translate. We have enough genuine books to work on without resorting to fake ones. Until she makes up her mind, I hear that she is going to stay with Della in the township.'

'But what of Drón and Sétach? Has Blathmac mentioned what he intends to do about them and Cill Ria? If I were the king, I would do all I could to have that place destroyed and its community dispersed to religious houses where fear and punishment are not incorporated into the rules and beliefs.'

'As you suggested, Blathmac is taking them back to Ulaidh, to Ségéne of Ard Macha, and telling him of the facts of the case. I think he will advise the Comarb of Patrick that before he starts asserting Ard Macha's moral authority over the churches of the five kingdoms, he should be careful whom he appoints as his emissary.'

'I do not think that Ard Macha will be strong enough to insist on that moral authority during our lifetimes,' replied Fidelma with gravity.

'Speaking of Sister Sétach, you never explained to me exactly what she was doing in Dúnchad Muirisci's chamber when you and Eadulf went to see him?'

'Exactly what they told us she was doing.' Fidelma smiled. 'She had gone to see him on Drón's behalf, Drón believing he had succeeded as the new abbot of Cill Ria, to reach some sort of truce in the disagreement between Connacht and the abbey. Sometimes, even the most suspicious circumstances turn out to have a simple explanation, and those involved tell the truth.'

There was a silence between brother and sister for a few moments, and then Fidelma asked: 'I presume that Brother Berrihert and his brothers still have permission to stay in the glen of Eatharlaí?'

'Miach has given assurances that can do so. They can remain there for the rest of their lives in peace if they so wish. But speaking of life –' Colgú suddenly grinned, '*your* life, Fidelma – before everyone disperses, we still have several distinguished guests awaiting a celebration.'

Fidelma coloured faintly. 'I had not forgotten. I think that you may safely go ahead with the delayed arrangements for tomorrow morning. I'd better find Eadulf so that we can prepare.'

Eadulf was not in their chambers when Fidelma returned. Only, Muirgen was there, with little Alchú. Fidelma spent a short time playing with the baby before Muirgen took him away to allow her some time to rest. Moodily, she crossed to the window and gazed down into the courtyard. At that moment, the door burst open and an excited-looking Eadulf hurried in.

'Have you heard the news? Apparently Abbot Augaire has fled the fortress. I've just been talking to Caol. He was last seen heading south. No one seems bothered to go after him.'

Fidelma turned from the window. 'I don't think anyone is unduly worried about Augaire.'

Eadulf stared at her calm features in disbelief.

'You don't believe that he should be punished? he demanded in surprise.

'Our system is not about punishment but about recompense for victims and rehabilitation for the culprit,' she reminded him. 'You should know that by now, Eadulf.'

'I understand that, but . . .'

'Ultán and Muirchertach should have faced the consequences of their evil deeds before now. Their Nemesis was Augaire. No one is mourning their passing and no one is going to lament the fact that Augaire has escaped to continue the life that was interrupted when he saw that poor girl, Searc, kill herself. He has probably suffered enough.'

Eadulf shook his head in bewilderment.

'Can a man really feel such strong emotion for someone he does not even know? You said yourself that he saw her once, passing by, and then he saw her again after her death. Can he really have felt such strength of emotion for her that he waited all these years planning vengeance in her name?'

'Love and hate are strong emotions, Eadulf. They strike in different ways. An idea is born in our minds and the idea then persists; it sometimes becomes uncontrollable. We cannot rid ourselves of it. It cannot be suppressed until we find that we are so obsessed that we are compelled to follow that idea wherever it leads us. Augaire fell in love with a shadow. Perhaps to us it was an insubstantial one, but to him it was very real. He became obsessed by it and was driven by his compulsion. To you and me, it was probably illusory. But then a lot of actions that are precipitated in our lives are but the children of dreams – our dreams or other people's. Maybe that is what is meant when the fathers of the Faith talked about damnation? Well, I think we should all find a moment in our hearts to utter a prayer for the damned.'

Eadulf was not entirely persuaded by her argument.

'Talking of love and hate, I suppose Marga and Fergus Fanat will get together now?' he asked. 'Even after the hearing, Fergus Fanat still pronounces his love for her.'

Fidelma turned back to the window where she had been looking down on the courtyard of the fortress below.

'He thinks that he loves her,' she replied. 'I am not sure that it is good enough for Marga, because at the very moment she needed the great essential quality of love – belief in the beloved's integrity and support for her against all adversity – he failed her. How can you love someone you think is a liar and a killer? For Marga, to find that the man who claimed he loved her also disbelieved her, even going so far as to denounce her while claiming it was for her own good . . . well, how can Marga ever trust that man again?'

'Do you mean that love must be blind?'

'I mean that love is not a superficial emotion. Love is knowing someone, their faults as well as the good, and, above all, understanding them. Fergus Fanat did not know Marga. And Marga, if you recall, finally recognised that fact. No relationship can be built on mistrust.'

'So there is no forgiveness for him?'

'I would say not,' confirmed Fidelma, glancing down through the window. 'In fact, Fergus Fanat has missed his opportunity.'

Eadulf frowned. 'You sound very positive about that fact.'

'Come here and look down into the courtyard.'

Eadulf moved across the room to join her.

Below he could see Sister Marga standing, her head thrown back and apparently laughing at something a tall, broad-shouldered warrior with dark hair was saying. Eadulf raised his brows and glanced at Fidelma.

'Gormán?'

'Why not?' She smiled. 'I understand that the girl is going to stay with Della for a while before considering where her future lies. I do not doubt that Gormán might convince her that she could have a worthy place at Cashel. Our library stands in need of another good scribe, for the girl writes a fair hand and translates in several languages.'

Eadulf watched the warrior and the young girl turn and, walking close together, move towards the stables. They could hear the girl's warm laughter answering Gormán's masculine tones.

It suddenly reminded him of something and he turned back to Fidelma. Before he could say anything there was a sharp knock at the door. Eadulf groaned. In answer to Fidelma's call, the door opened, and old Brother Conchobhar put his head round it. He smiled brightly as he saw them standing together by the window.

'The aspects were contrary,' he said in an apologetic tone. 'That was why you had the trouble during these last few days. But planets move on. Like time itself. Now all is well. The aspects are very favourable. It is the right time now. I thought that you might like to know.'

Eadulf grinned, glancing towards Fidelma.

'It was always the right time, Brother Conchobhar,' he said.